BETTER OFF WED

MARSWOOD HARBOR
BOOK 1

LILIAN MONROE

Published by Method and Madness Publishing PTY LTD
PO Box 186 Subiaco, WA, 6008, Australia

Print ISBN: 978-1-923187-69-6

Editing by Shavonne Clarke at Motif Edits and Paige Kraft PK Edits
Cover design by Talina at Bookin It Designs

PROLOGUE
ETTA: AN OLD WOMAN WITH A PLAN

I listened to the chatter around the dining room table, gathering myself to drop a bomb on the table right between the roast beef and the mashed potatoes. The smell of pepper and wine tickled my nose as cutlery clinked and voices mingled. I set down my knife and fork, and a ripple of silence spread over the table.

"Mom?" Angela asked as the silence became thicker. She'd always been the brashest of my six children. The one most likely to take the lead, especially after Mark died almost twenty years ago. I'd blinked, and time had jumped.

"Next year, I'll be ninety," I started, looking over the expectant faces surrounding the table. Only eleven of my eighteen grandchildren were at Sunday lunch this week, but it would have to be enough. Getting the entire family together usually took a wedding or a funeral; I didn't have time to wait for the next wedding, and the next funeral might very well be my own. "I don't have long left in the world."

"Mom," Angela repeated, reproachful. "You're healthier than ever. You could have another couple of decades with us."

I lifted a hand, and Angela stopped. "Marswood Harbor has been my home since I was born," I continued. "And it, like me, will die soon."

An uncomfortable tension pulled at everyone around the table. My grandsons Gideon and Jack exchanged a long look, then glanced at their two other brothers and then at their cousins. Darby, my only great-grandchild, leaned into Jack's side and whispered a question to her father. Jack comforted her with a few murmured words. Gideon glanced at his niece, then met my gaze, suspicious. I saw so much of Mark in Gideon, and it was a gift to have pieces of my late son at this table all these years after Mark's passing. My family meant everything to me.

My eldest son, Walter, narrowed his eyes at me. He'd always been perceptive; maybe that's why he kept to himself most of the time.

I had their attention.

"The population of our town is in decline. Businesses are closing down as people retire or die, and no one is stepping in to run them." I leaned back and spread my palms. "There's no one left here who can. Just last week, Ivan Popov told me that his daughter won't move back here to take over the antiques shop. That's another decades-long business that will close down when he goes."

"Grandma," Jack said, leaning forward. "We're all here. We'll keep the town going when you're gone, if that's what you're worried about."

"What I'm worried about," I said, "is that you'll do your best, and your best won't be good enough."

Jack opened his mouth and clamped it shut again.

I gestured to the door, and a slight man in wire-framed glasses walked in. He carried a laptop under his arm and ducked his head as the stares of more than a dozen people landed on his face and back. "This is Alex," I said. "He's been helping me with a little project these past months."

"A project?" Angela prodded, then looked at Jennifer, my youngest. Jennifer's kids shifted in their seats, impatient; they were only teenagers, so it couldn't be helped. They wouldn't be affected by my plans for a while yet. Not directly, at least.

"The project is a proprietary algorithm Alex has worked hard to design to my exact specifications," I explained, watching frowns grace the faces around the dining room table. My beloved family was so very suspicious of me. As well they should be.

"What does that mean, exactly?" Angela's frown was the most pronounced. She could feel that something big was coming.

"I have eighteen grandchildren, and only one of them is married," I finally proclaimed. I nodded at Ben and his wife Wendy, whose belly had started to swell as they awaited their first child. The first child to be born in the Mars family for over a decade. The second child born in Marswood Harbor in over two years. It wasn't enough. The town would die, and my family would scatter. My legacy would be lost. All the decades of my life, the sweat and tears and blood I'd poured into this town, this family, would be for naught.

But I wasn't dead yet. I still had my wits—and more importantly, my money.

"I've decided to bequeath my fortune to the national parks,"

I announced, and paused as outrage exploded all around the table. I lifted my hand, and a tense, angry silence followed. My lips curled into a humorless smile. "Unless."

A dozen and a half sets of eyes stared. Waited.

"Unless what?" asked my great-granddaughter Darby. She was only twelve, and she was the bravest of them all.

I could feel Gideon's glare from across the table. Brave Gideon, who hadn't been the same since the fire. He deserved happiness, and the poor dear would never go out and find it on his own. I would have to meddle.

I decided now was the time to detonate that bomb. My smile widened, my gaze meeting my eldest grandson's. "Unless you all start getting married and having babies, of course."

While the rest of the family exploded, Gideon leaned back in his chair, his shoulders relaxing. I could see his decision in the lines of his body. He would give up his inheritance in a blink. He wouldn't be manipulated by the pot of gold that would come with my passing.

No, Gideon would need extra encouragement. I knew just the thing that would persuade him to play along.

ONE
SADIE

As I turned the corner and faced the petal-strewn aisle that separated me from my soon-to-be husband, I realized I might've made a mistake in the wake of my latest heartbreak. I should've done the usual thing and given myself bangs while sobbing over my bathroom sink. Instead, I'd signed up for an arranged marriage.

My heart punched a slow, heavy rhythm against my ribs, and I inhaled the scent of the rose petals scattered at my feet. I gripped the stems of the flowers in my hands, my freshly painted nails digging into my palms. Sweat dribbled down my spine. It was as warm inside the church as it was outside.

For a single, suspended moment, I observed my husband-to-be without being seen in return. Light from the stained-glass windows behind him haloed his head, the chandelier above the aisle sending flickering lights dancing over half of his face. His expression was closed off as he stared at a spot on the floor in front of him, his sharp jaw clenched. He was tall, with a straight back and perfect posture. His lips were pinched. Tension radiated from him, streamed through the space between us, and struck me in the solar plexus. I inhaled sharply.

He wasn't feeling great about this whole wedding thing either, apparently. At least we had that in common.

I couldn't blame him; Gideon Mars had agreed to marry me based on the results of matchmaking software that was the brainchild of his billionaire grandmother. A powerful algorithm had matched us with each other. We were meant to be.

Allegedly.

At the very least, we were meant to repopulate the town of Marswood Harbor, which had been suffering from a slow descent into bankruptcy and oblivion for at least two decades. The matriarch Etta Mars's grandfather had founded this town around his logging company and sawmill, and now she was watching her family's legacy wither and die. Fortunately for Etta Mars, the little enclave in coastal Maine had an overabundance of Mars men, all of them strapping and handsome and in need of wives. We the wives would flood the town with fresh blood and inject new life into its streets. In exchange, we'd get a new home, a new start, and a shot at true love.

So I'd left everything behind to end up here, in a tiny, decrepit New England town, tying my life to her eldest grandson's. I had the wedding dress, the veil, and the flowers to prove it.

My heart gave another thud of warning, and I wondered if it was a sign to turn around and leave. This wasn't wise, even for me. I wasn't a stranger to bad decisions, but marrying a man I'd never met might've been one step too far. This was the mother of all rebounds.

But what choice did I have? I'd exhausted all my other options. My business was failing. My personal life was a wasteland. It was either this, or move back in with my parents at the tender age of thirty-one. I was teetering on the edge of a crumbling cliff face, and this was the only path back to stability. I wondered if my desperation had a stink. If the congregation would wrinkle their noses as I walked past. If my husband would be able to smell it when he stood in front of me and said his vows.

Then Gideon looked up.

If the graffiti and vacant shop fronts on Main Street hadn't scared me away, my husband-to-be's obvious hostility probably should've. His attention hit me like a sledgehammer. His glare was so intense I rocked back on my pearlescent white heels, my fingers spasming around the bouquet of red roses I'd bought at my favorite florist in Manhattan before driving up here yesterday.

From where I stood, I couldn't tell the color of his eyes, but I felt their intensity. His lips flattened even more, and my stomach clenched at the open animosity in his gaze. Unfortunately, my sense of self-preservation had died along with my last relationship, and his glare didn't make me run off screaming. I'd come this far. I wasn't changing my mind—even when the other side of his face came into view.

His chin-length hair had been tucked behind his ear, revealing a jagged hairline. Even from a distance, I could tell that there was something odd about the shape of his ear. The skin tugged at the corner of his eye, dragging it down slightly, scarring running across the side of his head and neck to disappear beneath his collar.

He watched me watch him, and his hard lips curled into a sneer. Because of his scars? Because he thought I'd run away screaming? Thinking I couldn't possibly agree to marry someone who didn't have a perfect, unblemished body?

Anger flared in my chest. He thought I was shallow and stupid and easily scared.

A familiar, almost-forgotten spark kindled to life in my gut: that driving stubbornness that usually led me straight into trouble. The little devil who used to be my constant companion tapped my shoulder and whispered in my ear, *Are you going to let this one slide?* I hadn't spoken a word to Gideon, but I was insulted that he thought so little of me. That he was so quick to reject me like everyone else had. I lifted my chin and straightened my shoulders, then I narrowed my eyes right back at him.

My body wasn't perfect, either, but my scars were hidden from view.

Electricity snapped against my skin as he held my gaze. He was challenging me, those eyes blazing from the other end of the aisle, prodding the fight-or-flight instinct inside me.

Fight, the little devil urged.

My lips curled into a smile I knew didn't reach my eyes. A notch appeared between his brows. The smell of roses filled my nose, cloying.

Somewhere above and behind me, an organ began to clatter out the opening notes of Mendelssohn's "Wedding March." The noise echoed and bounced off the arched ceiling, chaotic and loud and overwhelming. The small crowd of guests shifted in their pews. Their gazes raked over my skin like pinpricks, but I kept mine glued on Gideon. His stare was harsh. Angry. Hostile. It made my blood turn thick and hot, sent a buzzing sound rattling around my head. The longer he stared at me, the more I wanted to snarl. The more I was alive. My breath burned in my lungs, and my legs twitched and bounced beneath the simple silk dress that hid them.

For the first time since Henry sat me down and told me he was calling off the wedding, a rush of life went through me. I wasn't just putting one foot in front of the other. I wasn't just swept up by grief and shame and heartbreak, carried along on a current of my own misery. I wasn't scrambling to scrimp together enough to pay this bill or that one, or despairing about my dwindling client list as a wave of doom threatened to crash down atop me.

No; right now, I *burned*. My soon-to-be husband lit a blaze in my gut. It ignited in an instant and spread, all the way to my fingertips and my toes. His eyes drilled holes into mine, the line of his shoulders as rigid as a plank. The weight of his stare bore down on me until I couldn't breathe. Until I felt like I was flying or drowning or dying. Until I had to look away.

Damn it. I hated showing weakness.

Beside him, three groomsmen studied me. They were obviously all related. Brothers, probably. The best man beside him resembled him the most. He tilted his head at me, curious. Guarded. A couple of inches taller than my groom. No scars. The one next to him was about Gideon's height, but he was as broad as a bear. I'd never seen a man so gigantic. His face was utterly blank and unreadable. And when my eyes flicked to the third and apparently youngest brother, he flashed me a quick, reassuring smile.

Gideon drew my gaze like a magnet. His brothers fell away, fading into the background as soon as my attention landed on him. He angled his head slightly, showing me the mottled, too-shiny skin that made up the left side of his neck and part of his head. Thinking I'd run away screaming, probably.

He didn't want to marry me, obviously. *Well*, I thought, *join the freaking club, big guy.* There was a long list of men who'd met me, slept with me, and said, *No thanks.*

This time it would be different.

After today, I'd have a ring on my finger, a new home, and a fresh start.

Gideon would just have to deal with the fact that he'd been matched with me. Boo hoo. Poor him.

As if he could hear my thoughts, his eyes turned to blazing, hostile slits, sending my pulse hammering. His fists clenched and released, and his gaze finally tore away from mine to rake down my body and back up again. Goosebumps flared where he looked. I wore a slip dress that I'd designed and sewn myself. The expert seamstresses I'd previously employed had left for greener pastures. By which I meant pastures that paid them actual money for their time instead of only the empty promises I had to offer. Such was life when your wedding dress business collapsed.

My design style was all about clean lines and perfect tailoring, but I wasn't opposed to taking on more elaborate projects if the price was right. For myself, though, I'd gone simple. The thin straps framed my neck, the neckline a gentle curve. The fabric was cut on a bias, and it fell like water around my restless legs.

I knew I looked good. My hair was gathered at the nape of my neck, my face framed with perfectly imperfect tendrils. My makeup was as expertly applied as usual. It was fate's cruelest prank that men found me beautiful and interesting and attractive until they got to know me. Still, I had expected my groom to be pleased at the sight of me. At least until I opened my mouth. So as Gideon's eyes snapped back up to mine and flared, his lips flattening in displeasure, I was more than a little insulted. The devil on my shoulder whispered, *Wouldn't it feel so good to make him pay for that reaction?*

Unfortunately, the devil on my shoulder was only in charge of my impulses and not the reality of the world around me. So when I gritted my teeth and put one foot forward, the shiny red bottoms of my shoes connected with the velvety red petals sprinkled all along the aisle. I was so focused on returning Gideon's glare that I didn't notice until my beautiful satiny shoe slipped out from under me.

A startled yelp fell from my lips as I tried to overcorrect, stumbled sideways, and stomped the bottom of my other shoe on another flower petal. I was flexible, so I didn't injure myself when my legs did their best to split apart, but I sure as hell didn't look very graceful doing it. I jarred my tailbone on the hard tile floor as I finally landed, and the bouquet in my hands went flying a fair bit earlier than it was supposed to. The comb holding my embroidered veil in place bit into the back of my head as I whacked it on the floor, and little twittering birds started circling my head.

What the hell. *What the hell!*

Gasps filled the space as the organ played a discordant chord and stopped. Silence pulsed in the seconds that followed, alive and malevolent. I looked up at the big iron chandelier from my spot on the floor, wondering if this was an omen. A bad one. *Another* bad one, if you counted the groom's reaction to my arrival and the general air of decrepitude that hovered over the town.

Then Gideon was there, looming over me, huge and broad and unhappy. His presence tore out what little breath was left in me. Hard, pale blue eyes scanned me from head to toe, and his jaw clenched a little bit harder. He sure knew how to make a woman feel terrible on her wedding day. The scarred side of his neck was tight and shiny, with some odd lumps here and there. Burn scars, I guessed, before shifting my gaze back to the eyes raking over me. He'd noticed me notice his wounds, and his cheek twitched as he ground his jaw.

I gulped. For once, I was speechless.

"You think it's a sign?" he asked, echoing my thoughts from earlier, voice low and rough, gaze flicking down my body once more.

Heat flared where he looked. When I spoke my voice was hoarse. "A sign of what?"

"Maybe we should pull the plug before it gets any worse."

"You sound a little too hopeful for my liking."

"You hit your head pretty hard there," he noted conversationally, tugging at the cuffs of his shirt as he finally stopped staring. "Maybe you're not thinking straight."

"I'm getting the impression that you don't want to marry me." I narrowed my eyes at him as I pushed myself up to my elbows.

He glanced over again, following the movement of my body with hostile eyes. His smile was cold. "Just trying to save you from making a mistake."

"How altruistic of you. Forgive me for not quite buying it." I made a show of looking around. "Someone got a gun to your head, or something?"

Gideon didn't laugh. His eyes returned to mine. A resigned sort of grimness settled over his expression. "You want this."

"You don't." It wasn't a question.

His eyes skated over my curves again, a sharp, hungry movement, until he tore his gaze away and grimaced at himself. Like he hated that he'd checked me out.

And wasn't I just a conceited little egomaniac for thinking he was interested in me at all?

Familiar shame and mortification simmered in my gut, burning up the back of my throat. Even a man who was supposedly algorithmically perfect for me didn't want me. That was just great. But I'd come this far. I *would* be married by the end of the day. And no one—not even the groom—could stop me.

Yes, that was a ridiculous thought. If I'd been thinking clearly, I might've reconsidered. What kind of foundation was *this* for a marriage? At what point over the past six months had my brain actually leaked out of my ears, and why hadn't I noticed the lumps of gray matter on my pillow every morning? What the actual hell was I doing here? Living with Mom and Dad again wouldn't be *that* bad, surely. As long as I didn't care about feeling good about myself, or anything.

But it would be bad. Like, really bad. Existential bad. Slow, suffocating death bad.

Gideon Mars was the better option every day of the week, even if he hated my guts. Besides, I wasn't one to back down from a challenge. So instead of calling it quits, I straightened my arms and wiggled my fingers at my soon-to-be husband. "Help me up," I commanded.

Gideon let out a quiet sigh, then wrapped his big hands around mine and pulled me to my feet. I teetered slightly, catching myself against his chest, and inhaled the complicated, spicy scent of him. Thoughts scattered from my addled mind. His hand landed on my waist, warm through the layers of silk dress and nylon shapewear. I tilted my head up, startled at how good it felt to be this close to him. Caught in the intensity of his cold, blue gaze. Struck by the fact that despite his scars—or maybe because of them—Gideon was an exceedingly handsome man.

His jaw was emphasized by neatly trimmed stubble. His inky hair curled enough to look unruly, and the dark slashes of his eyebrows made his eyes all the more striking. He was muscular. I could feel the shift of his bulk under my palms, the strength that lurked beneath the suit jacket. His grip tightened slightly on my waist, maybe to steady me. Or maybe it was unconscious, and Gideon just liked the way it felt to have his hands on me, the way I liked having my hands on him.

His thumb pressed into my rib, a couple of inches below my breast. Suddenly, it was hard to breathe. His throat bobbed on a swallow. The scant few inches of air between us turned electric. Little shocks jolted through me, every atom of my being focused on the warmth of his hand against my side and the feel of his chest beneath my hands.

Gideon's eyes dropped to my lips. I licked them before I could stop myself, and his chest rose with a quick, silent inhalation. My fingertips curled slightly, nails pressing against his lapels. His thumb moved an inch. A millimeter. It barely qualified as a stroke, but the touch sent a blast of heat scorching through me. Under the dress and the shapewear, my panties grew damp. My thighs trembled and clenched, but not because they wanted to run away. They trembled because they wanted to spread in desperate need.

And that's when I remembered that I'd told an itty bitty lie on the application. A lie that had seemed inconsequential at the time. Something that I had thought would work out to my advantage in this marriage, and I was now realizing was actually a Very Big Problem.

Because my body was on fire, especially the spot where Gideon's hand still gripped my waist. My pulse had begun to throb—in my fingertips and my throat and my cunt.

The worst had happened. A disaster of unrivaled proportions.

I was very, *very* attracted to my soon-to-be husband.

GIDEON

She was the kind of perfect that turned heads. From the moment I'd seen her at the end of the aisle, I hadn't been able to take a full breath. I wanted to kiss her. Claim her. Possess her.

None of that could happen. I wrenched my eyes off her indecent, tempting lips. She would run, just like the rest of them. I wouldn't let her take a piece of my heart when she did.

The lie was actually a series of lies, and they'd started when I'd reached the section in the application about sexual compatibility. On a scale of one to ten, I'd marked my desire for sex as a one. The lowest possible score. At the time, it had seemed appropriate, since I was freshly dumped and men were generally awful.

I was also harboring a secret second lie, which was the fact that my body didn't work like it was supposed to. I had a condition called vaginismus, which I'd neglected to mention in the medical history portion of the application. With sexual desire marked as nonexistent, I'd figured I was covered.

I'd figured wrong.

Vaginismus caused my pelvic muscles to spasm and clench involuntarily, which led to extremely painful penetrative sex. It was curable, supposedly. With relaxation exercises, meditation, stretching, and cognitive behavioral therapy, the brain could be rewired to stop the vaginal muscles from clenching so hard.

Apparently. But all the money and effort and therapy and dilator kits and manual stretching and various homeopathic concoctions that may or may not have been actually poisonous had never worked for me. Penetrative sex always hurt. I could do other things. I could orgasm with clitoral stimulation. I could use my hands and mouth and toys with enthusiasm, and my previous partners had always assured me that they would wait for me to fix myself. Inevitably, though, the sighs and eye rolls and frustration would build up, the pressure made me shut down, and my desire for any sort of intimacy cratered. Resentment ballooned on both sides. Weeks or months—or, in Henry's case, three and a half years—would go by, and a breakup followed.

That was the pattern of every romantic relationship I'd ever had. As consistent as the sunrise. As predictable as the tide. If I'd loved myself a little more, I probably would've given up on finding a partner by now and instead found a way to make a life on my own. Unfortunately, I'd always wanted my happily-ever-after to include someone else. I'd always wanted what I couldn't have.

So I was here, trying this. The compromise I'd made with fate was that my happily-ever-after wouldn't include sex. I'd given up: Sex was off the table, and I thought I'd finally found peace with it. But it wasn't so much that I didn't *want* sex. It was more that I found sex to be unbearably, unfailingly painful, if it was done the way that men typically wanted to do it.

After Henry broke things off with me, I figured that part of me had withered away to nothing. I hadn't experienced any inkling of desire in so long that I couldn't quite remember how it was supposed to feel.

Until now.

Until Gideon stared at me, scarred and big and vaguely threatening, his touch on my waist sure and soft. Like he was holding something precious.

The expression in his eyes was as thunderstruck as I felt. No, not thunderstruck. It was *hungry*. The intensity of it made my head spin. Lust crashed into me, staggering in its violence. Desire tore a hole through me, carving out a space in my gut that instantly filled with tight, hot need. I wanted him to look at me like that all the time, forever, until I died.

But he dropped his hand from my waist and twisted his lips, angling his face away from me. He *recoiled*. The space between us widened and filled with the chill of his expression, and I sucked in a deep breath. Logic provided me with an explanation: We were supposedly a perfect match, which meant his sexual desire was low. He didn't want me that way. Probably, he didn't want me at all. He was disgusted with me. He'd seen how desperately turned on I'd become with the press of his thumb against the space below my breast, and he'd wanted to get away.

An alarm clanged in my head. Now it really was time to turn back. Time to run.

I'd been prepared for a marriage of convenience. We would've found some sort of middle ground, lived our own lives, and reached a kind of companionship that wasn't quite love but was still mutually beneficial. That's what I'd told myself. I would never have the everlasting love of a perfect marriage that I so desperately craved. No man would shackle himself to me when I could never meet all his needs. Time and time again, I'd had that lesson beaten into my battered heart. Sex really was that big a deal. No man had ever looked at me and said, *You're worth it, even if I can't put my penis in your vagina.* For a long time, I hadn't thought it was too much to ask, but now I'd finally come to terms with reality. I wasn't ever going to be enough, with my stubbornness and my big mouth and my malfunctioning lady parts.

That was why this arranged marriage had seemed like such a good idea. This marriage wouldn't be about love, but it could be full of respect and perhaps, someday, affection. Sex wasn't supposed to come into it.

But now I was attracted to him. Now it wasn't just a parallel life and companionship. Now it was one-sided desire. Unrequited lust. Now it was *torture*. I hadn't signed up to be edged for the rest of my life.

Because the reality was, I *loved* sex. I loved touching and being touched. Up until it had been worn out of me by constant pain and rejection, I'd been horny all the time.

I stood next to Gideon as he glared at the altar, my body leaning toward him like it knew it would feel so good to have those big, warm hands on it again. My pulse pounded. I teetered on my heels. The wetness in my underwear clung to my intimate flesh, cold, uncomfortable, a reminder of Gideon's rejection.

And I still wanted him. Wanted him to turn his head and look at me so I could feel electrified again. Wanted him to throw me over that broad shoulder and take me to his lair.

I was a mess. This wouldn't end well.

Time to do as Gideon suggested and pull the freaking plug. Panic nipped at me, sending my heart thumping all over again. He would be relieved. I'd be doing us both a favor.

But then what?

My life in New York was in shambles. I'd lost my business's studio space because I hadn't been able to afford the rent. I'd sold off all my furniture and packed all my belongings into two suitcases and one cardboard box. I had no friends. I had no home. I very nearly had no business, unless a horde of brides suddenly appeared and told me they wanted to throw money at me.

I could go back. I could scrape by, pretending to be a raging success while doing last-minute balance transfers and praying for a new client in order to pay the most pressing bills. Fake it until I made it. Work until the holidays, when I would go on my family's yearly ski trip so I could see them all being blissfully married while I was relegated to the air mattress on the chalet's living room floor. Endure the little comments and jabs about my spinsterhood, pretending they didn't hurt. Explain *again* why Henry had dumped me when he would've been the perfect addition to our family, him being a successful hotelier who owned the most popular wedding venue in the state of New York. Move in with my parents. Die a little inside. Date someone else. Get dumped by someone else. Rinse and repeat, year after year after year.

With wedding singers as parents, a florist for a sister, and a superstar videographer for a big brother, my failure to acquire a ring for my finger wasn't just embarrassment. It was existential. I didn't belong in my own family. My success as a wedding dress designer had been a lie. I was a big ole hypocrite. And now that my business had finally fallen apart, the reality would be exposed.

I had nothing left to lose.

"Let's do this," I said, throwing my shoulders back. I took one single step—and winced as pain sparked up my ankle.

Gideon shifted, the line between his brows turning into a chasm as he frowned. "You're hurt," he rumbled.

I straightened, glaring at him. *Nice try, buddy.* He wasn't going to use this as an excuse to call off the wedding. "I'm fine."

"You're clearly not." His arm extended slightly toward me, as if he wanted to touch me. Then he dropped it, because I was repulsive to him.

"Do you make it a habit to tell women how they're supposed to feel?"

He faced me fully again, and the weak, spineless, self-destructive part of me preened; all his attention was back on me. "Put your weight on your foot, Sadie," he said, voice deep and unimpressed.

He knew my name, and it sounded lewd when he said it like that. Not that he was saying it in some special way—that was just his voice. And of course he knew my name. He would've gotten the same profile that I got. Name, occupation, likes, dislikes. A three-page distillation of everything that I was and had and wanted.

Barring a few little fibs, of course.

Still, I was so far gone that the sound of my name on his tongue made my heart convulse. He watched me, waiting for me to tap out. But I wasn't going to let him use a measly twisted ankle to call off this marriage. I wouldn't allow it. I would make it to the end of the aisle if it freaking killed me.

I gritted my teeth and took a step. As soon as my heel bore my weight, pain darted up my leg. Not unbearable, but not exactly comfortable either. It throbbed, but I lifted my chin and met Gideon's glare. I was sure that I hid my pain—I had a lot of practice, after all—but his eyes still flashed as his jaw tightened.

"Fucking hell, woman," he muttered, then swept me into his arms. It shocked me into silence, and all I could do was cling to his shoulders and hang on. Warm arms banded around my back and under my knees, his chest a solid wall by my side. I stared at his face, startled and on fire. Apparently, I loved being manhandled by him.

That's when I realized that fate's cruelest prank wasn't the fact that I was beautiful but sexually dysfunctional. No. Her biggest laugh was that I'd never been more attracted to a man who wanted nothing to do with me.

Gideon didn't spare me a glance. In a muttered breath, he said, "Stubborn as all hell. Fucking figures."

"I'm pretty sure you're not supposed to swear in the house of God," I pointed out.

"I'm already going to hell," he said, and turned us toward the altar. "It can't get any worse than this."

"Wow," I said. "*Wow*."

That made his hard blue eyes slide over to meet mine. Our lips were inches apart. My hands had found their way to his neck, my forearms propped on his shoulders. His skin was so *warm*. I curled my fingernails against his nape, relishing the way his chest moved with a sharp inhale. I could feel every finger of his hand pressed against the backs of my ribs, every heartbeat thumping against my side, every harsh breath filling his lungs. "You know this is a bad idea," he told me.

"So it's a compulsion." I nodded in understanding.

"What is?"

"Your habit of telling me what I think and feel."

He stopped and set me down on the first step of the dais that held the altar. In my heels, on that first step, I was slightly taller than him. I used the opportunity to look down my nose at him, which was very satisfying but didn't seem to bother him one bit. He just met my gaze and snorted. "Maybe I made the mistake of assuming you were a rational person, but you're here, so."

"So, what? Finish the sentence."

"So obviously you're out of your mind."

I planted my hands on my hips. "Oh yeah? And what's your excuse?"

"I'm a hopeless romantic," he deadpanned. "Emphasis on the hopeless."

Outrage burned the inside of my ribs. The little devil sank his claws into my shoulder, cackling as he held on. I opened my mouth—

"Gid," his brother and best man cut in. We both turned to glower at him, and he lifted his palms in response. "You guys good?"

"Peachy," I bit off just as Gideon snarled, "Fantastic." Then we looked at each other again and narrowed our eyes.

"Okay, well, I thought I might remind you that you've got an audience." The best man tilted his head toward the pews.

I blinked, and my stomach bottomed out. I'd forgotten. I'd— what had actually just happened to me? I'd been so taken with Gideon that nothing else had registered in my brain. Not the murmurs, or the rustle of clothes, or the creaking of the pews, or the scent of burning candles, or the light of the stained-glass window, or the three outrageously large peacock feathers that trembled a few feet above an old woman's head in the front row.

The feathers were attached to the wide-brimmed royal blue hat that crowned her riot of ice-white curls. The woman's gaze was utterly steady as she watched the two of us. She blinked once and graced us with a serene, beatific smile.

Etta Mars. Gideon's grandmother, the mastermind behind this whole thing, evidently approved of me—of whatever was happening between me and Gideon. Or she was getting ready to stab me in my sleep. Or she was senile and busy watching monkeys swing around the vines growing inside her brain.

I turned back to my husband-to-be, and once again was stunned by the intensity of his gaze. He met my eyes for a long moment, then, very quietly, murmured, "Last chance, Sadie."

I decided I hated when he said my name. It threw me off-balance a little too much for comfort. "For what?" I managed to grate out.

"To back out."

My smile held no humor. "Nice try. Won't be that easy to get rid of me."

At my words, energy zapped between us. It must have only lasted a second or two, but it felt like every atom of my body, every cell living and growing and dying in that moment, was utterly focused on Gideon. The harsh light in his eyes. The shape of his lips. The bob of his throat as he swallowed once, twice. The decision that came over him, that almost audibly snapped an invisible thread that had been holding him back. "Suit yourself," he said, and wrapped both hands around my waist to lift me up to the top of the dais. I wobbled, and his hands tightened as he joined me there and faced me. My own hands landed on his arms, clenching against the hard muscle I found there. He was so tense I worried he was made of stone.

Breath sawed in and out of my lungs, and I couldn't stop staring. Light flickered on both sides of his face, colored by the stained glass over the scars, white over the unblemished skin. His hair was thick, and I itched to run my fingers through it. He was brutal and pitiless and magnetic. I was pretty sure I was halfway in love with him already.

"Like what you see?" he grated, lips twisted. I knew he was referring to the damaged skin on his left side.

"Yes," I told him, and it was the truth. The scars were just scars—we all had those. Only mine weren't visible on my body.

My response didn't seem to please him. His jaw tensed, his eyes searching mine as if to try to expose my deception. Looking for a way out, even now.

"DEARLY BELOVED," boomed a voice beside me. I jumped, and Gideon dropped his hands from my body. I did the same, feeling a rush of cold sweep through me. I turned to see a short and very round man in white robes. He looked like a marshmallow. He was entirely bald, and his head shone with various colors from the stained-glass windows behind him. He thrust his arms out to the sides, robe sleeves billowing like wings. The church organ rang with a dramatic chord, the noise echoing into the high arches above us. "WE ARE GATHERED HERE TODAY—"

"Reverend Strife," murmured the best man. He handed over a microphone. "Here."

"He won't need that," Gideon interrupted, intercepting the microphone, turning it off, and passing it back to his brother. "Strife, just cut to the chase."

The reverend's head went red all over, his arms falling back to his sides. "Pardon me?"

"Man, wife, kiss." A muscle on Gideon's cheek spasmed when he said the last word, but his gaze remained hard as he stared at the minister. "You know the drill. We don't need theatrics." He turned to look over the church, face angled up at the balcony above the front door. "That goes double for you, Marigold!"

The organ played a sad *womp-womp-wooommmp* sound, and I had to roll my lips to stop from laughing. Gideon didn't look quite so amused. He glared at the balcony, then at me.

A thrill went through me, dive-bombing through my stomach and landing somewhere between my thighs. We both turned to the reverend.

Reverend Strife looked at me as if to say, *Control your husband*, which was a bit rich considering I'd met Gideon five minutes ago. I shrugged and said, "I do?"

"Was that a question?" Gideon asked, ocean blue eyes blinking over to meet mine. "You better be sure about this, because as soon as we sign the wedding certificate, you'll be my wife."

He made it sound like a threat, which I didn't appreciate. I narrowed my eyes. "And you'll be my husband."

"Poor you," he said, shifting his gaze back to the reverend. "Do it, Strife."

The reverend arched a brow. "Take the bride's hands in your own."

Gideon gritted his teeth. The reverend waited. Finally, Gideon huffed a breath and grabbed my hands. His gaze touched mine for an instant, then turned back to the reverend. I tried to pretend I wasn't trembling, the pads of my fingers nestled in his big, callused palms.

"Do you, Gideon Mars, take Sadie Geo"—the reverend frowned—"Geog"—he cleared his throat—"*gee-oh-hee-gan*—"

"It's pronounced gay-gun," I said, forcing another smile. After today, I wouldn't have to correct people on the pronunciation of Geoghegan every time my last name came up. I wouldn't have to spell it over the phone while failing to remember the NATO phonetic alphabet. From today onward, I would be Sadie Mars. Four letters. Nice and simple. That upgrade was worth a lifetime with a sexy grump who found me repulsive. I hoped.

Reverend Strife glared at me. "Why is it spelled like this if it's pronounced gay-gun?" he demanded.

"*I do,*" Gideon interjected forcefully. "Now do her."

"This is not how things are done," Reverend Strife complained. He rose up to his full height, which hit right around Gideon's ribcage. "Gideon Mars," he started again, eyes flashing as if daring Gideon to interrupt him again. "Do you take Sadie Geoghegan to be your lawfully wedded wife? Do you promise to love and cherish her, in good times and in bad, in sickness and in health, for richer, for poorer, for better and for worse, and forsaking all others, keep yourself only unto her"— the reverend inhaled, and in a solemn, echoing voice, intoned— "*until death do you part?*"

Gideon paused, and my heart began to rattle. Stormy blue eyes met mine. He studied me for an endless moment, and the breath in my lungs turned solid. Despite the application and the forms and the interviews that had led me to this moment, all the hours of packing and planning, it was only now that things felt truly real.

Today was my wedding day.

After everything—all the chaos and the heartache and the pain—I would be married. The vow's words echoed in my mind. Until death. *Until death.* This wasn't just a promise for a week or a month or a year. It was a promise for life.

That meant something to me.

Finally, in a low rumble, Gideon vowed, "I do."

Breath slid past my lips in a rush. I blinked rapidly, hand tightening around Gideon's. His eyes searched mine, a slight frown etching lines in his brow. His thumb made a slow sweep over the back of my hand, the touch so gentle that I almost thought I imagined it. Then his scowl deepened, and he turned to glare once more at Reverend Strife.

"Sadie Geoghegan," the reverend boomed, my name echoing around the church. "Do you take Gideon Mars to be your lawfully wedded husband?" He repeated the vows, and they swirled around me, settling over my shoulders like a weight.

I was promising Gideon eternity, and he was looking at me like he couldn't wait to get rid of me. That had to be inviting some sort of cosmic curse into my life. But how could things get any worse than they already were?

Gideon watched me, as if he were suddenly not bothered by the minister's theatrics or the low rumble of the organ accompaniment. "Having second thoughts?" Gideon murmured, a little mocking and a lot bitter, his voice so low that only I and the minister could hear.

I narrowed my eyes at him, not liking the resigned, unsurprised note in his voice. He sounded like me backing out was exactly what he expected. Because of his scars, I gathered. I was so superficial and shallow as to leave him at the altar because his skin wasn't a perfect, unblemished canvas. Did he think so little of me?

I swallowed past the boulder in my throat and lifted my chin. When I spoke my vow, it was with a strong voice that rang clear and bright over the assembled crowd: "I do."

"The rings," Reverend Strife prompted, and Gideon turned to his brother, who produced two simple gold bands. Behind the best man, two other brothers—had to be, with all of them being tall, broad, and handsome—peeked their heads around the first brother's shoulders to watch. My left hand only trembled a little as Gideon took it in his.

The gold band slid past my knuckle. A perfect fit. I'd filled in my ring size on one of the endless forms that had been sent to me, but it still surprised me when the ring slid on so easily. The gold warmed against my hand within moments.

I took the bigger ring, noting the clenching of Gideon's jaw as he lifted his left hand. His wrist was mottled with scar tissue on one side, and it crawled all the way up along his pinky and ring fingers. His eyes narrowed slightly, as if challenging me to touch him.

I resented that. I wasn't afraid of a few scars. He'd soon learn that my body wasn't exactly perfect, either. Maybe. If we ever made it that far. If, by some chance, Gideon had lied on his application too.

Clenching my jaw, I shifted the ring to my left hand. With my right, I held the scarred side of his hand to angle it so I could slide his wedding band on his third finger. As soon as my skin touched his, he stiffened. I gentled my touch, but I didn't let go, even when he tried to pull away.

The ring fit perfectly as it slid onto his finger, and before

Gideon could move, I slid my hands into both his palms and held him there.

I wasn't going to let him ruin this for me. I'd made a vow; I was all-in.

"I now pronounce you man and wife," Reverend Strife announced. "Gideon, you may kiss the bride."

My pulse took off. There was a creak from the pews, as if everyone had leaned forward at once. The air seemed to still, and even Marigold's organ remained silent for one single, pregnant moment.

Gideon pulled gently on my fingers, and I leaned toward him. He angled his head, and I parted my lips. His body blotted out the light behind him, the stained glass painting his scarred side in pink and blue and green. Some of the coldness left his eyes as he dipped his gaze to my lips, and I swallowed convulsively.

Gideon Mars was *very* attractive. It hit me again, all at once, in that moment where our heads angled in preparation to fit together. I didn't think he knew the effect he had, and I was sure it wasn't just me. He looked dangerous and strong. He looked like he could face down any enemy without flinching. A warrior. A survivor. And in that moment, right before our first kiss, when he softened...

My heart fluttered. The scent of his skin filled my nose. Spicy and woodsy and male—intoxicating.

The last person to kiss me had been Henry. And he'd been nothing like Gideon. He had none of the raw, powerful energy that my new husband possessed. None of the potent maleness that seemed to press against me like a physical weight.

This kiss wasn't just ceremonial for me. Desire spread over

my lower abdomen like warm butter, the feeling as unfamiliar as it was heady. A low, flickering fire continued to build in the pit of my stomach.

Gideon leaned in. I felt his breath on my mouth, and I closed my eyes, tilting my head up to accept the kiss...

Only for Gideon to angle his head at the last minute, pressing a chaste kiss on the corner of my lips. He angled our heads to block the guests' view of us, so it looked like he was actually kissing me. As a cheer went up, Gideon moved his lips to my ear.

"You're welcome," he said, and pulled away. For not kissing me for real? His eyes were as hard as ever, a challenge blazing in them.

I narrowed my eyes before I remembered we had an audience. A familiar, bright smile stretched over my face—my best armor against the world—and I turned to face the crowd of strangers that had just witnessed my wedding.

Just because I knew it would annoy him, I gripped Gideon's arm and pressed myself up against it. And, fine, it wasn't *just* to annoy him. His biceps were magnificent, and the clench of his hand against mine was delicious.

Then the doors to the church burst open, and an old, balding man stood in the entryway, breathing hard. He had stringy brown hair clinging to the sides of his head, and he wore a short-sleeved button-down with wet patches under his arms, evidence of the sweltering July sun still beating down on the town outside. The congregation turned to stare. His eyes widened slightly at the sight of everyone looking at him.

Marigold pounded out a dramatic chord on the organ, and the man straightened. "Mr. Titty," he said between pants, when the organ had quieted down. "Mr. Titty struck again. Got the front of the church."

I got so far as to ask "Who's Mr—" before the force of a very small, round man barreling down off the dais knocked me off my stiletto heels. It was only Gideon's arm wrapping around my waist that stopped me from falling to the base of the stairs and being trampled by all the elderly people rushing to get outside in their orthopedic shoes. I clung to the front of his suit, got my feet back under me, and looked over my shoulder as the doors swung shut behind the last guest. Silence fell like a sack of bricks. My pulse was beating hard, and my breath sounded too loud in the empty church.

I lifted my gaze to Gideon's, watching the way the high, flickering chandelier's lights kissed his unblemished right side. His stubble had been shaped to highlight his jaw and cheekbone, and I knew that he must have been incredibly handsome before the event that scarred him. Then he turned his head to meet my gaze, and the other side of his face came into view.

He was still handsome, just...different. And really, I wasn't one to judge. My problems were internal, but they still shaped my life the way I imagined Gideon's marks had shaped his.

He watched me scan the scars, and his gaze went hard. Again. I wanted to scream, explain that I wasn't judging him, I just—they were part of him! I was captivated. But I already knew he wouldn't believe me.

I gulped. His arm was still around my waist, my own hands pressed up against his chest. Just like the first time, my world narrowed to the space between us. The points of contact between his hard body and my much softer one. This was the closest I'd been to a man—to anyone—since Henry. I'd forgotten how good it felt to be in someone's arms. Forgotten how blank my mind could go when I felt comfortable and at peace. When I felt safe.

It was a brain malfunction to feel safe with a man who so clearly didn't want this. I should've been guarded and hesitant. I should've pulled away. Gideon's pale eyes were flinty, but his touch was warm. He held me softly, his palm flat against the back of my hip, his fingertips grazing the curve of my waist.

That warm-butter feeling spread lower, dripping along the insides of my thighs. I swallowed, index fingers tracing the edge of his collar while my other fingers remained curled in his lapels, body leaning toward his.

There was *something* here. The way he'd looked at me...the flashes I saw in his gaze... He *was* attracted to me, at least a little. Wasn't he? A one out of ten wasn't a zero. Maybe—

"You're wrinkling my suit jacket."

I jerked back. "Oh. Sorry."

He used his big, rough hands to yank at the lapels to try to smooth them out. Without looking at me, he said, "This is our best opportunity to slip out of here before the reception."

"You don't want to go to your own wedding reception?"

He gave me a flat look.

I blinked at him, then at the empty church. I was at a loss, trying to come to terms with the dawning horror of being very attracted to a man who was definitely not attracted to me. A man who was now my husband. I gulped, eyes landing on the big wooden doors at the other end of the aisle. "Who's Mr. Titty?"

GIDEON

She did the one thing that people had been afraid to do since the fire: She looked at me and didn't hide it.

There was no furtive glance that bounced away the minute I noticed. No pity. No barely-hidden disgust. No pretending the scarred area didn't exist, avoiding it so completely that it only made me feel more self-conscious about the marks on my skin.

No. Sadie saw me, all of me, and I suddenly felt human again after living five long years as a ghost.

THREE
SADIE

Mr. Titty was a graffiti artist with a penchant for drawing bosoms. His latest tag was bright blue against the carved wood of the church doors, two gigantic globes with teeny tiny nipples, one on each door. His name was signed in stylized font on the bottom of the right-hand door, with some blue overspray staining the bottom hinges and the surrounding brown brick. All of us—the reverend, me, Gideon, and all the guests—stood on the grass in front of the church to admire his latest work.

"Reminds me of myself about fifty years ago," said a woman with the most gigantic breasts I'd ever seen, her voice wistful and pleased. She had hair dyed fire engine red, and her breasts were lifted and smooshed together, displayed prominently above the low neckline of her navy dress.

"Fifty years is a long time," another older woman grumbled, earning a glare from the well-endowed redhead.

"Jealous, Betsy?"

"Of what?" the other woman sneered, turning her nose up. "Your only accomplishment was growing those huge knockers."

"This is a travesty," yelled the reverend. "Mr. Titty must be stopped!"

"Hear, hear!" someone called out.

A hand slid over my arm. Gideon leaned closer. "Let's go," he said, a moment before a voice called out, "Gideon can figure it out. Right?"

Gideon let out a small, exasperated breath, eyes circling my face, lingering on my lips, then shifting away to look at the place where the voice had come from. His hand stayed on my arm, but he loosened his grip slightly, holding onto me as if he were afraid I was going to run away. He angled his head so his good side was to the crowd, and his voice carried as he said, "The team is investigating."

"This has gone on long enough," someone else yelled. The man who'd interrupted our wedding came into view. He was in his late fifties or early sixties with a big potbelly and a red, mottled nose. He pushed his way toward us to point at Gideon. "We all trust your family with security, and you can't even stop some tagger from drawing tits all over town. We're supposed to believe you have our safety in hand? Or maybe you only care about your more important clients. The ones that are ruining this town! And maybe this marriage is nothing but a sham—"

"Ivan, that's enough."

The crowd immediately settled, people shifting on their feet. They parted as if two enormous, invisible hands had shoved them aside, and Etta Mars appeared in the resulting space. She wore a calm expression—but her eyes scanned the townspeople with a sharpness that betrayed a mile-wide ruthless streak.

She was coming our way.

The three groomsmen drifted over, flanking Gideon and me. The best man leaned in to Gideon and said, "We'll handle this. You can take off before it gets ugly." His eyes skittered over to me, studying, assessing, and then he winked. A little girl, I guessed eleven or twelve years old, came running up to him. His face transformed—it softened and lost its guardedness.

"Daddy," she said in a loud whisper. "Mr. Popov looks mad."

The best man just put a protective arm around his daughter and held her near. Gideon watched his grandmother and said nothing.

Grandma Mars stopped in front of the old man who'd complained while the youngest—and friendliest—of Gideon's brothers leaned in to whisper in my ear, "Ivan Popov. Owns an antique store in town. Mr. Titty hit his shop earlier this week, so he's mad." I turned to nod at him, and he smiled, just like he had when I was about to walk down the aisle. He had nice hair, light brown and slightly curly, with the same blue eyes as Gideon.

I turned back to the standoff with the irate antique shop owner, watching the way Grandma Mars tilted her chin up, making the peacock feathers tremble and sway. She was shorter than Ivan, but he still looked intimidated. Then he stuck his jaw out. "You walk around here like you care about cleaning up this town, Etta, but Mr. Titty is getting bolder. You need to fix this, or else."

Grandma Mars didn't raise her voice, but when she spoke, I

was sure every single person in the street heard her. "Or else *what*, Ivan?"

"Or else!" A bead of sweat rolled down the side of his head. He was tall and thin apart from the potbelly, and he wore a striped button-down that looked like it was at least a few decades old. Wispy hair stuck to his skull as he glared at the woman in the big blue hat.

She stared right back, her voice as cold as Gideon's stare. It was quiet, but it whistled through the street and echoed off the buildings. "You come to me on my grandson's wedding day and complain about a bit of graffiti."

The threat in her words was unsaid, but we all heard it. Ivan blanched.

What in *The Godfather* kind of situation had I gotten myself into?

I stole a glance at Gideon, who looked grim. His best man was rubbing his temples. To my left, the two other brothers seemed to be trying to do some damage control by tapping furiously on their phones.

"Grandma Mars," Gideon said, finally letting go of my arm so he could step forward. He nodded at the old man. "Mr. Popov. The team's on it. I'll check all the CCTV on the street and find out who did this."

"You just got married," Grandma Mars reminded him. She gestured to the best man. "Jack will handle it."

Gideon sighed, exchanging a glance with Jack, who nodded.

"Not soon enough," Reverend Strife said, marching his marshmallow self toward us. "Look at my church doors!"

Gideon lifted his arms, and he was swallowed by angry townspeople. The brothers drifted away—the best man to follow

Gideon, and the two others off to a quiet place to the side to make phone calls. I looked at the boobs on the church doors, wondering what kind of omen *this* was meant to be. I doubted it was good.

"Welcome to Marswood Harbor," a sardonic voice said beside me. I turned to see a woman about my age—late twenties or early thirties—with dark, shoulder-length hair, bright hazel eyes, a bitter twist of her lips, looking over the mob with a bored expression. She wore an apron that said Knead More Bread, the name of the bakery a few doors down. Not a wedding guest, then. She glanced at me and arched her brows. "Regretting your decision to marry into the craziness yet?"

I surveyed said craziness. Gideon had managed to settle some of the more irate townspeople. He hadn't flown off the handle the way Henry did when things went wrong, or even raised his voice at all. He spoke, and people calmed down. That was a good sign, wasn't it? The late afternoon sun seemed to settle lovingly over his features. The crowd eddied around him, like he was the nexus of all that mattered. I was as bad as them all, unable to tear my gaze from him. "Not yet," I admitted.

She snorted. "Give it a few days." She stuck her hand out. "Caroline. I work at the bakery. Come by tomorrow and I'll let you know who to avoid. Although you might have a hard time, considering you're married to one of them."

"Uh-oh."

She grinned, and it transformed her face from angular and intimidating to something witchy and captivating. "This is your chance to slip away. Don't worry; Gideon will find you."

That sounded appropriately ominous. I let out an exasperated sigh. "Why is everyone assuming I want to skip my own wedding reception?"

"Maybe we're assuming you've got a brain in that pretty head of yours." She laughed, and I couldn't even be mad at her. "See you around."

She drifted away, and then Gideon was there, looming, huge, unsmiling. Everything in me tightened, squeezing the breath from my lungs. "I have to fix this," he told me, angling his head toward the graffiti. "There's food in the church basement. The mob will end up there once they've settled down. They won't pass up a free meal. I'll find you once I'm done."

His grandmother slid her hand over his shoulder as she joined us, stopping his escape. Her sharp blue eyes scanned me, then moved to Gideon. She put wrinkled hands on his stubbled cheeks and pulled him down to press a kiss to his forehead. "My eldest grandson. You've made me a very happy woman. I'm sorry about this ugliness."

"I'll handle it," he said.

"Let Jack take the reins," Grandma Mars commanded in that soft voice of hers. "It's your wedding day. Which reminds me, we need to sign that wedding certificate. Reverend!"

Gideon's lips pinched, as if he'd hoped we'd all forget about the formalities. The minister hobbled over, and the four of us shuffled back toward the church. My ankle was still a little sore, but I forced myself not to limp. It would be fine by the morning. It wouldn't stop me from signing the paperwork, that was for sure.

Grandma Mars grabbed the grumpy old woman, Betsy, who turned out to be her sister. She nodded at the busty redhead, who was still needling Betsy. "Mrs. Gretzinger," she said.

The other woman smiled at Grandma Mars. "Congratulations, Etta." Her gaze flicked over to me, assessing. Gideon's hand pressed between my shoulder blades, leading me up the church steps. I felt like a circus curiosity paraded around on display for everyone to gawk at.

We took a detour to a small table set up in the atrium, where our marriage certificate waited. Reverend Strife's head was still very red, and he waved at the certificate as his eyes strayed toward the door. He wasn't happy about the graffiti.

While Grandma Mars watched, Gideon signed, then handed the pen over to me. Our fingers brushed, and I ignored the tiny thrill that raced up my arm at the contact. It would fade; it had to. I wouldn't want him forever. I signed the certificate, which was then witnessed by Betsy and Etta. Then Etta took a crisp white envelope from the corner of the desk, slipped the marriage certificate inside, and gave us both a tight smile.

"Six weeks from today, I'll file this at Town Hall."

I inhaled, dipping my chin in a nod. This was the get-out-of-jail-free card written into our contract. In Maine, we had ninety days from the date of the ceremony to file the certificate in the town where we were married. However, *our* marriage contract had a different deadline: If either of us decided we needed out of the marriage within the first six weeks after the ceremony, we could push the eject button. The certificate would be torn up, and our marriage would never be registered. It would be as if it never happened.

I gulped, glancing at Gideon. His eyes were hard, and his back was straight. He looked resigned—and determined. I guessed he was thinking he only had to endure the sight of me for a matter of weeks.

Heat flared in my chest, but it wasn't lust. It was shame and embarrassment and determination. This was my one way out. My *one* shot. I had to make it work. That meant, no matter how much Gideon thought he would be free of me within six weeks, he was wrong. I would make sure that certificate got registered at Marswood Harbor Town Hall if it killed me.

Etta Mars slipped the envelope containing my future into her purse, then turned to Gideon. "My boy," she said. "Congratulations."

He simply grunted in response, not looking at me.

Then she turned to me, spearing me with a look. It was my turn to feel the warmth of her hands and the hardness of her rings against my cheeks. She kissed my forehead and said in a voice so low I had to strain to hear it, "If you hurt him, I will ruin your life."

Startled, I pulled back from her. Gideon was listening to Betsy complain about vandalized windows at the front of the local beauty salon, and Grandma Mars's face returned to the serene, harmless grandmother I was sure she wasn't. She gestured to the door. "Shall we?"

The reverend was out before anyone could say anything else, his dramatic sigh immediate as he took in the state of the church's doors. The four of us streamed out after him, and I stood at the top of the steps, looking out over the mostly elderly population, the overgrown grass median, the trees in need of pruning, and the graffiti visible on a number of buildings. I took a deep breath. Half the shops on Main Street were vacant. This was not a quaint, touristy town. This was a town on the verge of death.

A warm summer breeze swept down the street, ruffling through the overgrown trees whose leaves were green and cheerful as they danced in the wind. My dress fluttered around my legs, and I inhaled the scent of summer and the fresh, briny air. A weight lifted from my chest; I hadn't even known it was there.

There was no business to save and astronomical rent to scrape together. The biggest worry in Marswood Harbor was a pair of breasts spray-painted in blue behind me. Life was slow and small and lovely.

I wanted to stay here, I realized. I'd married into this town, and I would make sure that when six weeks were up, I *could* stay. When I glanced at my husband, I found him watching me. He arched a brow, and I lifted my chin. Then he sighed, resigned, and nodded to the stairs. We made our way down and joined the crowd. Gideon left me to go confer with his brothers, presumably about Mr. Titty.

I was mobbed by aunts, uncles, and cousins. I retained none of their names. They lied about how beautiful the ceremony was and tactfully avoided asking me about my fall. They all knew I designed wedding dresses. I'd obviously been Googled before arriving here to marry the eldest grandchild in the Mars clan.

I'd just met another of Grandma Mars's grandchildren— Lola, a girl of about fourteen with silky blond hair and a bright smile who bounced up the steps and gushed about my dress and veil—when the roar of many engines cut through the ruffling of leaves on trees and the chattering of birds and people. As one, every wedding guest turned toward the noise.

A dozen motorcycles came over the crest of the nearest hill, taking up both lanes of traffic, not bothered by the fact that half of them were going the wrong way down the street. Their motorcycles rumbled and roared, echoing off the buildings and drowning out the murmur of the crowd.

From the corner of my eye, I watched Gideon stiffen. His eyes were on the leader, a bearded man riding a Harley who wore a leather jacket and dark sunglasses.

"Cash Bridges," Lola muttered in my ear. "He's not supposed to come through town with his gang like this."

According to whom, I wondered.

Cash revved his engine, grinning at Gideon in a bald taunt. Gideon watched on, impassive. Then Cash slowed his bike, flanked by two lieutenants, and turned his head toward me. I felt his gaze rake over my body as a gust of wind blew my hair off my shoulders and stuck my dress to the front of my body. His grin widened, his eyes hidden behind those dark shades.

In an instant, Gideon started forward, only to be stopped by Jack's hand on his shoulder.

Grandma Mars stood next to me, her peacock feathers blowing in the breeze, her eyes taking on a hard, flinty look that told me she hadn't become a wealthy woman by chance. She'd fought for everything she had—and now she was fighting for her legacy.

The bikers' gazes moved to Mr. Titty's work on the church doors. Cash barked out a laugh, the sound of it rough and just audible over the rumble of the engines. The rest of his posse laughed in response, and the whole crew accelerated down the hill, around the corner, and out of sight. The noise of their engines faded as conversation swelled again, bolstered by fresh gossip.

"Grandma Mars, do you think Cash Bridges is Mr. Titty?" Lola asked, wide-eyed.

"No," the older woman replied before sliding a soft, wrinkled hand over my elbow. Her grip was surprisingly tight; I wouldn't escape it. "Let's go inside," she said, and turned me toward the side of the church where we could access the basement.

"He's gloating, Etta," Betsy said, glaring down the street at where the bikers had disappeared. "Making a show of strength on your eldest grandson's wedding day. He's Mr. Titty, and he's getting more brazen by the day. He's trying to stop you from cleaning up the town so he can keep running drugs and whatever else he does in that clubhouse of his. You know he's trying to expand his territory."

"Petty vandalism is beneath him," Grandma Mars replied, her grip on my elbow tightening. "Cash Bridges isn't worth talking about."

"Except for the fact that the minute he rolled into town four years ago was when everything started going downhill."

Grandma Mars sighed. "It started going downhill long before that. But we're changing that now." She smiled at me. "Aren't we, dear?"

I gulped and dipped my chin. "Trying to."

"Good," she said. "Now let's go inside. It's time to cut the cake. Gideon!"

His face was like thunder when he turned in response to his grandmother's voice. My heart thumped, and even with the pressure of Etta's hand on my elbow, I remained rooted to the ground, my heels sinking into the soft earth. Gideon's jaw clenched, and I wondered if he was angry about the motorcycle gang riding by. Or why he'd reacted so intensely, like he wanted to rush into the street and punch Cash Bridges right off his hog when the other man had grinned at me.

Heat circled inside me, concentrated below my navel. We watched each other, a little patch of grass separating us, and I was absolutely sure that Gideon lied about being a one out of ten. There was fire in his gaze. He'd been mad about another man's lecherous gaze on my body. He *wanted* me.

Didn't he?

Or was I just making another mistake?

GIDEON

I hovered over her like a lovesick fool in the church basement. Every time she moved, I inhaled the scent of her skin, and my want grew. I watched her lick a smear of icing off her lip, my cock a hard bar against the placket of my pants. It was unbearable. Electrifying. Awful. Incredible.

All I had to do was make it through the reception, and then I could take her to my apartment and tuck her into the spare room. Stay away from her for six weeks. Fulfill my end of the bargain with my grandmother, and let Sadie find her happily-ever-after somewhere else, with someone else.

The thought made my stomach curdle.

But how could someone as beautiful as Sadie want someone

as broken and ugly as me? How could I even think to put my scarred hands on her body?

I watched her take a sip of champagne, caught by the movement of her lips. I was sick with wanting her. Wanting what I could never have.

FOUR
SADIE

The wedding reception was a whirlwind of new names and faces. My new husband glared at his plate and occasionally at me. I caught him glancing at his watch for the thousandth time, so I asked, "Anxious about something?"

"It's almost five o'clock. The oldies will be wanting to go to bed soon, so we'll be free to leave."

I pinched my lips, casting an eye over the mostly elderly crowd. They'd picked the food tables bare and were lounging around drinking bucketfuls of coffee. One old man was already snoring in his chair, his mustache hairs fluttering with every breath. "Funny."

"I wasn't joking." Gideon straightened in his chair as two gangly boys approached. He introduced them as Connor and Glenn, brothers of Lola. His younger cousins. I was pretty sure I'd met their mom (Jennifer, maybe?), but I needed a diagram to keep all the family ties straight. There seemed to be an endless supply of cousins to meet.

Gideon nodded at Connor, the taller, dark-haired one. "Report."

Connor held a tablet in his hands. He turned it around and pressed play on a video. We watched security footage of the front of the church doors. A person darted in, spray-painted a pair of boobs, and snuck out. "Mr. Titty knows our blind spots," Connor said. "Snuck into the frame and hid his face at exactly the right moment. We've got nothing." He grimaced. His dark hair flopped over his eyes, and his suit looked a couple sizes too big for his gangly body. But he had the steely Mars eyes, and I thought he'd probably grow into a handsome man in another few years. Glenn already had a bit more bulk, but he still had the awkwardness of a teenager.

"It's not nothing," Gideon said. "It's the first time we've got him on video. Good work, Connor. Glenn."

The boys straightened at the praise, a flush darkening their cheeks as they glanced at each other and fought smiles.

"Connor." Grandma Mars's voice made me jump. I glanced over my right shoulder in time to see her come to a stop between me and Gideon. "I don't want to hear any talk about graffiti today. Let your cousins take care of it."

"But I'm the one who accessed the town's CCTV feeds—"

"Not today," she repeated, voice infinitesimally firmer. Her eyes were sharp, and her grandson's lips clamped shut. Grandma Mars ruled her family—and, by the looks of it, this town—with an iron fist. Her expression softened again as she turned to me, but I didn't quite buy the kindly grandmother act. "Connor is excellent with computers."

I smiled. "That's a very useful skill."

Gideon caught Connor's eyes and gave him a solemn nod.

Connor straightened, trying—and failing—to hide his glow at his older cousin's wordless praise. He and his brother slunk away, and Grandma Mars put her hands on Gideon's and my shoulders.

"Now," she said. "You'll need the keys."

Gideon stiffened. "The keys?"

"To the cottage."

"No." Gideon's refusal was unyielding, and Grandma Mars simply smiled.

She reached into her pocket and dangled a key ring between us. "Yes," she replied.

"I'm staying at my place."

I glanced between them, frowning. "What's going on? What's the cottage?"

"My dad's old cottage," Gideon gritted out. "We're not staying there."

"Do I need to remind you of the things you promised me?" Etta Mars asked sweetly.

My frown deepened as Gideon glared at a spot on the table. Etta Mars had something on Gideon. Was that why he'd married me? Gideon's jaw bulged, but after a long moment, he took the keys from his grandmother.

"Good boy," she said, and patted his shoulder. "You'll stay there until the certificate is filed, and then we can reconsider. Now it's getting late. Give me a kiss and go."

Dutifully, Gideon got out of his chair and kissed his grandmother's cheek. His fist was clenched around the keys. I stood and said goodbye to her, then grabbed my small purse from the back of my chair.

"See you both tomorrow," she said. "Until then..." She

smiled at the two of us, and the night looming ahead pressed against the edges of my consciousness.

"Tomorrow?" I asked.

"Family lunch," Gideon provided. "Every Sunday." He nodded at the older woman, looking utterly unhappy as his hand slid over the small of my back. I tried to hide the shiver that went through me. Tried and failed, apparently, because his eyes flicked over me. We made our slow way through the church basement, accepting well-wishes and goodbyes, and finally went up the steps and out the door. Gideon's hand stayed on my back, fingers splayed, palm warm.

He dropped it when we got outside. The sun was low in the sky, the shadows deep. Cold rushed over me, and I wrapped my arms around myself. Had he been pretending to want to touch me? For whose benefit?

"I'll follow you," I said, nodding to my vehicle in the church parking lot. "Is the cottage far? Why didn't you want to stay there?"

"Where's your jacket?"

I jerked back at his harsh tone. "Excuse me?"

"You're cold."

I dropped my arms to my sides and blew out a breath. The evening wasn't *cold*, exactly; the asphalt was still giving off heat from baking in the sun all day, but there was a chill in the air. A chill in my bones. My shoulders and arms were covered in goosebumps, but it didn't stop me from saying, "I'm fine. I'll be in my car in a minute."

He grumbled something unintelligible and stripped off his suit jacket. I lifted my palms, protesting, but the warm weight of it landed on my shoulders before I could back away. Gideon jerked the lapels closer together, and I couldn't help the small moan that slipped through my lips. The garment engulfed me in warmth and the scent of Gideon. The scent of safety.

His big hands were still on the lapels as I pushed my arms through the sleeves. He held me there, scowling, as I snuggled into the warmth he gave me. I looked up at him, wondering if there was a chance—any hope at all—that he felt a spark for me the way I did for him.

"Can you drive in those things?" Gideon demanded, glowering at my very beautiful shoes.

I clicked my tongue to hide my embarrassment. There was no spark. He found me as ridiculous and repulsive as he had when he first clapped eyes on me. I waved him off. "You know, I'm not *completely* useless." I stomped past him, dress fluttering around my legs. "You're treating me like I'm a liability, and it's getting real old—"

"Sadie."

I clicked the fob to unlock the car and wrenched open the driver-side door. "I get that you didn't want to marry me, but give me a *chance*. I'm not some useless woman who can't handle a car—"

"Sadie."

"I'm not a *complete* moron—"

"*Sadie.*"

"*What!*"

Gideon prowled closer, then crouched down beside the front wheel of my car. The completely flat front wheel of my car that I'd walked by without noticing. His finger traced a clean slice in the rubber, and a brow arched before he lifted his gaze to meet mine.

I blinked at the slash in my tire. Cold fear filled my belly. "What's that?"

Gideon's jaw tightened as we stared at the flat tire. His narrowed gaze flicked from my wheel to the church doors, the blue of the spray paint just visible at this angle.

"You think it was Mr. Titty?" I asked.

"Not his M.O.," he answered gruffly, but his eyes stayed glued to the boob graffiti.

A gust of wind blew past us, and I wrapped Gideon's jacket tighter around me. Gideon's gaze snapped over to me, and the valley between his brows grew deeper. "How's your ankle?"

I blinked at the change in subject. "It's fine."

"Don't lie to me, Sadie."

I planted my hands on my hips. "How long is it going to take you to figure out that I mean what I say?"

He huffed. "That would make you the opposite of every other woman I've ever met."

"Rude." I turned back to my car, glaring at the gaping wound in the tire. "I need to get these fixed. Is there a tow truck in town?"

"I'll handle it," Gideon said, reaching into his pocket for his phone. He shifted closer as he made a call, his free hand moving to the middle of my back. He murmured into his phone, then met my gaze. "What do you need from the car? We'll move it over to mine."

I blinked at him, then at the tire. "But—I don't—I need to... There's a spare tire in the back..."

"Sadie."

I looked up at him, wide-eyed. Someone had slashed my tire. On my wedding day. Why? Who?

His touch was gentle as he curled a finger under my chin. "I will handle this."

Oh, wow. I stood there, struck by the surety in his voice. It was the first time in a long time that I hadn't had to deal with every disaster on my own. Gideon was shouldering the burden, even though he clearly didn't want to be married to me. I didn't know what that meant.

"Tell me what you need from your car."

I pointed to the two suitcases I'd brought with me, and Gideon hauled them out of the trunk as if they weighed nothing. The one cardboard box had work stuff in it; I wouldn't need that right away. I grabbed the big tote bag from the front seat, wondering at the vandalism. Someone could have smashed the window and grabbed my stuff. But nothing was gone. The tire had simply been punctured, as if in warning.

Gideon put my bags in the trunk of his car, then opened the passenger door and loaded me up. He waited until I was clicked in, his jacket oversized and bulky under the seatbelt. With one hand on the doorframe and the other on the edge of the door, Gideon stood in the opening, watching me.

"Am I in danger?" I whispered.

"No." His voice was resolute. Intractable. "We don't know this was directly targeting you. Petty crime has been on the rise. You've got a nice car. Could just be bad luck."

It made me feel a bit better. "Okay."

"I'll find out who did this." His words were gritted out through clenched teeth; there was nothing warm about them. Still, they caused a wave of soft, gooey heat to go through me. It felt a little pathetic, to be so affected by a man acting like a big, macho provider. I didn't need a provider; I needed a partner.

Still, coming to Marswood Harbor had been impulsive, and the whole day had been full of such conflicting emotions that I felt like I had whiplash. Gideon's words eased some of that discomfort, made me feel like I had somewhere safe to land. Like I had a home.

And wasn't that just the silliest thing to feel in a situation like this?

My desire to be independent lost to the desire to feel safe. So I nodded, and Gideon closed the door. His car smelled like him, and I took a deep breath into my lungs as he circled to the driver's side. We turned out of the lot and headed down the hill toward the water. Then we turned again, left the town limits, and snaked along a tree-covered hillside. The ocean glittered to my right as the last sliver of the sun went down behind the hills.

Gideon's presence filled the car. It was a choking, heavy thing. I thought of the touch of his finger on my chin and the way he'd snapped into action when he saw the slashed tire. A big, strong man taking control. Making sure I was safe. Taking care of me.

And I realized I was turned on.

I gulped, thinking of what was to come. Him and me, at some cottage in the woods, alone. On our wedding night. I worked to keep my breathing steady. I thought I was doing a pretty good job until Gideon asked, "What's wrong?"

"Huh?" I replied, cheerful, smiling big.

His dark gaze flicked over, then back to the winding road. "You're breathing faster than before."

I blinked. "Oh."

"Regretting the choices that brought you to this moment?"

Gideon asked, sardonic and bitter, and I was pretty sure he wasn't looking for an answer.

I gave him one anyway. "Not exactly," I hedged. *Not because of you.*

There was a long pause.

"It was probably some dumb kid," Gideon finally said in a low voice.

"What?"

"The tire. I don't think it was directed at you, specifically."

"Oh. Right." I let out an awkward laugh. "Yeah."

Gideon glanced over, frowning, then back at the winding road. He was quiet after that. My breathing slowed a bit, and I felt better.

The big, looming problem of tonight was still there, though. Soon, we'd be at the cottage, and we might progress to the part of the evening where married people were supposed to do what married people did. And I wouldn't—*couldn't*—do that. Sex was something I desperately wanted and could never have.

And he was a one out of ten. Even if I *could* have sex, Gideon wouldn't want to. He'd made that abundantly clear. Every time he touched me, it seemed like he couldn't get away fast enough. Every time he looked at me, he grimaced.

It should have been a relief to know that my new husband didn't want me in that way—wouldn't subject me to pain and pressure—but it only made me feel worse. Small and sad and rejected.

We turned down a narrow road, a few low-hanging tree branches brushing against the roof of the car, and then a dark house appeared at the end of the drive.

It was a small, gorgeous stone building nestled in the trees, with a little patch of overgrown lawn at the front. A two-car garage had been built onto the house, almost as big as the rest of the building. I slid out of the car and looked around, eyes flicking to the hill that sloped down toward the water. The sky was deep blue over the water now, a few stars flickering to life.

Even without it being fully dark, there were more stars than I'd ever seen in Manhattan. My throat went tight as I listened to the wind in the trees and the distant lapping of waves on the shore. Crickets chirped, and the trees creaked as they bent and swayed. This place was isolated. Peaceful. No one would find me here.

I could turn my phone off, and all the pressure of the business and my family's expectations would be gone. Until this very moment, I hadn't realized how much I needed that. How heavy the pressure to perform had weighed on me.

Nestled in this forest, hours of road away from everything I knew, I felt like I could simply *be*.

Similar to the feeling I got when I stood at the top of the church steps, a wave of yearning hit me. I was so *tired*. I wanted to stop and rest. I wanted to curl up in a nest of pillows and blankets and sleep for an eternity. I wanted to cut myself off from the world, from my family, from my obligations, and start over. A new life. A new *me*.

I didn't want this to end in six weeks.

"I'll show you inside," Gideon grumbled, grabbing one suitcase out of the trunk. I turned away from the view, and he hit a button on the wall to close the garage door. We went in through an interior door, took off our shoes, and padded on hardwood floors toward a decently sized open kitchen/living/dining room. Big, comfy couches framed a gigantic fireplace, with a wall of windows showing the starry sky and darkening view beyond.

It was clean, but it had the smell of closed-off, barely-used spaces. Framed sketches decorated the walls—portraits, landscapes, and one particularly good sketch of a curled-up kitten—and a big basket of neatly folded blankets sat near the fireplace. Cozy. *Adorable*.

My heart soared as my eyes scanned the space. I was in love.

I turned to watch Gideon set my bag down and head back to the garage to haul in the last one. His back shifted, muscles visible through the thin white fabric of his button-down shirt. I remembered I was still wearing his jacket, and I took the opportunity to sniff its collar one last time when he was out of the room. Then I took it off and draped it over the back of the sofa before trailing my fingers over the knotty pine dining table and crossing to the wall of windows.

While I was admiring the view, my phone chimed. I dug through my tote bag, which I'd dropped on the couch with the jacket, and found my phone. When I turned the screen toward me, a familiar pit opened in my stomach. It was the family group chat.

> **MOM**
>
> Making plans for Christmas. This place looks perfect!

A link followed. Even though I knew what to expect, I still clicked on it. Still looked at the accommodation my mother thought was "perfect" for our yearly trip. Still felt the need to point out the obvious.

SADIE

That place only has three bedrooms.

MOM

The couch pulls out.

Because my favorite activity was bashing my head against the wall, I replied:

SADIE

Who's sleeping on it this year?

The rest of my family joined the chat, as well as their partners. I could see five people online, which I guessed were my mom Sandra, my sister Christine, her husband Mark, my brother Lucas, and his wife Lucy. None of them bothered replying. They just reacted to my message with a rolling-on-the-floor-laughing emoji.

Because it was a given that I would sleep on the couch in the living room. Because I was single, and therefore less valuable.

"What is it?"

I jumped, turning to see Gideon standing in the mouth of the short hallway leading to the garage. It was all darkness behind him, with only the light of the nearly-faded sun illuminating his front. He looked menacing and dangerous, but not in a way that made me afraid. He could take on whatever threat was thrown at him and come out ahead.

And I had the sinking feeling that I was nothing but a burden. First the wedding, which he obviously hadn't wanted. Then the tire. And now my petty familial problems. How much more could he take before he threw his hands up and decided I wasn't worth the trouble?

He wouldn't be the first man to toss me away like garbage.

I *wanted* to trust him, but I'd learned my lesson. I knew I couldn't. He'd probably think my being on the brink of tears over a pull-out couch on a family vacation was ridiculous. I mostly agreed, but I couldn't help the way I felt. But add to that the fact that my body was defective, and he obviously found me repulsive?

We wouldn't last six weeks. We wouldn't even last six days.

I exhaled, and the tears receded. "Nothing," I croaked.

He set my last suitcase down and prowled toward me. He moved quietly for a man his size, scanning my face and body before casting an eye around the room. He came to a stop in front of me, then reached over to press my chin up with his curled index finger. I hated that. I *loved* that. Forcing my eyes to open, I met his gaze. Heat rolled off his body, searing my front. His touch was gentle, barely an inch of contact between us, and it made me dizzy.

And his eyes, as always, were cold and hard and suspicious.

"You should stop lying to me," he suggested in a quiet rumble.

"I'm not—" I cut myself off as his brow jumped. I gulped. "Don't you find this all a bit overwhelming?" I finally asked, my voice squeaking at the end. I blinked rapidly, mortified by the prickling returning with a vengeance behind my eyes.

He dropped his hand and took a step back. "Not the Prince Charming you were expecting?"

"Stop doing that," I snapped, regaining control over my emotions.

Gideon blinked at me. "Stop doing what?"

"Saying that kind of thing. You treat me like I should be afraid of you."

"Maybe you should be."

I paused, holding his gaze. The thing was, I'd dated a manipulator. Henry was charming and perfect on the outside, but he'd taken a chisel to my self-esteem and carefully carved out chunks of it over the course of our three-and-a-half-year relationship. When he'd broken up with me, I'd been devastated, but a part of me had been relieved. I hadn't *quite* shaken the voice in my head that told me no one would want me—a voice that sounded eerily similar to Henry's—but I was working on it. And I'd been able to recognize that his leaving me had been a good thing, even though it hurt. Some men were users, consumed with selfish desires and a need for control.

Gideon was not that. He was angry and guarded, but he didn't look at me like I was something he could use. History taught me I shouldn't trust him, and maybe I didn't—not completely. But I wasn't *afraid* of him.

I stuck my jaw out. "Like it or not, we're in this together, Gideon."

He blinked when I said his name, and his eyes dropped to my lips. Sparks flitted through my middle as we stood there, suspended in time. Warmth dripped like melted wax across my lower abdomen and down the insides of my thighs, but I knew the space between my legs remained as malfunctioning as it always had. The new me hadn't grown a different, more operational vagina.

Didn't mean I couldn't want, though. Want and fantasize

and touch. The problem was when a man wanted more. Or, in Gideon's case, when a man didn't want anything at all.

Gideon tilted his head toward the small hallway off the kitchen. "I'll show you the bedroom."

That's when I realized this house was gorgeous, but it was small. Like, one-bedroom small. He grabbed both suitcases and led the way into the bedroom. *Our* bedroom.

I stared at the bed, neatly made, two pillows lying flat at the head, and my throat went tight.

"I can"—Gideon cleared his throat, suddenly dropping the whole *I'm-a-scary-monster-and-you-should-be-scared-of-me* act —"I'll sleep on the couch."

"That's not—" I stopped. "I don't want to kick you out of your own bed." I knew how it felt to be relegated to the couch. I wouldn't do it to my own husband. I swallowed, straightened my shoulders. "We're married," I finally said, but didn't have the guts to finish the thought. *We should be sharing a bed.*

Gideon set my suitcases down in front of the closet doors, then turned to face me. The room was so small that he'd only had to lean over to do it, and my bags now blocked the path to the other side of the bed. Gideon made it feel even smaller. He was just so...*big*. Broad shoulders and thick legs. A muscular chest. Easy, powerful movements. He towered over me, and I couldn't bring myself to dislike the feeling.

Why hadn't I just accepted his offer to sleep on the couch? That would've solved all my issues. I wouldn't have to tell him about my viselike, malfunctioning vagina, and he wouldn't have to realize that my body was defective and useless. *You look like you're built for sex,* Henry told me more than once, clicking his tongue, eyes sympathetic. He'd make it sound like a compliment, until he'd add, *It's such a waste*.

If Gideon slept on the couch, we could coexist, reach some sort of understanding, live our parallel lives. Easy. Simple. Clean.

But then what? What if Gideon was my best chance at a good life?

I loved this cottage in the forest. I loved the run-down town and the kooky, elderly inhabitants. I loved that the biggest problem was Mr. Titty and a few overly loud motorcycles. The slashed tire wasn't great, but I could deal with that. I *wanted* to stay. For the first time in years, it felt like I was choosing something for myself. I wasn't just picking a slice of the wedding industry and carving out a business because that's what my family expected. I wasn't dating a man who would be my perfect match on paper, even though he was a different person behind closed doors.

Coming to this little town had been an act of rebellion, and I wasn't ready to tuck tail and run.

Vaginismus could be cured. Every doctor said so. My old therapist said so. My brain just had to get the memo to not make those muscles clench when they were supposed to relax. Problem was, my brain had never cooperated, and I was starting to think it never would.

And what were the chances of Gideon hanging around while I tried to fix my malfunctioning brain and my stupid, nonworking vagina?

But maybe...maybe tonight was the night? I was married now. My husband was there, big and broad and male, and there was no reason for us not to try.

"What do you want, Sadie?" Gideon asked. The room was dark, with only a sliver of light coming in between the curtains, highlighting Gideon's cheekbone, his jaw, his hair. The scarred side of his face was in shadow. His voice vibrated across the space between us, sliding over my skin like velvet. He had a great voice.

My own came out like a whisper when I said, "I want to *try*. I don't want to give up before we've attempted to make it work."

His eyes glittered in the dimness, studying me. The light was fading fast, and we hadn't flicked on the lamp. Licking my lips, I lifted a hand to touch his jaw. I remembered how he'd flinched when I'd grabbed his left hand, and I regretted making him uncomfortable, so I made sure to touch the unscarred right side. Maybe the skin on his left side was oversensitive or sore, or maybe he just didn't want to be touched there. I, of all people, should've understood that. I resolved to do better. I'd take note of his boundaries and stay on my side of them. Stubble rasped against my palm, and I traced the line of his beard up to his ear, combing my fingernails over his temple and down to the nape of his neck. His hair was like heavy silk against the backs of my hands.

A low, rumbling groan sounded in Gideon's throat. The sound was tortured and needy and *hot*. He did that from me touching the side of his head. What sounds would he make when I touched the rest of him? Liquid heat scorched down my thighs, and I found myself moving closer. My front pressed against Gideon's as his hands slowly slid up my flanks and came to rest on my waist.

I focused on my breathing. My body was healthy, and it

would work. That's what my therapist had said. My body was healthy. My body was healthy. *My body was healthy.* As long as I stayed relaxed, my brain wouldn't panic and cause my pelvic floor to seize up.

It helped that Gideon's touch was gentle, that he seemed content with stroking the bottom of my ribcage with his thumbs, that his eyes circled my face and softened. I could do this. In one of my suitcases, there was a set of graduated dildos—a dilator set—that I'd bought to try to stretch things down there. I'd gotten to the second one out of five, about the thickness of my middle finger and a little longer. It was still uncomfortable, but it was getting easier. I *could* have sex. I *would* have sex. Tonight was my wedding night! I would *not* mess it up.

Looking up at my husband's face and unable to read his expression in the darkness, I asked, "Why didn't you kiss me before, at the altar?"

He was silent for a long moment. I felt his jaw clench against my palm, and then he finally replied, "Didn't think you'd want to."

I exhaled softly, my heart throbbing violently. "I did," I admitted. "I do."

GIDEON

I thought I'd heard wrong. With my hands on her waist and the soft press of her breasts against my chest, my heart was thumping so hard I couldn't trust my ears.

She had to have an angle. She wouldn't want me, ugly and scarred as I was. This was a ruse. A ploy. For what? What was she trying to gain?

But I was weak, and she was temptation incarnate. My resistance crumbled. I couldn't go the rest of my life without tasting her lips at least once.

FIVE
SADIE

Time stood still. I trembled in my new husband's arms, balancing on a cliff's edge. Vulnerability wasn't something I was comfortable with. I'd built a moat around myself over the years, an attempt at self-preservation. My work persona was glamorous and untouchable. Around my family, I was sardonic and unflappable. I didn't have friends to be vulnerable with. Not real ones.

Henry had slithered through my defenses by creating hairline cracks in them that he pried open with comments and criticisms. Over the years, I'd exposed my soft center to him; all the ways that I felt I wasn't enough. How much it hurt that I couldn't be the woman he wanted me to be. How much of a failure I was for having a body that just wouldn't do what it was supposed to do.

He'd been loving and understanding...until he wasn't. He'd used his connections in the wedding industry to send a steady stream of brides to my business, then almost gleefully cut them off when we broke up. He'd made me trust him with my secrets and then used them to control me.

I'd vowed to never put myself in that position again.

And yet in just a couple of hours, Gideon had managed to get me to open the gates and drop the drawbridge. I was asking —begging—for him to kiss me. Hold me. Love me.

Sex was never just sex for me. It had always been a complicated knot of emotion and compulsion. But I still wanted it right now, with him.

His throat bobbed on a hard swallow, eyes studying mine. Around my waist, his hands tightened. Warmth soaked into my skin at his touch, and I couldn't help the soft exhale that slipped past my lips. Gideon's hair was silky and thick between my fingers. My body bowed toward him as I ached for more contact.

Just when the threat of rejection loomed large enough to make panic tighten around the base of my spine, Gideon let out a harsh breath, murmured a curse, and kissed me.

The world tilted. Heat scorched through me, and both my arms tightened around his neck. His hands spasmed around me then slid lower, pawing my curves in a rough, possessive grip. Gideon's kiss was claiming. He groaned into my mouth and swept his tongue against mine. He pulled me closer. Tighter.

Nothing had ever felt so good. I panted his name as he kissed my jaw, my neck. His hands grabbed and squeezed, and a line of fire blazed down the middle of me. I *ached*. Then he slid a hand up my side to grip my breast. I gasped at the possessiveness of his touch, pulling my head back slightly to look into his eyes.

They were dark. Black. "This what you want?" he rasped,

his voice making everything from my shoulders to my knees go numb.

I nodded. "Yes."

"You want your husband to fuck you on your wedding night?"

The rumble of his voice made desire spike inside me, but a thin tendril of fear began to snake through me. I hadn't told him about my issue. But I swallowed convulsively, and the words couldn't come. So I just told him the simple truth, pushed it past my lips in a breathy rasp. "Yes."

He grunted, then tugged the strap of my dress off my shoulder, exposed my breast, and took it into his mouth. His other arm banded around my waist as I arched back to give him better access. His hot tongue laved my nipple, his free hand plumping my breast. I could feel his thumb sinking into my flesh, his fingers splayed over the side of my chest and across my ribs. It was like a brand. His skin was so hot I could think of nothing except how good it felt to feel it against mine.

My fingers curled into his hair and clawed at his shirt. My thighs rubbed together, restless, needy.

He hummed, pleasure vibrating in his tone. "Desperate for it," he murmured.

I tried to huff out a laugh, but it was hardly more than a short exhale. "No need to gloat."

"Been a while," he said, and I wasn't sure if he was talking about me or himself. I thought I detected a bit of vulnerability in his tone too. I pulled back to search his eyes, and he took the opportunity to kiss my lips once more. I lost myself in the taste of him, the strength of his arms, the scent of his skin. There was need in the way he palmed my breast. Desire in the low, rumbling groan that sounded as if it were ripped from his throat.

A little voice began to whisper, *What if he lied on the questionnaire too? What if he wants this as badly as you do?*

A man who was a one out of ten for sexual desire didn't kiss like this. He didn't stroke and palm and touch the way Gideon did. He didn't make noises like touching me was the last thing he wanted to do before dying happy.

Gideon was more than hungry. He was *famished*. He drank in our kisses like I was the best thing he'd ever tasted. He touched me like my body had been crafted from his wildest fantasies. I clung to him, lust building inside me like an electrical storm. My thoughts were nothing but a low hum, and my body moved of its own volition.

When my fingers wrapped around his clothed cock, Gideon bit out another curse. His hands slid to my waist, fingers tightening to hold me there, and he glanced down between us. My fingers clenched around his hard length as my chest rose and fell with every exhale. My nipple glistened, wet from his ministrations, my carefully crafted dress a rumpled mess.

Tension pulled taut between us. There was still time to recover. Sure, I was half-undressed, but I could scoop my strap back onto my shoulder and cover myself. That would be the safe thing to do. The smart thing to do. I couldn't take another rejection.

But Gideon moved first. His hands slid to the back of my dress, where the invisible zipper held the fabric closed. He tugged it down and brushed the other strap from my shoulder. I shifted, letting the fabric puddle at my feet.

Then he blinked.

"It's shapewear," I explained, fumbling. I slipped my thumbs into the top of the nylon fabric where it rested just below my breasts. I shimmied, embarrassed. "I have proper lingerie in my suitcase. I meant to change into it, if we...if this..." I stopped talking when Gideon took over, sliding the tight fabric over my hips and down my legs, taking my underwear with it. Then his hand was there, between my thighs, and my ability to speak stumbled and died. He crowded me against the bed, stroking at the wetness of my core, his free hand digging into my hair to tilt my head back so he could kiss me.

And just like the moment when he picked me up and carried me down the aisle, I realized I loved being manhandled by him. I loved the way his strong thighs bracketed mine and kept me from spreading my legs the way I wanted to. Loved how he curled his fingers into my hair and caused little pinpricks of pain on my scalp. Loved the way he kissed, wet and messy and hard.

Loved his big, hot hand between my legs.

This was nothing like the sex I'd had before. My mind was utterly blank. All my attention was focused on the feel of his fingers stroking my clit and his teeth closing around my bottom lip. His clothing felt coarse against my bare skin, and I fumbled with the buttons of his shirt before giving up and going for his belt. He smiled against my mouth, and a dart of pleasure went through me.

"This is a dream," he murmured, kissing down my neck, sucking the pulse throbbing there. "You're not real."

"Please," I panted, already begging. My hips gyrated against his fingers, and little fireflies of pleasure flitted through my veins. It was as if a decade of unspent lust suddenly crashed over me. All the times that my head had gotten in the way. All the times I hadn't been enough, or been worried about how I looked or smelled, or been anxious about the pain that would surely come. All the times that I'd put my partner's pleasure above my own, because I felt like I had to make up for my deficiencies.

All of it welled up inside and bore down on me, transforming me into a creature made of need. My fingers curled into Gideon's shirt as I pulled him down on top of me, my back hitting the mattress, my knees spreading and folding to accommodate his hips. He propped one elbow beside my head and kept the other hand between my legs. I moaned, my fingers wrapping around his wrist to keep him where I needed him, my hips grinding to chase the fire building inside.

"Beautiful," he murmured, eyes circling my face. "So fucking pretty, Sadie. Can't believe you're mine."

I dropped my gaze from his eyes down to his hand. The skin of his hand looked dark beside my pale inner thighs, knuckles and tendons shifting as he stroked me and stroked me and *stroked* me. My breath caught. The pads of his fingers slid over my clit then circled it, and I wanted to cry, it felt so good.

I pawed at his shirt, managing to rip the sides of it apart. Three buttons came undone. His chest was bronzed and breathtaking. I put my hands on him, loving the hard pack of muscle I found there, the soft abrasion of his chest hair. The tattoos on his arms crawled over one side of his chest, the right side. I slid my palm over them, avoiding his left side. He didn't like me touching his scars. I wouldn't do it now, when everything felt so good. When I was so close. When I couldn't bear the thought of him pulling away.

An orgasm shimmered, a glittering haze that promised something good. I felt it building in my blood, pounding against every door in my mind. I started on his buttons again, needing to feel the heat of his skin against mine. Wanting to lick and taste and consume. I managed to get two more buttons undone before Gideon shifted his fingers.

"You're so wet," Gideon marveled, letting his fingers slide down to tease at my opening before returning to my bud. A small, distant alarm went off in my mind. He bent down to nuzzle at my neck. "Can't wait to get inside you."

"Um—" I gasped as he pressed my clit, hips arching off the bed as far as they could beneath the weight of him. The alarm grew louder.

"Can't wait to fill you with my cock," he went on, scraping his teeth against my pulse. "Feel you come apart when I'm deep inside you."

Uh-oh. My eyes flew open to stare at the ceiling above.

"Gideon—" I moaned as he rubbed my clit, but the orgasm wasn't getting any closer. Fear had started to rise inside me, and it was impossible to ignore. I had to come clean. Had to tell him the truth. "Gideon, I have to tell you something."

"Right now?" he asked, stroking just the right spot. But it was too much now. Too sensitive. The pleasure that had been so close began to draw away from me like a wave being sucked back into the vengeful ocean.

Then his hand shifted, and he slid a finger inside me. The stretch of the intrusion was a familiar burn. My hands flew to his shoulders, fingernails biting into his skin. I could feel the smooth, hard muscle of his right shoulder, and the tight, mottled scar tissue on his left. He grunted. "So fucking tight," he said, and dropped his forehead to my shoulder. "Fuck, Sadie. Gonna have to stretch you a bit before I—"

Panic spiked. *"Wait,"* I screeched, and quickly released my fingers as he pulled away. My chest heaved as Gideon levered his top half off me, emotions quickly flitting across his face.

Confusion. Worry. What looked like a flash of understanding—and disgust. I reached for him, because I didn't want him to *stop*, I just needed to explain.

Explain that I'd lied. Explain that my body wasn't fully functional. Explain that all those things he wanted, those dirty promises he'd made, he could never make them come true.

And I thought he'd agree to file that wedding certificate once he knew? I thought I'd still get my happily-ever-after?

Tears welled in my eyes, burning my eyelids. My throat clogged up, and the words wouldn't come.

It had felt *so good* to be wanted as badly as he seemed to want me. I must've been weak-willed and cowardly, because I just couldn't manage to find the words to tell him that he'd married a dud.

I took too long to answer. He twitched away with a shrug and angled his head so I couldn't meet his eyes, keeping his scars facing the wall so his good side was to me. I could sense his fury in the room, a physical weight pressing against my naked body, making it hard to breathe. "Couldn't go through with it after all?" he spat out, shrugging his shirt back on before turning to face me.

My brain still wasn't working right. What was he talking about? "It's not—I'm—I need to tell you about—"

"I don't want to hear it," he snapped, then turned and

slammed the door on his way out. The walls crowded in on me, the air close, too cold now that he was gone, too thick.

I rolled onto my side, buried my head in my hands, and sobbed.

GIDEON

She'd stiffened as soon as her hand had slid over my left shoulder. She'd felt the knobby scar tissue, and the sensation of it had doused her lust in an instant. She was disgusted by me.

I should've known. Should've fucking seen it coming.

SIX

SADIE

I cried. I heard the garage door open and an engine rumble down the drive, and heavy sobs tore out of me. Then I wiped my face, found the bathroom, took a shower, and got my favorite pajamas out so I could sleep. This kind of hurt was familiar, and I could deal with it. Sex always sucked; this was no different. I didn't believe any of those silly romance books that talked about explosions and passion and waves of sparks. Complete bull, as far as I was concerned. Sex was awkward, painful, and, unless you were one of the lucky ones, it always involved men. *Blegh.*

Despite the tragic lack of pillows on the cottage bed, I slept. Around midnight, I woke up with my bladder about to burst and my head in an even greater amount of pain—crying always did that to me—so I crept out of the room and went to pee. When I couldn't find any Advil in the bathroom, I expanded my search to the kitchen. The cottage was dark and quiet. Gideon still wasn't back from wherever he'd gone, and that was *fine.* Completely fine. I wasn't hurt, or worried, or jealous. I was *glad,* actually, because I didn't have to see his stupid, handsome face and try to find the words to explain what had happened a few hours ago.

Okay, I was a little hurt. I'd kind of gotten wrapped up in the whole wedding thing and started to think this was meant to be. Marital bliss. Not.

When I woke up around five, it was still dark out. I padded out of the room to find the living room undisturbed; Gideon was still out.

I was *not* making up stories of him shacking up with a hypothetical ex on our wedding night. I wasn't going to spiral. That was not happening, no matter how badly my brain wanted to take me there. So my last ex had cheated on me on top of everything else? It didn't mean Gideon would. I was a grown woman, damn it. I wouldn't be reduced to petty jealousy about a man who obviously didn't give two shits about me.

No.

What I did instead was make myself a strong cup of coffee from the stash in the cupboard and take stock of my situation. As I sipped my coffee and watched the sky lighten to gray, then purple, and finally blue, I came to a conclusion.

I couldn't stay here.

Yes, I'd had fantasies of happy endings, but they were just that: fantasies. There was no basis in reality for those feelings, and I refused to put myself through one more minute of torture. I was clear-eyed as I watched the sun rise over the water, taking deep, cleansing breaths to let the decision settle over my shoulders.

I'd tap out. I'd go to my parents and ask them for help. They would look at me like I was their biggest disappointment as usual, but I would survive. I'd go to the family holiday and sleep on the pull-out couch and endure comments and criticisms, but I would *not* debase myself by staying with a man who wanted nothing to do with me. Marriage ceremony or no.

Air filled my lungs, and my spine straightened. The crumbling tower of my self-worth repaired itself just a bit with the decision. I took my coffee to the bedroom, where I packed up the few items I'd taken out of my suitcases. Then I tossed my toiletries back in their case and packed that away too. I zipped everything up and planted my hands on my hips. It felt good to take action. I rolled the suitcases out and stood them next to the hallway to the garage.

Back in the living room, I looked around to make sure I hadn't missed anything. As soon as my tire was fixed, I'd get on the road. Until then, I'd book a hotel room so I wasn't stranded in the middle of nowhere. That meant I needed a taxi.

Before I could call one, a car swung into view at the bottom of the drive, and my heart began to thump.

Gideon was home.

I forced myself to sit down on the couch and resist the urge to run to the bathroom to make sure I looked presentable. How I looked made no difference. Gideon would never be my husband —not really. This was a blip in the story of my life. A funny anecdote that I would tell at parties.

Nothing more.

I sipped my cold coffee and stared at the glittering surface of the water, pretending that every fiber of my being wasn't focused on the sound of the garage. The car engine stopping. Footsteps on concrete. The squeak of a door hinge.

Breathe in. Breathe out.

I turned in my seat, looking over the back of the couch.

Gideon stood in the mouth of the hallway, looking like he hadn't slept all night. He had dark purple circles hugging the bottoms of his eyes. His stubble had grown out overnight. His hair was a mess. His shoulders were slumped. He carried a tray with two huge cups. The logo on the cups proclaimed they were from Knead More Bread.

But it was his expression that made my breath catch. He was...careful. His eyes skated over my face, then moved to my packed bags. He went still for a beat, then swallowed. "You're leaving," he said, voice nothing more than a scrape.

I stood to face him. "I think it's for the best."

His pause was excruciating, but Gideon finally nodded. "You're probably right." His fingers covered the logo as he grabbed the cup on the left, sliding it out of the tray before extending it toward me. "Matcha latte, half sweet, made with almond milk," he said.

I blinked at him. He'd gotten my favorite coffee order exactly right. "How did you know?"

A dusting of red bloomed on his cheeks, and his gaze slid away from mine. "It was in your profile," he said, then cleared his throat.

I frowned. "It was?" I didn't remember reading about *his* coffee order in his profile, and I'd combed through those three pages like my life depended on it.

He grunted.

And then I remembered. There was a section in the application where I was asked to describe my perfect day. I'd written a bunch of drivel that held a kernel of truth: With my husband, I'd watch the sun rise while drinking a half-sweet almond milk matcha latte, have a leisurely breakfast consisting of a fat stack of pancakes with way too much whipped cream, spend some time outdoors, sketch wedding dresses in the sunshine with my head in my husband's lap, and then have dinner at home and curl up together to watch a movie.

After I'd written it, I'd laughed, because it was so different from the fast-paced, pressure-filled life I'd built for myself in the city. And then I'd cried, because I wanted it *so badly*.

But if Gideon had read that...it meant he'd read my application. And not only that, he'd *remembered it*. I blinked at him, then at my drink. "Thank you," I croaked, and he replied with a sharp nod.

"I'm sorry about last night," he said after a moment. He looked at my suitcases. It took long, sticky seconds for him to meet my eyes. He swallowed. "I know how little interest you have in sex. I shouldn't have pressured you into that. Especially not when I know you aren't interested in having sex with *me*."

A frown pulled at my brows. There was a lot to unpack there, and I didn't know where to start. What came out of my mouth was, "You didn't pressure me."

"You don't have to do that." He waved a hand. "Make excuses. I know what I did last night, and I feel like I need to scrub the skin off my body for how ashamed of myself I am."

Confusion clouded my thoughts. I couldn't follow what he was saying. "What you did last night?"

"*Forced myself* on you." He spat the words, gaze sliding to the side. "God. I don't know... I don't even recognize myself."

"You didn't force yourself on me!"

"Stop it, Sadie—"

"No, you stop it." My voice was sharp as a blade. "You're

doing that thing again, where you tell me what I'm supposed to be thinking. How about this time, for a change, you listen to me. I wanted to...to do what we did." My cheeks flushed. I couldn't say anything more crass than that, or I'd burst into flames. I certainly couldn't tell him that I'd wanted him from the moment I'd seen him, or that I'd lied on my application, or that even now, when I had decided to leave, I wanted to push him down onto the couch, straddle his lap, and kiss him.

I took a deep breath. We stared at each other. The truth hovered on my lips, but I was nothing more than a coward. Now that Gideon was here, it was *so hard* to tell myself I never wanted to see him again. No one had ever made me feel as electric, as alive, as he did.

But that was because he didn't know the truth about my body. My shortcomings.

I already knew the *real* truth. The truth that was as consistent as the sunrise and predictable as the tide.

I would never be enough.

Gideon proved it by shuttering his expression. "Either way, at least now we know that this was never going to work."

There was a boulder in my throat, so all I could do was nod.

"Where will you go?"

I took a sip of my drink. Delicious. It made me want to cry, but instead I shrugged. "I guess I'll move back in with my parents." Even as I said it, I couldn't help my grimace.

Gideon watched me as he took his own drink out of the tray. He tossed the cardboard onto the kitchen counter and made his way to the opposite couch. He sat, took a sip, then said, "You could stay here." As soon as the words left his mouth, it was

Gideon's turn to grimace. Because the thought of me being near him was repulsive.

I wasn't *that* much of a masochist. I just laughed and replied, "That's okay. I'll figure it out."

"I mean, we have six weeks."

"Five weeks and six days."

"Right." He swallowed. Tugged at a thread on his jeans, then adjusted the collar of his long-sleeve tee where it sat over his scars. I wondered how much of his chest and back were covered in them. The sliver of chest I'd seen last night had been unmarred, other than his left shoulder. He caught me looking at him and narrowed his eyes. "Why did you sign up for this in the first place?"

Because I was off-balance and tender, knowing that I wanted him and he definitely didn't want me, I went on the attack. "I'm a hopeless romantic," I said, echoing his words from yesterday. "Emphasis on the hopeless."

His glare was flat and unimpressed. "Come on, Sadie. I think by now we can be honest with each other."

There he went, saying my name again in that indecent, dark velvet voice of his. I squirmed and tried to cover it up by taking a sip of my drink. Finally, I said, "You first."

I expected him to brush me off again, but instead, he studied me for a beat and said, "My grandmother blackmailed me into it."

Shock stole my words. I gaped at him, then recovered enough to ask, "What do you mean?"

"First, she threatened to cut me out of the will."

My brows jumped. "Wow."

"To be fair," he added with a grin, "she threatened to cut us all out of the will."

"You were...okay with that?"

A careless shrug. "I wasn't going to let her manipulate me like that."

By all accounts, Etta Mars was a very wealthy woman. Gideon had been prepared to walk away from hundreds of thousands—millions?—of dollars to avoid having to marry someone. To avoid marrying *me*.

Throat tight, I asked, "So what happened?"

Gideon's eyes slid to the side, and he let out a long sigh. "When I was young and dumb, my security business was failing, and I went to her for help. I agreed to sell her half my business. Fifty-one percent, actually. She has a controlling stake."

"She threatened to take it if you didn't get married?"

He let out a bitter snort. "She threatened to chop it up and sell it like a venture capital vulture," he told me. "My livelihood. My *brothers'* livelihoods. We built Marswood Security together. We saw all these rich people building second and third homes on the outskirts of town—homes they barely visited—and we decided they wouldn't ruin us. They were a new market that needed security, and they were happy to pay for it. My grandmother said she was proud. She said I reminded her of my grandpa. And then she told me she'd take it all away unless I did what she wanted."

"She's ruthless."

"Oh, you have no idea," he agreed, leaning back against the couch. He took a sip and shook his head. "She wants these weddings to happen, no matter what. I agreed to six weeks. If I get to the end and my bride decides not to go forward, she'll let me be—and let me keep the business running as-is."

Embarrassment swallowed me whole. I'd thrown myself at him last night, made a mess of everything, and now I was learning that he'd married me under duress. Of course he had! Wasn't I in exactly the same situation?

"What if you don't go the full six weeks?"

"She'll use her judgment as to whether I made enough of an effort," he answered, sardonic and bitter.

"Oh."

He grunted in response.

He could lose his business if I left today. And still, he was willing to let me go. Because he wanted me to leave that badly? I was *that* awful?

Or was he just that kind?

"What's stopping her from cutting you out of the will even if you go the full six weeks and don't stay married?"

Gideon let out a humorless laugh. "Nothing. She'll always have this leverage over me." A tense silence followed. His blue eyes were suspicious when he met my gaze. "What's your excuse?"

"Same story, kind of. My business is failing. I needed a way out. The only other option was moving back in with my parents, and that was an absolute last resort. Which, I guess, is where I'm at now."

He clicked his tongue, ripping his gaze away to stare at the fireplace. It sounded like the words were torn out of him, but he finally said, "Stay, Sadie."

"I wouldn't want to put you through that," I answered, caustic.

Gideon let out a bitter laugh, like my words had been a joke only he could understand.

It was clear he had agreed to be married against his will, and meeting me hadn't changed his mind. Last night had been an aberration. We'd both gotten carried away.

These embers inside me would die. I wouldn't be attracted to him forever.

It was a terrible idea to stay...but I was tempted. It was a soft place to land while I figured my life out. I'd loved everything I'd seen about this town. Would it hurt to explore it some more? I had six weeks of free housing. Maybe I'd find a third option, and I wouldn't have to crawl back to the family fold.

"How would that look," I started slowly, "if I stayed."

Gideon cleared his throat. Shifted on the couch, like he couldn't get comfortable. "We would live here for the next six weeks," he said, spreading his arms to indicate the cottage.

The cottage with only one bedroom. Only one bed.

I sat very still. "Okay."

"I'm busy with work," he said. "You'd barely see me."

That was a blessing and a curse, but I nodded. "Right. And at the end of the month and a half, we decide what we want to do next."

He frowned like he didn't understand.

I took a deep breath and grasped at the only thing that was left between us. "I wasn't expecting to find true love here," I admitted. "All I wanted was companionship."

"I see."

I licked my lips. Companionship. That was achievable, wasn't it? If true love was a silly fantasy, then mutual respect was the real-life equivalent. "Maybe we can have that. We can come to an understanding," I said, then straightened, nodding, my own words convincing myself. "We both need this for our own reasons. It doesn't have to be a—a regular marriage. And then your grandmother's leverage would be gone, so you'd be free. And I...I like it here. You know?"

His eye twitched. "Right."

"Last night was messy," I continued, "so how about we just—"

"Pretend it never happened?"

"You need to keep your grandma off your back. I need a fresh start. We've got six weeks to see if we can live with each other. Like...friends. Or business associates."

His jaw ticked. "And after that?"

"If we're happy with how things are going, we file the certificate. Stay married on paper. Live our best lives." I gave him an uncertain smile. "And if we decide we're better off apart, then we go our separate ways."

It made sense. We couldn't just walk away from each other. I had nowhere to go, and Gideon would be at his grandmother's mercy. We could use this time as a test. I could stay in Marswood Harbor, see if it was really where I wanted to stay.

What happened last night wouldn't happen again.

His eyes bore holes into me. I couldn't tell if he was furious about my suggestion or relieved. Then it was his turn to smile without humor. "See if you still want to stick around after family lunch, and then we can talk about forever. We'll leave in an hour."

Without another word, he got up, turned around, and disappeared outside.

GIDEON

She would never be mine—not in truth—but the edge of panic that had ridden me hard when I noticed her packed bags had eased.

She was staying. For now.

I inhaled the loamy scent of the forest and cursed myself for wanting her so badly. The only way this plan would work would be to keep my distance. Build up my walls. Never, ever kiss her again.

SEVEN

SADIE

The drive to Etta's house was silent, giving me ample time to work myself up into a tizzy. Would they like me? Would I make a fool of myself? Would I remember anyone's name?

Finally, we arrived. Tall, wrought-iron gates were open to allow us entrance onto a long, tree-lined drive that opened onto a perfectly manicured lawn. A gigantic house stood guard over the land. The colonial mansion had a dramatic white colonnade framing the brick structure, with wide white window sashes. It was gorgeous. And huge.

Gideon turned off to the side and parked in one of the massive garages. He got out of the car and opened my door, then stalked beside me like a silent, looming bodyguard as we headed for the front entrance. This time, there was no hand on my back. No touch at all. He didn't knock when we got there; he just pressed the lever on the handle and walked in.

The foyer was grand, with two sweeping staircases covered

in plush red Turkish rugs. A round table bearing a vase of flowers gave the entryway a burst of fresh scent and color. The sound of chatter and peals of laughter guided us to a big living room at the back of the house.

The room had various sofas and chairs arranged in two conversation areas, with French doors thrown open to reveal a plant-filled solarium beyond.

All along our walk to the big living room, I gaped, suddenly realizing just how much money Etta Mars must've had. Her house was gorgeous.

Two dozen or more people sat on various sofas, chairs, or on the floor, and all of them turned to look when we walked in. A cheer went up.

"The newlyweds!" one of Gideon's brothers said—the youngest, whose name I'd learned was Bennett. "We weren't sure if you'd show up today."

"It was touch and go for a minute there," I admitted, then flushed when loud hooting sounded in response. Gideon threw me a dark look as one of his cousins clapped him on the back, congratulating him on a successful wedding night.

When my embarrassment faded, I realized that meant none of them knew where he'd been last night, either. They all thought he'd been with me.

Where had Gideon gone?

"Here," Jack said to me as he handed me a crystal glass full of fizzy water. A juicy wedge of lime balanced on the thin edge. "Don't mind them," he said, tilting his head to the crowd. "They mean well."

"Do they?" Gideon answered darkly. His gaze swept over

the room. I saw him glance at an antique mirror in a gilded frame beside us, then quickly away. He scowled. Because he'd seen his reflection?

"Cheerful as usual," I quipped.

Jack barked a laugh. "She's got you figured out already." He threw his arm around my shoulders and gave me a squeeze. "You'll fit in just fine, Sadie," he said.

Gideon's gaze lingered on his brother's hand on my shoulder for a moment, and then he sneered, "Date didn't go well last night?"

Jack dropped his hand from my shoulder, his gaze sharpening. "My date was great." He glanced at me, then away, and took a step to put some distance between us.

I glanced up in time to see Gideon's jaw clench and release as he glared at his brother. Jack snorted and rolled his eyes.

Some unknown communication had just happened between them. I frowned, wondering what it was. Gideon was angry at his brother?

Jealous?

Surely not. He'd made it abundantly clear that he didn't want me in that way.

"Are you not participating in the marriage scheme?" I asked Jack.

He gave me a tight smile that had none of the warmth he'd had a moment ago. "No. Grandma Mars knows I have a daughter to take care of." He motioned to his daughter reading in the corner, under the leaves of a big plant. "I've already done my part in repopulating the town."

"Any news on Mr. Titty?" Gideon asked, evidently wanting to change the subject.

"Nothing. And no sign of whoever punctured Sadie's tire." Jack nodded at me when he said my name. "The Blanchard mansion had an alert last night. Knox checked it out." He tilted his head toward their other brother, the big, broad, silent one who reminded me of a bear.

Gideon touched my elbow and told me he'd be right back, and he and Jack went to the other side of the room to confer with Bennett and Knox. I watched the way they spoke to each other, and could tell by their body language that they were utterly comfortable with each other. Knox was a quiet presence, and Bennett was all quick smiles and sarcastic quips. At first glance, Jack seemed like the leader. He took control of the conversation, and the others nodded at his words. He was the face of the company—professional, charming, and put together. He was the one who was plastered all over their website photos. But Gideon was the eldest. When he spoke, the others listened and deferred to his judgment.

"They're somethin' else, huh," a woman said to me. I turned to see a brown-haired woman with a kind smile standing next to me. She wore a plain white tee and jeans, and in her arms was the cutest, chubbiest baby I'd ever seen. "Wendy," she introduced herself.

"Sadie," I replied. "Your baby is adorable."

"Do you want to hold him?" she asked, and she didn't wait for an answer before passing the bundle of baby rolls into my arms.

I spluttered, heart taking off, and settled the baby in my arms after a moment of pure panic. He looked at me with big blue Mars eyes, then reached up to touch my mouth. Laughing, I gently moved his hand away. "Hi, buddy."

My sister had two kids, but she'd never let anyone but my mom hold them when they were babies. Certainly not me, who wasn't considered a fully functional human in the family. And after all my breakups, I'd mostly resigned myself to never being a mom.

Now, after last night, I was almost sure that was still the case. As I held the baby, my heart ached for what I would never have.

Wendy smiled. "He's such a Velcro baby that I'll take any chance I can get to have a minute to myself," she explained, but her eyes stayed on her son. Then she looked at me. "I'm married to Gideon's cousin, Ben." She nodded at a slight, tall man who sat talking to another, older Mars man. One of the uncles, I remembered. Wendy touched her baby's head, stroking his downy hair. "Sorry I couldn't come to the wedding yesterday. Ollie lost it in the car on the way over and I had to bail."

"That's all right," I said, not wanting to admit I hadn't noticed her absence.

She kept her eyes on her baby and said, "Ollie is only the second baby born in town this year," she said, then glanced at me. "Are you and Gideon thinking about kids yet?"

I blinked. We weren't even thinking about *friendship*, let alone children. "I mean, we got married yesterday," I replied with a laugh. "We haven't gotten that far." But then I looked down at the warm bundle in my arms, and my heart went all gooey and soft. Baby Ollie had spotted my necklace and was busy grabbing and tugging at it. I pried his surprisingly strong grip open and distracted him with babbles.

"I always thought Gideon would make a great dad," Wendy said as she watched me play with her son.

"Oh yeah?" I asked, flicking my glance from her to my new husband. He was frowning at something Knox said, shaking his head in response.

"He's so reliable," she replied, and a pain went through my heart. He hadn't been reliable last night, when he'd taken off after rejecting me.

But he'd given me his jacket and taken care of the tire. He'd asked about my ankle and got me my favorite drink in apology.

Complicated, confusing man.

Wendy went on: "I was stranded twenty miles away when I ran out of gas." She shot me a self-deprecating glance. "I called Gideon because I knew he'd at least wait twenty-four hours before giving me shit about it."

I laughed. "How generous of him."

"Right? But no matter what, with Gideon, you just know that he'll have your back."

My throat was tight. I wasn't sure Gideon felt that way about me. One matcha latte did not a marriage make. But when I glanced up again, Gideon was watching me.

There was an intensity in his gaze. I moved baby Ollie's fingers away from my mouth again—he really wanted to stick them in there for some reason—and glanced down to smile at him. He cooed, then suddenly remembered I wasn't his mother. His face went red, and a silent scream shaped his mouth.

"Oops! Time's up," Wendy said, and took him out of my arms just in time for an ear-splitting shriek to rend the air. She settled her baby, murmuring soft words, then excused herself to feed him. I watched her go, feeling oddly emotional, like I had to grieve something I'd never realized I wanted.

I shook the feeling off as someone else swept me up into

conversation. Two of Gideon's aunts, Susan and Angela, came up to talk about the wedding. Jennifer (she *was* Lola, Connor, and Glenn's mom, I confirmed with subtle questioning) joined the conversation and complimented my dress and hair. Then the ladies were called away and I met Luca, who informed me my car would be ready in the morning. I was pretty sure he was Susan's youngest son, but I was having a hard time keeping all the names and family connections straight. I needed Gideon to draw me a diagram.

Then Luca's older brother, Fletcher, came by to pepper me with questions. I learned he was a furniture maker with his own workshop in town. He had incredible green eyes and the kind of biceps that made me sweat. Another brother existed, apparently, and he lived in Chicago and only came back to Marswood Harbor very rarely. Too big for his britches, Fletcher said with a grin, nudging Luca.

"How could he resist, what with all the beautiful breasts on display everywhere?" I asked, laughing.

Fletcher shifted his body slightly, and I sensed all his focus turn on me. His green eyes twinkled, the color brought out by the dark green plaid shirt he wore. I knew in an instant that this man was a Grade-A flirt. And why wouldn't he be? He was gorgeous, like all the Mars men, although he didn't make my heart thump the way Gideon did.

"One might say there are simultaneously too many and too few breasts on display in this town," he replied with mock sadness.

"You could always ask Mrs. Gretzinger to give you a peek if you're hard up for other options," I suggested.

Fletcher barked out a laugh, and a few heads turned toward

us. Luca snorted, shaking his head. Then he gave in and laughed.

"You know, Sadie," Fletcher said, lips tugging up into a half smile once the laughter had faded. A dimple appeared in his cheek. "Things don't work out with you and Gid..."

"Then she sure as hell isn't ending up with you," a gruff voice said at my back. Shivers coursed down my spine at the sound of Gideon's anger and possessiveness, fire kindling in the pit of my stomach. The heat of his body touched my shoulder and back as the little hairs on the back of my neck prickled. Suddenly, I was panting. Lord have mercy.

Fletcher's smile turned blazing, his eyes twinkling as he held my gaze. He knew exactly what he was doing. Finally tearing his eyes away from me, he lifted his hands in surrender as he met my husband's gaze. "You don't know what you've got here, cousin," he said, indicating me.

"I know exactly what I've got," Gideon replied darkly.

"Oh, my favorite thing!" I cut in. "Being talked about like an object when I'm standing right here."

Still looking at Gideon, Fletcher's grin widened as he shook his head. "Maybe Grandma's pet dork isn't so bad at his job, after all," he mused, referring, I presumed, to the software engineer who'd designed the matchmaking algorithm for Etta.

Luca's brows jumped as he glanced at Fletcher. "You'd agree to get married? *You?*"

Fletcher glanced at me and baldly checked me out. Then he shrugged. "Might not be so bad."

Luca clicked his tongue, clearly skeptical. I finally stole a glance at Gideon, and saw the bare, simmering fury in his eyes.

Fool that I was, Gideon's reaction excited me. No, it *thrilled* me. It made me feel special and precious and hot. The other men faded away, and Gideon finally looked at me. But his eyes were shuttered, and there was nothing there. This arrangement would never work if I kept thinking he liked me that way.

Then his brothers came up, and talk turned to the graffiti and vandalism in town. I made another boob joke and made them all laugh. Low-hanging fruit, but I wanted to make a good impression. The noise and vibration of their deep voices trembled through me. I was surrounded by so much testosterone that I started to sweat. Wendy was right; the Mars men really were something else. Gideon touched my elbow with his fingertips and led me out of the pack.

"How many cousins do you have?" I asked when we'd escaped the crush.

"Seventeen."

I started. "And are all of them single men?"

"Why?" he asked, directing me toward the edge of the room. "You thinking of trading up?"

"Oh, stop it."

He shrugged, eyes sliding away from mine. I watched as he pressed a hand against his scarred neck, stretching his jaw like the old injuries were uncomfortable. Then he said, "Fletcher's a fuckboy."

"Okay. Thank you for that completely irrelevant piece of information."

"I'm just letting you know. But whatever, maybe that doesn't matter. You guys would look good together."

Outrage burned in the center of my chest. The wedding ring on my finger felt heavy and tight. "What the hell is that supposed to mean?"

He turned to face me fully, glaring. "As my 'business associate,' are you planning on sleeping around with all my cousins?"

I reared back. "Excuse me?"

"You were flirting with him. With all of them."

"I was *talking* to them."

"You made Fletcher laugh."

"Is that a crime?"

Gideon clenched his jaw, then relaxed. His eyes shuttered. "Lunch'll be served soon. I need to check on something for work," he told me, and stalked back toward his brothers.

I watched him go as I sat down on the nearest couch. I was offended by his accusations, and yet there was a sick kind of heat kindling in my gut. Gideon cared.

And wasn't that the most pathetic thing to be thinking right now? He didn't care about me! He just cared about saving his business from his grandmother's machinations. We had come to an agreement, and we were using these six weeks to see if it could work.

No sex. No love. No desire.

And that was *fine*. It was better than fine. It was *great*.

We could carve out a marriage that worked for both of us. Something safe and small, that would allow us both to live our own lives.

The thought made me ache with sadness and yearning.

"Will you design my homecoming dress?" Lola asked, interrupting my thoughts as she dropped into the seat next to mine. Today, the teenager wore a crop top and loose jeans, and her blond hair fell down in beachy waves. She smelled like fruity perfume, and it reminded me of the body spray I used to use when I was a young teenager. She kicked her legs out, staring at her white sneakers before glancing at me. "Or do you only do wedding dresses?"

"I usually only do wedding dresses," I admitted.

Lola pouted. "Dang. It's my first homecoming this fall. I'm a freshman this year."

"Maybe I could make an exception," I heard myself say.

Her eyes brightened, and I immediately regretted my rash words. Who knew if I'd even be here by the time Lola's homecoming came around?

"I looked you up online. Your dresses are *fancy*."

I huffed. "Thank you? I think?"

"I want to wear a pink dress. Macy Collins says pink is totally out this year, but it's my favorite color and she has no idea what she's talking about. She follows the *worst* fashion TikTokers, I swear."

I nodded. "Well, pink is classic."

"Right?" Lola agreed, huffing dramatically. She slumped back on the sofa and crossed her arms. Then she rolled her head on the back of the sofa to look at me. "Why did you get married to Gideon? Could you not find someone the normal way?"

Ah, the ruthlessness of teenage girls. I forced a smile. "No, actually. I couldn't."

"Oh. Like, no one would date you?"

"They'd date me, but they wouldn't marry me."

"That sucks."

I nodded. "It did, yeah."

"Kind of sad that you had to sign up to an arranged marriage."

I was not going to touch *that* comment with a ten-foot pole.

My ego would never recover. Instead, I asked, "You don't think your grandma should've started the program?"

Lola shrugged, twisting her foot into the plush rug covering the ground. "I just think it's weird. Like, why do we need a bunch of strangers coming to town, anyway?"

"I'm finding it hard not to take this personally," I said, laughing.

"Not *you*," she said, rolling her eyes. "You're cool. But just—everyone *else* that's going to show up. It's just weird."

I hummed, agreeing, and was thankfully rescued by the call to sit down at the table. We ate, talked, and laughed, and despite Gideon's animosity, I felt more at home with this big group of near-strangers than I ever had with my own family. By the end of the meal, I was full to bursting with good, home-cooked food, and my cheeks ached from laughing.

Leaving this town—and this marriage—would mean giving up a lot more than just Gideon.

I could build a life here. A rich, layered life with friends and family.

All I had to do was give up my desire for sex. Forever.

But wasn't that what I'd already resigned myself to do when I signed up to this scheme in the first place? Why did it feel like such a huge loss now?

Gideon was quiet in the car, but there was an edge to his silence. It simmered between us, raking against my skin. Finally, when we turned onto the cottage's gravel driveway, he blurted, "I thought you didn't want kids."

I started. "What?"

"In your profile." He parked the car.

"I—where is this coming from?"

"I saw you when you were holding Ollie. You didn't look like someone who didn't want kids." He turned to face me, his gaze hard. "Is that something you're going to want as part of this 'arrangement' you're proposing between us?"

"I'm not going to ask you to fucking *breed* me, Gideon," I snapped. "And by the way, I'm still mad about what you said earlier."

He clenched his jaw and wrenched his gaze away from mine. I watched his throat bob as he swallowed, a muscle feathering in his cheek. "You're right," he said. "I'm sorry."

"I'm not going to sleep with your cousins, or your brothers, or anyone else. Okay?"

"Guess six weeks isn't that long to go without."

I burned with outrage and anger. "You're so sure I won't want to stay married to you, huh? And by the way, my life isn't ruled by sex. If you know my favorite coffee order, you should know *that*."

He stared straight ahead, then closed his eyes. Finally, he jerked his chin down in a sharp nod and got out of the car.

Gideon slept on the couch. When I woke up the next morning, my car keys were waiting for me on the kitchen counter. I located my car—new tire and all—parked on the gravel drive in front of the cottage.

Gideon, however, was nowhere to be found.

GIDEON

Seeing Sadie with a child in her arms had hit my chest like a poison-tipped spear. I hadn't known it was possible to want something so badly...and be so sure I would never have it.

If it wasn't Fletcher who won her away from me, it would be someone else. The heartbreaking, infuriating, inevitable truth.

EIGHT
SADIE

Gideon worked long hours, and I had the sneaking suspicion he was trying to avoid me. He slept on the couch and was usually gone by the time I got up. And that was *fine*. Totally fine. We weren't actually a married couple, we were just making life easier for each other by staying married. So he owed me nothing.

Or so I kept telling myself.

I spent the next couple of days puttering around town, checking out the few shops that were still open, and visiting the bakery as often as possible. Caroline was sarcastic and friendly, and she made amazing matcha lattes. Main Street was a nod to a bygone era, with added graffiti, boarded-up shops, and big trees. The people were friendly, with a few oddballs who treated me like I was trying to ruin their town. The one time I went into Ivan Popov's antique shop, he looked at me with such disdain and suspicion that I left without buying anything, even though I spotted an amazing vintage dress form half-hidden behind a hideous lamp.

Gideon would come home late, and our conversations were stilted.

He didn't touch me. Not even accidentally. Not a hand between my shoulder blades or a touch of the elbow. I realized just how much physical contact we'd had in the first day of our acquaintance, and its disappearance made me feel hollow.

Those were my own issues to deal with; I was a lonely person who hadn't quite resigned herself to living a partnerless life. But this marriage was the best I could expect.

The family group chat was active, and I grimaced as they booked the Airbnb with the pull-out couch. We always celebrated the holidays a week early, since there were typically holiday-themed weddings booked between Christmas and New Year's, and we all had to be available for them. I didn't tell them I was married, and I wasn't sure when or if I would.

In essence, it was a week of stasis. I made the best of it, exploring my new home, going on long walks, and treating myself to daily coffees from Knead More Bread. I explored some of the restaurants in town: a Chinese place called Golden Chopsticks, an old diner out on the freeway. Everyone told me the one restaurant I absolutely had to try was a surprisingly fancy place called The Pier.

On Thursday evening, I dressed up and went to check it out. I sat at a balcony table and looked over the glittering ocean, sipping a crisp white wine. The day had been warm, and I was glad for the sea breeze. There were a number of people eating, more than I expected. A few older couples, one young couple, and one family. Over in the corner by a big fern was another single diner, a man in a blue baseball cap. I tried to glance over and nod at him in solidarity, us being two loners and all, but he kept his head turned toward the sea and away from me.

"How was your meal?"

I turned my head to see Mrs. Gretzinger standing next to my table. She wore a black pantsuit, her red hair gathered at the nape of her neck. Her ears were adorned with diamond earrings that winked in the fading light. Her substantial cleavage was difficult to ignore. She gestured to a waiter, who hurried over to refill my glass, and I gathered that she was the boss.

"The halibut was fantastic."

"Fresh-caught," she said with a nod. "Our head chef was thrilled with it." Her eyes were brown and very sharp as she looked me over. "I'm surprised Gideon isn't here with you. Newlyweds should be spending all their time together. I told Etta she should ship you off on a honeymoon as soon as you said 'I do,' but she insisted that you'd need to get to know the town to decide if you wanted to stay."

Her stare was birdlike, and I knew she was fishing for information. I played with the stem of my wine glass and reached for the polite smile that I used to use with clients at my studio. "Gideon's working a lot these days. All that Mr. Titty business..."

It was a weak excuse, even to my ears. Gideon should've been here. We should've been getting to know each other...if we were trying to be a real married couple.

But this was what we'd agreed. Separate lives. A marriage on paper.

Could I really survive this way?

The other woman nodded knowingly. "He really threw himself into work after…"

Now it was my turn to fish for information. "After?" I probed.

Mrs. Gretzinger gave me an assessing look. She enjoyed having more information than me. "After the fire," she said quietly. "And everything that followed."

I had no idea what she was talking about, but I tried to keep my face neutral as I nodded. "Of course."

"It was very hard on him."

"I can only imagine."

"We're all so happy that Gideon's found someone else," she said. "He's a good man, and he deserves a good woman by his side."

There was an edge to her voice; a hint of a threat. Just like Etta whispering in my ear, *If you hurt him, I will ruin your life.*

But that wasn't what caught my attention. I got stuck on one particular word that she spoke: She'd said, "someone *else.*"

Which meant Gideon had been with someone before me, and something big had happened between them. Was that why he had no interest in me? Because his heart was broken beyond repair?

Was he with her on our wedding night?

"Well, you'll have dessert," Mrs. Gretzinger said brightly, drawing me from my whirlwind of thoughts. "On the house. And I'll have a talk with Etta. She'll get Gideon's head screwed on straight again, and we won't have you eating dinner all alone every night anymore."

I burned with embarrassment. Of course everyone had seen me wandering around on my own this past week. But what was the alternative? I wasn't going to live my life as a shut-in. I wanted to at least *try* to be happy, or at least content.

I left The Pier and walked along the beach for a while, then climbed up over the scrub-covered dunes and headed back up toward Main Street. The air smelled of salt and seaweed, and the breeze was strong. Sea birds cried above as waves crashed behind me. Only a handful of cars passed me as I made my way up the hill, and once again, I was filled with yearning.

I loved it here. These days of lonely wandering had been peaceful—the first bit of rest I'd had in years.

My phone buzzed. I pulled it out of my pocket, half-expecting more annoying texts from the family group chat. But it was a call from an unknown number. As a general rule I didn't answer those, but something made me swipe.

"Hello?" There was a silence, and then a click. I pulled the phone away and saw that the call had ended. Strange. Probably spam. I put my phone away and kept walking.

I passed Knead More Bread, dark and closed at this hour, and looked across the street at a small hardware store, but my feet took me where they wanted to go.

A shop a few doors down from the bakery had plastic stuck on the windows to darken them, with one corner of it peeling down enough that I could see inside. A round sign hung above the sidewalk, showing a logo of a needle and thread surrounded by curved writing: Life's a Stitch.

The vacant seamstress's shop still had two sewing machines on a long work table, a couple of dress forms, and big cabinets lining the back wall. On the window was a sign that said, "FOR RENT," with a phone number handwritten in the blank space beneath the words.

I'd walked by every day this week, stealing glances inside, wondering, wishing. It was a good space. I probably wouldn't be able to afford it—the only reason I could afford my life right now was that I had no housing expenses while I was here—so it was pointless to even consider it.

But it was a huge space, and it was already set up for sewing.

Shaking my head, I made my way to my car and drove back to the cottage. As I crossed the garage toward the interior door, my gaze snagged on the cardboard box full of work stuff I hadn't bothered to bring inside. Impulsively, I opened it up and grabbed a sketchbook, then went inside.

The pencil scraped across the thick paper as I drew the familiar proportions of a female figure. A dress appeared on the page, draped and gathered to flatter the body. I'd drawn a million of these before; I already knew it wouldn't ever get made —but it was the first time I'd put pencil to paper since I shut the doors on my studio in Manhattan six months ago. My movements were stiff and awkward at first, and soon became easier. I flipped to a fresh page and drew some more.

That's how Gideon found me: curled up on the couch with a sketchbook on my lap, drawing pretty dresses that only existed in my imagination.

For some reason, I was embarrassed. I slammed the sketchbook closed and sat up. "Hi."

His gaze flicked to my lap, then up to my face. "Am I interrupting?"

"I was just sketching dresses," I said, shrugging.

"A new client?"

I shook my head. "No. Unfortunately." I huffed a laugh. A new client would definitely help my bank account right now.

He grunted, then headed to the opposite couch where he'd made his bed. His sheets were neatly folded on top of the pillow, and he dropped into the seat, propping his leg on the coffee table that separated us. "Can I see?" he asked, nodding to the sketchbook.

I slammed my hand on top of it. "No!"

Gideon blinked. "All right."

"It's not... They're not good."

"Last I checked, you had an entire business designing wedding dresses. They can't be that bad."

"Key word: *had*."

The bitterness in my tone made him tilt his head. "What happened?"

I chewed my lip before answering. I didn't want to tell him about the shame of my failure. But if this was going to work between us—if we were going to coexist, maybe become friends—then didn't I owe him at least a piece of me? So, hesitantly, I said, "My target market was wealthy brides. I charged a lot, but I provided a luxury service. My overheads were too high, and eventually I just couldn't sustain it. For a while, the business was propped up by..."

"By?"

My chest burned, but I told him anyway. "By my ex. He owns this really popular wedding venue. He got to meet a lot of brides who were right at the beginning of their wedding planning journey—his place gets booked out years in advance. So he'd send them my way."

"And once you broke up, that ended."

I touched the edge of my sketchbook, running my thumb along the corner of the cover. "My turnover dropped to about a third of what it was before we started dating. I guess I'd gotten lazy about finding clients for myself. And then everything fell apart really quickly."

"And now you're here," he murmured. I flicked my gaze up to meet his, and Gideon lifted his palms. "Hey," he said, "I get it. No one signs up for an arranged marriage unless they're at least a little desperate."

We studied each other. I still found him stupidly attractive. Sighing, I asked, "Are we crazy to be doing this?"

"Yeah."

I laughed. "I'm serious."

He shrugged, then winced and dug a knuckle into his lower back.

"Sore?"

"Just this busted-up old couch," he grumbled. "If my grandmother wasn't a tyrant, we could each have our own bedroom right now."

I snorted, then tilted my head toward the bedroom. "Why don't you take the bed tonight?"

"No," he said. "I get up earlier than you. Makes sense for me to be out here."

"Well, we could both..." I gulped. "I mean, not, like... We could both sleep in the bed."

His gaze was steady, eyes intent. "I don't think that's a good idea, Sadie."

I burned with shame. "Right. Of course."

"This only works if we stick to the plan."

I remembered his reaction to me speaking to his cousin, and

I narrowed my eyes. "Maybe we should discuss some more particulars if this is going to work out long term."

"As in?"

"You went all macho possessive at Sunday lunch. In this arrangement of ours, are we not allowed to see other people?"

His eyes twitched. "Is that what you want?"

"Is that what *you* want?"

"I asked first, Sadie."

I blew out a sigh. "Well, if we're being honest, what I want is to meet the love of my life, fall head over heels, and have him treat me like a princess for the rest of my life so we can both live happily ever after."

His face went still. "Seems like this marriage is doomed, then. Why bother going through with the next five weeks?"

I exhaled as I dropped my head in my hands. "Because if we don't, your grandmother will chop your business into pieces and sell it off. And I've got nowhere else to go."

When I looked up again, Gideon was watching me. I couldn't read his expression. Finally, I pushed myself up to my feet. "Are you sure you don't want the bed tonight?"

He shook his head and started spreading the sheets over the couch. Throat tight, I retreated to the bedroom.

GIDEON

Maybe I was a fool for refusing her invitation to sleep in the bed beside her. But before I lay on the couch, I opened her sketchbook and flicked through her designs. I wondered how quickly she would drop everything and leave Marswood Harbor—leave me—if the opportunity presented itself. If someone wanted her to create one of these dresses for them. If she got any chance whatsoever to go back to her old life.

She said it herself: She had nowhere else to go. This was her very last resort in a life that had crumbled apart.

If I got attached, it would only hurt that much more when she left. It was easier to shut her out and wait for these torturous weeks to pass.

NINE
SADIE

On Saturday, feeling restless and not wanting to have yet another meal in town by myself, where I knew my movements were watched and gossiped about, I spent the evening at home and decided to deep clean the cottage. I started in the kitchen, scouring every surface including the inside of the fridge, microwave, and oven. I tidied the living room and fluffed the ancient couch cushions. I washed the bathroom, swept the hallway, and made the bed. The home finally lost its shut-in smell, and I looked around with deep satisfaction.

I needed a shower. I headed to the linen closet in the hallway for a fresh towel and paused when I spotted an old storage container on the top shelf. It looked like it had scraps of fabric in it. Pulling it down from its shelf, I unclasped the clips and opened it to a waft of nostalgic scent—fabric that had been shut away for a long time.

A sharp inhale slid past my lips. I touched the old pieces of fabric—some of them barely the size of a coaster, some of them yards of untouched fabric—and felt the stirrings of inspiration.

It felt like the tingling of a limb that had been asleep. A little painful, but an intense relief; I hadn't lost my will to *make*.

I touched the cotton fabrics, the jersey, and the stiff canvas. I emptied the container and laid it all out, gasping when I found a bolt of pristine pink silk at the bottom.

My thoughts jumped to Lola. This was her homecoming dress. I let out a startled laugh, unfurling the fabric to see how it draped. Gorgeous. I folded it up again and went treasure hunting in the box of scraps.

That was how Gideon found me: kneeling on the floor in the hallway, surrounded by a multitude of fabrics. He wore dark jeans and a black, long-sleeve T-shirt. I'd never seen him in anything but long sleeves, even when the days were sweltering. He looked great. I, on the other hand, was filthy from my cleaning spree, sweat and grime soaked into the fabric of my T-shirt and decade-old sweatshorts. At some point over the course of my manic scrubbing, I'd forgotten about the awkwardness of my situation and the grief of never having a real marriage. And now, when I looked up to see him dark and brooding at the end of the hall, beautiful and mysterious and familiar, I couldn't help the smile that stretched over my lips when he stopped short and met my gaze.

"Can I use this?" I asked, lifting the pink silk. "Lola wanted me to make her a homecoming dress."

Gideon opened his mouth. Frowned. Closed it. Finally, a big shoulder lifted in a half shrug. "Don't see why not."

I smiled, and he simply stared at me. Tension teased at the threads binding us together, reminding me that this was my husband—in name, if not in truth. Before my mind could drag me into eddies of desire, I dropped my gaze to the piles of fabric around me.

In this town, I was waking up to life again. I was sketching. Dreaming. And now, I wanted to create. I felt like myself again. The woman who existed before Henry. Before my business failure. Before I forgot that actually, I loved designing wedding dresses.

I would never have a real marriage or true love, but wasn't that a fair price to fall in love with myself again?

"It's been a long time since I felt inspired to make something," I admitted.

The floor creaked as Gideon shifted. He took a step forward, crouching down to pick up a square of navy fabric covered in planets and spaceships. He rubbed the fabric between his thumb and forefinger and said, "I thought you made wedding dresses for a living."

"I do. I did," I corrected myself; my business was as good as dead. Wasn't that why I was here? Throat tight, I stroked the pink silk and let my lips curl into a bitter smile. "When I was little, I would go with my parents to the weddings they were working." I glanced up and explained, "They're wedding singers."

Gideon watched me, that little piece of fabric still clasped in his hand. He nodded.

Wanting to do something with my hands, I started folding up all the dozens of pieces of fabric and putting them back in the storage bin. "My mom and dad tell the story of their own meet-cute at every wedding," I added, arching a brow. "It was a beach in Costa Rica. A coconut fell on my dad's head, and my mom found him passed out on the beach with a big lump on his temple. She nursed him back to health, and the rest is history."

Gideon snorted. "For real?"

"So the story goes," I said, laughing. "I've seen a picture of my dad with a bandage on his head with my mom by his side."

He laughed, and the sound warmed me down to my toes. I couldn't resist my answering smile.

"My sister is a florist and my brother is a videographer," I continued. "I'm the youngest, and I always felt such pressure to follow in all their footsteps. And it made sense; my parents had tons of connections. The wedding industry is huge. We could get a head start if we carved out our own niches." I folded another piece of fabric, and then I said, "I *did* enjoy it before. The dresses, the look on the bride's face, the sheer *drama* of it all."

Gideon watched me. "But?"

"But then..." I flushed, embarrassed. "Then I went through breakup after breakup. In my family, if you aren't married, you're nothing. And with all our livelihoods tied to weddings, I started to feel like a fraud." I couldn't meet his eyes. I stared at the clear plastic container of fabric, suddenly nauseous. "I *loved* seeing the bride make her entrance. The dresses—God, they used to give me shivers every time. And for a long time, when I was hustling to build my brand, that spark was still there. I loved seeing a bride's face light up when she came in to choose her dress. I loved the look on her face at the final fitting, when she could imagine herself walking down the aisle. But..."

"The joy went out of it at some point."

I grimaced, nodding. "Yes. Designs that I was proud of wouldn't move off the shelves, so I started following trends. My overheads grew as the business grew, and then I was stuck designing dresses that I didn't love but knew would sell."

"And now?"

I leaned back on my heels, laying a piece of chambray on my lap. Gideon sat on the floor, his back against the wall. He had one knee bent with his arm propped against it. The cottage was silent except for a soft creak with a gust of wind. It smelled like lemon cleaning products and old fabric.

I smiled at him. "Now, for the first time in about four years —maybe longer—I feel excited to make a dress."

He was silent for long moments, and our gazes remained stuck to each other. I knew I should've looked away—nothing good would come of me feeling this kind of connection—but I couldn't help myself. I felt like Gideon understood me. Saw me. Knew me.

He turned back to the scrap of fabric in his grasp. Something crossed his expression—a flash of pain.

Suddenly, I remembered this cottage had belonged to his father. And I hadn't met his father at the wedding or at Sunday lunch. Which meant...

"Oh my goodness, I just went rummaging through your father's old things. And he's...he's not around anymore, is he?"

Gideon shook his head. "He died eighteen—almost nineteen years ago."

"I'm so sorry. I should never have snooped—"

"It's fine, Sadie." He tossed the scrap of fabric back in the box. "We lived here when I was a baby, but my parents moved out as soon as my mother got pregnant with Jack. Dad had plans to fix the place up, expand it, but..." He shrugged. "Never happened."

His mother hadn't been at the wedding either, and no one had mentioned her. I wanted to ask about her, but Gideon's lips had twisted when he'd mentioned her. I could sense him closing himself off, and I knew we didn't have the kind of relationship where we shared that depth of pain with each other. So I let it go, even though I wished he'd trust me with it.

Finally, he tilted his head toward the main room. "Thanks for cleaning."

I straightened. Henry had never thanked me for doing any chores. I shrugged and said, "It's no problem. The place needed a bit of freshening up."

"I'll make dinner," he said. "You like salmon?"

"You can cook?"

I must have sounded a little too incredulous because Gideon gave me a flat look and said, "Yes, Sadie. I can cook. Do I not look like I can cook?"

"You look like you eat microwave meals that say things like 'MUSCLE BULK' and 'ULTIMATE FITNESS' and 'OPTIMIZED MACROS' on the packaging."

His lips twitched. "That was rude."

"It's a compliment!" I gestured at his biceps. "These things don't grow themselves."

He growled low in his throat, and a spark lit between my legs. Bad Sadie! We weren't doing that. We were never doing that. We were just testing out a convenient arrangement where we both got to live our lives without other people's unwanted involvement.

Gideon stood in an easy movement, then extended a hand

toward me. Before I could reconsider, I slipped my palm against his and let him tug me to my feet. We stood inches apart, and I fought to forget how good it had felt to be in his arms.

This feeling would fade. It had to. Gideon didn't want me that way; I was only torturing myself by wanting him. I tore my gaze away and tilted my head toward the bathroom. "I need a shower," I said. "Then I can help you prep dinner."

He made a noise of acknowledgement, then stalked down the hallway toward the kitchen. I couldn't resist the urge to watch the movement of his body as he retreated, then cursed myself and disappeared into the bathroom. A cold shower brought my brain back online, and then I was able to make it through dinner without imagining Gideon's hands on my body. Mostly.

THE FOLLOWING DAY, there was a half-sweet almond milk matcha latte waiting for me on the kitchen counter when I woke up. Gideon was gone, only returning to pick me up for Sunday family lunch. I brought the bolt of pink silk as well as a sketch-book I unearthed from the box of work things I'd left in the corner of the garage. Lola's eyes lit up when she saw me approach with the fabric, and she leaped up from her seat beside Wendy and the baby to come see me.

"Is that what I think it is?" she asked excitedly.

I grinned. "I thought we could come up with some ideas today. You like the color?" I set my sketchbook down on the nearest table and unfurled the fabric, holding it up under Lola's chin. We turned toward the gilded antique mirror hanging on the wall, and her hands stroked the soft pink silk.

"I love it," she whispered.

"It looks great against your skin tone," I agreed. "I found it at the cottage. It was meant to be."

Lola beamed at me, then did a little excited dance and reached in her pocket for her phone. "I'll show you what I like," she said.

We found the nearest chairs—stuffy, carved wood chairs with backs that were too straight—and bent our heads toward each other to look at inspiration photos. I put my sketchbook on my lap and started jotting down ideas. Half an hour later, we had the beginnings of a design.

"Ohmigod!" Lola clapped her hands, and I couldn't help but grin in response. She reached over and wrapped her arms around my neck, squeezing me in a tight hug.

Over her shoulder, I met Gideon's eyes. I couldn't read his expression, but I thought he might have been pleased with me. Happiness glowed like hot coals in my belly for the rest of the day. When we got home, I unpacked my sewing machine from the box and set it up in the corner of the dining room table where the light from the windows was best. I would need muslin to start drafting Lola's dress, and some new thread. My machine needed to be oiled and cleaned. Other than my own wedding dress, I hadn't sat down and sewn anything for ages. Certainly not something for someone else, where the details mattered and I couldn't ignore mistakes.

I decided to practice by making some cushion covers. The couches were in desperate need of fresh throw pillows, and it would give me something to do while my brain worked on how to construct Lola's dress. I got to work, only looking up when

Gideon dropped a glass of water and a plate bearing a cut-up apple and a few slices of cheese next to me.

Shock made me blink. "You made me a snack," I said.

"You haven't stopped working since we got home," he grumbled. "You need to eat something."

And you have to stop doing things like this for me, I almost replied. My heart had gone all gooey and soft, and it was hard to swallow my first bite of apple past the lump in my throat. "Thank you," I croaked.

He grumbled something in reply and stalked off, leaving me to my work. I could feel myself wanting to fall for him. Wanting to imagine the fairy tale where we fell in love and lived happily-ever-after.

But I'd been through this before. I fell too hard for men who tossed me aside. This time would be different. This was my fresh start, my new home. I wouldn't wreck it by letting my feelings get in the way, especially when Gideon was just being nice. Hadn't Wendy said he was the most reliable of the Mars men? This was simply who he was; it didn't have anything to do with me.

These little thoughtful gestures didn't mean anything special. He didn't magically find me more attractive than he had before. Any evidence to the contrary was just my wistful imagination running away with me.

I'd only been in this town a week, and I already felt more inspired and more at ease than I had in years. Pursuing a man who clearly didn't want me would only ruin my chances at a decent life. As long as I kept my wants small and reminded myself to be grateful for what happiness I could find here, I would be safe.

My attraction to Gideon would fade. And if it didn't, I would just have to deal with it.

GIDEON

I tried and failed to avoid looking at Sadie. The light from her sewing machine illuminated her face as she frowned, moving a thread up, down, and around the complicated gears inside the machine. She was beautiful when she focused. When she was inspired. When she was happy.

I should've left the cottage, because staying here watching her was torture when she would never really be mine.

But I couldn't make myself leave.

So I busied himself by clearing her plate then making dinner. I set a serving of roast chicken, potato, and vegetables next to her, then grabbed a book and read on the couch while her sewing machine hummed. Occasionally, I glanced up to make sure she was eating.

The cottage had felt empty since my dad had passed away nearly two decades ago. It had been a cemetery of broken dreams, of plans that had never come to fruition. Dad had meant to retire here, when my brothers and I were grown up. My father would come here when he needed peace and quiet. He'd talk about the plans he had for the property—a small orchard, a new workshop, a pier where he could tie a boat. In the summertime, the five of us had set up tents in the backyard and camped on the property. It was a refuge for all of us.

Then my father died, and the cottage had been frozen in time. It had never become what my father had dreamed.

Now it was alive. It was a home. Sadie had given me that.

The ache in my chest was new; it was painful but sweet. I wondered if I could be satisfied with this half-life with her, and decided that it was better than not having her at all.

Two more days passed in the same way, though Gideon began to come home for dinner. Still he kept his distance from me, both physically and emotionally. We hardly spoke, but we moved around the cottage in mostly comfortable silence. It was for the best. Slowly, day by day, we were finding an equilibrium. The burning passion of our wedding night was becoming a distant memory.

Sort of.

Except when he was in the kitchen, cooking with that intense, serious competence that never failed to make me squirm. Or when I caught him watching me sew from his usual spot on the couch. His gaze prickled between my shoulder blades, and I struggled to focus on my projects. His attention was an aphrodisiac, and I found myself thinking of him when I lay in the bed at night all alone. If I listened closely, I could hear the couch springs complain as he moved. The soft grunts he let out as he tried to get comfortable. The creak of the floorboard and the sounds of the pipes when he got up to get himself a glass of water.

He was so close, and I wanted him so badly. But that wasn't meant to be.

Still, I burned.

My restless legs clenched together, and I finally gave in and touched myself, remembering how it had felt to be in this very bed with his weight atop me. The desperate rasp in his voice when he spoke dirty promises to me. The way my body had bowed toward him, one line of ragged tension from head to toe.

I bit my pillow to muffle my whimpers. When I was done, I lay in the silence of the night, breathing heavily. I felt no better than I had before. If anything, I felt worse. Needy, restless agitation made me toss and turn when I should have been lax and satisfied. Finally, I sat up.

Buried at the bottom of one of my drawers was the dilator kit. I stared at the pale pink silicone devices as my heart thrummed. The smallest was about the size of my ring finger, the biggest a little smaller than most penises I'd seen. They all had a finger loop at the end to grip.

I took the smallest one out of the case and bit my bottom lip. I was supposed to use them regularly to try to stretch things down there, but I'd gotten lazy. Or maybe I'd become resigned to my sexless, painful fate, and I hadn't believed my body could actually change.

But now, there was no pressure. Gideon didn't want me, and there was no other man tapping his foot as he waited for me to fix myself so he could get inside me. I'd had a week and a half of solitude, rest, and decent food. No one had asked me for a thing, other than Lola wanting me to make her a pretty dress. I was more relaxed than I'd been in years.

And that made me curious. What if my therapist had been right? What if the problem wasn't really *me*? It wasn't some innate failure of mine as a person, it was just my brain being a brain, getting its wires crossed. What if I *was* fixable?

In the still darkness, I reached for my lube and winced at the noise of the cap opening. It sounded like a gunshot in the silent house. Then, heart pounding, I squeezed some clear goop onto the smallest dilator and lay back on the mattress. With my knees bent, I forced myself to take deep, calming breaths.

Just beyond the door, Gideon slept. It felt indecent to be doing this in the same house as him, even if he was my husband. Indecent—and exciting.

I pushed the dilator inside.

The little silicone shaft was no bigger than my ring finger, but it still burned as my body clamped around it. I stopped, letting my muscles adjust, while my ears strained for any noise from the living room. Was that a creak of the couch? A deep murmur from beyond the doorway?

I breathed through the burn and let the silence pulse around me.

It would have been better to imagine anything else, but the only thing that came to mind was my wedding night. I imagined what it would've felt like not to stop. To invite Gideon into my body. To feel him shudder and gasp as he slid inside me. To watch him come apart, and to be able to chase my pleasure wherever it would lead.

The burn lessened as the minutes passed, and I began to move the dilator in and out in long, slow strokes. My breaths were ragged. My other hand moved to my bud, and a fine sheen of sweat covered my body as I touched and stroked. I sucked in a hard breath, and a whimper escaped my lips.

Pleasure tightened in the pit of my stomach. Shock warred with delight inside me; this didn't usually feel good. My brain tried to tell me that it wasn't anything worth celebrating. After all, wasn't it the smallest dilator? Barely the size of my third finger? And it had taken me almost ten minutes to even feel okay with it inside me. Longer than any man would wait, that was for sure.

But even my most judgmental, self-acrimonious thoughts couldn't win this battle. Not when I remembered the look in Gideon's eyes, or the way his hands had felt on my breasts and my waist and my core. The bitter thoughts dissolved like the smoke of a blown-out candle, and pleasure crested inside me. I gasped, half-laughing, arching on the mussed sheets of my bed. I couldn't quite help the low moan that escaped my throat.

For the first time in my life, I'd orgasmed with penetration as well as clitoral stimulation. I hadn't had to stop from the pain. In fact, at the end, it hadn't been painful at all. I'd felt full and stretched and *wonderful*.

I lay on the bed in shock, squirming at the sensation of the dilator still inside me, and tested the limits of my body by shifting the end of the shaft against my tender flesh. Stretching. Exploring. Learning the new limits of my body. Little sparks coursed through me, and I wondered how it would feel to move to the next size up. A scandalous thought. Thrilling. Unheard of.

And then, to my horror, I heard the soft snick of the bathroom door, followed by the patter of water hitting the shower tiles.

Gideon was awake, and he'd been just outside my door when I'd finished. There was no way he hadn't heard me.

GIDEON

Hell. I was in hell.

I'd survived the warehouse fire and its scars, my rocky childhood, my ex's cruelty, and my grandmother's schemes.

I wasn't sure I'd survive this.

ELEVEN
SADIE

Today was a big day in town. It was the third Saturday of July, also known as the Marswood Harbor Fair. I'd seen flyers go up over the course of the week, and the regulars at Knead More Bread had talked it up. It was the event of the summer. And at the very least, it was an excuse to get out of the house that wasn't just wandering around town, wondering what I was doing with my life.

But when I ventured out to the kitchen, Gideon was there. "Morning," he said, nodding to a takeaway cup from Knead More Bread.

Half-sweet almond milk matcha latte. Still warm.

My heart turned over. "Thank you," I said, voice choked with emotion, then cursed myself. He was just being nice. It wasn't some declaration of everlasting love; it was a hot drink. I sat down on the couch facing the water to enjoy it.

"What's your plan today?" Gideon asked.

Surprised, I looked over to where he stood in the kitchen. "Why?"

Gideon huffed a laugh. "Don't sound so suspicious, Sadie. I'm making conversation."

"Oh. Do we do that?"

He gave me a flat look. "I'm currently regretting my decision to try."

I rolled my lips to keep from laughing. "If you must know," I finally replied primly, "I'm attending the Marswood Harbor Fair. A dozen people have told me it's the best day of the summer."

"Oh yeah?" Gideon snorted.

"What? It's not a good event?"

"It's fine," he said, grabbing a pan from the cabinet. He put it on the stove, turned the burner on, then opened the fridge to get some eggs. "It's just...remember that this is Marswood Harbor we're talking about."

"A fair is a fair."

"Said like someone who's never lived in a small town."

"Said like someone whose bitterness has taken over," I shot back.

Gideon tilted his head to concede the point. "You want eggs?" He lifted one up as if I needed extra help understanding what an egg was.

I considered being snarky, but he'd gotten me a matcha latte and was offering to make me food, so I just nodded. "Sure. Thanks."

Gideon made deliciously creamy scrambled eggs and perfectly golden toast. He even cut it into triangles and didn't judge me when I smothered my eggs in ketchup. Well, he might've judged me, but he had the decency not to say it out loud. Henry had hated my liberal use of ketchup as a condiment. He thought it was uncivilized. And why was I still thinking about my ex-fiancé? We'd broken up half a year ago, and I was now married to another man. I should've been over the pain of it by now.

"Ready?" Gideon asked when we'd put our dishes in the dishwasher.

I frowned. "For what?"

He looked at me like I was dense. "For the fair?"

"You're coming?"

His lips twitched. "I'm driving, babe. Wouldn't want to miss your reaction to the biggest event of the summer." His sarcasm was so thick I could've cut it like jello.

"They should really put you on the Marswood Harbor marketing committee," I snarked. "You'd have droves of tourists flooding the town with that attitude."

He laughed, and we went out to the car. It was an easy drive along the coast, and I was once again captivated by the beauty of the region. The ocean was a wild crash of waves against the shore, and the hills were a tangle of dense forest. The air smelled so clean I wondered what poison I'd been inhaling in the city all my life.

We stayed on the coast road and parked on the far side of Main Street. The Pier was just visible behind us where it overlooked the ocean on top of a bluff. Gideon waited as I hooked my cross-body bag over my head, then nodded toward the seaside road.

And then we were at the fair.

It was about a hundred feet of ragtag stalls. Half of them

were empty. To my right, the words "Petting Zoo" were spray-painted on a piece of plywood that leaned against rickety-looking pens. Two angry geese were in the first one, followed by a goat, a llama, and finally someone's dog. A small stage had been set up at the far end of the road, with a small cluster of people setting up microphones and speakers.

As far as fairs went, it was pretty pathetic. Gideon's aunt, Angela, sat behind one stall full of frankly mediocre floral watercolor paintings. There was a stall selling little pucks of hard-looking bread. An angry woman sat at the table, glaring at the Knead More Bread stall across the road. I spotted another stall of secondhand clothes, and one final one with beeswax and honey products. The rest were empty.

"So?" Gideon asked.

He wore sunglasses, but I could see the crinkles at the side of his eyes. "Are we early?" I asked.

His lips spread. "Nope."

"Why are there so many empty stalls?"

"It's a first-come, first-served kind of thing, and the people of Marswood Harbor are optimists."

"Other than you, you mean?"

He laughed. "Where do you want to start?"

I nodded at Caroline manning the bakery's stall. "Might as well get another drink."

We ambled up to her stall, and she arched her brows at me. "I don't have matcha capabilities here, I'm afraid," she told me, and put her hands on two big silver carafes of coffee. "I have dark roast and darker roast."

"I'll go with dark," I answered, then glanced at the bread stall across the way. "What's the story with that bread lady?"

"Eat at your own risk," Caroline answered, and Gideon snorted.

We got our coffees, paid, and then faced the fair. "I was expecting more," I admitted, which made Gideon laugh again. I couldn't help staring at him when he did, my own lips curling in response.

"This is as good as it gets in this town, I'm afraid," he said, looking down at me. The sun gilded his dark hair, and I couldn't help the yearning that ached in my chest. I still wanted him as badly as I had two weeks ago, when we were married. He arched a brow. "Regretting your decision to stay?"

"No," I answered, and turned toward the pens. "Let's go see the animals."

Gideon followed me as I gave the geese a wide berth—devil creatures, as far as I was concerned—and started with the dog. He looked like a collie crossed with something big. A lab, maybe. He had dark fur with gray eyebrows, floppy ears, and a whipcord tail that wagged violently. He came panting up to the fence and put his paws up on the edge of it, aggressively happy to see us. The whole pen tilted as he did, and Gideon leaned against the wire frame to stop it from toppling.

"Hey, boy," I said, scratching the dog behind the ears. "Aren't you gorgeous?"

Gideon reached over to pet the dog, making clicking noises with his tongue and grinning when the dog licked his fingers.

An older man walked up to us, wearing faded jeans and an old T-shirt. "Still a soft touch with animals, eh, Gid?"

"Can't beat a loyal dog," Gideon replied, then nodded at me. "Sadie, this is my uncle Walter."

"Congratulations," Walter replied, and I recognized him as the snoring mustachioed man at the wedding.

"Thank you. I haven't seen you at Etta's Sunday lunches."

"Too busy with the animals," Walter said. "And too many people at them lunches. Mom doesn't care that I don't go as long as I show up for the important things."

Gideon grunted, and I went back to petting the dog. "Etta is your mother?"

Walter nodded. "Me, then Angela, Susan, Peter, Mark, and then Jennifer."

I'd met everyone but Mark. I guessed that was Gideon's late father. I was starting to make sense of the family connections. "I see. You're the eldest. Do you have any kids?"

"Sure do. Two boys and a girl. Their mother took them away when we split, but they come and visit often enough now that they're all grown up."

"Hard to keep people in this town," Gideon replied, and it had the sound of an old, familiar line. How many people had they seen come and go? Was that why Gideon was so sure I wouldn't want to stay?

Walter made a noise in agreement. "Mom's gotten some crazy ideas in the past, but this is a new one," he said, nodding at me. "But you've lasted two weeks, so you might last two more."

"I actually really like it here," I said, oddly offended.

Walter just laughed. "Can't say that until you've had a winter here."

Gideon grunted. "You coming to Grandma's birthday party?"

"That, I can't miss," Walter said, and he laughed. "See you both there?"

Gideon nodded, and when Walter went to chat with someone else, I asked about the birthday party. "She's turning ninety next week," he told me.

"Do I need to get her a present?" I asked, looking around a little frantically. There weren't even any knick-knacks at this terrible fair.

Gideon just smiled. "No. As long as we go, she'll be happy."

I nodded, gave the dog one last pat, then moved to the next pen. The llama looked a little angry, so I just gave it a tentative smile and went to the goat. It munched on the grass in its pen, then hopped up onto a bucket and bleated. I jumped back, startled, and laughed. Gideon chuckled beside me.

A moment later, the llama made a noise, and a stream of spit came flying toward me. I screamed, throwing my hand up too late, and stumbled sideways. Gideon tried to reach for me, but he bumped the goat's pen. The goat leaped from the bucket, jumped the divider, and landed between the two geese.

Covered in llama spit, I watched as the geese began to honk with fury.

"Oh, my God," I said, a moment before the goat panicked and leaped toward the pen's wire fence. I saw its hooves, the whites of its eyes, and its little horns, and then the whole pen collapsed and the goat made a run for it.

Leaving me standing four feet away from the devil creatures.

The closest goose's neck extended toward me, and a loud honk came blaring out of its beak. Its wings spread and started beating, sending flutters of goose-scented wind toward me. I screamed.

Gideon tried to put himself between me and danger, but

one big, brawny man was nothing against two angry geese. Walter came hobbling toward us, but it was too late. The lead goose bit Gideon on the thigh, and he swore.

"Run!" I screamed.

Gideon ripped his pants out of the goose's beak, picked me up around the waist, and threw me over his shoulder. And then he ran.

By the time we tumbled between two big dunes of sand that separated the fair from the beach, I was laughing so hard there were tears streaming down my face. I lay on sand and long grass as Gideon rolled into me and leaned his forehead against my shoulder as he laughed.

"I hate geese," I wheezed.

"I didn't think it would attack me," he admitted.

"Have you ever met a goose before? What else would it do?"

Gideon laughed harder, rolling onto his back in the sand. We lay there until the giggles subsided. Finally, I turned to look at him. He'd lost his sunglasses at some point, and his eyes were glimmering with humor. His smile was unguarded and bright. He was gorgeous.

We stared at each other for a long time. I licked my lips, and Gideon followed the movement with his eyes. Slowly, as if he was waiting for me to flinch back, Gideon reached over and tucked a strand of hair behind my ear, neatly avoiding the globs of llama spit. His finger was warm as it traced the shell of my ear, coasting down the side of my neck and drifting away.

I ached for him to touch me again, but he just looked at me.

"Thoughts on your first Marswood Harbor Fair?" he asked.

"Ten out of ten," I replied, and he grinned. He pushed himself to his feet and helped me up, and we did our best to brush the sand from our clothes and hair. Stumbling out from between the dunes, we nearly ran into grumpy old Ivan Popov.

The old man scowled at me and then at Gideon. "Beauty and the beast," he sneered, and then brushed past us to limp toward the fair. I frowned after him, offended.

But it wasn't until I looked at Gideon that I realized that little comment had overshadowed all the laughter that had come before. His jaw was tense, and he was doing that thing where he angled his head away from me, like he didn't want me to look at his scars. He wore long sleeves today too, despite the beating sun, and I watched as the fingers of his right hand twitched at the left cuff to pull it down over his scarred wrist. It made me want to scream.

He met my gaze after a long pause and said, "You want to stay longer, or should I drive you home?"

The bubbly, effervescent feeling in my chest went flat. "Gideon..."

He shrugged off the hand I reached toward him, then stalked toward his car. I followed, trying to find the words to tell him that Ivan had been rude, and that wasn't at all how I saw him.

"He's wrong, you know," I finally said when we reached the vehicle.

Gideon shot me a glance. "Is he, though?"

This time, he angled his head so I could see the scars. And that pissed me off, because how did he expect me to react? Did he think I'd run away screaming? The scars were just different-textured skin! They didn't change the fact that he was funny and warm and a great cook, he was reliable and beloved and respected in his family, and he had an amazing body, and his *voice*, and oh, God, I was falling in love with him.

My mouth clamped shut before I could reply, the horror of my realization staying my tongue.

"I need to go to work, so..."

"It's Saturday."

"We've got thousands of hours of video to review to try to find Mr. Titty."

"Can't a computer do that for you?"

Gideon just stared at me. "You want a ride home, or no?"

"I'll find my own way back," I said.

His eyes were flat. Unsurprised. "Fine," he said. His anger—or was it hurt?—lay heavy between us. He got behind the wheel and went to close the door, then seemed to reconsider. He glanced at me and, a little more gently, he said, "Call me if you need a lift."

I nodded and watched him drive off. Glancing back at the fair, I didn't have the heart to go back. I did spot Gideon's sunglasses on the ground by the dunes, so I circled back to grab them, then made my way up Main Street.

My head was a mess. I walked under the dappled shade of the big trees lining the street, barely seeing the new additions to Mr. Titty's oeuvre. I passed boarded-up shops and the vacant apartments above, and I nodded to passers-by who greeted me by name.

As I walked, my anger grew. Anger at myself for falling for yet another unavailable man. Anger at Gideon for thinking I was so shallow. Anger at Ivan Popov for being a rude son of a bitch who couldn't be civil for three seconds of the day.

Anger had always been a great motivator of mine. It's what

had made me sign up for this marriage, after all. So when I reached Life's a Stitch and saw the "For Rent" sign still hanging in the window, it was my anger that made me pull out my phone. I was mad when I swiped away yet another spam call from an unknown number, then typed in the phone number on the sign.

"Marswood Harbor Property Management, how may I help you?" a woman's pleasant voice sing-songed the greeting over the phone.

"Hi, I'm calling about Life's a Stitch. Is the space still available to rent? How much are you asking for it?"

"May I have your name?"

"Sadie Ge—Sadie Mars," I said, and I swallowed thickly.

There was tapping on a keyboard, and then the woman said, "Life's a Stitch is available to rent." She named a price that was modest but still out of my budget. My heart sank. "Would you like to meet to have a look at the space?"

"I'll have to think about it," I said, and my anger deflated like an old balloon.

I didn't have enough money to reopen the doors on Sadie Bridal, even in this tiny town. I'd need a serious injection of cash to be able to sustain a new location until I got a steady stream of clients. If I ever got a steady stream of clients without someone like Henry propping me up.

Maybe I just wasn't good enough to run my own business.

Dejected, I started the long walk back to the cottage. I waved at Mrs. Gretzinger, who was standing by the front sign of The Pier with a contractor, then continued on my way. I passed two cars going into town, and I could tell only one of them was a local because he lifted two fingers off the steering wheel of his beat-up pickup in greeting as he passed me. The other car was a fancy Mercedes with dark-tinted windows whose driver ignored me. An out-of-towner.

The thought made my shoulders slump. An out-of-towner like me.

Ten minutes later, a third car drove up toward me, slowed, and stopped. Gideon rolled down his window. "You were supposed to call me," he rumbled. His expression was still guarded.

My silly heart soared at the sight of him, thumping wildly at the thought that he'd gone out of his way to come pick me up. It took so very little to make me fall for a man. I smiled. "Did the Marswood Harbor Watch call to tell you about your dereliction of duty as my husband?"

"Three phone calls and six texts about you walking down the road on your own," he grumbled.

I laughed as I got in the car, but sadness pierced my chest. In an alternate universe, he would be my husband in truth. I would open up to him, and he would accept me for who I was. He would stop thinking I was going to leave as soon as our trial period was over. He would believe me when I told him that I found him wildly attractive.

But this was real life. We had four more weeks to figure out if this was what we wanted forever. And if things kept going the way they were, I already knew my heart would break. If I stayed, I'd be married to a man I loved who didn't love me back. If I went, I'd leave the man who had my heart.

I watched Gideon cook dinner, and then I worked on sketches of Lola's dress to show her at Sunday lunch the following day. It was the kind of quiet evening I'd imagined when I wrote about my perfect day. But when it was time to go to bed, I went to the bedroom, and Gideon stayed on the couch.

That night, when all was quiet, I tried the dilators again. Thought of Gideon, even though I knew I shouldn't. Dreamed of a life that involved the love of a good man, a successful business, a big family, and a cozy home. Fell asleep knowing I would never have it.

GIDEON

I should've thanked Ivan Popov, I realized. I'd needed a reminder that Sadie and I weren't on the same level. But it was easy to forget when she looked at me with glittering brown eyes and lit up the room with her smile.

TWELVE
SADIE

I was starting to look forward to Sunday family lunch. Both my parents were only children and they weren't close with their own parents, so I'd never had any cousins or grandparents around. As the family outcast, it had been a lonely upbringing. Gideon's family was loud, overwhelming, and warm.

Lola grabbed me as soon as I walked in, and we went over her design. She bounced on her seat and changed her mind a million times, making me laugh.

"So, no straps?"

"No. Strapless. But this dress looks so good with the sleeves."

I sketched on some sleeves and glanced at her.

She hummed. "No," she finally said. "Definitely strapless."

I couldn't help my smile. It was worse than working for a bridezilla, but I was enjoying myself. Then I glanced up and met Gideon's gaze across the room. He stood in a knot of people, silent, his left side turned to the wall the way it always was. Even in his family, he hid himself.

My heart ached for him.

"Sadie."

I turned at the sound of Etta's voice, straightening. "Grandma Mars," I greeted. "Hi."

"I'd like to speak to you for a moment," she said with a smile, gesturing toward the door leading to the hallway. I handed Lola my sketchbook and followed the older woman out. When I stepped into the hallway, I turned back and saw Gideon frowning at me.

Etta and I walked down the hall and around the corner to another wing of the house. She brought me to a study lined with floor-to-ceiling bookshelves that were filled with leather-bound books. The floor was covered in a plush rug, and a gigantic desk faced the window.

Etta sat down in one of the visitor's chairs and gestured to the other. "My property manager told me you were inquiring about a shop in town," she said without preamble, her blue eyes sharp.

I gaped at her. Life's a Stitch belonged to Etta Mars? After thinking about it for a second, I felt like a dolt for even being surprised. I recovered and said, "I was curious about the rent."

"Are you thinking of opening a business in Marswood Harbor?"

The question was posed as if she were genuinely curious, but her eyes told another story. This woman was as shrewd as anything, and she was sniffing for information. I relaxed my grip on the arms of my chair and nodded. "I'm considering my options," I hedged.

Her smile was small, but I saw it. "I'll speak to Melinda," she said, naming the property manager with the sing-song voice. "I'm sure there's wiggle room on the rent price."

My brows jumped.

"You ran a business in Manhattan," she said. "Wedding dresses."

I nodded. "I did."

"There will be lots of weddings in this town in the coming months. Seems like a good time to open up shop in Marswood Harbor. A clever woman might even consider investing in such a business, if the opportunity were to present itself." She leaned her elbows on the arms of her chair and touched one of the rings on her fingers with the opposite hand. Watching me.

I was not mentally prepared for this conversation. "Are you offering me a deal, Etta?"

The small smile hiding at the corners of her mouth spread. "You closed up your business and sold all your assets. You haven't worked on a wedding dress since you've been here, and your company doesn't seem to be doing any active advertising. I'm thinking you're short on capital, but your inquiry about the shop tells me you haven't given up. I admire tenacity in a woman. It's a necessary quality if she's to make anything of herself."

This woman was dangerous. I thought of Gideon being beholden to his grandmother, getting married under duress. This business deal would come with a whole lot of strings.

But. But it would be a way to start over. Right now, I didn't see any other way. It wasn't like Marswood Harbor was awash with employment opportunities. I had to consider it.

"I'm interested," I finally said.

"But, of course," the older lady continued, "we would have to wait four more weeks before signing anything official."

I exhaled. There it was: the catch. In four weeks, Gideon and I would either file our wedding certificate or go our separate ways. Etta would give me cheap rent and invest in my business...as long as I remained married to Gideon. If I didn't stay married to him, there would be no future for me in this town. I couldn't help the humorless smile that curved my lips, and Etta arched a brow, smiling serenely. A woman in complete control.

I inhaled. Exhaled. Met her gaze. "That makes sense," I said. "But maybe we could come to an agreement for the next four weeks. I'd like use of the space to work on your granddaughter's homecoming dress. I wouldn't do any trade from the shop; I'd only use it as a workspace for the project. And I'd gift Lola a custom dress in return."

Etta gave me the first genuine smile I'd ever seen on her face. She laughed, then extended a hand toward me. "Deal. I'll get Melinda to give you the keys this week." She gestured to the door. "Send Gideon in next."

I frowned. "Gideon?" I asked, but when I opened the door, he was pacing the hallway outside the study.

His head snapped up when I appeared. He searched my face, looking a little frantic. "Is everything okay?"

I couldn't help the smile. "Everything's great, actually. She's waiting to speak to you."

Gideon's gaze lingered on me, but he finally nodded and stepped into the study. I listened to the door click shut, then padded down the hall to see what Lola had decided about the sleeves.

I had a space. I had an investment opportunity. I had a *chance...*

As long as Gideon and I filed that wedding certificate and stayed married in four weeks' time.

GIDEON

I loomed over my grandmother where she sat. "What was that about?"

"That's between me and your wife," Grandma Mars replied.

Had Sadie come in here to talk about the wedding certificate? She wanted out already, after only two weeks?

Frustration made my blood simmer. Was that why Sadie had seemed so happy when she walked out of the study? I gulped back my retort and asked, "You wanted to speak to me?"

"Take a seat, Gideon, and tell me how things are going with your wife."

I knew that calm, unruffled tone. My grandmother would get her way. I sighed, considered storming out and chasing after Sadie, and finally gave up and took a seat.

THIRTEEN
SADIE

My head whirled for two full days, and then on Wednesday morning, I got the keys from Melinda in front of Life's a Stitch. "Here's my card," the auburn-haired woman said. She wore a bright blue suit and a wide smile. "Call me if you need anything. Ta-ta!"

"Thanks," I called out as she hurried back to her car. I turned to the door, slid in the key, and walked in.

The air was thick with dust. The far wall was covered with storage cabinets, and there were two long worktables to my right, with a small reception desk straight ahead. Two sewing machines sat silent on the worktables. I flicked the lights, then made a slow loop of the room. There was a small staff bathroom and a tiny storage closet at the back, with a door through to the alley behind. The worktables were solid, but both machines looked like they needed to be serviced.

I took out my phone and started making a list. I'd need a new fluorescent bulb to replace the one that was flickering overhead. While I was at it, I might as well buy a good desk lamp to clamp to the edge of one of these worktables. I tested one of the chairs and decided it would do, then checked the storage closet for cleaning supplies.

Nothing.

Looked like another marathon cleaning session was needed. I sighed. But first, matcha.

Knead More Bread was only three doors down. I smiled as I inhaled the scent of coffee and fresh baked bread, getting in line behind the man who owned the hardware store. He gave me a friendly nod and made a comment about the weather.

When it was my turn, I smiled at Caroline behind the counter. "The usual?" she asked, and my heart soared. I'd been in town just over two weeks, and the local café knew my order.

Things with Gideon weren't amazing, but they weren't *bad*. Maybe in the next four weeks, we'd find our groove. Maybe I'd get to reopen my business. Maybe everything would work out, even if I didn't find true love.

At least there were plenty of friendly faces in town.

"I'm still shocked that a small town like this has matcha lattes," I said, pulling out my card to pay. "I mean, I wasn't even expecting you to have almond milk."

She gave me a strange look, a smile with a confused frown, and I flushed. I'd basically just called her town a backwater dump that hadn't entered the era of alternative milks. But Caroline just shook her head, charged my card, and started making my matcha latte.

"Gid tell you about Mr. Titty's latest artwork?" she asked me over the hissing of the espresso machine.

I shook my head. Gideon hadn't told me much of anything

lately. But that was our deal, wasn't it? My heart and body would get the memo eventually.

Caroline tilted her head toward Main Street. "Up the road a few blocks. Huge tits." She set the jug of steamed milk down to gesture with her hands. "Gigantic. Over on the museum's facade."

"Mr. Titty does not care about Marswood Harbor's historical significance."

Caroline snorted, like she wanted to laugh but knew she shouldn't. She shook her head. "I think it's a message. That museum was paid for by Etta Mars."

My brows jumped. "You think whoever's doing this graffiti isn't happy about the marriages." I'd heard chatter about more matches being in the works. Wedding bells were going to be ringing with great regularity in town, if Etta got her way.

Hopefully they would be more successful than mine.

Caroline shrugged as she poured the milk into the cup. "Lots of people just want to keep to themselves. They don't like change."

"And you?"

She slid my drink across the counter and smiled. "I like the extra business you're bringing to my bakery."

"That's all I am to you, huh?" I asked, clicking my tongue.

She laughed. "There's a trivia night at Bertie's tomorrow night," she said, naming one of the three bars in town. "We need another person to have a full team. You should come and join. Then maybe you can become more than a frou-frou drink to me."

"You are so rude," I said, and took a sip. "You're lucky you make good matcha."

Caroline laughed, and I told her I'd join her for trivia the following night. I walked out into the sunshine outside, holding the door open for Gideon's giant brother, Knox, who nodded at me as he headed inside. The door was just closing when I heard Caroline shout, "*Out!*"

Startled, I glanced through the window. Knox was smiling at her, his hands up in the universal sign of "Don't shoot!"

I'd never seen him smile. It transformed him from scary-stoic to breathtaking.

Caroline was pointing an espresso portafilter at him.

I pushed the door open again. "Is everything okay?"

"The spawn of Satan was just leaving my fine establishment," Caroline hissed, glaring at the big bear of a man.

He clicked his tongue. "Come on, sunshine. Sadie's not *that* bad."

"Funny," she said. "Now get out."

Knox had actually spoken multiple words. And it had been a *joke*. I blinked at him, feeling like I'd never seen him before. He'd spoken no more than a handful of words—mostly barely intelligible grunts—in my vicinity up until now.

Caroline wasn't fazed by his smile. She reached into one of the display cabinets, grabbed a Boston cream donut, and hurled it at Knox's head.

He caught it, laughed, then bit into it and waggled his eyebrows as the filling oozed out.

"You're disgusting," Caroline said.

"Thanks for the donut, sunshine," Knox said, and then he took another bite of donut, turned around, and left. On his way past, he said to me, "Good luck with the new shop."

I gaped at him. How had he found out so quickly?

"What did he say to you?" Caroline asked, glaring after the big man. "Did he threaten you?"

"No," I said, and couldn't help the curl of my lips. She was being protective of me. I had a friend. I hadn't had a friend in a long time.

I left Knead More Bread with a beaming smile on my face. I loved this town. I had a sliver of a chance at reopening my business, and the sun was shining. Life was good. Actually, it was *great*. I had more to look forward to than I'd had in *years*.

I had to let go of this desire for Gideon. Only then would I be free to start a life here, in this adorably shabby town, with these people who had already made me feel welcome. But telling myself to stop wanting him felt like telling myself to cut off my own hand. I couldn't do it.

Halfway back to my car, which was parked down a side street just past Life's a Stitch, my eyes landed on one of Mr. Titty's many pieces. He'd spray-painted the side of a dumpster with a pair of breasts, these more oval-shaped with large nipples. The signature barely fit on the side of the green bin.

I frowned. Something about the signature looked strange to me. And the breasts themselves...

Slipping my car fob back into my purse, I wandered over to the alley and stood in front of the dumpster. I snapped a picture of the graffiti, then walked back to Main Street, where I knew there were more examples of the graffitist's work. I took pictures of each, and with each my certainty grew. Gideon and his brothers had missed something important about this guy. If he even was a guy.

As I walked up the hill, I spotted Ivan Popov's antique shop. The breasts on his front window were similar to the ones that had graced the church doors. Gigantic, tiny nipples, angular writing. I spotted the beauty salon down the street and studied the boobs gracing its frontage. My camera shutter clicked, and I found myself walking up and up and up, all along Main Street and a few offshoots, snapping pictures all the way.

That's how I ended up at Rock Bottom. The dive bar was a squat, dark building with a flickering neon sign that stood at the back of a vast parking lot. Half the parking spaces were taken up by motorcycles, gleaming in the summer sunlight. An old pickup was parked around the side, and in front of it was another stunning piece of artwork by the breastacular Banksy wannabe.

I was busy snapping a picture of Rock Bottom's boobs when I heard the scuff of a boot. Turning toward the sound, I gulped at the sight of a muscular man in a leather motorcycle jacket, a flaming skull on his breast.

Cash Bridges.

The biker was broad and tall, like most of the men in this town. A beard hugged his strong jaw, and tattoos snaked over his knuckles. He radiated danger, and the way he looked at me made me feel like my feet had grown roots and anchored themselves to the ground. I didn't know if I should run or stay very, very still. He had brown eyes that sparked with interest when he saw me, and his voice was a low rumble. "Can I help you?"

"Just admiring your artwork," I said, using my phone to point at the painting on the brick wall. I still held my matcha latte in my other hand, and I clutched it like it was a shield.

Cash's smile was a quick flash of white in a dark beard. "One of Mr. Titty's better pieces," he noted. He brought his hand up to his chin like he was an art dealer at a fancy gallery.

I turned back to the boobs and tilted my head. "This piece does evoke strong emotion," I said, picking up on his joke and running with it. "Yearning. Tension. The play between the vulgarity of breasts on a bar wall and the restraint of the art itself."

"Don't know about any of that," Cash said, "but they're a fine pair of tits."

I snorted, and he flashed me a smile. I remembered what Etta had said after the wedding—she didn't think that Cash was Mr. Titty. But still, I had to ask. "Did you do it?"

"Do what, sweetheart?"

"Are you Mr. Titty?"

His smile widened. "Are you Nancy Drew?"

He was mocking me. Knowing that to show fear would give him the upper hand, I pretended to be shocked and said, "You read books?"

He barked out a laugh and shook his head. "Gideon's got his hands full with you, huh."

"Unfortunately, no, he doesn't," I mumbled, and immediately regretted it when Cash's brows jumped. He smiled at me, and I suddenly realized this man was charming. Like, very charming. Sure, he was gruff and a little scary, but he was handsome and had bucketfuls of charisma. He tilted his head toward the bar. "Buy you a drink?"

"Thank you, but no," I said, then pointed at a camera on a pole that surveyed the parking lot. "This thing catch Mr. Titty in the act?"

"Maybe. But if I didn't show the cops the footage, and I didn't show your hubby either, what makes you think I'll show you?"

"I'm asking really nicely?" I blinked at him, smiling.

Okay, yes, I was flirting a little. But if Gideon hadn't gotten footage from this camera, maybe it could help him catch Mr. Titty. And also...I was enjoying myself. My husband was ignoring me, and by now I was pretty sure whatever spark had lit between us on our wedding night and at the Marswood Harbor Fair was destined to die. I wasn't going to do anything with Cash Bridges—I wasn't actually *into* him, and I would never cheat on anyone, even if they clearly didn't want me—but I really wasn't in the mood to clean when the weather was so good, and I was pretty sure I'd figured out something important about Mr. Titty.

He rocked back on his heels, studying me. Then he shrugged as if to say, *What the hell, why not?* Tilting his head toward the building, he invited me inside.

I looked at the dark building and hesitated. Going into a biker bar didn't seem like an impulse I should follow. Then again, it was ten o'clock on a Wednesday morning. How bad could it be?

The bar was as dive-y inside as it looked outside. It smelled like stale beer with an undertone of piss. Peanut shells littered the ground, and grizzled old men in motorcycle jackets sat along the bar. The back wall was dominated by a gigantic skull with flames coming out of its eyes and mouth. A few younger men clustered around a pool table, looking hungover and grumpy. Other than me, there were only two women inside: one standing behind the bar wearing a white tube top and short denim shorts, her bleached blond hair teased out past her shoulders, and the other an older woman wearing a motorcycle jacket of her own, sitting at a booth near the pool table with one of the younger men.

Every single person turned to look when I walked in with Cash. I was in over my head. Then again, I'd felt this way since I drove into town two weeks ago, and at least I was doing something productive.

Cash walked to the bar and leaned on the polished wood surface, angling his body toward one of the gray-haired, bearded men sipping a bottle of beer at the bar. I put a hand on the surface beside him, then gingerly took it back when I felt how disgustingly sticky it was.

"This little bird wants to see some footage from our camera outside," Cash said to the man, whose dark eyes swung over to look at me. "Wants to see who tagged our wall outside."

"That so," the older man replied, less of a question and more of a statement.

I gave him a winning smile. "I'm working on a theory," I explained.

"And why should we help you? You're Gideon Mars's woman, aren't you? One of them mail-order brides?"

"More like email-order bride, amirite?"

He snorted, and the corners of his eyes crinkled even though his lips didn't curl. "I think Etta's out of her mind," he said. "No way this whole thing works out." He nodded his head at me, and I understood that "this whole thing" meant the arranged marriage scheme, of which I was lucky number one.

The old man turned away from me and tilted his bottle against his lips. Cash gestured to the bartender, who put two bottles of beer down on the bar top. Cash slid one over to me. The younger men at the pool table had drifted closer, and I glanced over my shoulder to see the three of them watching me. I felt like a piece of meat, and I was starting to think I shouldn't have come inside this place at all.

Cash shifted his body slightly and made a subtle hand gesture, and the men stopped advancing. He sipped his beer and watched me, all dark eyes and danger. With one arm leaning against the bar, he looked like a lion at rest. A smile creased his cheeks. Uh-oh.

"You ever been on a bike, sweetheart?"

"Like, a motorcycle?" I squeaked.

His smile widened. "Yes, babe. A motorcycle."

I shook my head.

"You want to go for a ride? Feel the wind in that pretty dark hair of yours?" He reached over and touched a lock of my hair.

Before I could answer, the door banged open. I knew, by the shiver that went through me, who was standing on the threshold.

"Touch her again and lose your hand, Cash," Gideon growled.

I turned to see my husband silhouetted in the doorway. His face was in shadow, but even so, I could tell he was furious. It emanated from him in dark waves, filling the space with brutal tension. My spine snapped straighter, and it became hard to breathe.

Everyone else felt it too. The men shifted on their feet, puffing their chests as they faced Gideon. Hands went to waistbands, and I wondered how many of them were carrying guns.

Suddenly, I felt very, very stupid for having come in here. The tension ratcheted up. Breathing in the air in the bar felt like trying to inhale noxious soup. Cash shifted behind me; I felt him straighten and move closer. I clutched my coffee cup in one hand, hoping no one could see me trembling.

Gideon didn't care about the dozen other men in the bar who were doing their best to intimidate him. He stalked across the floorboards toward me, and bikers shifted out of his way rather than try to stop him. They glared at him, and as he got closer they glared at me. I felt their gazes on me like rakes of dagger-sharp claws, but I could look at no one but Gideon.

His hair was pulled back, his scars on full display. That, combined with the ire written in every line of his face and body, made him look like wrath personified.

I expected him to stop in front of me. Maybe tilt his head and order me around, tell me it was time to leave. As he moved even closer, my heart tripped, and I was sure he was going to throw me over his shoulder and carry me bodily out of the bar.

He did none of those things.

Instead, Gideon buried his hand in my hair, tilted my head back, and crushed his lips to mine. This was not the same kiss as our wedding night. It had nothing to do with wanting; this was Gideon staking his claim. Proving a point. I felt it in the way he held me, how he angled my body so everyone could see I belonged to him, how he kissed me so hard it felt like a bruise.

When he pulled away, his eyes were black. "We're leaving," he growled. "*Now*."

I could do nothing but nod my agreement. He'd reduced me to a puddle of simpering need. I *knew* I should've been humiliated, or at least outraged, but all I could feel was desire. I wanted to be wanted so badly that Gideon couldn't help himself, the way I couldn't help myself.

Sliding his hand down to drape across the back of my neck,

his palm pressed between the top of my shoulder blades, Gideon led me toward the exit.

Then Cash said, "Hey, sweetheart, you forgot something."

I turned to look at the man surrounded by all his threatening biker friends. He flashed me that scary-hot smile and tossed something through the air. I disengaged from Gideon in time to catch it with one hand, then let Gideon tow me out the doors where the air was fresh and the sun was shining. I gulped down a deep breath as my mind reeled.

"You going to tell me why the hell I found you in Rock Bottom talking to Cash fucking Bridges?" Gideon demanded, dropping his hand from my back. And, hey, turned out Gideon was still really mad.

And that made me mad, because what the hell! I planted my hands on my hips. "How did you even know I was there?"

He leaned closer, so I could see the sparks of anger in his blue eyes. "Why were you at Rock Bottom with Cash Bridges, Sadie?"

"What the hell do you care?"

His anger snapped against my skin like a thousand elastic bands. I welcomed it. It was better than the cool avoidance I'd gotten from him so far. The push and pull. The little droplets of affection that kept me on the hook.

At least, it felt better in the moment. Because at least now I knew I wasn't the only one who *felt* something. And who was he, to demand anything of me? Who was he to *care* so much?

Gideon's jaw tensed. His chest rose and fell with a sharp breath, his eyes scanning my face, my body.

Fool that I was, I wanted him to grab me and kiss me again. I wanted him to wreck me. To take my heart and crush it in his hands. At least then I wouldn't be drifting through life feeling like a shell of a person.

For a moment, I thought he would. I felt his desire like a rope around my wrists, keeping me tethered to him.

Then he swore and tore his gaze away from me, and the moment was over. I exhaled, confused by the hurt that sawed into my chest like a serrated blade.

But what was confusing about the truth? Gideon didn't want me. He never had.

With tears stinging my eyes, I shoved the item Cash had thrown me against Gideon's chest. "Here," I spat out. "I was in there to get this for *you*."

GIDEON

I caught the little piece of plastic against my chest before it could drop to the ground, but my eyes remained on my wife.

My stubborn, angry, breathtaking wife.

Fury still coursed through my veins at the thought of Cash touching her. I wanted to go back in there and tear the other man's limbs clean off his body, then come back and kiss her until she promised she belonged to me. Tell her to get on her knees and apologize for making me chase her across town like this, for making me feel so out of control.

I managed to look down at my palm, and the haze of anger was eased with a breath of confusion.

She'd given me a flash drive.

I wasn't expecting Gideon to jump up for joy or anything, but even so, his reaction disappointed me. He stared at the flash drive like it was a dead cockroach, his lip curling as he scowled.

"You went to Rock Bottom for *this*?"

"Okay, let's try that again." I gave him a sharp, humorless smile. "Instead of being an absolute jerk about it, you can say something along the lines of, 'Wow, Sadie, you're so clever and resourceful. I'm so glad to have you around.'"

"Wow, Sadie, you walk into a biker bar with no backup for a flash drive of questionable origin that may or may not contain anything of value."

Curling my fingers into a fist, I held back a growl. Anger sizzled inside me as I glared at Gideon. "That," I hissed, "was *rude*. You still don't have any footage of Mr. Titty, right? Other than our wedding day? Well, *that* is video of him tagging Rock Bottom!"

"I didn't ask you to go gathering evidence for me," he replied through clenched teeth.

"You didn't ask me for anything!"

"Exactly!" Gideon puffed out big, angry breaths, glaring at me with those ice-blue eyes.

Marrying him had been the biggest mistake of my life. I wasn't going to be able to think straight for a decade, just from the effect he had on me. "While we're airing our grievances, how about you tell me what the hell that was, in there." I tilted my head toward the bar.

"What are you talking about?"

"What am I talking about?" I screeched. "What am I *talking* about!"

"Yes, Sadie! What the hell are you talking about?"

"You kissed me!" My voice, mortifyingly, was shrill, and it broke on the last word.

Gideon's glare intensified. He stood close enough that I could feel the heat of him. Close enough that I had to tilt my chin up to meet his stare. "Yeah," he replied in a low voice. "That bother you?"

It didn't bother me; that was the problem. But kissing Gideon hadn't been part of our agreement. We were supposed to be married on paper. He'd get to keep his business. I'd get my fresh start. That was the deal.

But every time Gideon did something nice for me, it made my thoughts rush toward married bliss and love and rainbows and butterflies and unicorns. And a kiss? It set me on fire. It made me forget all the ways that I needed to keep myself safe.

Sex and intimacy needed to be off the table. We were

married in name only. That was the way for me to survive this without breaking my own heart in the process.

The alternative was admitting to Gideon about the vaginismus. Admitting to myself how much I craved intimacy with him—emotional and physical. And once I did that, I'd have to see his endless disappointment in me. Just like everyone else.

No. I liked it here. I wouldn't ruin it by letting him in. This right here—how fucking *rude* he was—was proof that I couldn't open up to him, ever.

I would never have it all, so I had to carve out a little sliver of life where I knew I could be content. A friend or two. My business. A place to stay. That was enough. It had to be enough; I would never have anything more.

"It bothers me that you marched in there and made a show of kissing me," I finally replied. "It bothers me that even now, you haven't thanked me."

"Maybe you wanted to ride Cash's bike," Gideon replied with a curl of his lips.

"Oh, no," I said, brushing past him. "We're not doing this. You're not turning this on me and making me feel bad for being a woman who exists in proximity to other men."

"He was *touching* you."

I whirled around. "That's more than you've done!"

As soon as the words were out of my mouth, I regretted them. He wasn't meant to touch me; that was our agreement. The fact that I couldn't stop myself from falling for him was an inconvenience. It was my problem to deal with.

But now he stared at me like he'd never seen me before. Like he was trying to read something in me that he couldn't quite believe. "You *want* me to touch you?"

Yes. The word was on the tip of my tongue, but I couldn't say it out loud. That was one step toward vulnerability. One step toward mess. One step toward disaster. I turned my back on Gideon again and mumbled, "Forget it."

"Sadie!" His steps hurried after me, but I didn't turn to look at him. If I did, he might see the tears I tried to fight.

"Leave me alone, Gideon," I said. "Take the USB and go to work. I know you'd rather be there than here with me." I marched back down Main Street without looking back. I found a garbage can and tossed the rest of my matcha latte away. My stomach was in knots; I couldn't finish it.

A minute later, Gideon's SUV rolled along the road beside me. "Sadie," he said softly. "Get in the car. I'll drive you back to town."

"No."

"Sadie. Please."

"No."

He sighed, but he didn't drive off. He just rolled alongside me at a walking pace, even when two cars came up behind him and honked. I tried to wave him on, but Gideon was stubborn. He just kept driving beside me, occasionally glancing over and arching his brows like he was asking me to get in the car.

I wouldn't. Couldn't.

All these little acts of service were weakening my resolve. I couldn't let these silly feelings win. I could *not* fall in love with Gideon. Not truly. Not in the deep, everlasting way that I'd always dreamed of. What a disaster that would be! I had to keep him at arm's length, or else this whole arrangement would fall apart.

So, despite the honking and the ridiculousness of Gideon

rolling at three miles an hour beside me, I walked all the way back to Life's a Stitch and turned down the side street where I'd parked my car.

And stopped short.

One ugly word had been scratched into the white paint across the passenger side of my car:

LEAVE

This time, there was no doubt. The vandalism *was* deliberately targeting me. And it was escalating.

I never heard him get out of the car, but suddenly, Gideon's arm went around my waist, and he wrenched me against his side to hold me close. I was sure he could feel the fine tremors going through my body as I stared at the damage, read and reread the word. His phone was in his other hand. "Jack," he growled, "check every camera we have near the bakery. Everything. Someone just threatened Sadie."

GIDEON

I would find the person who did this. Hunt them. Hurt them.

FIFTEEN
SADIE

Marswood Security was housed in a three-story glass building on the edge of town. The first floor was all glossy reception and sleek conference rooms. Lots of gray, white, and black, with the company's logo subtly displayed on walls, stationery, and screens.

Gideon guided me up the stairs to the second floor. He pressed his finger to a security pad, waited for the beep and the click that told us the lock had disengaged, and then opened the door to a high-tech lair. His brothers were sitting at a command station along with Connor, the whiz-kid cousin, and a couple of people I didn't know. All of them buff men with an air of no-nonsense industry.

"What have you got?" Gideon asked when Jack stood to greet him.

"Nothing so far," his brother replied, grimacing. He nodded at me. "How are you holding up?"

"I'm okay," I said, which was the truth. Surprisingly.

Gideon's hand pressed against my shoulder blades in response. He led me to a chair, then grabbed the arm of it to roll it closer to him as he took a seat next to me, never more than two feet away from me. After my experience with Henry, it should've felt suffocating, but instead, it felt nice. Comforting. Safe. Gideon's hand moved from the armrest to my knee as he spoke to Jack. "I drove by about fifteen minutes before I called you, and the car was intact. That gives us a time frame."

Jack grunted in response, running a hand through his hair and making it stand up on end. "We have limited coverage down that road. Our closest camera is at Fletcher's shop at the end of Marswood Drive," he said, naming the cross street two blocks away from where I'd parked. "That leaves a big area that's unsurveilled. Connor, you think you can get us eyes anywhere closer?"

"I'll work on it," the teenager replied, tapping furiously on a keyboard.

To my left, Knox was staring at a sped-up security feed from a traffic camera on Main Street. There was no sign of the mirth he'd shown with Caroline—and no sign of the donut. I watched his screen for a moment, then asked, "How did you access that? Wouldn't that belong to the DOT?"

Knox glanced at me. He wore glasses, which he hadn't had on any of the other times I'd seen him. His lips twitched in response, barely a movement in his stoic face.

"Knox doesn't like divulging his secrets," Jack answered with a grin. Connor let out a cackle from across the room, his hands flying over his keyboard as his eyes stayed trained on his screen.

Gideon's hand gently squeezed my knee, and I turned to see him watching me. "You want something? Tea? Coffee? Water? Food?"

I shook my head. My stomach was one big writhing mass of stress. Putting anything in it was out of the question.

His eyes were intent. "We'll find out who did this," he vowed.

I believed him. He held my gaze for a long moment, and it became harder to breathe. His eyes were intense, but the anger in them was gone. He *cared*. It made my heart swell, which was so typical of me and so utterly disastrous. I just couldn't help myself from falling for him, even though I *knew* he didn't want me that way. Every time he touched me, he wrenched himself away from me. And still, I wanted more. I was a fool.

But here he was, directing every member of his company to find out who had keyed my car. When was the last time someone had cared so much about my safety? When was the last time someone had recruited any amount of resources to helping me with a problem?

I couldn't remember. I'd been on my own for so long, even when I'd been in a relationship.

Gideon sighed, stood, and extended his hand toward me. "Come with me," he said gently.

I slipped my palm against his, and he threaded his fingers through mine. He turned to toss the flash drive I'd procured to Jack, then tugged me up to my feet and kept hold of my hand as he guided me toward a closed door on the other side of the room. Holding his hand felt natural and thrilling all at once. I never wanted him to let go.

But he did let go when we got inside the room. It was a

small meeting room, with a couch, two armchairs, a low table, and a big screen on the wall. Gideon sat me down on the couch and took a seat next to me, his expression serious.

"You didn't sign up for this," he started without preamble. He licked his lips and swallowed thickly, gaze sliding away from mine for a moment. Then he took a deep breath and met my gaze again. "I'll understand if you just want to grab your stuff and go, Sadie. No hard feelings."

I reared back. "What?"

"I'll find out who did this either way. But I know this isn't what you thought you were getting when you agreed to marry me. We can rip up that certificate, go our separate ways. I know this changes things."

"You're trying to get rid of me?" My words were breathless.

Gideon's brows slammed down. "I'm trying to keep you *safe*. If someone has it out for you, the best thing for you to do is go back to the city."

I crossed my arms and stuck out my jaw. "Nice try, Gideon. Still isn't gonna work."

"What the fuck is that supposed to mean?"

"You've been trying to get rid of me since the moment you saw me at the end of the aisle." An idea dawned. No—not possible. But still, I had to ask. "Did *you* vandalize my car? You're trying to scare me off?"

He stared at me, disbelieving and furious. Then in a low voice, he said, "I've married a lunatic."

"That wasn't a no," I observed, leaning back on the couch. "You could just tell me you don't want to stay married to me. No need to cause property damage."

Then he was there, caging me against the arm of the sofa. His scent filled my nose. His arms strained against the fabric of his shirt on either side of me, his jaw twitching from how hard he clenched it. All that existed was him. The heat of his body blazing against me. The closeness of his features. The feel of his warm breath ghosting across my skin. "I did not key your car, Sadie," he enunciated. "I didn't slash your tire. And the last thing I'm trying to do is get rid of you."

I gulped, heart thudding in my throat. My body was ablaze, even though no part of him touched any part of me. My gaze dropped to his lips, and I remembered how they felt against mine. Remembered the way his stubble abraded my skin. Remembered how badly I wanted to feel the rasp of it against my inner thighs. "You've got a funny way of showing it," I answered, and it came out as a whisper.

His fingers tightened against the couch, causing the leather to creak in protest. "I'm trying to give you a *chance*, Sadie. A chance to make the right decision."

My pulse was still too fast. I narrowed my eyes. "And what's that?"

"Get away from this town. Find something better for yourself." He paused. "Some*one* better."

I clicked my tongue, shoving his chest so he'd back away. I stood up, restless and on edge. Crossing the room, I stared out the window at the trees surrounding the building. It took several long moments for my heartbeat to settle. Then I turned and found Gideon watching me. His gaze held an edge of desperate hunger, but the line of his shoulders was resigned.

I lifted my chin. "No."

He jerked. "What?"

"I'm not leaving."

Where would I go? I'd closed up shop on my business. I'd moved out of my apartment. My parents' guest room beckoned, with all the emotional damage that would come along with it.

I was *tired*. Life in the city was a grind, and most of the time I was pretending to be a savvy, put-together woman that I was pretty sure was entirely false. Marswood Harbor was the first place that had ever felt like home.

And then there was Gideon. He looked at me like he saw right through to the heart of me. We'd known each other just over two weeks, yet he'd managed to make me feel appreciated in a way that none of my partners or family members had before. He'd *apologized* after our horrible wedding night. Henry had never once apologized like that. Sure, my ex might've told me he was "sorry he made me feel that way," but he'd never come to me with a half-sweet almond milk matcha latte in his hands and a simple apology on his tongue.

Maybe this wasn't a love story for the ages—maybe once our six weeks were over, we'd settle into companionship. We'd never truly fall in love. I'd eventually accept that love just wasn't in the cards for me.

Or maybe not. Maybe this little kernel of connection between us was real.

Didn't I deserve to find out?

Slowly, Gideon shifted his body and stood. He crossed the room and came to a stop in front of me, his toes an inch from mine. My heart began to rattle. I sucked in a hard breath, and Gideon's lips twitched. They tugged into a half smile, pulling at the undamaged skin on his right side. Then he lifted a hand and softly, so softly stroked my cheek with the backs of his fingers.

My heart took off.

I closed my eyes and leaned into the touch, sighing when he turned his hand to cup my cheek with his palm. His thumb rubbed my lips, a gentle brush, and I parted them on an exhale.

"If you stay here much longer, Sadie," he rumbled, "I'm not going to be able to let you go." His thumb pressed down on my bottom lip, and I opened my mouth. Pupils flaring, Gideon watched the movement. His chest rose and fell unsteadily, his thumb still holding my lips open. "You should leave," he whispered.

My body was a bowstring, ready to be plucked. My nipples were hard points beneath my bra, and wetness soaked into my panties. The last thing I wanted to do was leave. I wanted Gideon's ravenous gaze on my body again. I wanted his hands to touch and claim and possess. I wanted everything—wished I could have everything. The everlasting love of a happily-ever-after. The pleasure of good sex. The ability to take his body into mine the way I knew he wanted. The way *I* wanted but could never have.

Most of all, I wanted him to know me—all of me, secrets and flaws and all—and keep looking at me exactly as he was in this moment, forever.

My tongue slid out to lick the tip of his thumb, and his body went rigid from head to toe. Drunk on the intensity of his reaction, I swirled my tongue around again, tasting the salt of his skin.

"Sadie." His voice was a tortured groan, as if he wanted me

to stop. But instead, he pushed his thumb into my mouth. I fastened my lips around it and sucked. He grunted—

And the door flew open. "Gid—oh, shit. Sorry! Sorry!"

"*OUT*," Gideon bellowed, his eyes on mine, his thumb sliding out of my mouth as he shielded me from view of the door.

"That flash drive Sadie got did have footage of Mr. Titty on it," Jack said from the doorway. It sounded like he'd stepped around the corner but had stayed near. "Thought you'd want to know."

Gideon let out a shallow breath, his eyes blazing as they circled my face. "Fine."

"Yep," Jack said, and closed the door to leave us alone again.

"This isn't over," Gideon warned, sending a thrill rushing down my spine. Then he tangled his fingers with mine again and dragged me, face flaming, out into the other room.

We all watched the video on the screen. A hooded figure dressed in all black other than a pair of white shoes darted into view. They spray-painted breasts onto the side of Rock Bottom with a few smooth, practiced movements, signed their work, then glanced over their shoulder and sprinted off toward the forest behind the bar. A moment later, a motorcycle came to a stop in the frame. Cash got off his bike, stared after the graffiti artist, then considered the new breasts on his clubhouse's wall.

"That's it," Jack said when the video stopped. "Do we think Mr. Titty vandalized Sadie's car?" Jack asked, leaning back in his chair. It squeaked slightly as he spun around to look at us.

Connor glanced up sharply. "What? Why would he do that?"

Jack shrugged. "He knew, somehow, that she was getting this footage, and got spooked?"

Gideon was staring at the still frame of Cash on screen. "Mr. Titty has a motive. He wouldn't be so prolific if it was just the thrill of tagging all these buildings. He's trying to make the town look unappealing to newcomers."

"Newcomers like me," I said, finishing the line of thought.

Gideon's palm slid up my spine. It was embarrassing how much I loved that touch. How much I'd missed him reaching for me like this, especially when Gideon didn't even seem to notice what he was doing. His brows were drawn and his eyes were still on the screen. "We know that whoever vandalized Sadie's car wants her to leave. That could be Mr. Titty escalating to direct threats. Instead of making the town unappealing to new residents, he's trying to scare them off directly."

Knox hummed from his chair, his hand coming up to rub his jaw. "Could be a coincidence."

"I don't believe in coincidences," Gideon said darkly.

"Cash doesn't want newcomers in town," Bennett, the youngest brother, piped up to say. "If Marswood Harbor grows, his territory gets threatened."

"You think he orchestrated this?" Jack asked, waving a hand at the screen. "Got someone to tag his bar so he could give us the footage? If that were true, why wouldn't he give us the video when we asked the first time?"

"I don't see him for it," Gideon said, shaking his head.

"What if Mr. Titty is multiple people?" I asked. All eyes turned to me, and I cleared my throat. "Would that change your opinion?"

Gideon frowned at me. "What do you mean?"

"I started looking at the graffiti today," I said, pulling out my phone. "That's how I ended up at Rock Bottom. I was taking photos of every tag I could find because I noticed something strange. There are two styles that Mr. Titty uses, and to me that says two people."

After selecting all the photos I'd taken, I handed Jack the phone so he could transfer the pictures to the big screen. A moment later, they were up, and Connor's fingers were flying over the keys. It took him less than two minutes to get all the pictures dropped onto a map of town so we could see the distribution of photos.

"The breasts on the church doors are one style," I said, pointing to the spot on the map. Connor clicked the photo and dragged it over to one of the many screens. I gestured to another photo. "Compare that to the tag on the hair salon."

We went through all my pictures, and I categorized them on two screens. All the men were silent and watching.

"One style favors large breasts with tiny nipples. The signature is always angled upward, and there's a lot of overspray." I pointed to the other screen. "These breasts are more pear-shaped, and the nipples are more realistic. The signature is clearly different, and the spray is much more concentrated."

"It's two different people," Gideon agreed, staring at the screens. "Maybe three." He gestured to the big breasts, subtly different in a few of the images.

"The other thing I noticed was the location of the tags. Most of them are on Mars family buildings." I felt the weight of everyone's attention turning toward me, and I fought not to fold under the pressure. "I got curious," I said, a little defensively. "I mean, I married into the family, right? And then Caroline made a comment about the museum being paid for by your grandmother, so I started Googling buildings in town when I found a tag. Most of them belong to your family, or at least have some sort of historical significance."

Knox's fingers flew over the screen, and at least two-thirds of the graffiti locations lit up. "She's right," he rumbled.

Bennett clapped me on the back and wrapped me in a hug, laughing. "I gotta go talk to Grandma Mars's computer guy. He did something right when his algorithm picked you, Sadie."

"It's just a theory," I protested, but I was struggling to fight my proud grin.

I glanced over to look at Gideon, who had a strange look in his eyes. When Bennett dropped his arms from around me, he reached over to tug me closer. His hand went around my arm, thumb stroking the inside of my elbow. "Good work," he murmured.

"So who are they?" Jack asked, returning to the issue at hand. "And are they the ones who threatened Sadie?"

"And how do we find out?" Knox added in a quiet rumble, his brow drawn in a deep frown. Silence settled over all of us in the wake of his question, and I glanced at the brothers and cousins, waiting for someone to answer.

Finally, I couldn't take it anymore. "Isn't it obvious?"

Gideon, who'd been scowling at the screens, lifted his head to stare at me. "What's obvious?"

"We need to set a trap," I said.

They all turned to look at me. Gideon understood me first,

and his scowl deepened as he crossed his arms. It was Connor who looked most confused; he was the one who finally asked, "How would we do that?"

I spread my arms. "Easy. Use me as bait."

GIDEON

She was out of her mind if she thought I would allow her to put herself in harm's way. Out of her fucking mind.

SIXTEEN
SADIE

"Absolutely not." Gideon's voice was a whip crack in the small room. Stillness followed his words. Computers hummed in the resulting silence.

The rustle of my clothes sounded loud as I crossed my arms to face Gideon. "You got a better idea?"

"Yeah," he said, stalking closer. "I lock you in a room until you stop walking into danger."

"When have I ever walked into danger!"

"I found you at Rock Bottom an hour ago, Sadie."

"I wasn't in any danger! I mean, those guys were a little scary, but I didn't think they'd *hurt* me. Not until you barged in all macho aggressive and threatened to kill Cash Bridges."

And kissed me, I refrained from saying.

"You *what?*" Jack asked, eyes widening as he glanced at his brother. Gideon ignored him and kept those blue eyes trained on me.

Bennett whistled. "Shit," he murmured.

Knox just sighed and said nothing as he rubbed the bridge of his nose.

I pointed at the screen. "We have a problem," I said. "Someone is targeting me, and we don't know if there's any relation to Mr. Titty. Mr. Titty is also getting bolder and seems to be going after your grandma's properties. First, we need to figure out if they're related. Then we need to stop them."

"I like her," Bennett said to Knox. Knox ignored him.

"We're not using you as bait," Gideon growled. His eyes sparked as they held my gaze, and I felt a shiver course through me.

"It's the easiest way of finding out who did this to my car. And once we have them, we can get them to tell us whether or not they're Mr. Titty."

"No."

"Gideon."

"I said *no*, Sadie."

"Oh, and I'm supposed to just agree with you, am I? Because you say no?"

Tension was thick enough to slice. Bennett broke it with a low whistle and a laugh, and Gideon used the opportunity to close the distance between us. He wrapped a hand around my arm and walked me toward the exit.

"What are you doing?" I protested. "We haven't finished."

"Oh, we're done here, Sadie," he growled.

"I do *not* like this side of you," I said as he opened the door to the stairwell. It closed behind us with a bang, and I realized that was a lie.

I liked this side of him very much. I liked the fire in his eyes, and the way he couldn't seem to stop touching me. I liked the way he caught me around the waist and pushed me up against the bare concrete wall.

"You," he said in a quiet, dark voice, "are not bait. You're never going to be bait. Understand?"

"I am a grown woman," I answered, but my voice trembled. He was so close to me. So big. I wanted him so badly.

For a moment, I thought he felt the same. His eyes dropped to my lips and then skated away. I thought he was holding back from kissing me again.

But he wasn't. He dropped his hands from my waist and took a big step back. Like being so close to me repelled him. He could only stand it for a few measly seconds.

I wanted to cry.

He glared at me once more and said, "I'm taking you home. I'm setting up a perimeter around the cottage, and you're not going anywhere without me or one of my brothers by your side."

Horror dawned inside me. Instead of the pleasant, relaxing time I'd had so far in town, I'd be stuck with a man I couldn't help but desperately want. A man who clearly didn't want me back. No matter what had happened in that room upstairs, or in Rock Bottom in front of an entire biker gang, or alone in the bedroom on our wedding night, the truth was that Gideon always recoiled. It was like he was trying to force himself to want me, but he couldn't quite manage.

He was a one out of ten; he just didn't want me that way.

If he'd kept his distance all the time, I would've been okay. My own desire for him would fade, and I'd find some sort of stasis in town. I'd settle for an okay life.

But this hot-and-cold act was driving me insane. Especially when I knew that even if we *did* want each other, I still hadn't told him about my malfunctioning body. We were never going to get our happily-ever-after, but I couldn't stop myself from dreaming about it.

Maybe this whole thing had been doomed from the start. We weren't a perfect match because I'd lied on my application. Gideon was just a microcosm of the whole town and the easy, quiet life it promised: something I desperately wanted that didn't want me back.

"Let's go," he said, and led me down the stairs and out the door.

We drove home in silence, and I ducked into the bathroom to shower. I heard him banging around the kitchen, but I didn't have the heart to face him. An hour after I'd scurried back into my room, there was a knock on the door.

"Yes?"

"Food's ready. I made lasagna."

I freaking *loved* lasagna. But I didn't love the prospect of eating it with Gideon sitting on the other side of the table. "Thanks, but I'm not hungry."

The knob turned, and the door cracked open. I sat up in bed, glaring. "I could've been changing in here!"

"You should eat something."

"When are you going to stop ordering me around?"

"When you start taking care of yourself properly."

"I'm not hungry."

My sort-of husband glared at me from the doorway, then let out a sigh. "I've got to head back to work. Knox is watching the house; I've left his number on the kitchen counter. Call him if you need anything."

We watched each other for a moment, and then Gideon

turned and left. I slumped back in bed and listened to the engine of his car fade, wondering how the hell I'd gotten myself in this position. Was this worth the angst?

My phone buzzed, interrupting my thoughts. The family group chat. My sister Christine had sent a photo. I prepared to toss my phone aside without looking at it when a second message came through.

CHRISTINE

Sadie, is this you????

A second later, my mom chimed in.

MOM

YOU GOT MARRIED?

I had time to swipe up and see a screenshot of a news article. The headline read: ARRANGED MARRIAGE LAST DITCH EFFORT TO SAVE A SMALL TOWN. There was a picture of me and Gideon at the altar, glaring at each other as we held hands, with our names in small print in the caption.

Then my phone rang. I tossed it away like it was a live snake, and watched as it buzzed its way across the comforter, my mother's name lighting up the dim room.

It went still, and I let out a breath.

Then she called again.

With a sigh, I grabbed my phone and swiped to answer. "Mom."

"You got married? Without me?"

I closed my eyes and reached for patience. Trust my mother to make my wedding about herself. "Nice to talk to you too, Mom."

"Don't sass me, Sadie. Is that you in that article?"

I bit my thumbnail and scrambled for an explanation, and finally had to settle on the truth. "Yes." Bracing myself for her ridicule (what kind of desperate ninny needed an arranged marriage to finally tie the knot?), I tensed on the bed.

But my mother did not ridicule me. Instead, she let out a shriek of happiness. "FINALLY! BARRY! SADIE'S MARRIED! YES! I KNOW! AFTER ALL THIS TIME!"

I listened to her cheers as I sat on the bed all alone, and a piece of my heart withered and died. For my entire life, being married was the pinnacle of success. My parents had built their business, their very identity, on the love story that had bound them together.

Now that I was finally toeing the family line, the relief in my mother's exclamations was clear. I was finally one of them, and it didn't matter that I'd had to have an arranged marriage to achieve it.

Instead of feeling relieved or happy for it, I was numb.

She hadn't asked me if I was happy. She hadn't inquired about the groom. All that mattered was that I had a ring on my finger.

I looked down at the gold band that Gideon had slipped on my finger, touching the underside of it with my thumb.

"Well, we're going to have to get a bigger cabin for our family trip," she said, coming back to the call. "And I have to meet him! What's he like? I can't believe you didn't tell me. I didn't even get to make a speech! Your father and I always dreamed of singing at your wedding. We'll have to have a do-over reception. Christine will do the flowers."

I made vaguely appropriate noises and waited for my

mother to run out of steam. She eventually told me she had to run, after having asked me exactly zero questions about myself. I hung up the phone and tossed it aside, then got up off the bed and ate three servings of lasagna.

It was delicious, because I'd married a fantastic cook. Damn Gideon for being the perfect man. I found Knox's number and texted him about the lasagna. A minute later, the door creaked open, and he gave me a little half-smile. He ate half the pan then patted his stomach. "Good stuff," he said in his usual low grunt.

"Gideon made it," I said as I cleared his plate. "I can't take credit."

He nodded, watching me. "We'll find out who did that to your car," he told me quietly. "Anything you need, Sadie. You're one of us now."

My throat clogged up, and all I could do was keep my eyes on the dishes. I nodded, listening to Knox's footsteps fade as he went back to his post outside. Through the windows, I saw him get in his car and get comfortable. My own car had materialized beside his; someone had driven it over. I could see the scratches on the side from here. I slumped down on the sofa and buried my head in my hands.

I should've been grateful for the Mars clan's protection. I'd never had anyone—let alone a whole group of people—accept me so easily. Now they were spending their time and energy making sure I was safe. Contrast that with my own family, who only accepted me now that I was married. They didn't even care to whom.

I so badly wanted to stay here. I wanted Caroline as a friend. I wanted to get gossip from Mrs. Gretzinger. I wanted

Sunday family lunches and Scooby-Doo mysteries involving spray-painted breasts. I didn't even mind the vandalism on my car if it meant I belonged somewhere.

But I *did* mind the constant rejection from the man I'd married. A man who was perfect in every way, other than the fact that he didn't want me back.

Leaving would save my sanity and my heart...but it would mean admitting to my own family that my marriage had failed. I would go back to being an outcast and a failure. Only worthy of an air mattress or a pull-out couch.

I went to bed early and fell asleep. Alone.

GIDEON

The house was dark and silent when I drove up, waved at Knox through the windshield, and parked outside. I crept inside and listened at the mouth of the hallway for evidence that she was awake. I hadn't seen her in almost six hours, and the need to touch her made me twitchy and uncomfortable.

Behind her closed door, there was only silence.

Despite my aching back, I took my position on the couch and lay there, staring at the ceiling, wanting her.

But the only way to keep myself whole was to maintain my distance. A woman like her would tire of me as soon as she'd recovered from whatever had landed her here. She wouldn't want to stay with someone deformed and broken.

Better to guard my own heart while she figured that out on her own.

SEVENTEEN
SADIE

I woke up to a hot half-sweet almond milk matcha latte waiting for me on the kitchen counter and tried to pretend it didn't make my heart go all gooey inside. Then, despite my protests, Gideon went with me to the nearest city of Ellsworth so I could buy what I needed.

"You're leasing the place?" he asked when we were on the road.

"Not yet," I hedged. "Your grandma is letting me use it to make Lola's dress."

He nodded, eyes on the road. He'd insisted on driving us in his car, reminding me that someone had made threats against me, and I'd only weakly protested. Now I was ensconced in a car that smelled like him, aware of every shift of his body, being lulled by the smooth, easy way he drove, and I regretted my decision.

Every minute I spent with him made me like him more. It

had to be some kind of self-destructive instinct in me. Why would I be *so* into someone who didn't want me back?

"You thinking of restarting your business here?" Gideon asked a few minutes later. He glanced at me then back at the road. "Not really a huge market for wedding dresses here."

"Not yet," I said, laughing, which made his lips twitch. "But seriously, most trade is online these days. And I have this idea..." I shook my head.

"Tell me."

Biting my bottom lip, I hesitated. My heart banged against my ribs. Henry had had this *look* he would give me when he thought I was being stupid. It was a condescending, pitying look that he'd cover up if I questioned it. Once, I'd found a bridal show and wanted to prepare a small collection to attend the convention. He'd systematically poked holes in my plan, asking me where I'd come up with the money to make the dresses, how I'd manage the risk of not selling anything, what I would do with the clients I already had, who were taking up all my time...

I ended up not going, and Henry patted me on the head and told me I'd made the right decision. It wasn't until a few months after our breakup that I got angry about it. And this type of thing happened over and over and over again. I started questioning myself about whether or not I was hungry, or tired, or horny. He stripped away all my confidence to the point I didn't know myself anymore.

So telling Gideon my ideas felt dangerous. He waited, and finally, I decided that I had to speak. After all, wasn't he my sort-of husband? And if this marriage was going to work out, we'd need to have each other's backs, even if we weren't *really* husband and wife.

"I was thinking about The Pier," I finally said. "It's really nice. Like, surprisingly nice."

Gideon hummed, nodding. We took an exit toward the city, and I watched the forests melt away to reveal more buildings. "Lots of wealthy folks have second homes up here," he said, "away from the big cities."

"Right." Speaking quickly, I continued, "I thought maybe I could organize retreats. Or…I'll come up with a name. But basically, brides would come with their entourage, stay at The Pier or another nice hotel, and I'd have a couple of days with them to do designs, fittings, whatever. They could visit the area—it's *so* beautiful—and make a trip out of it."

Gideon's brows jumped. I tensed, waiting for him to start poking holes in my idea. But when he spoke, he sounded genuinely curious. "You think people would go for that?"

"People spend crazy amounts of money on their weddings."

That made him glance over. "Is that something you wanted?"

"To spend the equivalent of a house down payment on one event?" I asked, laughing.

He shrugged. "Yeah. The planning. All the little details. The—the romance." He cleared his throat.

We pulled into the Walmart parking lot and he slid into a space. I stared at the big blue building and shrugged. "Once upon a time, maybe, yes. But by the time we got married, I was kind of just happy to get it over with."

He looked at me then, and his expression was unreadable. Maybe a little sad. Maybe even heartbroken. For me? Or for himself? But he blinked, and I convinced myself I'd imagined it.

We went into the store, and I bought all the cleaning supplies I needed. Then we went to the fabric store, and I got supplies for Lola's dress.

We were back in Marswood Harbor by ten, and I went to work. Gideon set himself up at a table with a laptop while I cleaned, then disappeared to get us some sandwiches from the grocery store deli for lunch.

"You don't have to stick around here," I told him as we broke for lunch.

"Sadie," he replied patiently, unwrapping his sandwich with methodical care. "Someone vandalized your car *twice*. And no, I'm not letting you stay here on your own as bait," he added, giving me a dark look.

His protectiveness sent a shiver of delight through me. I got back to work cleaning and organizing the space, and Gideon did whatever he was doing on the laptop. As I cleaned the wall of shelves, I asked, "Any news on Mr. Titty?"

"He's gone quiet. Or *they've* gone quiet," he said. "Not a single new tag in the last couple of days."

"That's unusual," I said, and Gideon grunted in response.

We worked some more. By three o'clock, I was drenched in sweat and in desperate need of a shower. We went back to the cottage, took our turns in the bathroom, and then I told Gideon about my date with Caroline at Bertie's.

"All right," he said, and went to get his shoes.

"You don't have to come."

"*Twice*," he grumbled, and I knew he was talking about my vandalized car. A warm glow kindled in my chest, and I allowed him to drive me to the bar.

Bertie's was pumping. It was about halfway between Life's a Stitch and Rock Bottom, a block off of Main Street. Lights spilled from the open door, and the sounds of a man shouting into a microphone were audible as soon as we got out of the car half a block away. Then music started, and the hum of conversation and laughter added to the noise. We stepped into a cozy room with wood pillars and matching paneling, a long bar to the right, and lots of high-top tables. The edges of the room were lined with booths.

Caroline sat at a table by the tiny stage in the back corner with two other people. She spotted me immediately and waved, then scowled when she spotted Gideon behind me.

"Really?" she asked with an arched brow. "What, he wouldn't let you out of the house on your own?"

"Actually no," I said, laughing. "But he has a good reason."

Caroline pointed a finger at Gideon. "I'm only allowing this because of the matcha. You understand that, right?"

I frowned. "The matcha?"

"Nothing," Gideon grumbled. He nodded at the two other people at the table.

"This is Joanne and Ricky," Caroline said, introducing me to her friends, who were bright-eyed with interest. "Guys, meet Sadie. She's married to Gideon, but she's okay."

I laughed as I sat down in the stool Gideon pulled out for me, then watched him grab an unused one from beside the bar. Instead of sitting to my left, he circled around and slid the stool on my right. Then he angled his body so his scars faced the wall and his right side faced the table, legs bracketing my stool. Always trying to hide himself. He moved stiffly, and I wondered if it was discomfort at being in public or just his back being sore from weeks of sleeping on a busted old couch.

My eyes narrowed and flicked between him and Caroline. "I want to know what that matcha comment meant."

"He hasn't told you, huh?" Caroline asked. "Typical."

"What hasn't he told me?" I was starting to get worried. I loved those matcha lattes. Was something wrong with them?

"It's nothing," Gideon said.

"It's the only reason I'm allowing you to sit at this table," Caroline proclaimed, "so you might as well tell her."

"Nothing to tell," Gideon replied.

Caroline looked down her nose at him, then turned to me. "He buys the matcha and the almond milk and the sugar syrup for your lattes. Bought the bowl and whisk and everything."

I blinked. "What?"

"Loath as I am to admit it," Caroline continued archly, putting her hand to her chest, "it's nice. More than I would expect from a Mars."

I looked at Gideon, who was busy staring at a spot on the wall behind me. "Gideon?"

His gaze slid down to meet mine. "What?"

"Is that true? You bought everything she needed to make my favorite drink?"

His jaw hardened. "Is that a problem?"

"No," I answered, laughing unsteadily, which was a lie. It was a *huge* problem. It was the most romantic, incredible, thoughtful thing anyone had ever done for me. It was *wonderful*. It made me want to jump into Gideon's lap and kiss him until we both passed out from lack of air. It made me want to bat my eyelashes and smile like a simpering fool, because I was dive-bombing into love with him.

He frowned at me. "It's just a hot drink."

I narrowed my eyes right back at him, then lifted my index finger and poked his chest. "You," I said slowly, "*like me*."

I could feel Caroline's and her friends' gazes prickling on the side of my face, and I didn't care. All my attention was caught by the flash in Gideon's blue eyes, the challenge in his arched brow. "I like you?"

"You like me!"

"Did you think he didn't like you?" Caroline asked, sounding like I'd just admitted that I didn't know grass was green.

"Yes, I thought he didn't like me!" I cried, turning to stare at her.

"You thought I didn't *like* you?" Gideon repeated, incredulous.

I felt like I was going cuckoo. "You deny it?"

"Of course I fucking deny it!"

"This is better than my favorite trash TV show," Joanne muttered, and Caroline said, "Right?"

"I'm getting a drink. What do you want?" Gideon said, pushing himself to his feet and glaring at me. But I wasn't offended. I was staring at him like I'd never seen him before. He arched his brows at me, waiting.

I beamed. "I'll have an old fashioned with an extra orange twist."

"This is Marswood Harbor," Gideon reminded me.

"Right. I'll have a beer."

He nodded and stalked off. Caroline was grinning at me. I bit my lip, but I couldn't help grinning back.

"Girl," she said in a flat voice, and I laughed.

Then the music cut out, and someone started handing out sheets of paper and pens. Trivia night was starting. Gideon returned with drinks for the whole table while we were deciding who would write down our answers.

"If I see either of you pulling your phone out at any point tonight, you're both barred from Knead More Bread. We don't cheat at trivia night at this table."

I put my hand on my chest. "I would never."

"I wasn't talking to you. Mars?" Caroline narrowed her eyes at Gideon, and I could see the ghost of a smile on the corner of his lips. He was enjoying himself. He nodded, and Caroline was satisfied.

We came in second place, which meant we didn't win the free round of drinks. But someone kept refilling my beer, and my cheeks hurt from laughing. By the time we stumbled outside, I was pleasantly buzzed and feeling like I never wanted to leave this town.

Gideon was stalking toward his car, so I caught him by the hand to slow him down. "Did you have fun tonight?" I asked.

He looked at our joined hands, then at me. "It was okay."

"You're such a liar," I said, and he smiled. I loved it when he smiled.

"I had fun," Gideon conceded.

I leaned into him, inhaling his scent as I looked at the stars above. There were so many. The air was pleasantly cool, a breeze ruffling through the green leaves on the trees. "Have you ever seen Miss Congeniality?" I asked.

"The movie?"

"Hmm," I said, nudging him toward the car.

"No."

"Well, there's this part in it," I said, turning to walk backward as I faced him, my lips spreading into a smile as I quoted Sandra Bullock, "'You think I'm *gorgeous*, you want to *kiss* me... You want to *hug* me... You want to *love* me... You want to *smooch* me.'"

Gideon laughed, tugging on my hand so I crashed into him. His other arm went around me, and he looked down at my face like he'd never seen anything so beautiful. Then his smile faded and he said, "You're drunk."

"Only a little."

His warm hand reached up to tuck my hair behind my ear, and then he leaned down and pressed his lips against my forehead. "We can talk about this tomorrow," he murmured against my skin, then opened the passenger door so I could get in.

Disappointment crashed into me, along with something worse. The familiarity of rejection didn't ease its sting. It still hurt so freaking much to be tossed aside. Again. So when my phone started ringing, I used it as an excuse to shift away from Gideon and hide my face. I clicked my tongue at the spam call from an unknown number and pressed the side button to ignore it.

By this point, Gideon had come around to the driver's side and was buckled in. My phone rang again, and he glanced over. "Who is it?"

"Just these stupid spam calls," I answered, then frowned when a text came through.

Cold froze the pit of my stomach.

"Sadie?"

I tried to angle my phone away, but Gideon had already seen. He took the device from my hand and scowled at it. "Who's this from?"

"I don't know."

"Have they contacted you before? Why didn't you tell me?"

"Jesus, Gideon, I said I don't know!" My head pounded. I didn't want his protectiveness. It wasn't warm and safe anymore; it was suffocating. I felt so ashamed for throwing myself at him earlier when it was so painfully clear he would never want me that way. When would I finally understand that Gideon was a one out of ten, the way I'd lied and said I was?

"Sadie. Someone is threatening you. I need to know about these things."

"I thought they were spam calls," I snapped. "That's the first text I've gotten."

Gideon squeezed the steering wheel with one hand, glaring at my phone.

Because I was feeling tender and pitiful and self-destructive, I said, "They're not wrong, though," nodding at the text.

Gideon's eyes were sharp as he looked at me. He opened his mouth, reconsidered, and closed it again before handing me my phone. Then he turned on the car and started driving. "Let's go home," he finally said. "I'll get my guys to up the patrols around the cottage. We'll find out who's doing this."

I nodded, hollow inside. We drove home in silence, and when we got there Gideon started setting up the couch for sleep. When he dug a knuckle into his back, I clicked my tongue.

"Just take the bed, Gideon. Please."

"I'm not making you sleep on that thing," he replied, not looking at me.

"So sleep next to me! I won't touch you, I promise," I sneered. My headache had turned into a jackhammer on the inside of my temples, and I didn't have the energy to be civil. Besides, my ego was bruised and I was starting to think this whole experience was just one big bout of torture. I could glimpse my perfect life, full of friendship and laughter and joy, but I could never actually make it reality.

Gideon finally lifted his eyes and met my gaze. Then he glanced at the phone I still held clutched in my hand, and he finally nodded. "Fine," he said, and I wondered how much of his agreement was due to his sore back, and how much of it was because he was feeling responsible for my safety.

I rushed through washing my teeth and face, put my PJs on, and curled up in a ball. The bed dipped when Gideon got in beside me, and a pit opened up in my stomach. Even after all these rejections, I still wanted him.

I was such a fool.

GIDEON

I lay awake for a long time listening to the sound of Sadie's breathing. I stared at the lump in the blankets that was her curled-up body, wondering if I should have kissed her when she'd invited me to. She'd been radiant in the moonlight.

But would she still want me if there was no threat? If she didn't need a protector? If she had another option, any option but me?

My defenses were crumbling. Was there any point resisting her at all, if I already knew that when she left Marswood Harbor, it would destroy me?

EIGHTEEN
SADIE

Horrifically, I woke up with my face smashed into Gideon's chest and a puddle of drool dripping from my mouth and soaking into his shirt. Both his arms were around me, our legs tangled together. He was hard. I could feel it throbbing against my thigh.

The moment I moved, he released me. "Morning," he rasped, looking rumpled and sleepy and gorgeous.

I wiped the crusty line of drool at the side of my mouth and shuffled back to my side of the bed. "Morning," I said. "Sorry about that."

Gideon sighed. "It's fine, Sadie."

"No, I promised not to touch you and—"

"It's *fine*."

I clamped my lips shut, keeping my back to him as I swung my legs off the bed. By the time I was showered and dressed, Gideon was in the kitchen. There was a matcha latte from

Knead More Bread waiting for me on the counter. My heart ached as I grabbed it. "Thank you."

He nodded in response. Then we ate and headed into town. Gideon ignored me when I suggested that he go to the Marswood Security building and let me work at Life's a Stitch in peace, so I resigned myself to another day of torture. I managed to finish cleaning the front of the shop and start sorting through the bits and pieces in the storage room. Gideon helped me put up curtains at the back of the shop that I would use for a change room when Lola came to try on the muslin draft of her dress.

Jack came by to pick up my phone to see if he could figure out who had sent that text. He returned a few hours later with a grim shake of the head. Nothing.

By the end of the day, the space was clean and ready for me to start working. Despite everything that had happened between me and Gideon and whoever was threatening me, I was excited to make a dress.

Gideon and I cooked together, and then I spent the evening sketching ideas for the construction of her gown while Gideon read on the opposite couch. It was disgustingly domestic and I would've loved every minute of it if it hadn't been absolute torture. Then it was time for bed.

"I'll take the couch," I said decisively.

Gideon closed his book and looked at me. "No."

"No?"

"You heard me."

"Well—" I planted my hands on my hips, but there was no fight left in me. I followed him to the bedroom and climbed into bed beside him.

Despite all the work I'd done during the day, I wasn't tired enough to pass out. I couldn't help tossing and turning. He was so close and so warm and so *Gideon*.

With a huff, Gideon wrapped a big arm around me, pulled me into the cradle of his body, and grumbled, "Sleep."

Eventually, with the sound of his easy breathing behind me and the warm weight of his arm wrapped around my body, I slept.

THE NEXT DAY was Grandma Mars's birthday party. I had a half-day to start cutting pattern pieces out of muslin, which I did at Life's a Stitch while Gideon ducked into his company's office for an hour. This time, Bennett kept me company, asking a thousand questions about me, my life, sewing, and the plans I had for the shop. He had an easy smile, and I couldn't help liking him.

By the time it was time to get ready for the party, I was a little more relaxed. I wondered if Gideon had known his little brother would have that effect on me, and that's why he'd sent him to be my bodyguard. It would be a very Gideon thing to do, thoughtful and protective and perceptive.

My fingers skimmed over the black fabric that covered my hips, adjusting the fall of my cocktail dress. I turned to look at the back of my outfit, tweaking the way the one-shoulder strap fell across my chest. My earrings dangled as I moved, and my hair fell in gentle waves to the middle of my back. I'd taken my time with my makeup, emphasizing my eyes and lips.

With a deep breath and one last look in the mirror, I

stepped out of the bedroom. Gideon turned at my approach, wearing the same suit he'd worn to our wedding ceremony. The sight of him stopped me short. We looked at each other, and I felt it. I *felt it*. The strumming, tightening cord of tension winding around us. It was there, sliding against the bare skin of my arms, chafing, real. My lungs constricted. My heart took off.

Gideon took in my appearance with ravenous eyes, then suddenly shuttered his expression. "Ready?" he asked. "We're nearly late."

His gruff question was like a slap. And I thought there was a connection? I thought he *cared*? I blinked rapidly, forced a smile, and nodded. "Let's go."

We didn't speak on the drive there, and the air in the car was thick with tension, but not the delicious, addicting tension I'd felt with him before. This was strained. Gideon was shutting me out. For whatever reason, he wasn't interested in me. There was some drop of attraction, but he did his best to douse it.

That hurt. Rejection always did, even though I should've been used to it by now.

I stared out the window at the purple-navy sky and the deepening shadows between the trees. We drove through town, and I noticed no new sets of breasts decorating the town. Mr. Titty had gone quiet.

If Gideon noticed the same thing, he didn't say. He said nothing at all, actually, and as we drove toward his grandmother's house, it felt like he was slowly sucking the oxygen out of the car, leaving me gasping for breath like a fish flopping on the shore.

I had the awful feeling that it was my fault. It was because of Thursday night, when I'd been tipsy and thrown myself at him. And then I'd made it worse by forcing him to cuddle with me every night. He was sick of me.

We drove up to Etta's house, and I was at once struck by the beauty of her home. In the evening, the garden was illuminated by feature lighting, and the front of the house was dramatic and warm. Cars lined the circle drive, but we parked in the usual spot next to the garages.

Gideon led me through the home and into a big living area where most of the guests had gathered. It was the same room where the family ended up at the weekly lunches, but the space had been transformed. One of the large seating areas had been removed, and bar-height tables dotted the space. They were covered in white tablecloths, with delicate vases full of fresh flowers acting as centerpieces. Caterers in black vests and bow ties circled with nibbles and drinks. The doors to the solarium beyond were thrown open, and more guests mingled amid the greenery.

We found Etta holding court at one end of the room. She wore a glittering black gown cut high on her neck, her white hair swept back from her face to show off two sparkling chandelier earrings that appeared to be real diamonds and sapphires. She spotted us and shifted her body, and the crowd around her parted to let us through. She was an expert at commanding a room with nothing more than subtle gestures.

"Happy birthday, Grandma," Gideon said, pressing a kiss to her wrinkled cheek. The earrings winked in the warm light of the room as they dangled from her lobes.

"Thank you for coming." She smiled, patting his arm, then turned to me. "You look beautiful, Sadie," she told me, and I smiled. At least someone had noticed.

"Happy birthday," I replied. "Thank you so much for having us. I don't think I've mentioned this yet, but your home is incredible."

"Edwin was proud of the place, so I've tried to keep it maintained all these years since he died," she said, naming her late husband. "But if it were up to me, I'd move to something like that cottage you two are in." She smiled and I smiled back, but I didn't quite believe her. Etta Mars knew the power of wealth, and she knew what this big home on the edge of town signified to everyone who stepped across the threshold. It gave her authority. Gave her the right to set up arranged marriages for her grandchildren in the hope of keeping her town on the map.

Her gaze shifted from me to a spot over my shoulder, and it was my turn to move and let another newcomer through. I watched as a gorgeous blonde swept across the room, drawing every gaze. Her hair was glossy and golden, her lips full, and her body perfectly curved and taut. She wore a wine-red dress that hugged her body in a way that was just this side of lewd.

Gideon made a noise beside me. I looked over in time to see his shock, which he quickly wiped from his expression.

The blonde took in the room, then made her way toward us.

"Lenore," Etta greeted her, and I thought I detected a note of frost in the old woman's voice. She was so good at hiding it that I wasn't sure.

"Happy birthday, Grandma Mars," Lenore answered, kissing the air on either side of Etta's face. "You look wonderful, as usual."

"Mm," Etta replied, eyes sharp. "No husband today?"

"He's at work, I'm afraid," Lenore pouted, then turned in mine and Gideon's direction.

Well. She turned in Gideon's direction and entirely ignored me. "Gid," she said, fluttering her lashes.

The jealousy that I'd successfully tamped down after our horrible wedding night suddenly came back with a vengeance. It rose up inside me like a dragon huffing smoke, infecting every corner of my heart.

It was petty and ridiculous and shameful, but I couldn't help it. She was beautiful, and she knew him. Suddenly, I was sure they'd slept together. Was she the ex Mrs. Gretzinger had alluded to? Or some other conquest of his?

She walked over to where we stood.

"Lenore," Gideon greeted, unable to keep the emotion from his voice. "You're back."

"I'm back," she confirmed, smiling, and when Lenore tilted her head, he leaned down and pressed his lips to her cheek. She batted her lashes at him, her hand remaining on his arm. Gideon straightened, shoulders tense. Because of her? Because she'd come back to town after who knew how long? Or because I was beside him, watching their exchange?

I hated being jealous. *Hated* it. But Henry had scraped away at my self-esteem so much that all I'd had left to cling to was poisonous jealousy. He'd paraded women in front of me just like this, and I hadn't had the strength to leave him. Pathetic, grasping woman that I was, I endured the humiliation just because I couldn't bear the thought of being alone.

And now I was doing it again.

Why hadn't I left the day after the wedding? I'd let one measly matcha latte change my mind? What was *wrong* with me? Why hadn't I left in the weeks since? Surely a quaint small town and friendly brothers-in-law weren't worth *this*. Caroline was nice, but I could surely find one other human on this planet to be my friend.

"Lenore, this is Sadie," Gideon said, finally remembering that I existed. He angled his body to include me in the interaction, and the other woman blinked as if she hadn't even noticed my presence. He hadn't said, "this is my wife, Sadie," I noticed. Just my name.

"Oh," Lenore said, tittering. "The new wife." Her smile was perfectly pleasant, but her eyes shot daggers. "How is married life? It's so nice to meet the woman who replaced me." She laughed, flicking her hair.

Ah. So I was right. Not only had they slept together in the past, but they'd dated.

My chest was so tight I couldn't speak, so I just smiled. I was sure I looked like a fool.

Gideon cleared his throat. "Lenore moved away a few years ago," he said.

"I did," she agreed. "But it's *so nice* to be back in town." She beamed at him, and Gideon frowned. His gaze had shifted across the room, to where his brother Knox loomed. Knox nodded, and Gideon looked at me. "I'll be right back."

"Uh-huh," I answered, nodding like a brainless bobblehead. I watched him cut across the room, took a deep breath, and turned to see Lenore studying me.

Her smile had disappeared, and her eyes had narrowed. Even like this, she was beautiful. Gideon had downgraded when he married me. And he didn't even know the worst of it, all the ways I was dysfunctional.

I inhaled sharply and straightened my spine. I would *not* let those poisonous thoughts take control of me.

"When I heard about Etta's marriages, I wondered who would be matched with Gid," Lenore said, tilting her head, the movement birdlike, her eyes beady and flat. "How fascinating."

"You dated, I gather?"

"We were engaged." She smiled, and her eyes remained dead and cold. "He broke it off after the fire. He told you about the fire?"

I shook my head. "Not yet."

"Oh! That's...interesting. Well, I'm sure he'll open up to you at some point." Condescension dripped from her tone with such thickness that it felt like she physically patted my head. She went on. "When he was recovering in the hospital, he told me he wouldn't subject me to marriage to him. It hadn't been what I signed up for, he said." She sighed, adjusting a strand of hair against her cheek. "I couldn't talk him out of it. Couldn't make him change his mind."

He'd loved her so much that he'd let her go. The constriction in my chest worsened.

"I see," I said, bile rising in my throat. Did he still have feelings for her? Was *she* who he'd been with on our wedding night? "Excuse me."

I knew—and she knew—she'd gotten to me, but I couldn't find it in myself to care. I pushed through the crowd, stumbled around until I found a bathroom, and locked myself inside.

It only took a second for me to lose the fight with my tears. I cursed myself for being so weak, but I couldn't help the tears from falling. Three weeks, I'd been married to the man, and all he'd done was play hot and cold. But had there been any hot? Or was he just the wonderful, reliable person that Wendy had described, and I'd misread everything?

Maybe he'd never wanted me. Maybe everything was in my head.

Stop, I told myself. With a few deep breaths, I mastered my roiling thoughts, my fingers gripping the edge of the sink. I trembled as I reached into my clutch for my makeup and did my best to clean up the damage.

Staring at myself in the mirror, I wondered again what the hell I was doing here. Gideon had rejected me over and over again, and I thought he cared about me? I thought this marriage would last?

I was such an idiot.

I *knew* I wasn't enough. I'd been taught that lesson over and over again. Henry had been right about me. My mother had been right about me. No one would ever want me for me. Not when my body didn't work. Not when I was defective and stupid and silly.

It was the reason I couldn't keep a man. The reason my business failed. The reason I had no friends. I wasn't good enough for those things.

I shook the sound of my ex-fiancé's voice from my mind and filled my lungs. I had to get through this event, and then I could leave. There was no matcha latte that could keep me here after tonight. I was wasting my time and breaking my own heart by hoping for the impossible. I wasn't going to find a new home or a community or *love*, of all things. That just wasn't how my life was meant to go.

And that was okay.

I sucked in a long breath and let it out slowly as I counted to ten. Then I did it again. And again.

No one else would make me feel whole. I had to do that on

my own. Chasing men who didn't want me had never worked; why did I think a marriage ceremony would change that?

I could leave here, and that didn't mean I had to go back to my old life in Manhattan. I *could* start over—on my terms. Somehow. I'd figure it out. I had to. I wouldn't have Etta's offer of start-up cash. I wouldn't have free housing. But I'd have my self-respect. That would have to be enough.

Once I'd mastered my emotions, I straightened my spine and walked out of the bathroom. My heels clicked on the tile floors and then were muted when I stepped onto a rug. I re-entered the main party space, scanning the room for Gideon. His brothers were clumped in a corner, and Etta was still where I'd left her. More people had arrived, and the noise in the room pressed against me, vibrating into my skull.

I smiled at Betsy and nodded at Lola, who were sitting on a couch, and wove my way through to the solarium.

Mrs. Gretzinger accosted me. "You met Lenore," she said.

"I did. Excuse me."

"She was married within three months, you know."

I paused, shrugging. "Why are you telling me this?"

"I just thought you'd like to know how quickly she moved on," she said, and there was kindness in her intelligent gaze. "She pretends theirs was a tragic love story, but she moved on quicker than a snap of the fingers."

But did he?

I held back the question, choosing instead to dip my chin in a nod and excuse myself again. I had to get out of here. Needed some fresh air. I stepped into the solarium—

And stopped short.

Through the open French doors leading to the back garden,

silhouetted by the feature lights in the hedges, were Gideon and Lenore.

Her bottom lip was trembling. She said something, and Gideon replied. I couldn't hear their words. But I saw her fall into his chest, her arms clinging to his suit jacket. His arms circled around her, holding her carefully as she buried her head against his chest.

I took a step backward, and I must have made a noise, because Gideon's head shot up. His eyes went wide, and he dropped his arms from around Lenore's body.

I saw nothing more, because I'd already whirled around. I had to get out of this place. *Immediately.*

GIDEON

The look on Sadie's face speared me through the heart and ripped the breath from my lungs. She'd looked hurt beyond belief. Betrayed.

I couldn't make sense of it, couldn't understand why she cared so much. I just knew I had to fix it.

Panic stabbed its claws into my gut—and then I was running.

NINETEEN
SADIE

"Sadie!" Gideon bellowed as I hurried out the front door and down the long drive. Guests were still arriving, lining up outside the front of the huge estate, and I was sure I would be the hot topic of conversation in town for weeks to come.

I didn't care. I'd be gone, and I'd never be back. Coming here had been a mistake. Thinking I'd end up married and in love had been naive. Settling for a quiet life and some sort of arranged companionship had been misguided and ridiculous.

An arm snatched me around the middle, and then I was flying through the air. Gideon spun me around, planted me on the ground, and turned me so I was facing him. My heels stabbed the soft earth and sank in an inch. He kept his arm around my back, fusing the front of his body to mine. His chest heaved with every breath, his eyes burning as he stared at me.

"Let go of me," I demanded. Humiliatingly, I followed it up with a sniffle.

"No."

"No?"

His lips flattened. "No." He tightened his hold on me, and I pushed my palms against his chest. It was like shoving a brick wall. Gideon grunted, then said, "Not until you listen to me."

"Why should I?" I sounded petulant, and I didn't care.

He lowered his face so all I saw were his eyes. Furious, dark eyes, holding me in their unbreakable spell. "Because you are *my wife.*"

The words echoed through me, vibrating in my bones. My bottom lip trembled. "Am I?" I spat out. "Maybe you should tell that to your ex."

"You want to do this?" He backed away an inch, and I could breathe. But he didn't let go. "You want to do this right now?"

"Were you with her that night?" The question burst out of me before I could stop it. A hot tear rolled down my cheek. I was so embarrassed I wanted to die, but now that the question had been posed, I had to know the answer.

Gideon stared at me, not understanding. "What night?"

"Our *wedding night!*" I screamed. I dropped my voice again, knowing there were people all around. "Were you with your ex on our wedding night?"

"What? No! I haven't seen her in five years."

I scoffed. "Let go of me."

"Sadie." Something in his voice made me stop struggling against him. When I looked up at him, the fury in his eyes had faded, and there was an edge of panic. Fear. "I wasn't with Lenore. I wasn't with anyone. Not—not like that."

"So where did you go?"

"Portland," he said.

My shoulders dropped, and I clicked my tongue. "You went

to freaking Oregon and were back by morning?" Did he think I was stupid?

His lips twitched. "Portland, Maine, babe."

I blinked. "Oh." Maybe I was stupid.

"I'll prove it."

He stroked my cheek, catching a tear, then shifted a step back while keeping his arm around me. We walked toward his car, and he put me in the passenger seat before getting behind the wheel. He turned on the car, but instead of driving off, he pressed the screen on the console until "recent trips" showed up. He'd gone to the Maine Medical Center in Portland. A two-and-a-half-hour drive.

I frowned at the screen, then at him. "Okay? Did you have an appointment in the middle of the night?"

He rubbed his jaw, his other hand kneading the steering wheel. "Sometimes, I..." He gulped. Kept his eyes on the beam of the headlights shining over the trees behind the garage. He rubbed his hand over his mouth, stretching his jaw before he continued, like he had to push the stress out of his body with physical effort. "Sometimes I go to the burn unit," he said, his voice full of gravel. "The nurses aren't supposed to let me in, but they know me. I...sit there. With the patients." His hand kept moving over the steering wheel, clenching, releasing, shifting, over and over again. His body was made of tension. "When I was getting treatment for my burns," he said, "I couldn't sleep. The pain and the discomfort and the drugs...there was so much time where I just sat in that bed feeling like I was in hell. So sometimes I go there, and I try to make it easier for the people who are going through what I went through. That night, when I thought I'd pressured you into... I needed to feel like I wasn't a piece of shit." He let out a breath. Turned to face me. "If you don't believe me, we can drive there now and the nurses will vouch for me."

A breath slipped past my lips, and I shook my head. I felt unsteady, like I was balancing on a high wire suspended over a gorge. One gust of wind would make me fall. Blinking at Gideon, I tried to make sense of what he'd just told me. What it meant for him, for me, for us.

"I wasn't with my ex, Sadie," he said, his voice a warm, low rumble. "I promise."

"I believe you," I croaked. A wave of shame washed over me, bitter and familiar and suffocating. I couldn't look at him, so I leaned my elbow against the doorframe and put my head in my hand. "I'm sorry. I just saw you put your arms around her, and I felt... She said... I thought..."

I squeezed my eyes shut. Memories assaulted me, dragging me down into the darkness.

"She just went through a divorce, and she just—she was crying. When you walked out, I hugged her, but it didn't mean anything. I swear."

She was a damsel in distress, and Gideon had been the big strong protector. That was familiar. God, I was a fool.

A warm hand slid over my thigh. Gideon, anchoring me to the here and now. His touch felt so good I wanted to cry.

I owed him an explanation. I marshaled my thoughts and wrapped whatever courage I had around myself. Then I lifted my head from my hand and faced him.

"My ex cheated on me," I said. "So I'm...sensitive."

Gideon's hand tightened on my thigh, as if he'd spasmed at

hearing those words. Slowly, he released his grip, his thumb coasting along the outside of my leg. "I see," he said.

"He wanted to have an open relationship," I said, the words coming out in a rush. "When I refused, he did it anyway. Hooked up with a woman who worked with him. The one he'd wanted to open the relationship for. And he said... He made me feel like it was my fault."

I could taste Gideon's confusion in the air. "Why would it be your fault?"

I scoffed. Leaned my head back against the headrest. Closed my eyes.

Might as well rip off the band-aid. I'd already made a fool of myself and probably ruined things with Gideon tonight. He was the kind of guy who made a five-hour round trip to sit with burn victims in the middle of the night. And he'd done it because I hadn't been honest about my condition. He'd felt guilty about forcing himself on me when the whole debacle had been caused by me being a fucking coward. He wouldn't want to be with someone so petty, jealous, and defective as me.

If he wanted to call off the marriage after this, it would be exactly what I deserved.

"I have a condition called vaginismus," I said into the heavy silence of the car. "It causes my pelvic muscles to tighten involuntarily. Sex is... I wouldn't say impossible, but it's close. It hurts, so I don't usually want to do it. Henry wanted to open the relationship so he could get what he needed elsewhere. The things I couldn't give him. Maybe I should've agreed." I let out a bitter snort. "Maybe it's the only way..."

"Sadie."

I gulped, watching the way his hand looked against the

black fabric of my dress. His thumb still made slow sweeps over my outer thigh, his fingers splayed in a strong grip. My body was trembling so much that it took me long moments to realize Gideon's hand was shaking too.

"Sadie, I need to ask you something," he said quietly, "and I need you to be honest with me."

I inhaled, nodding. "Okay," I croaked.

"The night of our wedding, did you feel..." When he paused for long moments, I found the courage to look at him. He chewed the inside of his cheek, his eyes circling my face. He looked completely, unbelievably devastated. "Did you feel like you had to hook up with me? Like you had no choice?"

I let out a bitter huff and shook my head. "That's the thing," I said, letting my lips curl into a humorless smile. "I still *want* sex. I just can't have it. There was nothing forced that night. I wanted to hook up with you. I was so turned on, but then you started talking about—about penetration, and I kind of froze. And then you put your finger inside me, and—"

"I hurt you." His voice was strained. Tortured.

"It wasn't your fault."

"It was, Sadie. I fucking hurt you because I was too focused on how much I wanted you to even notice that you wanted to stop." He swore and took his hand away from my thigh, leaving cold in his wake. He rubbed both palms over his face.

It took me a minute to register what he'd said. *I was too focused on how much I wanted you.*

My heart began to hammer. I sucked in a breath and tried to push down the knot of hope and despair and desire that tightened in the middle of my chest.

"You...you wanted me?"

He gave me a look of confusion. Disbelief. "Could you not tell?"

"It's just…" I licked my lips. It was hard to speak, to put into words my deepest fears. I'd never had a conversation go like this. Usually, when I mentioned the vaginismus, men would ask me if it was permanent. I could tell they were thinking about what *they'd* be losing by dating me.

Not Gideon. He was upset that he'd hurt *me*. Actually, "upset" didn't touch the sides of it. He looked anguished. Tormented. Which made no sense.

I gulped. He'd wanted me that night, but…"What changed?"

"With what?"

His confusion *seemed* genuine, but how could it be? I dropped my shoulders and frowned at him. "You've been avoiding me. You recoil whenever we touch."

"I *recoil*?"

"You find me repellent."

"What—and I truly mean this—the fuck?"

"Oh, give me a break, Gideon." I shook my head, scoffing. "I know I'm not some sort of catch, okay? Especially with this." I gestured in the general area of my vagina. "But I know when a guy is interested. They don't jerk back whenever they touch me. They don't go out of their way to avoid me. They don't run the fuck away when I'm naked and spread-eagled on the bed beneath them. You are obviously not interested in me. Not that way."

He blinked at me, staring into my face like he was worried I was having a stroke. Then he exhaled and sat back, like he'd come to a decision. His voice was a low rumble in the car, vibrating in my bones. "Before I tell you all the things I've been wanting to do to you since the moment I laid my eyes on you, I need you to answer a couple of questions."

Oh. *Oh.* Oh, my God. I had misread this situation *severely.* My throat was suddenly dry. "What questions?"

"On a scale of one to ten, how would you rate your desire for sex?"

The question from the application. The one where I'd lied. My face flamed, and I tore my gaze away from his to stare out through the windshield. "Is this designed to humiliate me?"

"This is designed to figure out where the fuck we went wrong, Sadie. Answer the question."

My heart had started beating harder at some point over the past few minutes, and now it thumped against my ribcage like it was trying to escape. "Ten," I said in a raspy voice.

Gideon let out a short grunt. When he spoke next, it was all gravel. "So, just to be clear, on our wedding night, you didn't tell me to stop because you touched my scars?"

I blinked, jerking my head to look at him. "What?"

"Your hand touched my shoulder, and suddenly you wanted to stop," he grated. "I thought—I left because I thought you found me disgusting. And then I figured I'd forced you to go that far, and..."

I fought for my next breath, frowning at him. "No," I said, the word exploding out of me. "No, I never felt that."

"You wanted me to touch you, but you were worried about your body."

"That's right."

He exhaled, leaning his head on the headrest as he closed his eyes. Seconds rolled by, slow as molasses.

"Are you okay?" I finally asked.

"I'm processing."

"Oh. Do you want me to leave?"

He laughed. "No, babe. I don't want you to leave."

Something in the way he said it made me think he wasn't just talking about getting out of the car.

Then his eyes opened. He turned to face me and said, "We need to lay it all out. All our cards on the table. Are we together? Like a married couple is supposed to be?" He swallowed thickly, then continued in a voice that was a little more strained: "Do you want something different? A partnership, without intimacy, like you said the morning after? What do you *want*?"

I stared into his pale blue eyes. The eyes of a man who sat with burn victims because he didn't want them to feel as alone as he'd felt. A man who dropped everything to help a cousin-in-law who'd run out of gas. A man who was wracked with guilt over feeling like he'd pressured me. A man who hadn't hesitated to run after me, to hold me until I was honest with him, to listen without judgment.

He hadn't turned away when I told him about the vaginismus. Hadn't said anything about the fact that we couldn't have penetrative sex. Hadn't lamented the fact that I couldn't meet his needs. No—his first thought hadn't been about his own needs at all. He'd thought about *me*. He'd been worried he'd hurt me.

There was only one possible answer to his question.

"You," I whispered. "I want you."

GIDEON

She trembled beside me, looking tender and afraid, and I wanted to flay the skin off of my own flesh for hurting her. Find her ex and annihilate him. Tear the world apart and put it back together in the shape she most desired.

Anything—I'd do anything for her.

TWENTY
SADIE

All the air rushed out of me as I admitted that I wanted him. Gideon reached over to touch my cheek. His grip tightened for a second then suddenly softened, as if he'd had to master his own reaction with sheer force of will. His eyes bore into me, and I thought I would die from the tension strumming through my body.

Then he leaned toward me, parted his lips on a soft exhale, and kissed me. His fingers ghosted over my skin as he angled my face toward him. He leaned over the center console and deepened the kiss.

With the gentleness of his touch, my heart began to settle. I'd been so primed for rejection that this new development was almost dreamlike.

He kissed my lips slowly, thoroughly, and then moved his mouth over my jaw. And when his hand drifted down to my lap, my whole body shivered. His hand was so *warm*. I could feel the heat of it through the fabric of my dress over my upper thigh. His calloused palm snagged on the silky fabric as he shifted his hand to run his fingers over my inner thigh.

My heart rate spiked. On instinct, I reached across to put my hand on his crotch. I needed him to feel good too. That was the only way I knew how to do this, how to have sex, how to make it worth it for him despite my deficiencies. I always had to overcompensate.

But Gideon did something I didn't expect: he pulled away. He looked down at my hand as I gripped him, stroking clumsily across the center console, and then shifted his gaze to meet mine.

"What are you doing?" he asked curiously.

I froze. "I—I'm sorry, I thought—"

"I'm the one who fucked up, Sadie. I'm the one who's supposed to fix it."

I wasn't sure that was quite accurate, but as he spoke, he shifted the hand in my lap to grip the space between my legs, and my response died on my tongue. The fabric of my dress bunched under his fingers, and my legs spread on instinct.

"Take your hand off my cock," he rasped, and I shifted my hand to his leg. My chest heaved as he squeezed my cunt, lightning sparking in the pit of my stomach. Gideon hummed. "You've been treated badly, baby," he mused. "Haven't had someone take care of you properly. Myself included. I fucked up. Didn't understand what you needed from me."

"I forgive you," I said between pants. My knees were pressed as wide as I could manage, one shoved against the door, the other against the padded surface of the center console.

Gideon let out a harsh grunt, then took his hand away to press the ignition button. "We're not doing this here," he said.

He backed the car out of the spot, and then his hand was on me again. Even through the layers of fabric, the touch ignited a fire in me. I squirmed, arching my hips up toward him.

"Seatbelt," he said, driving with his knees while he put his on. I fumbled for mine as he turned off the long driveway onto the road. "Good girl," he said when it clicked.

I let out a shaky exhale, and his fingers rubbed in slow circles exactly where I needed them. I whimpered, glancing over at him to see him look entirely unbothered—other than a slight tension in his neck and the clenching of his other hand on the wheel. When we were on a straight patch of road, he took his hand off the wheel and pressed it against the bulge in his pants, his knees guiding the steering wheel to keep us on the asphalt.

All the while, his fingers rubbed and stroked and circled my clit. My panties clung to my body, soaked. I reached over to slide my hand over his inner thigh. His lips kicked in a small smile, the movement of his fingers increasing in speed and pressure.

I was so turned on my vision had gone hazy at the edges. Then his hand was gone while he drove around a bend, and I whimpered in protest.

"Patience," he chided softly, returning his hand to where it had been delivering sweet torture to me. My own fingers crept closer to the hard bar of his erection. I wanted to feel it, wanted this to feel good for him too. Wanted to show him that even though I couldn't take his cock inside me, I could still make it good for him.

But when I felt the seam of his pants in the middle of his spread legs, he took his hand away from my core and used it to grab my misbehaving wrist. "Not what we're doing, babe," he said, shooting me a glance that looked part stern, part amused, and part...something else. Something deeper.

"Gideon," I whined.

"Nearly there." He kept hold of my wrist, his thumb stroking the pulse on its underside, and I squirmed in my seat. Unbelievably, the feel of his hand on my wrist was almost as good as when it had been between my legs.

He turned onto the cottage's driveway. I would've said he was entirely calm, unbothered by our activities, except that he parked crookedly, half on the grass to the side of the driveway. Then he was out of his seat and coming around to my side. I fumbled with my belt as he wrenched the door open, and then I was unceremoniously hauled out of the car and thrown over his shoulder. My heels went tumbling to the ground as my legs kicked, Gideon's steps crunching on the gravel drive. His arm banded over my legs, and a big, warm hand gripped my thigh, the thumb pressing in the soft flesh near my core.

I panted, a breathless laugh falling out of me. "This isn't how I imagined things going this evening."

"No?" Gideon asked, reaching into his pocket with his other hand to grab the keys to the front door. "This is how I've imagined things going every day since you walked down that aisle. Every day, every night, every fucking second, Sadie. No matter how hard I try to stop it."

"What?" I breathed, confused, but the sound of my question was lost as Gideon slid me off his shoulder and brought me inside. He kicked the door closed behind him, hands bracketing my waist, and pushed me up against the wall.

I moaned into his kiss. Gideon was a torrent of energy and

desire. He pressed his thigh between my legs and pinned me against the wall with his bulk, kissing me like he wanted to consume me. Worship me. Make me his. I writhed against him, fingers curled into his hair, body arching and grinding as much as the position would allow.

"I didn't realize," Gideon rumbled, his lips coasting along my jaw. "Didn't realize what you needed." His hands slid down to my hips. As he pulled back, I saw that his pupils had blown out so there was only the thinnest ring of blue around them. With his fingers sinking deep into the flesh on my hips, he helped me rock them back and forth. I gasped at the pressure of his thigh against my clit. Gideon's lips kicked.

"You just need a man who isn't afraid to make you come," he said, reading my face for every reaction. His grip on my hips was inexorable, rocking, rocking, rocking. "This is what you need, isn't it, baby?"

"Gideon—" I dropped my hand to his crotch, and—

"Stop that," he said mildly, and I did, pressing my hand against his stomach instead. His smile widened. He looked drunk, but I knew he hadn't touched a drop tonight. I felt like I'd gone out of my mind. I was outside my body and simultaneously more connected to my physical self than I'd ever been before.

Heat snaked through my belly and tightened. Gideon shifted his leg, and I had no choice but to go up on my tiptoes. I clung to his shoulders, gasping, as most of my weight was balanced on the ridge of his thigh. It felt so good. So fucking good.

"How long has it been since you've been given what you need?" Gideon asked, dipping his face into the crook of my neck. I felt his breath against my collarbone, his nose tracing the line of my pulse. He inhaled like he wanted to imprint the scent of me into his lungs. "How long since a man has treated you right?"

I huffed a breathless laugh. "I'm not even sure what that means," I admitted. My fingernails had curled into his suit jacket, one hand on his shoulder, the other pressed against his stomach. The pressure on my clit was so intense my vision went white around the edges.

"It means this, right here, baby," Gideon answered. "It means you riding my thigh until you come. It means my face between your legs. It means you take every orgasm you need from me, every orgasm that you've been denied before, and you *take your hand off my cock.*"

I huffed, tears leaking from the sides of my eyes, and moved my hand back up from where it had drifted down. "I want you to feel good," I whined, leaning my head back against the wall. It sounded like a desperate whimper, and even as I said the words, tension gripped my chest like a giant's fist. I *needed* him to feel good. Needed him to get what he needed, because otherwise...

Otherwise what?

Otherwise he'd leave. He'd get sick of me. He'd look for pleasure somewhere else. He'd toss me aside like garbage, and I'd have no choice but to come to terms with the fact that I would never be good enough.

"Hey." Gideon squeezed my hips, then moved one hand to my jaw. His thumb pressed my chin, and I blinked until his face came into focus. He frowned at me. "You went somewhere. Stay here with me."

"I—" The words died on my tongue. I didn't know what this was between us. Didn't know how to take without giving. If I didn't give him something back, what use was I? Why would he ever want me to stay?

As if he could read my mind, the line of Gideon's shoulders softened. His eyes flicked between mine, and his thumb moved from my chin to stroke my cheek. "Do you trust me?" he finally asked, voice soft and low.

I gulped. Opened my mouth. Closed it again. My mind reeled as I tried to figure out what he was trying to ask me, what it meant, how I should answer. In the end, all I could say was the truth. "Yes."

His thumb stroked my cheek again. "Good," he said. "Trust this: When I want you to touch me, I will let you know."

This wasn't how sex had ever gone for me. In the past, it had always been more give than take. I always had to make up for my deficiencies. Give and give and give, and only ask for a little in return. That was the only way to keep a man interested, to make up for the fact that I could never offer him what he truly wanted.

But Gideon wasn't letting me give. He was telling me he wanted me to take. And take. And take.

I didn't know how to do that.

He shifted his leg, and my feet fell back to the ground. I hated the loss of pressure against my core. Hated the distance between us. Even still, a sick kind of relief ghosted through me. Maybe if we stopped, I wouldn't have to face the crashing wave, the unbearable weight of my desire for him.

But we weren't stopping.

Gideon tangled his fingers in mine and tugged me to the

nearest soft surface—one of the two couches in the living room. With a soft kiss on my lips, he lowered me down onto it, tugged my ass to the edge, then pushed my dress up so it bunched over my stomach. I felt his knuckles against my skin as he hooked his fingers into my underwear, and then the cold air kissing my damp, swollen flesh. Gideon's hands pressed against my knees, spreading them wide. He exhaled a shaky breath, his eyes trained on the apex of my thighs.

"I'm going to eat your cunt until you scream," he informed me.

"Oh," I said, mind utterly blank. Then he stripped off his suit jacket and slowly, methodically, rolled up his sleeves. All the while, he kneeled on the floor between my spread knees. I felt exposed and aroused and a little ashamed. When he swept his hands up my thighs and ran his thumbs over the moisture gathered between my lower lips, a full-body shudder went through me.

Then his face was there, and he was licking. Sucking. *Devouring.* His fingers sank into the fleshy curves over my hips, thumbs pressing into the crook of my thighs to hold my legs wide. His shoulders pressed against my inner thighs, and that stubble scraped exactly where I'd wanted it to on our wedding night.

But it was the noises Gideon made that sent me over the edge. When he tasted me, he groaned like I was the most delicious treat he'd ever had. When I couldn't help myself from tangling my fingers in his hair, he grunted, his whole body bowing toward me like all he wanted me to do was grab his head and use him to get myself off.

His eyes flicked up when I loosened my grip on his hair, and

I could tell in an instant that he was enjoying himself. Truly enjoying himself. This wasn't a chore that he was doing in order to get me to go down on him after. It wasn't something he endured in order to make things "fair" between us, or to use as a bargaining chip later when he wanted to push me past my limits. This was something he wanted. His face between my legs. Me, out of my mind.

I came, unable to hold back the cry that slipped through my lips. My hand scrabbled at the edge of the sofa while my back arched off the cushions, the only thing tethering me to the earth being his hands and mouth. When the tension went out of me, Gideon pressed a kiss to my inner thigh, then straightened. He used a palm to wipe his mouth, then let out a satisfied exhale, his eyes fluttering shut as if he wanted to savor the last taste of me on his tongue.

I watched him, chest heaving with every breath, hair clinging to the back of the sofa as I reclined, twitching. The orgasm had been like a perfect appetizer. I was ready for the main course—but history had taught me that there was no main course. This was all I was going to get. I arranged my face into a pleased smile to let him know that it had been great.

Gideon opened his eyes. Met mine. Smiled like he could see right through my bullshit. "Take off your clothes," he commanded in a quiet, sure voice. "You need another one."

I blinked at him, confused. Gideon stood, took my hands, and hauled me to my feet. He took my face in his hands and kissed me, then with his lips moving against mine, he repeated, "Take off your clothes, Sadie."

All of a sudden, all the desire that I'd tried to stifle came rushing to the surface. I flushed and knew my cheeks were bright red. And I took off my clothes. My dress dropped to my feet a moment before my bra landed on top of the crumpled fabric. Gideon's hands swept over my waist, and he pulled me down on top of him so I straddled him on the couch. I was entirely naked, and he was fully clothed.

I reached for the buttons of his shirt, but Gideon stilled my hand, grimacing. "Not—not yet."

His scars. I'd forgotten. I could see some of them on his neck and the side of his head, but I'd spent so long looking at him that I no longer really *saw* them. They were just part of who he was, part of the man who turned me inside out. But he was self-conscious, and he didn't want me to see his body.

I couldn't help the sting of it; I'd bared myself to him—literally—and told him all my dirty little secrets. He evidently didn't feel comfortable enough to do the same.

But with a deep breath, I let go of that feeling and moved my hand away from his shirt buttons.

"I'm sorry," he murmured. "I just—not tonight." His hands swept up my sides and back down again, learning the shape of me. "Not when you're here, like this."

"This all seems very one-sided," I quipped, arching a brow as I tried to use humor to hide my disappointment.

Gideon hummed, sliding one hand between my legs and making me gasp. "It's not one-sided," he said in a low voice. "Believe me, I'm getting just as much out of this as you are."

My breaths were coming faster now, hips rolling as he used his fingers to make sparks ignite between my legs. "I find that hard to believe," I answered.

He spread his legs wider, pushing my knees apart. It was just past the point of comfort, and it made his touch feel all the more intense. I clung to his shoulders and leaned my forehead against his, fighting for every breath. Gideon's free hand slid up my side and covered my breast. He squeezed it as he stroked me, then rolled my nipple between his thumb and forefinger. I shuddered.

"I could watch you like this for hours," Gideon told me in a low rumble. "So fucking beautiful, Sadie. I can't believe you're mine." The pressure of his hand between my legs increased. I gasped.

"Yours," I agreed, unable to form complex thoughts.

He hummed, pressing and rolling my clit with his fingers. "My wife." He pressed a kiss to my lips. My jaw. My neck. "My wife who's so pretty when she's desperate. Aren't you?"

"Rude," I panted. My hands curled into the fine white fabric of his shirt. My hips rocked, needing more. It was rude, but he was right. I *was* desperate.

It was as if his attention had opened the floodgates, and now I could see just how much I'd denied myself in my previous relationships. I'd kept score, and the score had always been lopsided. My partner got ten orgasms for every one that I allowed myself. I'd worry if it took me too long to reach my peak, thinking he was bored. I'd get on my knees and suck him off, but it was out of duty rather than desire. Trying to make up for the fact that my vagina didn't work right.

This was different.

Gideon looked at me with a mix of lust and reverence. He stroked my body until I whimpered and shook above him. As he exhaled, eyes hungry as they watched me, I finally believed that this was enough for him. That *I* was enough for him.

It was a feeling of safety that I'd never experienced before.

Here, in this room, with this man, I was enough. I didn't have to give him anything. I didn't have to work to make up for my body. I could just *be*.

The feeling overwhelmed me, and on its heels was an orgasm so intense it stole my breath. Gideon urged me on, his hands on my body, his lips on my shoulder, my clavicle, my neck. He murmured sweet words to me. "Beautiful," he rasped. "So beautiful, baby. Could watch you do this every day for the rest of my life."

He didn't mean it, of course. This arranged marriage was still on shaky ground. But it felt so good to hear him say those words, to bask in the feeling of being enough.

My orgasm ebbed, and I rolled my forehead against his shoulder. He smelled divine. Like sweat and spice and man. I wanted to lick him. My fingers clenched and released over his biceps, body still rocking gently against his. Gideon's hands swept over my thighs, stroking my ass and then up on either side of my spine. I loved the way he touched me.

"I want to make you feel good," I admitted in a whisper.

Gideon turned his head to brush his lips against my temple. "What part of you thinks I don't already feel good, Sadie?"

I huffed, leaning my cheek against his shoulder. Settling on top of him, straddled over his lap, I felt one specific part of him that seemed to be experiencing some hardship. I rocked against him, and fireflies of desire flitted through me once more.

"Insatiable," he chided, then grunted when I pressed my core down on his clothed cock. He leaned his head back on the couch cushions as I rode him in slow waves, watching me through half-lidded eyes. His cheeks were brushed with red, and the only sign of tension was the hard thudding of his pulse in the side of his throat. When he spoke, his voice was a low rumble. "You lied on your application," he noted, hands sliding back down to shape my curves.

I rocked against him and bit my lip. "A little," I admitted.

"You weren't supposed to want this." He exhaled as I ground myself against his crotch. "You weren't supposed to want me."

"It was a shock to us both," I quipped, a little breathless. Desire still coiled tight in the space below my navel, and I chased it with every rock of my hips. I'd orgasmed harder than I had with any partner before, and still I wanted more. That was greedy, wasn't it? But how could I stop, when Gideon looked at me like that? When he touched me with those hands like he never wanted this to end?

"I feel like I'm going to wake up any minute here," he said, fingers spasming on my curves. He gripped me harder, spreading my cheeks, changing the angle of my hips so the pressure increased where I needed it. I whimpered, half out of my mind.

"I wish I could—" I stopped myself as my eyes began to prickle. "I wish—"

"Hey." His hand swept up to my neck, my jaw, my cheek. He tangled his fingers in my hair and brought me closer for a kiss. "You're perfect, Sadie. Just like this."

"Let me feel it," I begged in a whisper.

Gideon huffed, closed his eyes, and sucked in a hard breath. His neck was corded with tension, his jaw bulging as he ground his teeth. It lasted endless seconds, this moment suspended in time. Then the tension went out of him, and he reached for his belt. I propped myself up on my knees, hands on his elbows, and watched as he shimmied his clothes down to his knees, where they dropped to his ankles.

It was lewd. His thighs were dusted with dark hair, and his cock sat heavy and hard against his stomach. He gripped it in a big hand, squeezing the base as moisture leaked out the tip.

"You keep licking your lips like that, I'm going to have to tell you to suck it," he said, his voice a harsh rasp.

My eyes flicked up to meet his, and my breath caught at the sight of him. He was so beautiful, teetering on the edge of control. Wanting me so badly his whole body was one taut line. I lowered myself back down on top of him, exhaling at the heat of his cock against my center, pinned between my core and his stomach.

"Maybe that's what I want," I whispered, burying my face in his neck. "You to tell me to...to..."

I couldn't say it. I'd done it so many times before, but the act had become—at best—a chore. At worst—disgusting. Right now, though, it was the opposite. It didn't feel like I *had* to suck Gideon off just because he'd made me orgasm. It felt like an overwhelming desire, something I actually *wanted* to do, because I wanted to taste him. I wanted to see him lose control.

Gideon's teeth raked down my neck and bit into my shoulder. His hands guided my hips to rock against him. "You want me to tell you to get on your knees and suck, baby?" His hands tightened on me, pressing my weeping core harder against his cock. I slid against him, my slickness coating his hardness from root to tip.

I shuddered. "Yes," I admitted—and there was something wrong with me, wasn't there? To want him to use me like that when it was being used that had made me feel so worthless. But somehow, it felt like going down on Gideon would rewrite all those bad experiences. Like it would be something new with him. Something better.

I felt rather than heard Gideon's chuckle in the vibrations of his chest. He sighed, hips rocking against me, the tip of his cock pressing against my bud over and over and over again. He tangled his fingers in my hair and pulled my head back so he could look in my eyes. "My wife is a horny little thing, isn't she?" He must have seen the effect his words had on me—the pleasure of being called his wife, the embarrassment of being read so easily, the spark of hopeful yearning at finally being understood—because he grunted and added, "What am I going to do with you?"

I'm not sure why that little musing sent me over the edge. Maybe it was the promise of a future with him, or the fact that it implied he wanted to figure me out. To please me. Whatever it was, a final orgasm gripped me, and I shuddered on top of him. Gideon swore, grabbing my hips, and dragged me down harder against his body.

And then he did use me.

He used his hands to rock my boneless body against his cock, his own hips punching up into me. Another shudder of pleasure washed through me. As I clung to him, his body went rigid, and I felt the warm wetness of his release against my stomach.

We lay there until our heart rates settled. Then I peeled myself off his chest, swallowing thickly as I met his gaze.

Gideon's hand came up to tuck a strand of hair behind my ear. He looked thunderstruck. In a gravelly voice, he simply said, "Let's clean up and go to bed."

GIDEON

Her skin was silver in the moonlight. I brushed her hair off her cheek as she slept, listening to the soft sound of her breaths.

It couldn't last. She'd come to her senses. She was a beautiful, intelligent, brave woman from the city. She'd never settle for me, for this.

But she was here for now. I vowed to make the most of it until she inevitably left.

TWENTY-ONE
SADIE

I woke up with the warm, heavy weight of Gideon's arm around my waist. This time, instead of letting me go, Gideon pulled me tighter as he mumbled a good morning, then rolled me over so he could kiss me softly. I'd half expected to wake up and realize that yesterday had been a dream. It didn't seem possible to finally be here, with him, like this.

Within moments, Gideon proved me wrong.

I arched off the bed as he stroked me, my legs scrabbling at the sheets, my hands curling into the soft, long-sleeved tee he'd worn to bed. He watched me with his head propped against his hand as he lay on his side beside me, a soft, satisfied smile on his lips. When I came back down to earth, he pressed a kiss to my shoulder and promptly intercepted the searching hand I'd sent over toward his crotch.

Bringing my fingers up to his lips, he kissed them gently. "None of that, now."

"Why don't you want me to touch you?" I asked, and it sounded embarrassingly close to a whine.

He just smiled at me, eyes circling my face. "I want you to touch me," he answered, but he didn't let me move toward that goal. "But not when it feels like you're just doing it because you think you need to."

My brows slammed down. "That's not how I feel."

"Every time you come, you jump toward me like you think you owe me one."

"Well—" I clamped my lips shut, heart hammering. Finally, I whispered, "Isn't that how it works?"

"Not here," he said. "Not with me."

"I don't understand."

He smiled again, his expression full of fondness, and touched his nose to mine. "That's okay. You will."

Rattled, I let him pull me out of bed. I'd thought last night had been the exception. He'd wanted to give me pleasure because he'd felt guilty. He was trying to apologize.

But was Gideon saying that this was what he wanted...all the time? For me to just take what I needed without offering anything in return? *Why?*

He tugged me to the bathroom, turned on the shower, and set me inside.

"You're not coming in?" I asked.

He hesitated and finally tilted his head toward the door. "I'll get some coffee started."

The door closed behind him, and I knew what had happened; Gideon still wasn't ready for me to see his scars. It hurt to be shut out like that, and it made it harder to understand what was going on between us.

We moved slowly through the morning. When we sat down for a breakfast of scrambled eggs, bacon, and toast—made by Gideon, of course—he looked at me and said, "I think you should talk to Mrs. Gretzinger about your wedding dress retreat idea."

I blinked, eggs turning to glue in my mouth. I swallowed with difficulty and said, "Why?"

"Because she's a good businesswoman, and I think she'd be on board."

It was hard to breathe. "You...think it's a good idea?"

"To talk to Ida?"

"No, the wedding dress retreats."

He watched me for a moment, then nodded. "Yes."

"Oh."

"Is that a problem?"

"It's just—" I licked my lips. Why was my heart thumping so hard?

"I looked your company up online," Gideon continued as he piled some scrambled eggs on a triangle of toast. He took a bite, chewed, and swallowed. "You're good, Sadie."

"Don't sound so surprised."

He huffed a laugh and shook his head, arching a brow. He saw too much.

"If I'm so good, why couldn't I stay in business? Why did I have to shut everything down?"

Gideon shrugged, like my failure was no big deal. "Why does any business go through a rough patch? When I started Marswood Security, I only offered security system installation and maintenance. I struggled. I almost didn't make it through my second year in business. It wasn't until we started offering on-site surveillance to some of the wealthy property owners outside of town that things changed. That's when I hired my brothers, and things grew from there."

In my travels around town, I'd noticed that there were huge properties outside the town limits. I'd read into it and learned that the area was dotted with a lot of huge mansions belonging to people who lived in Manhattan or Chicago or Boston. They'd spend a week or two per year in the area, if that, and usually maintained a full staff at their properties. One of the reasons Marswood Harbor had been in decline was because the cost of living here had increased substantially when more estates were built in the surrounding area. It was hard for locals to make ends meet.

"Is that when you asked your grandmother to invest?" I asked. "When you almost lost your business?"

He hummed, nodding, as he took a bite of bacon. "I sometimes regret it, but I wouldn't have made it without her investment."

My throat went tight. That sounded ominously familiar. Did I really want my entire livelihood beholden to Etta Mars? But what other option did I have?

"I can take you to The Pier to talk to Ida," Gideon suggested. "Or give you her phone number."

I nodded, part uncomfortable, part so hopeful it hurt to even admit it to myself. "Thanks."

When Henry had helped me by sending brides my way for consultations, he'd made me feel like I owed him something. I wondered if Gideon would think the same. If all these wonderful things he was doing for me—and to me—would start adding up too much. He'd start thinking that he wasn't getting anything out of this relationship at all, and he'd toss me aside just like Henry.

"Unless you don't want to reopen your business in this town," Gideon asked, his voice raspy. He watched me, tentative, like a heavy weight hinged on my answer.

I gulped. "I'm not sure I want to reopen my business at all." Speaking the words out loud made fear thrum inside me. It felt like a big bass drum being hit in the depth of my gut. Without my business, who was I? Just a defective nobody. Unsuccessful. Unlovable. "I'm afraid," I admitted in a small voice.

I caught the edge of an emotion on Gideon's face. A kind of resigned devastation that he hid in an instant. "What would you do instead?"

I huffed a bitter laugh. "I don't know. Be a housewife?"

"For this?" The derision was thick in his voice. He flicked a hand, indicating himself. The marriage.

That pissed me off, because he was doing the same thing he always did. Making it seem like his scars were a dealbreaker, and I must've been out of my mind to put up with them. But his scars were a part of him! How could I look at them and not see the man who'd held me so tightly last night? The man who'd finally made me feel safe?

"Stop doing that," I snapped. "You make it sound like I'm so shallow."

"Isn't everyone?" he answered, bitter.

We stared at each other, and I bit back half a dozen retorts. I could see the shape of the walls he threw up around himself, and I knew in that instant that attacking them would do nothing. He was so sure that his scars defined him, and I wasn't going to change his mind.

He hadn't even let me see them.

So instead of fighting him, I pushed myself off my chair and circled the table. Gideon frowned at me, suspicious, until I plopped myself down on his lap and wrapped my arms around his neck. I rested my head on his shoulder and felt his heartbeat against my palm. It took a few long seconds for his arms to come around me, and slowly, the tension eased out of his body. When he stroked a thumb over my side, I spoke.

"What happened," I asked softly, "with the fire?"

His body went stiff, then, muscle by muscle, it eased, as if he were consciously trying to drain the stress out of his body. His hand resumed its stroking, and I let my fingers drift over the soft fabric of his shirt. He smelled like himself, clean and male and delicious.

"It was a warehouse fire. One of the old derelict warehouses on my grandma's land. Used to be where they let the wood dry out after it was milled. I got an alert that some kids broke into the building one night, so I called the cops and drove over. Three of them had gotten in. Teenagers who were bored with nothing to do on a Friday night."

I kept my head on his shoulder even though I desperately wanted to see his expression. "They started a fire?"

He grunted. "The warehouse was almost a hundred years old, and it was full of sawdust and half-rotten wood. They found some old solvents in a box that hadn't been stored properly and started messing around with them. They had lighters. It went up within seconds, and one of the roof beams collapsed in front of the exit."

My heart thumped. "You got there first."

His throat bobbed with a thick swallow, and he dipped his

chin. "I could hear them screaming," he answered, his voice hoarse. "And then they stopped." He shrugged and stretched his neck, as if his scars had started itching. "I was able to break a hole in the wall at the back, where the wood had almost rotted away. By that point they'd passed out from the smoke, so I had to drag them out one by one."

Three times. He'd gone into a raging inferno three times to save them. This time, I couldn't resist the urge to sit up. I kept my hand on his chest, even though I desperately wanted to stroke his face, to touch his skin, to tell him how incredible he was.

But Gideon's eyes were faraway, as if he were reliving that night. "I was lucky," he finally said, shifting his gaze to meet my eyes. "I only got burned on my last trip in, and I was able to put my arm up to protect most of my face. My forearm and shoulder got the worst of it. The doctors said I was fortunate. The firefighters said I was an idiot." He huffed at himself and shook his head.

Blinking back tears, I exhaled a shaky breath. "Wow. That's awful. Were the kids okay?"

"Few weeks in the hospital and they came out fine." He gave me a small smile. "One of them was Cash Bridges' nephew. After that, we reached a bit of a truce. They stopped going for rides through town, intimidating the residents. Stayed up near their clubhouse and in the surrounding hills. That's one of the reasons I don't think Cash or any of his people are Mr. Titty," he added. "If he knew one of his guys was tagging all over town, he'd put a stop to it."

I accepted this change in topic, even though I wanted to ask him more about the fire. I wanted to tell him how brave he was and how much I admired him for what he'd done. Instead, I laid my head back down on his shoulder, and we both drifted back into silence.

He held me tightly, and my body eased against him. I'd never felt so comfortable with anyone, especially not a man. But how could I *not* be comfortable with Gideon? Someone who put others first, always. He'd run into a burning building three times to save a bunch of delinquent teens. He'd driven hours to sit with burn victims. He'd gotten married to me so that his brothers wouldn't lose their livelihood when his grandmother sold off his business.

He put me first every time we got physical. Even his rejections had been his way of prioritizing my needs. He hadn't thought I'd want him that way.

The magnitude of Gideon's selflessness was staggering, even if it sometimes seemed misguided. After all, he'd pushed me away the same way he'd done to his ex. He'd broken up with Lenore because he thought she deserved better.

Then my mouth opened, and words vomited out of it before I could hold them back: "Do you regret breaking up with your ex?"

There was a pause. "What?"

I could taste his confusion in the air, and I lifted my head to look at his expression. There was a deep furrow between his brows, and he scanned my face like I'd just started explaining the finer details of quantum physics. I gulped. "She told me you broke it off with her when you were in the hospital because you didn't want to subject her to a life with you."

Gideon blinked. His frown deepened. "That's what she told you?"

I rushed onward, knowing that if I didn't get the words out, they'd stay stuck halfway up my throat. "And now you and I are together, and I'm starting to... I've developed feelings for you, Gideon." I inhaled. "I know how it feels to be betrayed by your body. It's not the same thing," I added, "because my problems are hidden and yours are on full display. But I still feel like a lesser person because of my issue. And if you feel the same way...and you only broke up with Lenore because you wanted to let her go..." I shook my head. "I guess I'm just asking if we've got a chance. You and me. Or if you still have feelings for her. She's back now, so maybe that changes things for you."

He looked at me like I'd been speaking a foreign language. "I didn't break up with Lenore because I wanted to set her free of a life with me," he grated. "*She* broke up with *me*."

I frowned.

He let out a bitter huff. "Maybe not in so many words, but I could see the disgust in the way she looked at me when she came to see me in the hospital. It was a whole month after the fire when she finally showed up." His eyes slid away from mine, lips twisting bitterly. "I waited and waited and waited for her, and she showed up with her hair done and a new designer purse on her arm. She looked at me like I was vermin, and then she told me she wasn't the nursing type. So yeah, I said we should go our separate ways. I told her I wouldn't hold her back. But it wasn't because I *loved* her. In that moment, all the love I thought I had for her died. Like a switch flicking."

Cold seeped into my bones. He'd been at his lowest, lying in a hospital bed with burns all down his left side, and then he'd been through *that*.

As if he wanted to drive the point home, he met my eyes

and said, "I didn't break up with her because I was some sort of selfless martyr. It was because I could tell her new man had bought her that purse, and there was nothing that would make her stay with—" His hands lifted off my body and settled back down again. A helpless, hopeless gesture. *There was nothing that would make her stay with* me.

"I'm so sorry," I whispered.

"Don't be." His eyes were remote. He was still in the past. "That's what people do. They let you down. Use you."

The hell of it was, I *agreed* with him. I'd said those same words, thought them countless times. But hearing them spoken by Gideon in such a bitter tone made me want to rebuke them. I didn't want to use him, and I hadn't felt used by him. He'd let me down on our wedding night, but he'd more than made up for it.

Not everyone was like Lenore and Henry. Gideon wasn't. *I* wasn't.

He sighed and met my gaze. Pale blue eyes circled my face, and he let out a long sigh. "I don't know if we have a chance, Sadie," he finally said. "I keep waiting for you to up and leave."

Like I almost had twice already.

But that was before I'd bared myself to Gideon. Before I told him everything about me, all the lies and the secrets and the things I hated.

Now he knew, and he hadn't turned his back on me.

"I'm not going anywhere," I vowed.

He searched my face, looking for the lie. His grip on me tightened almost to the point of pain, and then suddenly he was standing. I yelped, wrapping my legs around his waist so I didn't fall to the ground.

He marched us to the bedroom, kissing me the whole way. Then he threw me on the bed, took off my shorts, and used his mouth in other places. I gripped his hair and ground myself against him, breathless with pleasure. Wild with it. Through hazy eyes, I watched Gideon rut against the bed as he ate me out, like he couldn't help himself. Like he was enjoying himself too much to stop himself from chasing his own pleasure any way he could.

I was so close. "Gid—"

He grunted in response as he sucked my clit. I gasped.

"Gid," I repeated. "Can you—"

"What, baby?"

"I want..." I squeezed my eyes shut, breathless with fear and need and desperation.

"Tell me."

"A finger. Just—I'm afraid it'll hurt—"

He lifted his head. His hips stilled. Breaths gusted out of him, brushing over my sensitive skin. "You want me to put a finger inside you?"

I bit my lip. Nodded.

He gritted his teeth, frowning. Shook his head. "I don't want to hurt you."

"I've been practicing," I blurted, then flushed.

Gideon's eyes went wide. I could feel fine tremors in his shoulders where they pressed against my inner thighs. He dropped his gaze to my center. Licked his lips. "You'll tell me if it hurts."

I nodded.

"You'll stop me the second it's too much."

"I will."

He looked up. "I mean it, Sadie."

A breathless laugh fell out of me. How was this man real? Normally, an invitation like the one I'd just extended would never have been questioned. My previous partners would've used it as an opening to push my limits. But Gideon was letting me know in no uncertain terms that I was safe here. That this would only go as far as I wanted it to.

Every muscle in my body eased. Gideon felt it, his eyes skimming up to meet mine before dropping back down to my core. His thumbs spread me, stroking. Worshipping.

His finger was bigger than the dilator I'd been using. I tensed as he pushed it inside, only as far as the first knuckle. He stopped immediately.

"It's okay," I whispered, shaking. "Keep going."

He hummed, unconvinced. Then his mouth was on me, sucking, licking, caressing. His finger did not move. Not until I was rolling my own hips against it. Not until I was begging.

Only then did Gideon push his finger deeper. It stretched, but not in the painful way I was used to. No, this was something different entirely. And when he thrust it in and out of me in long, slow strokes, his mouth still moving over my clit, I couldn't help the disbelieving laugh that fell from my lips.

And then I came. My back arched as my hands gripped Gideon's head. I rocked against his mouth and his hand as he urged me on with wordless, urgent grunts. Afterward, I was glad we were in the middle of the forest, because the noises I made were unlike anything I'd ever heard coming from my own mouth.

"Now you," I said as soon as I could speak. My breaths

sawed in and out of my lungs. "And don't say no. Let me make you feel good."

Gideon extracted his finger from my body and huffed, pressing a kiss to my hip.

"I'm serious, Gideon. I want to."

He straightened, amused. A wet patch stained the front of his bottoms.

I blinked, my gaze flying up to meet his. He let out a long, gusting exhale, his hand moving up to comb the hair from his face. Satisfaction was written on every line of his face and body.

"You already...?"

He caged me against the mattress with his palms on either side of my head and pressed a kiss to my lips. "You think I'm able to listen to you make those noises while you're grabbing my hair to ride my face, and I'm not going to lose control in the process?"

I gulped, heart hammering. Words were beyond me.

Gideon chuckled, then gathered me in his arms and held me close. Eventually, I gave in and dozed.

GIDEON

I was done fighting against my desire for her. It had always been a losing battle.

Still, I wondered if her hesitation to pursue her business idea was more than just a confidence issue. What if she didn't want to set down roots here? What if all this time, she was planning on leaving the first chance she got?

TWENTY-TWO
SADIE

The floodgates had opened. In the days that followed, Gideon and I hardly left the cottage. We ate, laughed, slept, and screwed. Ducked out for groceries and matcha lattes. Came back and fell into bed together.

I'd never had so much sex in my life. Not in a way that always felt so good. Gideon was a generous lover, and he was committed to learning my body. He read about vaginismus and asked me questions. They weren't the questions I was used to; he never asked me how long it would take to get better, or talked about me getting better at all. He was curious and nonjudgmental. He respected my limits, and he sensed when I was pushing them out of a sense of misplaced duty. As the days passed, I began to believe him when he said he enjoyed making me climax just for the sake of it.

All was quiet on the Mr. Titty front—no new tags appeared in town. I received no threatening calls or texts. It was as if the world outside had paused in order to allow us to have this time together.

A week passed in a haze of pleasure. We finally left the cottage to go to Sunday lunch with the family, and left as soon as the plates were cleared. I ignored the wiggling eyebrows and wolf whistles that chased us out.

That evening, with my face burning, I showed him my dilator set and watched his eyes spark with interest. He grabbed the fourth one—second-to-largest—and turned it around in his hand.

"I haven't tried that one yet," I admitted.

"You want to?"

I blinked. "You mean—with you?"

His smile was wicked.

"I've never... It's not usually something I do with someone else..."

Gideon shrugged and put the device back in the box. Impulsively, I picked it up again. My heart began to gallop. I held the soft silicone shaft and realized I'd never believed that I'd actually be able to put it inside me. It was too big, being maybe an inch in diameter and four inches long. When a single finger of mine was painful, that size might as well be the girth of a soda can. No, thank you.

But that was before Gideon. Before a week of good sex. Before the safety of his affection.

I thrust the dilator at him. "Okay," I said. "Let's do it."

He softened, wrapping his hand around the pink silicone, then took me in his arms. He kissed me for a long time, then spent even longer stroking my body. By the time I'd taken my pants and underwear off, I was drenched.

Only then did he look at the dilator on the bedside table. My lube was beside it, and he flicked the cap open to squirt some onto his hand. It wasn't inherently sexy. In fact, it was a little awkward. Clear goop covered his fingertips, glistening in the light of the bedroom.

"Spread your legs, love," he murmured, and I did. His fingers were warm, but the lube was cool. I twitched at the feel of it, then exhaled when he pushed his finger inside me.

We'd done this a lot this week, but I still marveled at the feel of it. Gideon's other thumb moved to my bud, exactly where I needed it. He knew my body as well as I knew it myself. I writhed on the bed as he watched the movement of his hands on my core, mesmerized.

"Gideon," I whispered.

"Mm?"

"What if it doesn't work?"

"What if what doesn't work?"

"This. What if it's too big?"

"Then we stop."

"That's it?"

His gaze flicked up to meet mine. His hands stilled, and then one palm moved up to stroke my lower belly. His finger slid out of me, and he rested his hand on my inner thigh. "You don't have to do this, Sadie. I'm not going to be mad at you for something you can't control."

"But I *should* control it," I said, and tears gathered in my eyes. I squeezed them shut and threw my arm over my face to hide my shame. "I just want to be fixed."

"There's nothing to fix."

I snorted.

Gideon's hand wrapped around my elbow, and he pulled it off my face. He lay down beside me, silent. I turned my head on the pillow to meet his gaze, and we stayed like that for a long time. He had one hand on my stomach, the other curled under his head. He was so patient.

"In every romantic relationship I've ever been in," I whispered, "my partner has pretended like everything is fine until they realize that actually, my body isn't going to change. This is it." I gestured to myself helplessly. "Their penis isn't going to magically cure me. And then they start treating me like dirt, and they dump me."

"You think I'm going to do the same."

"Aren't you?" I blurted. "This is fun now, but how long until you just want to get your dick wet? Until you ask me to open the relationship because you need something I can't give you?"

My husband's eyes flashed. He rolled on top of me, pinning my wrists to the bed. "Don't fucking compare me to your loser exes, Sadie. Never again."

Tears leaked down the sides of my face. "I don't know what else to believe."

"Listen to me when I say this." He manacled my wrists to the bed, but his touch was soft. "You're it for me. You are my wife. For better or worse. And if our bodies aren't compatible the way men and women normally are, then we'll find a thousand different ways to enjoy each other. I've had plenty of practice getting my dick wet," he added, spitting my own words back at me. "Being with you is better than anything that came before."

My lip trembled. Gideon watched me, and then, coming to a decision, he swore and sat up. He straddled me, his hips pinning mine to the bed. With one harsh movement, he tugged his long-sleeve T-shirt off over his head and tossed it to the floor. There he stayed, a silent challenge in his eyes.

It was the first time he'd let me see his scars in their entirety.

My heart thrummed as I reached for him, then hesitated. "Will it hurt if I touch you?"

A muscle jumped in his cheek, but he shook his head. "I don't have much sensation over the scars. It feels...strange. I don't normally like to be touched. But—if you want—"

Tentatively, I reached for his chest, then traced the edge of the scar tissue along the front of his shoulder. Gideon watched me as I ran my fingers over the burn scars on his shoulder, then shuddered as I ran my hand down his arm and over the worst of the scars on his forearm. Stroking back up to his neck, I traced over his jaw and into his hair.

"For better or worse," he repeated bitterly.

"Better," I said, touching his shoulders then stroking down his chest. "Definitely better."

He frowned, searching my expression, then, slowly, relaxed. I explored his body, marveling at the hard pack of muscle, wondering at the pain he must have endured during the fire and in his recovery. His body was a work of art. It was the story of his bravery and his selflessness. It was finally mine to touch and admire and adore.

I realized I was truly in love with him, head over heels, never coming back. I wondered if he could see it in my eyes when our gazes met. Maybe that's why he shifted off me and slid his hand between my legs again. Maybe the reverence with which he touched me was his way of telling me he felt the same way.

This time, when he slid a finger inside me, there was nothing but pleasure in the touch. I reached for him, wrapping my arms around his shoulders and kissing his jaw as he slid his finger in and out. I spread my knees as wide as I could, arching into the touch. He hummed his pleasure, peppering my shoulder and neck with kisses. His skin was hot against mine as I rolled into him to press my chest against his, and I sighed at the ecstasy of finally feeling it against my own.

"My greedy wife," he murmured. "Greedy, horny, perfect wife."

Embarrassment was a hot flush that only heightened my pleasure. "You're so rude," I murmured, and he chuckled.

Then he pulled back to watch my face, and he added a finger. I clung to him, trembling, as he made shallow little movements and whispered, "Okay?"

I nodded, blowing out a breath, my fingers sinking into his shoulders. "Better than okay," I said, and he went a little deeper.

"You want to try the toy?"

His eyes were clear blue and patient. There was no ulterior motive in his question. It was entirely up to me. I inhaled sharply and said, "It's a medical device, actually."

His smile was a flash of white, and he dipped his face to kiss me. He pushed his fingers a little deeper and swallowed my gasp. His tongue brushed mine as he worked his fingers inside me until I was panting and writhing beneath him. Gideon was generous with his praise. He murmured in my ear about how brave and perfect and beautiful I was. He kissed my neck and hummed when I reached down to grab his wrist, rocking my hips against his hand. He made it feel good to let go, because there was no endgame other than my own pleasure.

I'd never been with anyone like this. I hadn't even known it was possible for sex to be like this.

I scrabbled at the bedside table, and Gideon got the message. He reached over to grab the dilator, squeezed some lube on it, then brought it to my core. He didn't have to tell me that he'd stop if I said so. It was right there in his eyes as he watched me.

The dilator slid in. Filled me up. I whimpered, but it wasn't from pain. Gideon's eyes skittered down my body to watch as he moved the shaft to penetrate me in slow, deep strokes. His breathing became shallow.

It was an entirely different experience to do this with someone else. Vulnerable in a way that amplified the pleasure. Every stroke of the shaft against my inner walls made me want more. I reached down to guide his hand, and he grunted in encouragement, shifting so he could watch.

There was nowhere to hide. Gideon knew all my dirty little secrets, and he wasn't afraid of them. He relished the opportunity to explore them with me. Suddenly, I wasn't trying to fix myself on my own. I wasn't racing against a ticking clock, knowing that when the time was up, he would be gone.

Gideon was here to stay.

I pushed against him, and he rolled onto his back, brows arching in surprise and concern. I saw the moment he realized I wasn't stopping him. It was right about the time that I had his jeans unbuttoned and tugged halfway down his thighs. He helped me get them off, and then I knelt between his legs and took his cock in my hands.

"Sadie—"

"Don't you dare tell me not to touch you," I warned.

His chest heaved with every breath. For the first time, we were both naked with each other. Equals. I stroked him with my hand, then, before he could protest, I took him in my mouth. He swore, hands flying to my head, and I sucked him with all the expertise I'd honed when I thought I had to make up for my body's quirks.

It didn't feel like I had a malfunctioning body anymore. With the dilator still inside me and pleasure winding tight in the pit of my stomach, it felt like my body was working exactly as designed, because we fit together like we were made for each other. My lips wrapped around his thickness and I took as much of him into my mouth as I could, wrapping my hand around the base when he bottomed out against the back of my throat. I doubted I'd ever be able to feel his cock between my legs; he was simply too big. But it didn't matter. There were plenty of other things we could do.

"That medical device still inside you?" Gideon asked between pants.

I gave him a hard suck in response to that insolence, and he let out a breathless laugh as he swore. I sucked up to his tip, released, and giggled, leaning my forehead against his hip as I stroked him with my hand. He gathered my hair in his hands and gripped it in a fist as he stared down at me—and I saw the same hungry look in his eyes that I'd seen the very first time we stared at each other, standing in the aisle on our wedding day.

He'd wanted me from the start, just like I'd wanted him.

And I realized something. "You must've lied on your profile too," I said, and straightened. I frowned down at him, my hand still wrapped around his throbbing cock. "Gideon Mars," I chided. "On a scale of one to ten, how would you rate your desire for sex?"

"Right now it's about a fucking million," he rasped, rocking his hips into my grip. He groaned. "Now stop talking and suck me off, babe."

"You are *so* freaking rude." But it turned me on when he talked dirty to me.

He laughed, and there was nothing but tenderness in his gaze. "I want you to come with my cock in your mouth and that toy in your pussy," he said, eyes dark.

It was the first time he'd asked me for anything during sex —and he was asking me to orgasm. My pleasure was his pleasure.

So I reached between my legs as I lowered my lips to his tip, and I got myself off while I sucked his cock. His grip on my hair tightened, and he came in hot spurts down my throat as I moaned. Then he pulled me up the bed beside him, rolled me onto my back, and buried his head between my legs. I moaned as he slid the dilator out of me and gasped when his fingers replaced it. He was desperately hungry, and he didn't stop until I was a boneless, sweaty, satisfied mess.

GIDEON

Her touch was as gentle as a butterfly's kiss. She traced the scars on my shoulder, down my triceps, and across my forearm. The deadened skin still had no sensation, but I could feel the pressure of her touch on my arm. Part of me wanted to tell her to stop; it didn't feel right for someone so beautiful to touch all the ugly parts of me.

But Sadie rested her head in the crook between my chest and shoulder on my good side, her arm draped across my body as she explored the boundary between healthy skin and damage. Her leg was thrown over both of mine, her nakedness a reminder of what we now shared. I would deal with the discomfort of being examined this way, because putting even an inch of distance between our bodies was out of the question.

"There's one good thing about the fire," she said suddenly, fingers ghosting up my forearm and lingering at the elbow.

My cock stirred. Her touch was addictive. With my eyes closed, I let out a low grunt. "What's that?" I asked.

"It spared your biceps." Her hands covered the muscle and stroked. Squeezed. "Losing them would've been a real tragedy."

My eyes cracked open, and I glanced down at my impertinent wife. Her eyes glimmered with humor, lips trembling as she tried to hold back her grin.

"You'll pay for that," I growled.

Her smile widened. "But is it a lie?"

She squealed as I flipped her onto her stomach and reached between her legs. Dripping wet. Lusty, perfect wife. Her gasp was my sustenance. I could listen to her make that noise for hours. I draped my body over hers, pinning her to the mattress as I stroked her to madness.

And when I used my knees to hold her legs together and fitted myself in the soft, fleshy space between her thighs, she whimpered so sweetly I knew I'd do anything for her. I rutted against her, grunting as she writhed and bucked beneath me. She was slick and hot and I'd never felt anything so good.

"Gideon," she whined, and I hushed her, brushing her long brown hair off her shoulders so I could kiss the nape of her neck. She pushed her ass into me, needy, desperate. I loved her like this. I loved her all ways, but I especially loved her like this. No one got this side of her but me.

Reaching around to her front, I pressed against her clit the way I knew she liked. She shuddered and cried my name, and I couldn't wait any longer.

I sat back, took myself in hand, and painted her curves with my release. Marked her—branded her—as pleasure shattered through me.

She turned her head and looked at me with one eye, her breath coming fast and hard.

In Sadie's gaze, I saw everything: How she wanted more, but she was afraid to ask because she'd learned she didn't deserve it. She thought I was keeping score. Thought this was over just because I'd had an orgasm.

I smiled. It would be my life's mission to make her realize that I was here to service her as often and as enthusiastically as she required. I grabbed her hips and hauled them up, then lay down beneath her swollen cunt and guided her back down to my mouth.

TWENTY-THREE
SADIE

On the Monday that marked the start of our fifth week of marriage, Gideon and I ventured out of the cottage and drove into town. I had agreed to meet Lola this week for the first fitting of the muslin draft of her dress, and I had a lot of catching up to do if I wanted to have anything for her to try on.

That meant we could kill two birds with one stone.

Gideon unlocked Life's a Stitch, did a sweep, and turned to face me. "I've got eyes and ears on you," Gideon assured me, "and either me or one of our guys is one minute away. If anything seems weird—*anything*, Sadie—you call for help."

I nodded. "Everything's going to be fine," I assured him. "I promise to be very responsible bait."

"I don't like this."

I wrapped my arms around his neck and smiled. "I know."

"Why is that funny?"

"It's not funny. I'm just smiling because it feels good for someone to care about me like this."

His hands drifted down my sides, and he kissed me again—hard. I let my own hands slide up his arms, loving the feel of his skin under my palms. For the first time since I'd met him, he was wearing short sleeves—and he was doing it in public. His T-shirt clung to his biceps and strained over his chest. He looked delectable, especially when he glared at me with protectiveness emanating from every pore. "Call for help, even if you're not sure," he reminded me, then stalked out the door.

I watched him go, eyes flicking to the cameras he and his team had installed in the shop. I gave the nearest one a wave, then moved to the worktable where I'd left my project. Working on Lola's dress was like learning to walk again after a long illness. It was uncomfortable almost to the point of pain, but also an intense relief. I made a ton of mistakes and almost ran out of muslin, but I finally got the pattern pieces cut and pinned together.

Standing back from the dress form, I tilted my head and considered my work. Not bad. The waist probably needed to be lifted a bit, but I'd leave it as-is until Lola came in. She had a pretty long torso, so I wanted to give myself fabric to work with. Excitement bubbled in my gut. It felt good to be back.

That was the moment Ivan Popov chose to walk in. I turned at the sound of the door opening and greeted him as he looked around the room with a sneer on his lips.

"Think you'll be able to make this place work, do you?" His lips curled into a cruel smile. "Good luck."

The best way I'd learned to handle this kind of sarcastic, passive-aggressive comment was to take it at face value. I beamed at Ivan. "Thank you! It's such a great space. I'm really enjoying working here."

His eyes narrowed. "I don't trust you."

My heart had started rattling as soon as he'd walked in, and now it began to bang. "Okay," I answered.

"We don't need any newcomers in this town. It's fine as it is. You should just pack up and go back where you came from."

"Oh yeah?"

"Yeah. Or else life here might get *real* difficult—"

The door banged open again, and a second later, Gideon had Ivan by the lapels of his faded plaid shirt. He backed the old man up and slammed him against the big window at the front of the shop so hard it rattled in its frame. Ivan's head went red, and he stammered, feet flailing as Gideon lifted him off the ground.

Knox was just behind him. He reached into Ivan's pocket to pull out a phone. He connected it to another device and started typing.

"Threaten my wife again and die, old man," Gideon growled.

"I didn't—it's not—she doesn't belong here!"

Gideon slammed him against the window, and Ivan whimpered. My husband glanced at his brother. "Anything?"

Knox just grunted, and the look on Gideon's face told me that was a negative. Gideon rattled the old man once more and said, "Did you key Sadie's car?"

"No!"

"Did you puncture her tire?"

"No!"

"Did you send her a threatening text?"

"A text message?" Popov answered, incredulous.

"Answer the question."

"No! I didn't do any of that! I just think she should leave!"

Gideon growled, animalistic. His neck muscles were stark, and his eyes were fully black. I drifted over to where Knox tapped on his laptop, downloading all the data from Ivan's phone. That looked...illegal.

My husband glanced over at the two of us, and Knox shook his head. "Phone was nowhere near Sadie's car at the time of the vandalism," Knox said. Then he angled the laptop toward Gideon and said, "It was there."

Gideon glanced over, then narrowed his eyes. "Betsy's house?"

Ivan spluttered. "We're just friends!"

"You're having an affair with my grandaunt?"

"If you tell anyone, I'll—"

"You'll *what*," Gideon growled. He set the old man back down on his feet, but he didn't move back an inch.

Popov trembled in front of him, his jaw jutting out as he glared. "It's not an affair. We're in love."

Gideon and Knox exchanged a glance.

Ivan slithered out from where he was pinned to the window and snatched his phone. Then he pointed at Gideon. "You should be the one telling her to leave. You think she'll stick around? After your mother and your ex both left you? When you look like *this*?" He gestured to Gideon's bare arm, where the burn scars were on full display.

My mood went from zero to apoplectic in the space of a breath. I was so angry I couldn't feel my face. Then, suddenly, calm descended over me, cold and distant. I took one step to the side and threw the lock on the door. Then I turned to face the old man.

"Apologize," I said, my voice sounding flat and strange, even to me. In my peripheral vision, I saw my husband and my brother-in-law shift their stances to face me, but my gaze remained trained on Ivan.

He turned to face me, lips curling down in an exaggerated frown, then slowly rocked back on his heels. "What the hell?"

"Apologize to my husband," I repeated in that same mechanical, horrifying voice. "*Now*."

Ivan blinked a few times, then lifted his chin. "Why should I?"

I gave him a terrible smile. It felt wrong on my lips when fury still made my blood pump hot. "Because what you said wasn't very nice, was it?"

Fear began to flicker in his expression. He shrugged, then tilted his head and mumbled, "Sorry."

"Say it like you mean it."

"You're a bitch, you know that?"

"Yeah," I replied, then waited.

Ivan grumbled, spun around, and said, "I'm sorry, okay? You people are crazy." Then he brushed past me, unlocked the door, and scurried out. I watched him until he moved out of sight, then sucked in a long breath and let it out slowly.

Finally, I turned to look at the two remaining men. Knox had an eyebrow popped. Gideon was looking at me strangely. He approached and put his hands on my shoulders in a gentle touch. "You good?"

"No," I said. "I'm furious. I wanted to deck him, but he's so old I was worried I'd kill him. And then I was thinking about how I'd happily kill him, but then I'd go to prison, and that would suck."

Gideon's arms went around my shoulders, and then he was shaking. It took me a moment to realize he was laughing.

I pulled away to glare at him.

He kissed the tip of my nose. "Remind me never to make you angry."

"You're on thin ice as it is."

He chuckled, kissed me softly, then let me go. Knox squeezed my shoulder with one of his giant hands, his eyes crinkling at the corners. "Badass," he mumbled, then took his gear and left.

"So it's not Ivan Popov," I said.

"No," Gideon replied.

"At least we know I make good bait."

He grimaced, then dragged me away from the shop so we could get lunch.

That evening, when we were curled up on the couch after dinner trying to decide on a movie, I remembered something Ivan had said.

"What did Ivan mean when he said your mother had left?"

With my head on his chest, I heard Gideon's pulse speed up. He put the remote on the arm of the sofa and swallowed. "She left when I was eight years old. My dad raised us. He had to work overtime to care for us, so a lot of the home stuff fell to me when my aunts or grandma couldn't come and help. It was a lot."

I licked my lips and said, "I'm so sorry."

"It was a long time ago."

I nodded, my face rubbing against his shirt. "Why did your mom leave?"

"My dad had met her when he was in the military, and

they'd settled here when he got out. She popped the four of us out within six years. We were four out-of-control boys. She was at home all day with us in this small town she'd never wanted to move to. I guess it was just too much for her."

With his arm draped around me, I felt the moment his hand spasmed on my arm. I wondered if he thought I'd be the same. If I'd cut and run back to the city at the first sign of trouble. But where would I go? *Why* would I go, when all my happiness was right here with him?

"I'm so sorry, Gideon," I repeated.

"It's fine," he replied, but the hitch in his voice told me it was a wound that still caused him pain. "I mean, I had my aunts and uncles. I had my grandparents. I had my brothers and my dad. And after my dad died, the whole family rallied. I'm lucky."

Like he was lucky to get out of the fire with only the burns he sustained. Funny kind of luck, I thought.

He flexed the hand that wasn't holding me. I watched the low light glint on the signet ring he always wore on his right hand. He shifted, pulling the ring off to hold it between his thumb and forefinger. "My dad got sick when I was seventeen. Pancreatic cancer. Died within four months of feeling an ache in his back."

"Oh, my goodness. I'm so sorry," I said for the third time. I wished there was something else I could tell him, but nothing seemed right.

"He gave me this ring and told me to watch over my brothers when he was gone. That's the Mars family crest," he said, gesturing to the design on the ring. "He said family's all we've got at the end of the day, and as the eldest it was my job to watch over my brothers and take care of my grandmother."

"Your grandmother doesn't seem like she needs taking care of."

Gideon huffed a laugh. "No, she doesn't, does she?"

I lifted my head off his shoulder and looked in his eyes. "That's a lot of pressure to put on a seventeen-year-old."

He stared into my eyes and said nothing.

I pushed his hair off his forehead, my heart aching for the little boy who'd been through so much. No wonder Gideon had been unsurprised when I'd told him I was leaving the morning after our wedding. It wasn't just his scars that made him believe everyone abandoned him. His mother had left when he was a small child, and his father had died suddenly—and that was before his ex had rejected him for the crime of saving the lives of three kids.

Gideon had started a business and expanded it in order to employ his brothers. He'd hired his cousin Connor. The only reason he'd agreed to an arranged marriage was for them and to make his grandmother happy. He dropped everything to go bail Wendy out when she ran out of gas.

He always put me first, and not just during sex. He'd plate up my food before his own and always give me the better cuts of meat. He was protective and tender and patient.

Everyone came before Gideon. He put every single other person ahead of him, as if his needs didn't matter.

Pressing a hand to his heart, I asked in a whisper, "And who is supposed to take care of you?"

There was a flash in his eyes. Pain and yearning, there and gone. Even now, he didn't understand. He didn't think he deserved someone to take care of him. Didn't realize that that someone was *me*.

Because this was love unlike anything I'd experienced before. How else could I describe the overwhelming feeling of fullness in my chest? The fear that I would lose something I so desperately wanted? The weightless, breathless feeling of being the one he chose? Of *finding* each other when life had seemed so bleak before I saw him standing at the end of the aisle.

"Gideon, I—" I stopped. Exhaled. Tried again. Failed.

Even though he was the best man I'd ever met, I was afraid.

How could I measure up to him? He who was so patient and brave and selfless and loving? He who was my perfect man, who demanded nothing of me? He who made me believe in a future that I had thought was only a fantasy?

Why would he want someone as thoroughly inadequate as me?

Because it had barely been a month. How could I trust that things would stay good? What if in another month or a year or longer, Gideon decided that actually, he *wasn't* satisfied with me? He needed more. He needed someone else. Someone better. What would happen then?

I would be heartbroken again, but it would be so much worse, because my feelings for him were immense and growing every day. If I didn't tell him how I felt, it meant I could hide a little part of me. Keep it safe.

Gideon sighed, his hands cupping my jaw as he lifted my face. He smiled softly at me, stroking my cheeks. "I know," he said. "It's okay, baby."

Even now, he was protecting me.

My heart cracked wide open, and tears fell down my

cheeks. He kissed them away then caught my lips in his, and I pressed myself up against him as tightly as I could. I couldn't say the words—not yet—but maybe I could show him. Maybe the knot inside me would loosen, and when it finally came undone, Gideon would still be there, loving me.

"Stop crying," he chided softly as he kissed my jaw. "I can't stand it."

"They're happy tears," I said. "I think."

He huffed a laugh and kissed me harder. We forgot about the movie we were supposed to watch and focused on showing each other what we felt with touches and kisses and strokes.

A while later, when we decided to wander down to the water to look at the full moon and the brightness of the stars, I leaned my head against his arm and felt the shell around my heart crack open.

I wasn't sure if I would design wedding dresses or plan retreats with Mrs. Gretzinger or take Etta's investment offer. I wasn't even sure if I'd do more than make Lola's dress. But I had the space and time to figure it out. There was no deadline looming in two weeks, because Gideon and I were meant to be. We walked back to the cottage in easy silence. I kept my fingers tangled in Gideon's. In my heart, there was the soft fluttering of hope.

And then we walked up to the cottage, and reality came crashing back down on top of me.

Blue spray paint covered the blank canvas of the garage door:

GO HOME WHORE

Gideon reached into his pocket for his phone, and Jack's face appeared a moment later. Gideon's grip was tight on mine as he said, "I need everything we've got surrounding the cottage."

"Why? What's... Oh, shit," Jack said when Gideon flipped the camera to show him. "Sadie okay?"

"I'm fine," I said.

"We'll find out who did this," Jack promised. "You're one of us now. Got it?"

I looked at Gideon, who was holding back his rage with every fiber of his will. His jaw was stone hard and his eyes blazed. I was one of them. For the first time in my life, I belonged.

I gulped and nodded. "Thank you."

We made it to the front door as Gideon hovered beside me, scanning the forest. Then we went inside and he told me to stay put, and he methodically cleared every room in the cottage. When he was sure there was no one inside, he came over to me, wrapped me in a hug, and said, "Take what you need for a few days. We're going somewhere more secure."

I didn't protest. I packed up one of my suitcases with the essentials and let Gideon lead me back to the car. He hauled the suitcase into the back once I was settled inside, then got behind the wheel and drove.

"Where are we going?" I asked.

"My place." Gideon's tone told me he was beyond words, so I sat back and watched the trees and the buildings and the hills go by. We parked outside the Marswood Security building and Gideon hustled me up to the top floor.

His apartment was spartan and clean, but there were a few

touches that reminded me of Gideon. He had a few pictures of his family hanging in the living room, and a fantastic kitchen with all the trimmings. As I snooped, Gideon brought my suitcase to the bedroom. He stalked back out when there was a knock at the door.

He checked the screen next to the door and unlocked the door to admit Jack and Knox. Knox carried a laptop. Bennett was absent.

"We've got a car turning onto Maple Street at 9:43 p.m. and back out twelve minutes later," Jack said, naming the road the cottage was on. "Plates are obscured. We'll find this asshole."

"Spray paint seems to be similar to what Mr. Titty's used to tag around town," Knox said as he opened his laptop and sat down at the kitchen island. "Can't be sure it's the same, though."

"We just can't get any footage of this guy—or guys," Jack added, frustrated. He crossed his arms as he stared at the laptop screen, where Knox was loading up the grainy footage of the car driving onto the cottage road. He pulled up security footage from the front of the house, where a man darted up to spray paint the garage, his face out of view. He looked taller than the other shots of Mr. Titty I'd seen, and his shoes were different.

"You guys think whoever did this is Mr. Titty?" I asked as Knox replayed the video.

"It seems like a logical conclusion," Jack said, shrugging. "Same spray paint. Escalation of threat."

Gideon was silent as he glared at the screen, where the video played on a loop.

"This person is wearing dress shoes," I said. "Mr. Titty had sneakers on in both other shots."

The three men looked at me. Jack grimaced. "Is that enough to draw any conclusions, though? I wish we had more. Just when we were making headway, they go quiet. Not a single tag this week, so we can't catch them. Using you as bait only brought out the town crazies."

Gideon agreed with a grunt. "Connor said it seems like they know our blind spots."

I looked from one brother to the other to the other to the other, waiting for one of them to state the obvious. When they didn't, I had to: "Maybe they do."

Three sets of blue eyes turned to stare at me.

I clarified: "Maybe they know your blind spots."

"Our systems are secure," Knox growled like I'd personally insulted his life's work. And hey, maybe I had.

I nodded. "Right. But what if Mr. Titty is one of your people?"

GIDEON

My ears were ringing, and it took me a second to understand what Sadie was saying.

Then the realization hit me like a sack of bricks.

There was a traitor in our midst.

TWENTY-FOUR
SADIE

My words were met with deathly silence...followed by chaos. The three brothers exploded into action, arguing with each other in half-sentences that only made sense to them.

"If one of our guys has been threatening Sadie, there isn't a place on this godforsaken earth they can go where I won't find them," Gideon finally snarled, silencing the other two.

Jack and Knox exchanged a loaded look. Jack obviously was used to playing peacekeeper, because he lifted his arms in a placating gesture. "Let's take this one step at a time."

Gideon vibrated like there was excess tension tightening his body. I stepped up to him and put a hand on his chest. When he met my gaze, his eyes were dark. "I mean it," he said. "Whoever is threatening you won't be able to hide from me."

A tendril of pleasure snaked through me. I'd never had anyone care about me so much. Not to the point that they'd blow up their own business to protect me.

I didn't want him to make any rash decisions, though. It was like him giving me the space and time (and snacks) to sew cushion covers with old scraps while I reacquainted myself with sewing; I knew he cared about Marswood Security, and he cared about his employees. I wanted to help him keep everything he loved while figuring out if anything needed to be scrapped. If there was a rat.

"I don't think Mr. Titty is the person or people who have been threatening me," I said, keeping my voice calm.

"You have no evidence of that," Gideon fired back.

"It makes no sense. If it was the same person, why would they keep drawing boobs around town when I got here? Why not escalate further right away? If the goal is to get me away and to stop the arranged marriage scheme, why not move to a bigger target? Why not go after you or your brothers or your grandmother?"

His eyes narrowed. He kept an arm wrapped protectively around my waist, but his gaze shifted to his brothers.

"It's a fair point," Jack said, and Knox grunted in agreement.

"The tags stopped after I got the footage from Cash. Mr. Titty knew we had more footage of them, and they got spooked. So, the way I see it, there are two problems here. One, someone in your inner circle is either selling information to Mr. Titty, or one of your employees moonlights as a breast connoisseur."

"This is not a time for fucking jokes, Sadie," Gideon growled.

I ignored him. "The way to solve this problem is to look at everything you know about Mr. Titty through the lens of a very short suspect list which includes everyone who works for your organization."

The three brothers watched me. Looked at each other.

I took a deep breath. "Once you've done that, you can determine whether or not that person has been threatening me. If they have been, we go from there. If they haven't, we start at square one. There are only so many people in this town. It can't be that hard to find out who's doing this."

The temperature in the room dropped a few degrees. Gideon stared at me, then lifted his gaze to his brothers.

Knox nodded and started packing up the laptop while Jack said, "Let's get to work."

"Um," I said, lifting a finger. All three men stopped what they were doing and looked at me again. I gave them a tense smile. "Can I make a suggestion with where you should start?"

AFTER TWO DAYS of being holed up in Gideon's apartment, he finally reluctantly allowed me to go out as long as he was right there beside me. He and his brothers had looped Bennett into the traitor-in-their-midst hypothesis, and they'd been busy gathering evidence.

I was pretty sure I knew what they would find.

We went for coffee—I'd missed my matcha lattes when shit had hit the fan—and then wandered up Main Street to the seamstress's shop. Despite everything, I'd made progress on Lola's dress and was ready to get her in for a first fitting.

The muslin draft hung on a dress form. The main goal of the fitting was to get the bodice nailed down. It was a strapless sweetheart neckline with quite a bit of boning in it that flared out into a full skirt. The muslin fabric didn't fall like the silk would, but the draft would allow me to cut the fabric with confidence.

I waited in the shop, working on sketches of another dress that had popped into my head. Finally, around noon, Lola walked in. Her blond hair had been slicked back in a low bun, and she wore dark sunglasses and a black tank top tucked into her loose jeans. She gave me a blazing smile. "Hi, Sadie!"

I smiled in response, then squeaked when she came up and hugged me. Her mom, Jennifer, entered behind her and greeted me with a smile. I'd spoken to her for a while at last week's family dinner, and had learned that she and her husband were both accountants who were born and raised in the area. I was vehemently informed that Lola was absolutely not going to follow in their footsteps.

"So, this is what I've come up with so far," I said, leading her to the dress form.

Lola frowned. "Okay..."

"The muslin is stiffer than the silk, so the skirt drapes differently. But I really just want to make sure it fits you, and then I'll deconstruct this and use it as a pattern to make your actual dress."

Lola tilted her head, interested. Her mom drifted closer and touched the silk fabric I'd folded on top of the work table. Lola went behind the curtains at the back to change into the dress.

"Lola's so excited about this," Jennifer told me. She was about fifteen years older than me, with thick-rimmed glasses and a calm demeanor. It was hard to believe her exuberant daughter came from the same stock.

I smiled. "I have to say, I'm pretty excited about it too. It's the first time in a long time that I've looked forward to creating a dress."

"You don't like doing wedding dresses?"

I chewed my lip. "I'm not sure anymore."

She hummed, nodding. "It's a lot of pressure."

We both turned as Lola walked out. The bottom of the dress dragged a bit, and she'd gathered it up to reveal her white sneakers. She marched up to us and stood in front of the floor-length mirror, then let her hands slide down her waist as she considered the dress.

"We'll take this in a bit," I said, repinning the waist. "And I'll make sure to get a lot of volume in the skirt so there's drama when you walk. Your inspo photos all had a thigh slit. How's this height?"

"Too much leg," Jennifer cut in, and Lola let out an exaggerated huff.

I nodded, pinning the slit a little lower to make the dress more modest. Lola clicked her tongue, rolling her eyes at her mother.

As I pinned, my eyes darted to movement outside. Someone was crouching near Jennifer's car. I looked away again and smiled as Lola said she loved the dress. She beamed at me in the mirror and did a twirl. "Omigod! I can't wait to see the final dress!"

"We haven't talked about payment," Jennifer said when Lola had gone to change back into her own clothes.

I shook my head. "There's no payment necessary. I didn't even have to buy the fabric."

"But—your time. Your expertise!"

"Trust me," I said. "It's been my pleasure."

"I'll make you some cookies," Lola announced when she came back out and handed me the bundle of muslin. "I make really good chocolate chip cookies." She beamed at me, then threw her arms around me for a tight hug.

My heart twinged. She really did seem like a good kid. That's why it hurt so much when Gideon walked in, looking grim. Jennifer and Lola turned at the sound of his footsteps, and Lola made a strangled gasp when she saw what he held.

"That's my backpack!"

"Gideon," Jennifer said, putting herself between my husband and her daughter. "What the hell is going on? Did you break into my car to get my daughter's stuff?"

The backpack's zipper creaked as Gideon wrenched it apart with his strong hands. He reached inside and, without a word, pulled out a used can of blue spray paint.

Lola screamed, turned around, and ran...

Right into Jack's chest, who'd snuck in the back door. He caught her around the waist and lifted her over his shoulder. Jennifer gasped. Gideon sighed.

I grimaced, disappointed that I'd been right. Recognizing the white sneakers had seemed like a long shot—so many people wore them—but it had been enough.

"Jennifer, you might want to sit down," Gideon said, gesturing to a chair. The mother obstinately remained standing, caught between shock and the desire to protect her daughter.

"You tell me what the hell is going on," she demanded. "And *you*." She pointed at me. "You had something to do with this!"

"She sure did," Gideon agreed. "She's the one who figured out that Lola is Mr. Titty."

"I'm not!" Lola screamed.

"One third of Mr. Titty," Gideon corrected. "The other two thirds are waiting for us at headquarters."

Lola suddenly went limp in Jack's arms, her head drooping in defeat.

GIDEON

When the hubbub had died down, Jennifer agreed to drive to the Marswood Security headquarters with Lola so we could get to the bottom of things. The look in my aunt's eyes told me that Lola would have a very unpleasant trip—worse than if Lola had ridden with me.

Beside me, Sadie was quiet as we drove up toward head-quarters.

"You okay?" I asked, not liking the curve of her shoulders.

Her eyes were sad as she looked at me. "Don't go too hard on them," she requested. "They're just kids."

I couldn't get the words out to answer. How could I, when I was choked with grief and betrayal?

My own family. My own kin.

I'd done everything for my brothers. I'd sold half my business to give them their livelihoods. I'd hired Connor and nurtured his talents from the start. I'd given so much, and this was how they repaid me?

It was almost easier when my mother had left. When my father had died. When Lenore had turned her back on me at my lowest. Because this? This hurt, this knife in the back? It was so much worse.

I glanced at Sadie once more, wondering what she was think-ing. If she still had dreams of a successful business in the city. If she'd be the next one to cut my legs out from under me.

When he spotted Lola being marched into Marswood Security, Connor folded like a cheap suit. The whole story came blubbering out of him—how he, Glenn, and Lola didn't want to be subjected to arranged marriages. How they'd concocted a plan to make the town look unappealing. How they targeted family properties because they didn't want to get other people involved, other than a select few who annoyed them. Ivan Popov had been rude to Lola, for example, and Glenn had tagged his shop in retaliation.

I watched Gideon bear the weight of the confession. He was quiet as we made our way up to his apartment on the top floor. I tried to reach him with soft touches and comments, but he remained closed off. I'd never seen him so withdrawn.

We ate dinner, watched TV, and got ready for bed in silence. Finally, when we'd lain beside each other for an hour, I couldn't resist any longer. "Talk to me."

Gideon pretended to sleep for a second, then gusted out a

breath. "My own family," he said. Grief threaded through his voice, and my heart ached for him.

"I'm sorry."

"Don't be. You're the only one who was able to figure it out. The rest of us were blind."

"I wish I'd been wrong."

"They're not the kids I thought they were," he said, voice dark.

His tone worried me. I could hear the weight of all his pain behind it. All the ways he felt betrayed. But Lola, Connor, and Glenn weren't criminal masterminds. They were teenagers with underdeveloped frontal lobes and poor impulse control. Yes, they should be made to bear consequences for their actions—but I didn't want Gideon to exile them from his own family.

Speaking gently, I said, "We all did stupid things when we were teenagers. At least we know they're not the ones who threatened me." It had been very clear from their denials that they had nothing to do with that. Connor's fear had been thick in the air as he swore up and down that they had nothing to do with the threats against me. Glenn had cried. Lola had looked devastated.

"So they say," Gideon growled. He lay on his stomach, and his voice was muffled in the pillows.

I sighed, curling up on my side beside him. I ran my fingers through his hair, feeling his body soften bit by bit. Finally, he turned around, wrapped his arms around me, and pulled me close. It was the first time he'd hugged me since the moment he'd pulled the can of spray paint out of Lola's bag. I sighed into his touch, some of the stress I hadn't even registered easing out of my body.

"Are you upset that they lied to you?" I asked. The street-lamp outside his window sent light slanting against the wall. I traced the edges of it with my eyes while I listened to the sound of Gideon's heartbeat.

"Yes," he replied. "Connor used my company to vandalize my town. He pretended to work on finding Mr. Titty while deleting or recording over half a dozen shots of him and Glenn and Lola. I trusted him, and he betrayed me. My own family."

I stroked Gideon's chest. I sensed that he didn't want solutions or even commiseration. He just needed time to sort through his thoughts and feelings. His hand slid up and down my arm as he lay in bed, staring at the ceiling. I could feel the tension in his body. The hurt.

Finally, he sighed. "I don't know what to do."

I stroked the hair off his forehead and cupped his cheek so he'd meet my gaze. "The worst thing you can do is ice them out," I told him.

He scowled. "I'm supposed to pretend what they did was fine? Using my trust to run around vandalizing the town? *Lying* to me over and over again?"

"You don't pretend it's fine," I said. "You come up with consequences. Make them clean up or repaint over every single pair of boobs they sprayed onto the walls of the town. Make them make a public apology. Don't let Connor into your command center until he's learned his lesson and you're sure you can trust him—that'll hurt him more than anything. But don't make them feel like outsiders in their own family. Especially when the family is woven into the fabric of this town. It's their home, Gideon. They were just afraid of losing it."

His eyes flicked between mine, and I knew that he could hear everything I'd left unsaid. He always did.

"The way your family made you feel like an outsider because you weren't married," he murmured.

"It really freaking hurts to feel like an outcast," I whispered. "Especially when you've got nowhere else to go."

He clicked his tongue and pulled me closer, then he pressed a kiss to my forehead. "You've got somewhere now," he said. "You belong right here."

He kissed my lips, and in that kiss I felt the hugeness of his emotion for me. I hoped he felt the same when I kissed him back. This wounded, gentle, kind, protective man was the most incredible person I'd ever met. He was the love of my life.

As he shifted me onto my back and propped himself above me, I let that realization settle into my bones. The love of my life. The man I'd married. The person I wanted to spend the rest of my days with.

With my hands draped over his shoulders, I couldn't help the smile that curved my lips.

"Are you smiling because you know you've won?" he growled. "I'll go easy on them," he added, disgusted with himself.

My grin widened. "That wasn't why I was smiling, no, but I'm glad to hear it."

"Can't say no to you," he complained, and dropped a trail of kisses down my neck. I shivered, spreading my knees so he could settle between them. He was hard, his erection pressing against my stomach.

All at once, I realized I was ready.

"Gideon," I whispered, kissing his jaw, his ear, his shoulder

—any bit of skin I could reach. "Gideon," I repeated when all he did was grunt in response.

He pulled away. "You want me to stop?"

My chest cracked wide open, exposing my beating heart. I was so in love with this man. I smiled at him and shook my head. "No. I want to try."

It took him a second to understand. I had to roll my hips against his hardness, and then his eyes finally widened. "You're sure?"

I nodded.

"Sadie—" A shudder went through him, and he dove down to kiss me harder. His hands palmed at my sides, running up to squeeze my breasts. He pulled the strap of my camisole down off my shoulder and took my nipple in his mouth. He kissed me there, his hips bucking, and I melted into the mattress beneath him.

He wore only a pair of pajama bottoms, and I had on a camisole and loose sleep shorts. So it took only a few seconds to strip off our clothes, and then it was all his warm golden skin on mine. It felt like heaven.

My heart began to thump. Nervousness and anticipation wrapped like a fist around my heart. A lump jammed itself in my throat, and all I could do was pant and moan and whimper.

Gideon took his time, even though I could see how much he wanted me in the throbbing between his legs. The head of his cock was nearly purple, seeping liquid onto the blankets. He ignored his own needs as he buried his face between my legs, making me come with a cry before he even went near my opening.

When he slid a finger inside, his hand was shaking. He

pressed a kiss to the soft flesh of my inner thighs, and I let out a trembling breath.

"Have I ever told you how much I love your pussy, Sadie?"

I huffed a laugh. "A few times, yeah."

"So wet and hot and perfect."

I sank into the pillows, my hand reaching down to stroke his hair. He probed my entrance with a finger, slowly, slowly, slowly, until I shivered and whined for more. Always ready to meet my needs, Gideon did as I asked. Another finger joined the first, and the stretch was just this side of painful. I wrapped my hands in the blankets and breathed.

"So beautiful," he said, kissing the top of my slit. "I could just keep doing this all night."

Tension slowly unwound from my body; I knew he was telling the truth. As I relaxed, he stretched me. His fingers spread and scissored, and pleasure began to wind through the pit of my stomach. Still, Gideon took his time. I tried not to think of what we were preparing to do, but the act loomed in my mind like a hulking shadow.

But I loved him. I trusted him. I could have penetrative sex with him. Why wouldn't I? Why would my brain throw up barriers between us, when he was the man I most wanted to be with? The man who made me feel safer than I'd ever felt before?

He groaned as my body eased, and when he inhaled, his breath was unsteady. I realized I'd closed my eyes, and I opened them now to look at him. His dark head was bent between my legs, his muscles stark in the low light of the room. His scars were lit by the streetlamp, muscle and sinew moving under the skin.

He was so beautiful. My husband. My love.

I reached down to touch his hair, and when I whispered his name, Gideon looked up. His eyes were black. Desire carved his features in stark relief. He was holding on by a thread.

"Ready?" he asked, his voice hoarse.

I panted out a few breaths and finally dipped my chin. Gideon searched my face for a moment, his fingers curling inside me, and I let out a breathless laugh. "Yes," I finally said aloud. "Yes, I'm ready."

It was the truth. I'd never felt so connected to another person. I wanted him inside me. I wanted to be able to do this with *him*, because he was the man I loved. He was my husband.

Slowly, Gideon moved. He reached into the bedside table and got a condom. Rolled it on. Paused. His chest heaved, and he closed his eyes as he knelt between my bent legs, as if it was almost too much for him to bear.

He wanted this so badly. I saw it in the line of his shoulders and the tension in his arms. I felt it in the gusting breaths that ghosted over my bare skin. I heard it in the tortured, barely audible groan he let out when he opened his eyes and looked at my cunt.

He'd been lying to me before, about being happy to do other things. About loving making me come in any way he could. *This* was what he really wanted. Just like every other man.

The thought was like a vengeful ghost winding its way through my brain, flicking on familiar switches that made electrical currents zip toward my pelvic floor.

I breathed in and out, trying to reach that place of calm again.

"Hey," Gideon said, one hand on his cock, the other stroking up my leg. "We don't have to do this, Sadie. Okay?"

A breath gusted out of me, and tears leaked out the corners of my eyes. Gideon bent over me and kissed me until I relaxed.

"You stop me anytime," he murmured. "I mean it."

Gulping, I nodded.

Then his cock was there. Probing. Huge. I sipped in little breaths, keeping my arms wrapped around his shoulders, staring at the ceiling as I focused on my breathing. Gideon kissed my shoulder and neck as his hips moved, slowly, gently, inexorably.

The stretch was intense, overwhelming. I loved him so much and I was ecstatic to be doing this with him. Because we *were* doing it. His cock pushed deeper and deeper, and the weight of him pushed my thighs apart. I sank my nails into his back and gasped. Trembling overtook me from head to toe.

"Okay?" Gideon rumbled, pausing.

"I think—yes," I said. "Yes, okay."

He pushed deeper still. I stiffened, and he retreated. A groan tore out of him as he dropped his forehead to my shoulder, his hands curling into the pillows on either side of my head. He swore then pushed back into me as he turned my head and kissed me. I felt the fine tremors in his back. The twitching of his thigh muscles. The clumsy, distracted way he kissed me.

And it was wonderful. It was exactly what I'd wanted. A connection I'd never experienced before. My body working as it was supposed to.

I tried rolling my hips and heard Gideon's breath hitch. His back went solid, as if every muscle in his body had seized, so I did it again. Rocked against his cock, taking more of him inside me. He swore again, louder and longer, and then we were doing it. *I* was doing it. I was having penetrative sex with a man—with my husband! A giddy sort of lightheadedness took over, and I couldn't help the laugh that tumbled out of me.

Gideon pulled back to stare into my eyes, looking utterly awestruck. He rocked into me then bent down and kissed me deep and long. I moaned into his mouth, wrapping my arms around his neck as he murmured in my ear about how good I felt and how hard he was and how he'd been dreaming of this since he saw me.

Then Gideon reached down and hooked his hand under my knee, pulling it up toward my shoulder. I gasped, and Gideon let out a groan unlike anything I'd heard before. It was the sound of pleasure. His hips drove into mine, pushing his cock so deep it stole my breath—and suddenly it was too much.

I scrabbled at Gideon's back, panic spiking inside me.

"So fucking good," he slurred, lips brushing my neck, hips rolling into me once more. It burned in a way that was horribly familiar. Pain speared into me, and I let out a whimper as my palms found his shoulders and pushed.

Gideon was off me in an instant. He propped himself above me, eyes wide, wild, and sucked in a hard breath. "You good?"

"No," I whispered, temples wet with tears.

"Fuck," he barked, and slid out of me. It burned as he did, and I couldn't help the mewl that escaped my throat as I curled onto my side. "Why didn't you say something?" Gideon demanded, taking me in his arms. "Fuck, Sadie!"

Words escaped me. I buried my face in his chest and shook my head. I was so embarrassed and ashamed. So fucking disappointed. Why couldn't my body just *work*?

Because I'd felt how badly Gideon wanted this. Every

tremor, every curse, every desperate roll of his hips. All those times we'd had sex before, he'd wanted *this*. And I couldn't give it to him.

Panic seized me, and I forced myself to wipe my eyes before lifting my head. I forced a smile. "It's fine."

"I hurt you," he said. He tried to pull me down to hold me, but I shook my head.

"It's fine," I repeated, and Gideon glared at me. "I'm sorry for stopping."

"I told you to stop me anytime," he snarled, angry. At me? At himself? I couldn't tell.

I gulped, then reached down to where he was still hard. "I'll—"

"No."

I pulled my hand away from him, hurt. He didn't even want me to touch him now. I hadn't been able to have sex with him, and now he was angry. Pulling away. Recalculating how much sacrifice it would take to be with me. Reassessing whether he really wanted *this* for the rest of his life.

My breath hitched, and then Gideon's arms were around me. He held me as I sobbed. As I tried to push him away. As I finally gave up and wet his chest with my tears. Finally, when the storm of emotion had passed, I found the courage to look up at his face.

He met my gaze calmly.

"I'm sorry," I whispered.

"For what, Sadie?"

"For stopping," I said, like it was obvious.

His scowl was deep, and it oddly made me feel better. "I

told you to stop me," he repeated in a growl. "How many times do I have to say it?"

"But..." I would *not* cry again. I bit my lip. "But you wanted to keep going."

"Not like *that*. Not when I was fucking *hurting* you."

"But you were enjoying yourself, and—"

"You think I *liked* causing you pain?" He was angry now, cheeks flushed red, muscles stone hard where they held me. "You think a fucking orgasm is worth *that*?"

I was at a loss. Because yes, history had taught me that my previous partners' orgasms *had* been worth the cost of my pain. Why would Gideon be any different?

Gideon must have seen how hard I was fighting my tears, because he clicked his tongue and gathered me in his arms. He held me until I softened, and until I finally fell asleep.

But deep in my heart, I couldn't shake the feeling that this was the beginning of the end.

GIDEON

I'd been a selfish piece of shit, and I was ashamed of myself. As Sadie slept beside me and her tears left traces of salt on my chest, I wondered if I'd just ruined everything. I'd hurt her, and I hadn't even noticed.

If she left after this, I would have only myself to blame.

We didn't try again. In fact, Gideon didn't initiate sex with me at all. He refused to continue with the bait plan and instead parked one of his brothers with me whenever I wanted to go out. I tried not to spiral about him wanting to avoid me and mostly failed.

I kept working on Lola's dress, because what else was I going to do? She'd still be going to homecoming, and making her dress was the only thing that felt good anymore.

Sunday lunch was the same as always, with a little more spiciness due to the Mr. Titty business. Gideon loomed beside me, silent. Glenn, Connor, and Lola were chastened and reserved. I suspected Bennett found the whole thing hilarious and was waiting for the minimum amount of time to pass so he could start cracking jokes about it. I felt like an anthropologist observing a clan from the outside.

Always on the outside.

Day bled into day, and I felt the fraying of the threads

that held us together. When I kissed him, Gideon kissed me back, and we did have sex, but it didn't feel the same. He was holding back. Sometimes it seemed like he was afraid of hurting me, checking in a thousand times if I told him I wanted to try a finger or a toy. But other times, I wondered if he'd realized what the future held if we were to stay together. What never having penetrative sex *really* meant for him.

Maybe he just wasn't that interested in me anymore.

Our sixth week of marriage started and plodded onward. On Friday, we would either decide to file the certificate or go our separate ways.

And I was still a coward, because I hadn't been able to broach the subject with Gideon at all. The sick feeling in my gut got stronger with every passing hour, sure that this was as close as I'd ever get to a happily-ever-after of my own.

By Thursday morning, I woke up and wondered if I'd imagined everything. The unbearable ache in my heart was my only evidence that at one point, I'd thought Marswood Harbor was forever. I'd thought Gideon was forever.

If I stayed here, I'd have to take Etta's investment offer. I couldn't afford to reopen my business without her, and there weren't exactly a ton of jobs in town.

But if she gave me money, I'd be beholden to her. If Gideon told her he was sick of me, she could ruin my life.

Gideon snored softly as I extricated myself from his hold. I'd tossed and turned for the first half of the night and didn't feel particularly rested. Bleary, I pawed at the nightstand and found my phone. My vision cleared as I saw a notification on the screen that caught my interest.

It was from my nearly dead business email; an inquiry had come in from my website.

SUBJECT: Need three wedding dresses (URGENT)

Leaning on my elbow with my back to Gideon, I swiped at my phone and read the email. My heart began to thrum. A big-name wedding coordinator had emailed me on behalf of one of her clients. The bride's dresses had been flown in from Paris and had been destroyed in shipping. They were unrecoverable, and the original designers wouldn't be able to get new ones made in time. She was desperately contacting any designer local to Manhattan for replacements.

The amount of money she was offering was eye watering. Nearly triple what I would have charged for each dress...and she wanted three of them. It was enough money to lease Life's a Stitch, give me some wiggle room to re-establish my brand online, and start over.

Without Etta.

Without strings.

With the most precious thing of all—*options*.

All at once, I realized what I wanted, and it wasn't to slink away and lick my wounds. I wanted Gideon. I wanted to stay and fight for him, for us, because he was the love of my life.

And I wanted my business. The magic hadn't gone out of weddings for me—it had been hidden beneath layers of insecurity and angst. I'd been so worried about myself, my marital status, and my failures that I'd forgotten what brought me joy.

I loved making women feel beautiful. I loved coming up with an idea and seeing it come to life on a dress form and then on a bride. I loved teary hugs and follow-up photos from my brides' big days.

And maybe I could expand. Seeing Lola light up had been the first thing that had made me feel like I was part of this town. Like maybe I had a future here, as part of this family. I had Ida Gretzinger's phone number, and I'd been working on that idea of a wedding dress retreat.

My business had failed once, but I could try again. I could lease the place, renovate it, and start over. The overheads would be a fraction of what they'd been before.

And if Etta refused to lease the space without the investment deal, I'd find some other space that she didn't own. Because I'd have enough money to make it on my own!

This time, I wouldn't be pursuing this business because it was a desperate attempt at fitting in with my family. After all, hadn't I found a new family? One who supported me instead of cutting me down. Who protected me instead of judging me. A clan who rallied around me at the first sign of trouble.

I typed a quick answer. I was available and I would drop everything to make this bride three incredible dresses. The wedding planner replied in an instant; she must have been under an immense amount of stress and tied to her phone. She'd call me in a few hours when she was with the bride, and we'd go over the particulars.

"What is it?" Gideon's voice was groggy with sleep.

I lay back on the pillows and looked at him, smiling. "I just got a request for three wedding dresses," I told him, giddiness making me wiggle. "A rush job. Huge."

The sleep cleared from his eyes. "In the city?"

I paused at the harshness of his tone. "Well, yes. I'd have to go and meet her, and if it's a rush job, I'd probably have to use suppliers and seamstresses I already have relationships with. And I'll have to find somewhere to work. Maybe a hotel, or I could see if I could get a short-term lease somewhere..." I trailed off. When Gideon didn't answer, I arched my brows. "Are you... mad?"

He sat up and swung his legs over the side of the bed. "I'm not mad. You need to do what you need to do," he answered. His back shifted as he moved, one hand reaching over to massage the stiff scar tissue on his left shoulder. He didn't turn to look at me.

"Gideon."

"I get it," he answered, standing.

"Gideon, stop. I'm not *leaving*. It's just—it's a huge job! It would be enough to restart my business."

He grabbed a T-shirt from the back of the armchair in the corner and pulled it on. His head popped through, and he ran a hand through his hair. He still hadn't met my eyes. "It's good," he said. "I'm happy for you."

My chest went cold as he walked out the door. I listened to him moving in the kitchen—the clink of a mug, the gurgle of the coffee machine, the scrape of a pan against the gas-fired range—and I fought against the panic that tried to build inside me.

This was his way out. Out of this marriage. Out of the contract that his grandmother had blackmailed him into. Now he could cut me loose and not feel bad about it, because I wouldn't be homeless and destitute. This client would give me a cushion.

If he wanted me to stay, he'd tell me. But he just...walked away. He was icing me out. Taking his chance to dissolve this marriage that was more of an inconvenience to him than anything. Had he ever really wanted me? Or had this just been a distraction to him? After that awful night, had he realized we had no future?

It was so familiar I started to laugh. Yes, putting his dick in my vagina *was* that big a deal. How had I believed it wasn't? How had I believed all his lovey-dovey words about just loving to make me orgasm? No one loved to make me orgasm! That wasn't the way sex worked. That wasn't the way relationships worked!

I had nothing to offer him, and now he was done.

Throat tight, I closed my eyes. I was *so sick* of feeling insecure. But how could I help it, when I was hit with rejection every time I thought I found The One?

On soft feet, I padded to the kitchen. The toaster popped, and Gideon slid a buttered piece of toast and a mug of coffee toward me, then turned his back on me to fix his own breakfast. There was a huge lump in my throat, and I stared at the mug without seeing anything.

"When do you leave?" Gideon finally asked, and he turned to look at me. His expression was stony, his eyes cold.

I flinched. "I haven't—I need to call the wedding coordinator and get more details."

He nodded. "It's probably the logical thing to do. We still don't know who keyed your car and spray-painted the cottage. If you leave, the threats will stop."

"Gideon, I'm not—" I frowned. "I'm not *leaving*. Unless... that's what you want?" My voice squeaked on the question.

My husband's expression didn't change. Could I even call him my husband? We'd had a sham of a wedding ceremony, and the wedding certificate was stashed away in Etta Mars's home. It wasn't real. Gideon had never actually wanted to file the certificate. He was just running out the clock so he could keep his business and his bachelorhood.

Gideon finally shrugged. "You need to do what's best for you, Sadie. I'm not going to stop you."

I stared at him, blinking. "What does that mean, exactly?"

His phone chimed. We both glanced at where it lay on the countertop, and Gideon reached over to grab it. Because of course he did. I mattered so little to him that he would use any excuse to get out of this conversation—out of my life.

Then he straightened, frowning, so I asked, "What is it?"

"Ida Gretzinger just texted," he replied. "Two people booked into a room at The Pier last night, and this morning they've been asking about you. She said they just ordered breakfast so if we head over now, we can probably catch them before they leave."

I didn't want to go see who had come looking for me. I wanted to stay right here and talk to Gideon until we figured this out.

But what was there to figure out?

I'd known the truth that night last week, when my body had failed me once again: It had been the beginning of the end. As soon as my body malfunctioned, the clock started ticking. It had taken three and a half years for Henry to pull the plug, but Gideon would be much more efficient. We were already over.

The pain was so huge that I went numb.

Five minutes later, we had our teeth brushed, our clothes on, and we were out the door. Gideon took the stairs two at a time as I hurried to catch up. He barely let me get my seatbelt on before accelerating out of his parking spot and turning in the direction of The Pier.

"You don't have to go to this trouble," I said, my casual tone a shock even to my ears. "I know my being here has been a huge inconvenience."

He didn't deny it. Instead he explained, "They threatened and vandalized you while you were in my town. I'm not going to let that slide."

I was surprised that I could actually feel worse than I had a few seconds earlier, and it was because of six little words in his sentence: *While you were in my town.*

Would he care if I was threatened again when I left?

I stared out the window, already knowing the answer to that question. It hardly sounded like he cared about me at all. He was just angry that someone had dared challenge him in the town that bore his family name.

GIDEON

My knuckles were white on the steering wheel. I was a fool for thinking she'd stay. Sadie had been desperate when she'd signed up to marry me, and she was taking the first lifeline tossed her way. She couldn't wait to get out, to get away from me.

Ice formed over my heart and spread to every inch of my body, muffling the world around me. I never should've let her in. I only had myself to blame.

The day got worse.

My mother jumped up from her chair as soon as I walked into the dining room at The Pier. Sun slanted in through the big windows, blinding me. But I still heard her.

"My baby is married!" she screamed, then did her signature arms-flailing jog-dance toward me. She wrapped me in a tight hug as I stared over her shoulder at my father, who smiled at me like he'd never been prouder.

"Introduce us!" my mother cried, pulling back. She turned to Gideon—and froze.

It only lasted a second, but it made me feel like dying. Her gaze caught on his scars, and her expression went stiff. The shock and disgust were clear.

Then, a second later, it was all wiped away with a too-bright smile. "Welcome to the family!" She hugged a tense Gideon, whose jaw bulged as he clenched his teeth. My dad gave me a one-armed hug, his eyes scanning my husband. He took in the breadth of his shoulders, his dark hair, his skin.

His scars.

My father stared at Gideon's forearm, frowning. I wanted to snap at him the way I'd snapped at Ivan Popov, but my tongue was heavy and my mind was dulled. Everything felt strange.

Why were my parents here?

When my mother let go of Gideon, my father stepped in to shake his hand. Mom took the opportunity to lean into me and say, "What happened to his arm? Are you sure about this, Sadie?"

"*Mom,*" I hissed, cheeks burning with shame. Who was she to judge Gideon? And simply because of his scars?

She gave me an exaggerated shrug. "I'm just saying, Sadie. After all this time, this is who you end up with?"

I could feel Gideon stiffen even more beside me. I put my hand on his back, and he flinched away from me. The cracks in my heart grew wider.

"Honey," my dad interjected. "Shall we?" He tilted his head toward the grand piano looming in the corner of the room.

"Absolutely not," I snapped, but my parents were already at the instrument. My father opened the key cover with a flourish, and my mother grabbed a microphone from a stand. She flicked the switch on it, then tested it by tapping. The sound echoed in the dining room, and everyone who hadn't already been staring definitely was now.

"We can go," I said to Gideon, tugging his arm.

His face was carved from stone. He shook his head. "I want to ask them if they know who might be threatening you."

"What?" I asked, frowning. "How would they know anything?"

The opening notes my dad played on the piano made my stomach drop. I hissed at my mom and made a neck-chopping sign. She smiled at me and waved, then put the microphone up to her lips and sang, "*Oh*-oh, *oh*-oh, *oh*-oh, oh-oh-oh!"

My dad accompanied her, his usual besotted wedding singer expression on full display as he beamed at my mother from his seat on the piano bench. The notes of Beyoncé's "Single Ladies" echoed in the dining room. My mother danced the classic "Single Ladies" dance as she sang, and I imagined my flesh melting into a gruesome puddle on The Pier's patterned carpet, a fitting end to a pathetic life.

Gideon stared at my parents, then at me. If the past week of distance hadn't convinced him, and this morning's tension hadn't done it, my parents surely had pushed him over the edge. He would never want to be with me. It had been foolish to think he ever would.

A pit opened up in my stomach. This really was the end. There was no coming back from this. Gideon had realized that I was more trouble than I was worth. He'd decided to let these six weeks come to an end so he could keep his business while we went our separate ways.

And now his decision was obviously the right one, because who the hell would want to marry into *this* family?

I burned as my parents performed, turning as Mrs. Gretzinger came to stand next to me. She watched the show, then looked at me. "Do you know these people? They were asking about you."

"It's generous of you to pretend like you don't already know they're my parents," I replied.

Her lips twitched, and that made me feel a little better. "Would you like me to ask them to leave?"

"They'll tire themselves out soon," I said, shifting my gaze to watch them again. I hoped they would, anyway. Glancing at Gideon, I tried to read his expression and failed. He wouldn't acknowledge me, and he looked completely blank.

Finally, I marched out of the dining room and plonked myself down on a sofa in the lobby to wait. My eyes stung. My chest felt hollow and cold. My parents' arrival was a stark reminder of what my life had been like before I'd come to Marswood Harbor.

And now I would have to go back.

Gideon didn't follow until the sound of my parents' song died down and scattered applause took its place. A moment later, he walked out with them. "And you have no idea of anyone who might want to cause her harm?" he asked.

"Sadie? God, no! No one would even care enough to want to hurt her!" My mother let out a laugh as she shook her head. "If you only knew the number of boyfriends who had dumped her. None of them were jilted lovers who wished her ill. They mostly just wanted to get away from her." She clapped her hands and turned to me. "Now," she said, smiling. "We've booked a new place for our little family shindig this year, seeing as we needed more room. Everyone is *so* excited to meet you, Gideon. Aren't they, Barry?"

"They surely are," my father replied, nodding.

And wasn't it the funniest thing, that the family ski trip would be the thing that put me over the edge? Not losing the love of my life. Not the thought of leaving the town that had become my home. Not the certainty that I had never been—and would never be—enough.

It was the fucking pull-out couch that did it.

"No," I said, standing up from my seat.

My mother blinked at me. "Excuse me?"

"I'm not going."

"Honey—"

"I'm not, Mom. I don't care if I get a real bed in a real bedroom this time. I'm sick of being treated like I'm inferior."

"We never—"

"I'm not going!" My voice echoed in the lobby, shrill.

"Honey, you don't have to be *embarrassed* just because your husband is, you know…"

"Oh my God! I'm not embarrassed by his scars! I'm embarrassed by *you*!"

My mother reared back, gasping like I'd slapped her. Her lips twisted, and she looked me up and down like I was worse than dog shit smeared on the bottom of her shoe. "I don't know what I did to deserve you, Sadie."

"Funny. I was just thinking the same thing."

She spluttered, then turned to my father, who put his arm around her and gave me a disapproving look. "Really, Sadie, after we came all this way—"

My mother sniffled and looked at Gideon. "You can do better," she told him. "In case you were thinking you had to settle because of your…" She gestured toward his neck and body.

It was so shocking that I laughed. And it wasn't shocking at all. Because hadn't that been exactly the type of thing she said about me all the time? That it was no surprise I wasn't married. That I would never find someone if I kept acting the way I did. That the problem was me, me, me.

And I realized it wasn't Henry who had taken a chisel to my self-esteem. It was my mother. She'd bullied me from the time I was a child and made me feel like I was worthless. Henry hadn't caused those cracks; he'd simply exploited them.

My dad, sister, and brother had stood by and enabled her, because it was easier to watch my mother torment someone else than it was to be in her crosshairs.

I'd lived my entire life feeling like I wasn't good enough, and it had started with her.

I would never speak to her again.

A weight dropped from my shoulders. "Goodbye, Mother," I said, and I turned toward the exit and walked out. A gust of wind hit me as soon as I stepped outside, the chill of autumn already in the air. I welcomed it, turning into the wind as I inhaled. It was crisp and salty, and it froze the tears in my eyes before they had a chance to fall.

I would never be my mother's punching bag again. I would never go on another family vacation. And I would *never* sleep on a pull-out couch for as long as I fucking lived.

Gideon stalked behind me, saying nothing as we got into his car. I stared out the window, feeling light and heavy all at once. He turned on the car and cool air started coming in through the vents, but he didn't start driving.

"I'm really sorry," I said. "You shouldn't have had to listen to that. My mother is a bully."

"Nothing I haven't heard before." He pulled out of the lot and said nothing more.

"She's wrong, Gideon."

"She's not." He shrugged. "It is what it is. We both know you can do better than me."

A disbelieving laugh fell out of me. "Better than you? Are you serious right now?"

"Come on, Sadie. We don't look right with each other. Ivan said it himself. Beauty and the Beast."

"Ivan is an asshole. And so is my mother, by the way."

"Being an asshole doesn't mean you're a liar."

"This is ridiculous." I crossed my arms. "You're the most attractive man I've ever met, and you're talking like you're some kind of ogre. And even if you were an ogre, you think that's a dealbreaker! Do you think so little of me?"

Gideon just scoffed and put the car in gear. The chasm between us widened. I wanted to reach over and touch him, but I felt like I didn't have the right. We drove in silence all the way to the Marswood Security building. When Gideon turned off the engine, he finally looked at me.

"When do you leave?" The warmth had gone out of him. He looked at me like I was an employee, or a customer, or a stranger.

I met his gaze. I wanted to cry. "Can we talk about this? I feel like you're taking it the wrong way."

"I'm just asking you when you're leaving, Sadie." He sounded tired as he stared at the concrete wall in front of us.

My throat tightened. "I have a call with the bride and the planner later to hammer out the details. But probably tomorrow. The next day at the latest."

A muscle bulged in his jaw and was gone again. He nodded. "Okay."

I couldn't take this—couldn't take being iced out by the man I loved. Desperate, I told him, "It's the only way of saving the business. Otherwise I'd have to take your grandma's offer."

His brows tugged together, and he finally met my gaze again. "My grandma's offer?"

I'd never told him. Why hadn't I told him?

But the answer to that was easy—it was because I'd been petrified of hearing what he'd say about it. If he tried to tell me to refuse the deal, I would've taken it as him telling me he didn't want me to stay. And if he'd told me to take the deal, I would've worried that he wanted leverage over me, the way Henry had wanted leverage by becoming my main client stream.

I hadn't trusted him. Not fully. Not with this.

"Your grandma offered me an investment deal," I finally croaked. "She'd help me reopen the business and lease me Life's a Stitch for an ownership stake."

His face didn't move an inch. His voice was flat. "It's what she does. What did you tell her?"

"That I'd think about it. The deal was contingent on us filing the wedding certificate, so I'm guessing it's a nonissue now."

Gideon flinched. Frowned. "Is that"—he cleared his throat—"Is that what this has been about?"

"What do you mean?"

"Is that why you've been acting like you're into me?"

I threw my hands up like I was Tim Gunn seeing a horrifying creation in the workroom on Project Runway. "First of all, *acting like I'm into you?*"

"You just wanted to get your business off the ground again. This had nothing to do with me." His lips curled, disgusted, as his right hand slid over his scarred left forearm. The signet ring glinted on his pinky finger.

"Okay, now I'm offended," I snapped. "I *am* into you. I have been into you since the moment I saw you. I...I—"

Even now, I couldn't say it. Why couldn't I say it? Why couldn't I tell this man that I loved him, that I saw a life with him, that I wanted everything with him?

He scoffed, disgusted.

I changed tack. "And I didn't even want to take your grandma's deal!"

"Because you didn't want to be tied to this place. You want 'options.'"

"Of course I want fucking options! I'm not stupid!"

"So go to Manhattan and make dresses for that bride." He looked at me like none of the past six weeks had happened. "See if you feel like coming back when you're done."

I opened my mouth. Closed it. Suddenly, the enormity of this fight felt like it sat in the middle of my chest. I couldn't breathe. "Do you..." I sucked in a wheezy breath. "Do you *want* me to come back?"

"What kind of question is that?"

"Ever since that night last week, you've been pulling away." The words burst out of me, and tears quickly followed. I brushed them aside as I said, "When I couldn't—when we couldn't have sex. You realized what it means to be with me. What you're giving up by being with me. I've been a burden and an inconvenience to you since I got here."

His fury was a physical thing. It pressed against my skin, choked me as I tried to inhale. "If that's what you think, then it's probably a good thing you're leaving town."

"Tell me you want me to stay," I begged, choking on the words.

"You need to do what's best for you, Sadie," he replied, then slipped out of the car and slammed the door.

I watched his retreat, and something tore in my chest. I felt it rip wide open, felt the pain of the tear and the jagged edges it left behind.

He was just another person who was ready to walk away from me. Another person who rejected me once they knew the real me. Another person who reminded me that I just didn't measure up. I wouldn't ever be good enough as I was.

I'd always been an outcast in my family. I'd felt like I had to make up for my flaws with my previous partners. And now, when I thought I'd finally found somewhere safe—some*one* safe—Gideon had pushed me away.

It was all well and good to be angry at me. But he couldn't just say he wanted me to stay? He couldn't tell me that he cared about me? Not even once?

Suddenly, I couldn't take it anymore. I rushed up to the apartment and started tossing things in my bag. My vision blurred with tears. If I stopped moving, I'd collapse. Once I'd cleared all my stuff out of the apartment, I got my car from the lot and went to the cottage. I needed to get out. Needed to run.

All my life, I'd been made to feel small. I was worthless and broken. Undeserving.

Maybe that was how things would always be. Maybe this was the reality of my life, and wishing for more was just a recipe for heartbreak. A sob tore out of me as I hauled my big suitcase out of the closet in the bedroom, keeping my eyes off the bed where Gideon and I had shared so much.

I'd actually thought he cared about me. I'd actually believed that he would see past my physical shortcomings and love *me*. Actually thought he'd make me feel safe and loved and cherished. How naive. How foolish. How fucking stupid. Why would he be any different from any man who came before?

With my arm, I scooped all my toiletries off the vanity into a bag, then tossed it into my suitcase. I grabbed my laundry from the hamper and stuffed it in a plastic bag, then struggled with the zipper as I tried to close it up. Frustrated when it wouldn't close, I opened the bag and wrenched out the sketchbook that had been catching on the zipper. Stupid thing. I didn't need this anyway. It wasn't like I'd be able to save my business after all this, new client or no.

Marching to the kitchen, I opened the cupboard under the sink to pull out the garbage, and my gaze snagged on the multitude of takeaway cups from Knead More Bread.

My matcha lattes.

Green liquid pooled at the bottom of one of the cups, and my bottom lip began to wobble. Gideon had gone out of his way to buy matcha powder for me and give it to Caroline, just so I could have my favorite drink when I moved to his town. It was the most thoughtful thing anyone had done for me.

In the past week, Gideon hadn't bought me a single one.

My legs collapsed from under me, and I sat on the kitchen floor. I buried my head in my hands and cried.

GIDEON

The world was a flat, gray wasteland. I'd seen this coming all along, and yet my devastation turned my lungs to stone, made it impossible to take a full breath. She was leaving me, and once she was gone, she wouldn't be back.

No matter what she said, if she drove out of this town, it would be the last time I ever saw her.

My mother had left me as a child. My father had died when I was on the cusp of young adulthood. My fiancée had abandoned me when I was at my lowest. My grandmother had blackmailed me. Lola, Glenn, and Connor had proven that even after I'd given everything to my family, they just didn't care about giving anything back.

Even after all that, I'd let her in. Allowed her to hurt me like this.

I deserved all the pain I got for being such a fucking fool.

TWENTY-EIGHT
SADIE

My last stop was Life's a Stitch. I unlocked the door and stepped inside, trying to ignore the lump in my throat at the sight of the sewing machines sitting dormant on the worktables.

This could've been my fresh start.

But maybe that had just been a silly dream. Nothing good could come of an arranged marriage. I'd come to this town out of desperation; that was no way to start a new life. I shuffled over to my own machine and started packing it up in its case. I moved on to my sewing paraphernalia next: pins, needles, measuring tapes, shears, seam rippers, trim, extra muslin fabric, zips, fasteners, and all the other items that needed to be put away.

When I was finished, I looked at Lola's dress hanging on the dress form. I'd have to finish it in the city and ship it over. She could find someone else to do alterations if needed.

The practical side of me knew it was the best way forward, but the thought still sent a dagger of pain stabbing through my chest. Creating Lola's dress had reignited my love of design. It had made me feel part of the town, the family. It had been the first thing that had felt *good*, other than being in Gideon's arms.

All that was gone now.

"Knock knock!"

I turned to see Caroline walking into the doorway carrying two mugs; one of them had a green tinge that told me she'd made me a matcha latte. She handed it over, and I wrapped my hands around the warm ceramic.

"You look like you're about to cry," she said.

"I am."

"Oh, God. Should I leave?"

I let out a watery laugh and shook my head. "I'll pull myself together."

Her gaze was incisive. "I noticed the bags in your car outside."

Bottom lip trembling, I nodded. "I'm leaving."

"Oh."

"It's not... It didn't work out with Gideon."

Caroline, my one good friend in the whole world, dropped her shoulders and sighed. "That sucks."

I huffed and sipped my drink. The taste of it made me want to cry; the only reason she'd been able to make it was because Gideon had bought the supplies. "It's okay. I got a big commission from a bride in the city. It'll be enough to get the business going again."

"Get it going...over there? Not here?"

I frowned. "I can't stay here. Gideon and I broke up."

"Last I checked, it's a free country. You can stay here if you want to."

"Come on." I scoffed.

"What! The Marses might own half this town, but we're not their loyal subjects. Make your life where you want, girl. You've got free will. Right?"

I stared at her. She stared right back. "That would be so awkward."

"Never stopped me." She dropped into one of the chairs next to the work table and it rolled back a few feet while she kicked her legs up.

"What happened between you and the Mars family, anyway?"

"No," she said, lifting a finger. "We're not getting distracted here. You're telling me why you need to run away when you've got a perfectly good shop right here. And the world is online, isn't it? So you can still sell your dresses all over the country while enjoying the affordable rent that Marswood Harbor provides."

"I'm not running away."

"Girl."

I huffed, staring at the wall. "I might be running away."

"It's kind of your thing."

"What the hell is that supposed to mean?" I snapped, whirling around to face her again.

Caroline arched her brows. "Oh, wow. Are we in our first fight?"

"I hate you, you know."

"No you don't. And yeah, you're running away. You ran from Manhattan thinking Gideon would save you from yourself. But you know what they say"—she smiled sardonically and swept her hands in an arch—"'Wherever you go, there you are.'

So you can run to the other side of the world and it won't change a damn thing. Why go through all the trouble? Just stay here to deal with your shit. Save yourself the hassle of moving somewhere new. Besides, I was just getting used to seeing a new face around town."

"I don't have 'shit' to deal with."

"Oh, so we're in *denial*, denial."

"Have I mentioned how much I hate you?"

Caroline gave me that witchy, evil smile of hers, and I couldn't help the laugh that fell out of me. She pushed herself up to her feet, set her mug down on the table, and came toward me. Her hands were heavy when they landed on my shoulders. "Sadie," she said, becoming serious. "Stop running. Face the big monster right here, where you're strongest."

"The big monster" was my own inadequacy. It was easier to make myself smaller instead of reaching out and grabbing life with both hands, shaking it, and seeing what fell out.

What if I really wasn't good enough? All the men in my life had been right to dump me. My mother had been right to disparage me. I was lacking in all ways—physical, mental, and emotional—and it wasn't going to get better.

The thoughts felt like the truth.

But Caroline was staring at me with her glimmering hazel eyes, and I wondered if this particular truth was mutable. What if I was enough...for me?

I *liked* my body. I liked my drive and my determination. I liked that I'd been able to start over multiple times, pick myself up after breakups, job losses, and business failures. I liked that I still believed in love, even when love kicked me around and left me for dead.

"There she is," Caroline murmured, smiling. "You don't need a man to give you permission to step into your power."

I straightened, then wrapped my arms around my friend. My only friend. My best friend. She squeezed me in a tight hug, then stepped back and said, "Should we go egg the Marswood Security building later? All that glass...it would be impossible to clean up."

I laughed, and then was mortified when it turned into a sob. Caroline made a horrified noise, and I wasn't sure if it was because of my distress or just the fact that I was crying in her vicinity.

"Sorry," I said, wiping tears that wouldn't stop coming. "It's just—I want to stay, but I don't know if I can stand seeing Gideon around."

"You're in love with him."

"Unfortunately," I blubbered.

"And, what? He's not in love with you?"

The incredulity in her voice made me pause. I shrugged. "No? He told me to leave."

"Oh my God." She rolled her eyes. "He is dumb as a box of rocks."

"Hey," I protested weakly.

"Sorry. He's really great except when he acts like he doesn't have a brain."

"If he wanted me to stay, he would've told me."

Caroline clicked her tongue, grabbed me by the arms, and shook me. "Sadie! Get it together! The man ran into a burning building to save three teenagers who thought throwing paint thinner around and then setting it on fire was a good idea! This is the level of people we're dealing with in this town! He wouldn't ask you to stay if he thought you could do better by leaving."

I reared back. "No. No, he was very clear. He iced me out! He told me that there was no future for me here."

Caroline gave me a flat look. "Right. Now say that again, but slower."

There was a long pause as we stared at each other. Finally, I whispered, "Oh."

My best friend patted me on the head and said, "At least you figured it out in the end."

"He doesn't hate me."

"The man has been obsessed with you since your wedding day. Remember when he chased you into Rock Bottom and threatened to rip Cash's arms off for touching your hair? He *loves* you, loves you."

"Well, he could have told *me* that."

She just laughed.

I started for the door, then stopped. Narrowed my eyes. Turned around to grab my purse, then marched to the exit.

"Where are you going?" Caroline asked. "And do you have protection?"

"Funny," I said, ushering her out of the shop. "I'm not going to talk to Gideon. I'm going to talk to his grandmother."

***

I FOUND Etta sitting between two giant palms in a sun-drenched corner of her solarium. She greeted me with a smile, then waved at her housekeeper, who brought us coffee and cake on a silver tray.

"You're here to discuss Life's a Stitch," she guessed.

"Yes," I replied. "I'll take the lease, but I will decline your generous business offer. Thank you, but I've decided to go it alone."

"I see." She picked up the delicate china cup and took a sip of coffee. "Have you found another investor?"

"I'm self-funding," I told her. "I need to leave town for a while to complete a few projects for a client, and then I'll reopen Life's a Stitch when I return."

Her brows jumped. "Ah. Gideon is aware of this plan, I assume."

"He is," I hedged. "And that brings me to the other thing I wanted to talk to you about."

Etta watched me with those piercing blue eyes of hers, shrewd and all-seeing. Her lips curled into a humorless smile. She was a raptor, ready to dive down for the kill. "Go on, dear," she said in a mild voice. "Tell me what's on your mind."

I took a deep breath—and spoke.

DETERMINATION WAS a strong tailwind that propelled me back into town. I made only one last stop before returning to Life's a Stitch. It was surprisingly quick but very necessary. Gideon would just have to deal with the consequences.

Once that was done, I continued on my way. I had sewing supplies to pack and a man to confront. Driving down Main Street sent elation floating through me. I loved this town. I loved the shabby vacant shops and the overgrown median. I loved how hard the residents tried to keep things together. I loved the terrible fair and the devil geese. I loved the patches of fresh paint that Lola, Glenn, and Connor had started brushing over their graffiti.

And I loved Gideon. His silent brooding. His big, beating heart. His strength. His kindness.

He was the man I would spend my life with, and that was just the way things were going to be. I was done making myself smaller because I was afraid of taking up space.

Gideon had told me—and shown me—that my vaginismus wasn't even close to a dealbreaker for him. I realized, as I loaded my machine into the back of my car, that the only person it had been a dealbreaker for was *me*. I'd used it as a shield to keep him at arm's length.

Not anymore.

If I wanted Gideon to trust that I would stay here for him, with him, then I had to trust him too. Trust that he would stay with me even if my vaginismus never got better. Even if I got sick someday in a more serious way. If I decided to change careers. If I got pregnant.

The only way this relationship would work was if we each took one big step toward each other, over the swirling abyss of the unknown.

I was ready. The question was... was he?

With trembling hands, I texted Gideon to ask him where he was. I even sent the dreaded, "We need to talk," and I didn't even feel bad about it.

Then I slipped my phone back in my pocket and re-entered Life's a Stitch. The last thing I had to pack up was Lola's dress. I carefully folded the muslin draft and set it in a bag with the pink silk. I pinned Lola's measurements to the side of the fabric bag, then took one last look around the room to make sure I had everything I needed.

The door opened behind me, bringing in a gust of cold air. I straightened, heart thumping, and took a moment to prepare myself for the conversation that would change the course of my life. Gideon was here.

I turned.

Frowned.

Froze.

Because it wasn't Gideon standing silhouetted in the doorway. It took me a few seconds to recognize him, even though my body's primal reaction was instant. Cold fear iced my spine. The back of my neck prickled. My legs tensed, ready to run.

With a gun clutched in his right hand, wearing old jeans, a dirty hoodie, and a blue baseball cap, and his beard grown out to a scraggly, graying mess, Henry looked like a stranger.

I blinked—and looked at his hat again. I recognized that hat. I'd seen it at The Pier during my very first week in town.

Horror and fear shocked me into inaction. Henry had been here the whole time.

"Hello, beautiful," he said, giving me an awful smile. His eyes were fevered, and his hands trembled as he gestured toward me with the gun, then used it to point at the door. "It's time for you to come home."

Sadie's ring waited for me on the bedside table at the cottage. She was gone.

After filling the home—and my life—with love and laughter and light, she'd taken everything and left. Just like I knew she would.

Well, not everything. When I pulled open the closet, I found a garment bag hanging on its own. With a tug, I unzipped it and let her wedding dress spill out over my fingers. A sound stuck halfway between a grunt and a whine escaped my throat as pain slashed across my chest.

It was as if she'd wanted to leave all the evidence of our marriage behind. Pretend it had never happened.

What had I expected? I slid the mirrored closet door closed and was confronted with my reflection. Ugly, scarred, disfigured reflection. It was just like Ivan Popov had said: It made no sense for someone like me to end up with someone like her. The old man had simply been saying the quiet part out loud.

Disgusted, I turned away, grateful when my phone chimed. I needed any distraction I could get.

But it was her. Sadie's name illuminated my screen, her text message saying she wanted to talk. What the hell did we have to talk about? Why couldn't she just leave? We'd both be better off when she was gone. I could focus on my company, and Sadie could find someone else. Someone better.

I stalked back out of the bedroom, ignoring the message.

Anger was a helpful buffer against the pain of my heartbreak. I used it as I grabbed the throw pillows she'd made and tossed them in the trash.

My phone rang, and I ignored it. I kept prowling around the cottage, remembering the way Sadie had looked when she sat and sewed, or how she'd laughed at one of my jokes when she lay on the couch just there, or how I'd kissed her in the kitchen against that cabinet, or how she'd moaned when I'd made her come in the shower and the vanity and the bed.

The vibration of my phone in my pocket only angered me. Would she not just leave me alone? She must've called a dozen times. How much clearer could I make it that I just wanted her gone?

Finally, I was in the bedroom again, staring at her wedding dress. She'd looked like a goddess that day, and I'd known I didn't deserve her. I never would.

I sat on the bed, staring at the white fabric, remembering how it felt to have her in my arms. To feel the weight of her fingers ghosting over my scars. She never shied away. She never pretended they didn't exist. She was the only person who looked at me and accepted me the way I was now.

My family still treated me like the old Gideon. The man from *before the fire. They pretended my scars didn't matter, but they did. My scars had fundamentally changed the way the world saw me. The way I saw myself.*

Sadie had seen me and loved me. All the broken pieces of her had fit into the hole in my heart like the two of us had been made for each other. And suddenly I didn't care whether I deserved her or not, because I still wanted her. Because she was mine.

My woman.

My future.

My wife.

If she didn't want to stay here, I'd follow her to the city. I'd follow her to the end of the earth, because life made no sense without her in it.

I huffed to myself. Yeah, we had to talk. I had to tell her that she could do whatever the hell she wanted as long as I could be right there beside her for every minute of it.

My phone buzzed again. A text.

The woman just wouldn't leave me alone—because she knew it too. We belonged beside each other. The world made no sense unless we were together.

But when I pulled my phone out of my pocket, it wasn't Sadie's name on the screen. All three of my brothers had called me, as well as my cousin Fletcher and one of my employees. And, strangely, the most recent three calls had been from Cash Bridges.

Something had happened.

Heading outside toward my vehicle, I glanced over the tree-tops and felt my gut clench. A plume of smoke marred the sky. Something in town was on fire. Dread walked down my spine on spindly, cold legs. Even from here, I could smell the smoke. I choked on it, though it was only the ghost of a scent. The ghost of a memory.

My phone was still in my hand, so when Jack called, it only took a flick of my thumb to answer. "Yeah," I said.

"Life's a Stitch is on fire," Jack replied without preamble. "Sadie's car is outside with all her stuff in it. We can't find her, and she isn't answering her phone."

My vision went funny, tunneling in the middle and fuzzy around the edges. My steps were awkward and too heavy as I stumbled to my car. I barely heard the engine start before I was tearing down the driveway in a spray of gravel.

She'd wanted to talk, and I'd ignored her. Was she still in the building?

Fear tasted like ash and accelerant on my tongue. By the time I slammed on the brakes outside the seamstress's shop, my back was soaked in sweat and my scars felt like they'd tightened to the point of pain. The heat of the fire assaulted me as soon as I opened my door. It prickled on my front, uncomfortable, familiar.

Time slowed, and I took in the scene in a single glance.

Fire licked at the upper windows like awful tongues. A dull roar filled my ears, and it might've been the fire or just the memory of those three trips I made into the burning warehouse five years ago. My breaths were fast, and cold sweat drenched my back.

Someone was screaming my name, and then all the windows in the building exploded out from the heat of the fire. I lifted my arm to shield myself, feeling the pressure of debris hitting my scars but not the pain. Sirens screamed in the distance, but it had to be cops because the closest fire department was miles away.

The building would be ash and rubble by the time the firefighters arrived.

Caroline Black sprayed the neighboring building with a garden hose. She yelled at me, but the words didn't register. Her eyes were wide with panic.

I shifted my gaze back to the building, knowing what I had to do.

All of my worst nightmares were rolled into one. I had to run into that building, feel the searing heat of the fire against my skin, and save the woman I loved. I had to endure more injuries, more destroyed skin and flesh, more weeks of recovery in the hospital, because she was in there. I couldn't lose her.

I had no choice. There was no other option. I had to go in.

Time snapped back to real speed, and I started sprinting. I made it three steps before a motorcycle blocked my path, screeching to a stop close enough that I felt the heat of the exhaust pipe against my calf when I stumbled into it.

Cash Bridges opened his mouth, and I saw red. I grabbed the man by his stupid leather jacket and hauled him off his bike while Cash yelled. I threw him to the ground, but I didn't have time to take care of Cash properly. I'd punch the biker in the mouth when Sadie was out of that building and in my arms.

Cash kept yelling, and I ignored him. I made it to the door, ducking as flames gusted out.

"I know where she is!" Cash yelled, and I whirled.

There must have been death in my eyes—there was certainly murder in my heart—because Cash scrambled to his feet and lifted his palms.

"She's not in there," Cash told me.

I didn't believe him. Why the hell would Cash care? Was this a trick? Did he want her to die in there?

"She's not in there," Cash repeated, calm and certain. It sounded like the truth, but I couldn't think straight.

"Where. Is. My. Wife." My voice was inhuman. I didn't recognize it. I felt like I was going to burst out of my skin at any second.

"Some asshole with a gun hauled her into a car and drove off. I've got two guys on her tail." Cash looked at the motorcycle that had tumbled to the ground when I'd pulled him off it. Cash gestured to the bike and said, "What the hell, man."

I grabbed the lapels of the leather jacket again. "If you don't tell me where my wife is in the next three seconds, you won't live to see the fourth."

Cash lifted his gaze to meet my eyes. His smile was cold and calculating, and he said, "I'll take you right to her," he promised. "As long as you do something for me first."

"What do you want?"

"How about part with something you care about?" Cash gestured to the signet ring on my right hand.

The ring my father had worn every day of my life. The ring that made me feel close to my father, that reminded me that I'd promised to take care of everyone but myself. Giving it to Cash was giving up a part of my past. It was opening a door for Cash to exploit me if I ever wanted it back. The last piece of my father I had for myself.

I didn't even need to think about it for a second. "Fine," I said, tugging the ring off and slapping it into Cash's palm. "Let's go."

Cash's smile was a slash of white in his dark stubble. His eyes were hidden behind sunglasses, but I knew they were gleaming with satisfied greed.

"You're a bastard, Bridges."

"I know," Cash replied easily. "It runs in the family."

I got in my car and followed the motorcycle into the forest.

THIRTY
SADIE

Henry kept the gun in his lap as he drove. His movements were jittery, his gaze glassy. His pupils were pinpricks that gave me shivers every time he glanced at me.

"It didn't have to be this way," he repeated for the hundredth time. "If you'd just come back to me like you were supposed to, this wouldn't have had to happen. But you *left*, Sadie. You left and got married. You shouldn't have done that."

Fear choked me. We were almost at the I-95 freeway that would take us down the coast and out of Maine. The forest was thick and green on either side of the road, the sky blue. Summer beat down on us, incongruous with the horror icing my veins.

He'd taken my phone and set fire to Life's a Stitch. I'd seen it go up in flames as we drove away. I never should have gotten into the car, but he'd held a gun to my waist and prodded me with the end of the barrel. Now I regretted my cowardice.

"You broke up with me, Henry," I said with a voice that only trembled a little. My fear was so big it made everything go still.

"You told me you didn't want to be with me anymore. You kicked me out of our home."

"You were supposed to *come back to me*," he roared, leaning forward as he gripped the steering wheel. His hand tightened on the gun, and I closed my eyes to suck in a slow breath. "You were so mad at me for fucking Erin, but what was I supposed to do? Live without sex for the rest of my life? This would have been so easy if you just *listened* to me, Sadie."

Erin had been the coworker he wanted to open the relationship for. My mouth was dry as I sat utterly still, watching him take a bend a little too fast. The gravel on the shoulder crunched under our tires, and he let go of the gun to wrench the wheel with both hands.

"You deserved to be punished for being so stuck-up."

"That's why you broke up with me." I kept my voice low and calm, as much to keep my own panic at bay as to keep Henry calm.

He exhaled. "You were supposed to suffer, Sadie. And then you'd come back to me and everything would be okay. You'd see the error of your ways, and everything would be okay."

We slowed as we reached the exit that would take us onto the freeway. Henry shook his head and guided the car onto the main road, then jammed his foot on the accelerator to speed up.

He'd wanted me to suffer. He'd *planned* it so that I would be so broken and desperate that I would come back to him.

As if from a distance, I realized that I was no longer the same person I'd been when Henry and I were together. I wasn't a broken shell of a woman who accepted the scraps of a horrible man's affection. I wasn't the little girl who grew up as her mother's punching bag.

I was better. I was whole.

Part of that had been my own work, my own healing. I'd learned that I deserved better.

But a lot of it had been Gideon. He'd treated me like I was worthy of being spoiled. He'd given without asking for anything back. He'd cherished me, held me, loved me.

No one had ever treated me like that before. I squeezed my eyes shut and prayed that I would make it out of this alive just so I could see him again.

"When you lost the studio, I thought it was only a matter of time," Henry ranted, speeding down the freeway faster than was safe.

Something in the way he said that made me pause. It was in the tone of his voice—that gloating, condescending note that used to make me feel small.

Now it only made me feel angry.

"Henry," I started slowly. "Did you have anything to do with the failure of my business?"

His smile was a wide, awful thing. "It was so easy," he said, bursting with glee. "Almost all your clients came from me. All I had to do was stop referring people to you. And then a few phone calls to the right people, and I knew you'd need me again."

"You badmouthed me in the industry."

"Come on, Sadie. You needed me from the start. I *made* you. You didn't deserve to be successful without me."

It was a strange feeling to be horrified and relieved at the same time. Horrified because I was trapped in a speeding vehicle with a madman. Relieved because finally, the failure of my business made sense.

I hadn't had to close up shop because I was awful at wedding dress design or because I'd mismanaged my affairs. I'd had to shut down because I'd been sabotaged. Henry had systematically made me rely on him for everything, and then he'd pulled the rug out from under me. He wanted me to be utterly reliant on him.

My ex-fiancé gritted his teeth. "And then you left. And you got *married*." He let out a scoff, and I flinched. His condescension had been constant when we were together. I'd accepted all his scoffs, his judgment, his derision.

Now I knew I deserved better.

But I was still trapped in a car with him. I took a deep breath in an attempt to keep the panic from overwhelming me. My fingertips trembled and my legs were twitching and restless. I swallowed convulsively, trying to stay calm.

I had to get him to stop the car. It was over seven hours to New York City, and I wasn't sure we'd make it that far. Henry would snap at some point. I needed to save myself—and soon.

"You're right," I said softly, using the meek voice I remembered from our relationship. "I always needed you."

He relaxed slightly. "Yes," he said. "You did. You needed me, baby. You still do."

"I still do."

He nodded, relaxing.

Behind us, I heard the roar of an engine. Glancing in the side mirror, I saw two motorcycles speeding up the freeway toward us. Was that...?

No. It couldn't be. I squinted at the mirror, but Henry glanced over at me, and I had to look away.

"Thank you for coming to get me," I said.

Henry smiled. "You're welcome. I knew you'd understand."

"I need you more than ever," I continued.

The motorcycles got closer, their headlights shining in the mirror. But not close enough for me to be sure of who they were.

Not until the sign for a rest stop came into view, and one of the bikes accelerated so I could see the logo on the driver's jacket.

A flaming skull. One of Cash's men. He dropped back so all I could see was the shining headlight in the mirror.

Hope flared in my gut, but I squeezed my eyes shut and forced my voice to stay small. "Babe?" I asked.

"Yes, darling."

"I really need to pee."

Henry's jaw tightened. "Hold it in."

"I'm so sorry, babe. I know I'm such an inconvenience, but I really need to go."

"You just can't make life easy, can you?"

"I'll be so quick."

Henry glanced at me, assessing. I kept my gaze wide and guileless, reaching deep in my gut for all the old insecurities that no longer felt like they fit. I hoped they showed in my gaze. Hoped he saw the broken, small woman he wanted me to be.

And then he wrenched the wheel toward the rest stop exit.

I stared straight ahead, afraid to check and see if the motorcycles had followed. What if I was wrong? Why would Cash have sent his men after me, anyway?

But even if it wasn't him, this was my best chance at escape. I breathed in and out in slow cycles as Henry slowed, turned into the gas station lot, and parked in one of the spots to the side of the pumps.

He shoved his gun in the back of his pants as we got out, then circled the car and grabbed my shoulder to lead me inside. The gas station attendant looked bored. I tried to communicate with my eyes. Tried to mouth *help*, but he just grabbed the bathroom key when Henry asked for it.

"Bathroom's around the side," the attendant said, gesturing out the door and to the left. "Bring the key back when you're done."

My heart pounded. My throat was dry. I needed to run, but where would I go?

"Be quick," Henry said as we walked out through the sliding glass doors.

"I will be," I promised.

He unlocked the bathroom door and glanced inside. There was no window or other way to exit but the door. I had no phone and no way to call for help. He shoved me inside and closed the door, keeping the key. I still locked the door, even though he'd be able to barge in any minute.

Knowing I needed to stall, I sat on the toilet and made myself pee. Henry knocked impatiently. "Almost done!" I called back as I moved slowly through the necessary steps. I washed my hands thoroughly, my heart in my throat.

In the distance, I thought I heard the rumble of engines. Closing my eyes against the reflection in the grimy mirror, I prayed that I was right.

Then I walked out of the bathroom and faced the man who'd almost broken me. The man who *had* broken me.

The man who hadn't expected me to put myself back together again.

GIDEON

I saw her walk around the corner of the gas station. Saw the other man's hand gripping her shoulder too tight. Saw the way she jerked her head up when Cash and his men drove up and stopped around them to cut them off.

Then I was out of my car, and I was running.

Henry got so far as reaching behind to the gun at his back before my elbow shot out and smacked him in the face. There was a crunch, and blood sprayed everywhere. It was disgusting. One of the bikers tackled Henry to the ground and disarmed him. Then Gideon was there. He grabbed my cheeks, squeezed my shoulders, and let out a big, gusting exhale. His hair was a mess and his eyes were wild.

"You're okay," he breathed, and I wasn't sure if he was saying it to me or himself.

"I'm okay," I replied, but my bottom lip trembled.

His jaw went hard, and he turned to the man still pinned to the floor. The biker holding him down scuttled away, and Gideon lifted my ex up by his hair. Without hesitating, Gideon gave him two hard punches to the gut and one to the jaw. Henry crumpled into a bloody pile.

Then I was back in Gideon's arms, clutching his shirt. "I

don't endorse violence, but that was pretty good," I said in a trembling voice.

"Did he touch you?"

I shook my head. His hands coasted over my body, over my back and arms, like he wanted to make sure I was whole. His chest heaved, and I found myself comforting him instead of the other way around. Sirens screamed, and suddenly there were cops pulling into the lot.

But all I could look at was Gideon.

"You came for me."

"Always."

I sucked in a trembling breath, and then Gideon was holding me. "I'm sorry, Sadie. So sorry for how I acted. Sorry for pushing you away. Sorry for not begging you to stay."

"It's okay." I sniffled.

"It's not." He pulled away. Looked in my eyes. "I love you. You hear me? I love everything about you, and I'm pretty sure I've loved you since you gave me lip on our way up the aisle."

"I did not give you lip," I protested, a watery laugh bubbling out of me.

"I think part of me died in that fire, and you brought me back to life." His gaze was solemn, his hands soft as he cupped my face. "You're everything to me. The reason I get up in the morning. The light and air and water I need to survive. I need you. I love you. You're my everything. Forgive me for shutting you out. Forgive me for not getting on my knees and begging you to stay or take me with you. I love you, Sadie, and I always will."

Gideon dropped to his knees. Cops jogged up to us and hauled Henry to his feet before slapping him in cuffs. We ignored them. Gideon stared at me with those incredible blue eyes, so full of emotion, and said, "I can't live without you, Sadie. Marry me. Officially. Come back and file the wedding certificate with me, and then I'll follow you to the ends of the earth. Till death, baby. Forever."

Smiling through my tears, I said, "I can't do that."

Confusion drew his brows together. Devastation began to creep into his expression, and he opened his mouth—but I cut him off.

"I already filed it, Gideon." I could tell he didn't understand. My smile was wild, uncontrollable, as it spread over my lips. "I spoke to your grandmother earlier. Got the certificate. Filed it at Town Hall. We're officially, legally, undeniably married." I poked his chest with every word as I hardened my expression. "If you want to get rid of me, you've got to divorce me. And I'm not going to make it easy on you, so be ready for the fight of your life."

Disbelief made his eyes wide. And then I was in his arms as he whooped, spinning me in a circle. Caught in the cage of his arms, I let myself melt into him. From somewhere far, far away, I heard Henry screaming. I blocked it out because it didn't matter what he had to say. He didn't matter.

My life, my future, my husband, was right here.

"I love you," I whispered, touching my nose to Gideon's.

Placing me back down on the ground, Gideon pressed his forehead against mine as he held me tight. "I love you." His eyes were closed, and for a moment, we just breathed each other in.

Then someone cleared their throat. Cash stood beside us, a sardonic eyebrow lifted. He gave us a slow clap. "Isn't this beautiful," he said. "The two lovebirds, reunited."

"What do you want, Cash?" Gideon asked, his arms tightening around me.

"I just want to tell you that now we're even."

Gideon frowned. "Even?"

Cash tilted his head toward one of his men. He was younger, late teens or early twenties, and below the cuff of his leather jacket, I saw the familiar texture of burn scars. He was one of the boys that Gideon had saved in the warehouse fire. "My nephew's life for your wife's," Cash stated.

"You never owed me anything for that," Gideon said.

Cash shrugged. "Regardless, now it's done." He glanced at me, winked, then gave me a little salute. On his pinky finger, a signet ring glinted.

I jerked my gaze down to Gideon's hand. "You gave him your father's ring?"

"He wanted something in return for bringing me to you."

"That *asshole*!" I tried to pull away, and Gideon jerked me back. I crashed into his chest and glared at him. "I'm going to go get it back. Let me go! I should've elbowed *him* in the face when I had the chance!"

Gideon huffed, stroking my cheeks with his thumbs. "Easy, Sadie."

"I need to punch him *right now*."

Gideon's smile was brighter than I'd ever seen it. "I love it when you get all protective of me."

"Well, no one else is going to do it, are they?" I gave up the fight and stayed in the circle of his arms. "You need taking care of, Gideon Mars, and I'm damn well going to do it. Stealing your father's ring when you were desperate!"

He tightened his hold on me, leaning his forehead against

mine. "I don't care about the ring. I would have given him my right arm if it meant I got you back."

"Still, that's not—"

"Sadie." Gideon kissed me, then pulled away. Smiled. "It's just a ring."

That's when I realized Gideon seemed lighter. Freer. I wondered how much his promise to his father had weighed on him all these years. All the responsibility for his family's well-being had been thrust onto Gideon.

Now, maybe, it was time to start a new chapter—with me.

Eventually, after multiple interviews with police officers, Gideon and I were on the road back to Marswood Harbor. We would spend the night at the cottage, then head to the city together in the morning, where I'd meet with my new client and earn enough money to reopen the doors of my business. In the meantime, Etta would deal with the nightmare of insurance, police reports, and construction required to rebuild Life's a Stitch.

As we drove past the gates of Etta Mars's estate, I said, "Your grandmother is kind of scary."

Gideon laughed. "Yeah."

"I didn't think she'd give me the wedding certificate without talking to you."

"She did talk to me."

"What? She was with me the whole time. I told her I wanted to file it, she listened, and then she got someone to bring me the paperwork. She didn't touch her phone."

Gideon smiled softly, slowing as he hit the town limits. The leaves on the trees fluttered in welcome, and Glenn, Connor, and Lola turned to wave at us from where they stood in front of the beauty parlor, scraping spray paint off the windows.

"That day she called me into her study," Gideon replied, pulling up on the side of the road in front of the burned-out husk of Life's a Stitch. "She asked me if I wanted to make it official. I said yes."

I stared at him. "That was only two weeks after the wedding."

"Yeah."

"It was before we...before anything. We barely knew each other."

"It was enough to know you were the one." His voice was soft. Sincere. He reached over to tuck a strand of hair behind my ear then leaned across to kiss me once, twice, three times. Then Gideon pulled something out of his pocket. My wedding band shone between his fingertips for a moment, and then Gideon took my left hand and slid the ring where it belonged.

Throat tight, I threw my arms around him and kissed him harder. Then we got out together and got my stuff out of the mangled wreck that was my car. Soot, ash, and dents marred the front of the vehicle. Both front tires had exploded from the heat, but most of my belongings seemed to be okay.

"I'm going to need a new car," I said.

"I'll handle it," Gideon replied, and I smiled, knowing he would.

THAT EVENING, Gideon and I moved slowly, enjoying the feel of each other's arms. He fielded phone calls from the whole family, and I was surprised to hear my phone ringing just as much. Finally, frustrated at the hundredth assurance that we were both okay, Gideon took both phones, turned them off, and tossed them in the junk drawer in the kitchen. His annoyance made me laugh, and I delighted in the tiny curl that tugged at his lips.

We ate, cuddled, and kissed. We touched each other and reminded each other that we were safe, and alive, and in love. Just like this—just as we were—we were enough. The certainty of it sank me into the deepest, most restful sleep of my life.

Waking up next to Gideon with early morning sun streaming through the bedroom window was one of the happiest moments of my life. He took his time to kiss and stroke me, until I was a limp body in the bed beside him. Then he grinned and tugged me out of bed...

And to the front door.

On the stoop, a reusable grocery bag waited beside a cardboard tray bearing two cups from Knead More Bread.

"Matcha!" I exclaimed, delighted.

"I got my brother to drop some supplies over," Gideon explained, handing me my drink while he took his coffee. He grabbed the bag, towed me inside, and told me to sit down on the couch while he cooked. I watched him move through the kitchen with that irresistible confidence, a soft smile on my face. He was so incredibly sexy, and he was mine.

Then the smell hit, and I sat up. "Pancakes," I said.

"With way too much whipped cream," Gideon confirmed. "Although you'll have to let me know what 'way too much' means."

My heart swelled so big it was hard to breathe. I stood on

shaking legs, my eyes already filling with tears. "My perfect day," I whispered.

"There's a nice walking trail that starts just behind the cottage," Gideon said. "I was thinking we could check it out once we've eaten. And I fished that out of the garbage." He nodded to the countertop, where my sketchbook waited. "But we can head over to Ellsworth and get you a new one. That one's a little stained with old matcha*aah*."

Gideon grunted as I slammed into him, my arms wrapped like a vise around his neck as I peppered his face with kisses. "I"—kiss—"love"—kiss—"you"—kiss.

His laugh sent shivers down to my toes, and then the kissing got hotter, and he had to flick the burner off before hauling me up so I was sitting on the edge of the counter. As I lifted my hips to help him get my pajama bottoms off, I gave him a smirk. "This wasn't part of the perfect day," I noted.

"I'm reading between the lines," he said with a grin, and then used his mouth for purposes other than talking.

We ate pancakes, walked through the forest, and then I sketched wedding dresses in the sunshine with my head in Gideon's lap while he read a book. We ate a home-cooked dinner, then curled up on the couch to watch a movie together. Gideon was never farther than arm's reach.

"Thank you," I murmured when we finally made it to bed.

Gideon smiled, pulling me closer. He kissed me languorously, thoroughly, and reminded me how much he loved me. That things progressed beyond kisses was inevitable. I could never resist Gideon, and he showed me just how much he enjoyed giving me pleasure.

When I was panting to recover from my second orgasm of

the evening, I wrapped my arms around Gideon's shoulders and squeezed my thighs against his hips. He settled his weight a little more heavily on top of me, a soft smile tugging at his lips.

"Is my wife not satisfied with my performance so far?" he teased in a low rumble.

I flushed, hips rocking. "Maybe just—just a little more," I said between breaths. Gideon's smile was wicked and bright, and then he met the movement of my hips with his own. I gasped. Spread my knees.

And our eyes met.

Swallowing thickly, I dipped my chin. "I want to try again," I whispered.

Gideon let out a shaky exhale. "You're sure?"

"Yes." My smile was a trembling, happy thing.

"I don't want to hurt you," he said, tracing my jaw with his nose. "I don't want you to feel like you have to do this for me."

"I don't feel that way," I answered, and I knew it for the truth. "I want to do it for me."

His breath gusted out, warming my neck and shoulder. His hips made small, jerky movements as he rocked against me, and I began to squirm. Gideon, as usual, would not be rushed. He took his time with me, his eyes dark, his focus on me.

When I was wet and begging, he pushed inside. I clung to him, shaking, as tears leaked out of my eyes. Gideon stopped.

"Happy tears," I panted.

"They better be," he growled.

I laughed, rocking against him, then locked my ankles behind his back. He groaned out his pleasure, burying his face in my neck. His body was all ragged tension and desperate need. Mine was its perfect mirror.

In the silence of the cottage, ensconced in the safety of the forest and my husband's arms, I let go of my doubts and insecurities. I trusted my body. I trusted Gideon.

He rolled his hips and drew a gasp from my lips. "Oh," I said. "Oh, wow."

"So deep, babe," he rasped, teeth closing on my earlobe. "I'm so deep inside you."

"Uh-huh," I replied, drawing a huff of laughter from him.

On stiff arms, his body trembling with the force of holding back, Gideon pulled away to look in my eyes. "You'll stop me the minute it hurts."

I smiled as my heart crowded out my lungs. "I love you so much," I whispered.

"Baby," he replied, teetering on the edge of control, "you got no fuckin' idea."

My laugh turned into a gasp which turned into a moan. I hadn't known it could be this good—and I suspected this was just the beginning.

GIDEON

It was hard to let Sadie out of my sight, those first few weeks after the kidnapping and the fire. I followed her to the city and acted as her bodyguard whenever she'd allow it. I bit my lip every time she went out on her own to meet her client or to work on the dresses that would re-launch her business. But she always came back, and I managed.

Soon enough, we were heading back to Marswood Harbor. I

watched Sadie's face as we left the city, searching for signs of regret. Would she really want to move to a tiny town on the coast of Maine? Could she really be happy there, with me?

When we crossed state lines and entered Maine, Sadie let out a sigh. Her shoulders eased, and a smile spread over her beautiful lips. "Feels good to be home," she said, and I reached over to tangle my fingers in hers.

Throat tight, all I could do was nod.

It was Sunday, so we went straight to Grandma Mars's house for family lunch. Sadie glowed in the warm welcome that my family—our family—gave her, and I could hardly believe that she was really mine.

"Gideon."

I turned to see my grandmother beckoning from the hallway. I followed her to her study, where a document folder waited on her desk. "What's this?" I asked, suspicious.

Grandma Mars smiled, and it wasn't the sharklike smirk I knew so well. This one was softer. Happier. "Your wedding present," she said simply. "Congratulations." She kissed me on the cheek and left me to read the documents on my own.

It took me a while to understand. I had to read through the pages twice to be sure.

Then I rocked back on my heels and let out a disbelieving huff.

My grandmother was surrendering the leverage she'd had over me, once and for all: She was selling me her share of Marswood Security—for just a dollar.

THIRTY-TWO
ETTA

Three weeks after Gideon's return, I sat behind the desk in my study and reviewed the report Alex had slid over my desk. I flicked through the pages, then leaned back and tapped my finger against my chin.

"It's remarkable," Alex said, pushing his wire-frame glasses higher up the bridge of his nose. "A ninety-nine point two percent match. The highest we've seen with either grandson's applicants. No one else came close."

I watched the young man for a beat, then returned my gaze to the pages. "Jack won't like this," I said. "He was very clear with me that he won't bring any woman around Darby until she's grown up and moved out. He only completed the profile because I twisted his arm."

And if needed, I'd twist it harder. It was for his own good, after all.

"I've finally gotten the information I needed from Knox, Bennett, and Fletcher."

I glanced up sharply, surprised. "Fletcher?" I hadn't expected my lothario of a grandson to complete his profile at all.

Alex nodded. "Your other grandchildren, however, have been..."

I arched my brows.

Alex grimaced. "Avoidant. I haven't heard from Walter's daughter at all. She never answered my messages."

"Not surprising," I murmured. Danae had shot out of Marswood Harbor when she'd turned eighteen and never looked back. It would take a cataclysm to bring her back to her hometown. Walter's two sons weren't much better.

Sighing, I placed a hand on the report and drummed my fingers. "We'll move forward with Jack," I decided. "The boy needs a push in the right direction, and we can't ignore the strength of this match."

If Alex disagreed, he didn't show it. He simply gave me a curt nod, stood, and went to work.

Single dad Jack is content living his life exactly as it is.

Then Ember shows up and offers him a side deal:
Marry her until she gets her million-dollar inheritance. Get paid. Get divorced. Go back to life as he knows it.

Ha. If only things were that simple...

Get Book Two: TITLE!

EPILOGUE

EIGHT YEARS LATER

After two years of planning, approvals, and construction, the extension on the cottage was finally complete. The two new bedrooms, one with an ensuite bathroom, were tucked at the back of the house, surrounded by lush forest. At the height of summer, birds sang, leaves rustled, and the sun dappled the forest floor with dancing shadows.

I stood outside the big sliding glass doors that led to our private patio and inhaled the scent of the loamy earth. My hand coasted down my baby's back where she was nestled against me in her carrier. She was three months old today.

"Mommy!" My son Grady came crashing through the new master bedroom and hugged my legs. "Come see! Me and Dad unpacked all my toys!"

I let Grady tow me back through the new part of the house and over to the room that Gideon and I had shared for the first two years of our marriage, before Grady was born. When our son arrived, we moved to Gideon's apartment to have more space, but we were finally ready to move back into the little cottage nestled in the forest that had always felt like my forever home.

Jack, Knox, and Bennett had been happy for us to buy them out of their share, and then we'd started designing the addition and the renovations. I could hardly believe they were done.

"Oh, wow," I said, admiring the shelves full of neatly arranged toys. I predicted it would last about four minutes before being torn asunder by the tornado that was our four-year-old.

"And this is the cars. My firetruck is right here. Mr. Stuffy goes right here, Mom, okay? *Don't* move him."

"Got it," I replied solemnly, then looked down as the baby stirred.

Gideon stood from where he'd been fiddling with Grady's bedframe. He kissed my temple, then peeked in the carrier at the sleepy baby who had already started rooting for milk.

"I'll go and feed her in the nursery," I said.

Gideon kissed me once more, his eyes soft. "Love you," he murmured, then turned to Grady. "Race you to the tree?" The tree was a big oak on the edge of the forest. Gideon had already installed a swing on one of the thick branches overhanging the yard. He had plans for an orchard in the clearing beyond, and he already had engineer's drawings for a new pier.

It wasn't exactly what his father had imagined, he said, but it was better. It was ours.

Grady jumped up from his toys and ran out with a yell. I laughed as Gideon followed, my heart overflowing with love. Padding to the nursery beside our new bedroom, I settled in the rocking chair and fed my baby. I was exhausted from sleepless nights and long days during the move, but my heart was calm.

This was happiness, I realized. I could hear Grady screaming and laughing through the open window. Gideon chased after him, his deep voice echoing. My daughter Etta smacked my chest with her little hand to get my attention, and I smiled down at her.

"Hi, baby," I whispered. "This is your new home."

Later, I was sure we'd have guests. Gideon's brothers and their wives were never far away. There were cousins and kids and friends to meet. Next week, I'd be going back to work part-time; I had a client arriving on Monday for a weekend retreat to design and start her wedding dress. The Marswood Harbor Fair was happening in three weeks, and I'd somehow been roped into the organization committee after last year's debacle—there hadn't been enough stalls for everyone who wanted to participate.

But for now, all was calm. I could listen to my husband play with my son and enjoy the way my baby played with me while she nursed. My life was full and rich and happy.

Then my phone buzzed, and I saw a link to an article from Lola. I clicked it and read the judge's decision to sentence Henry to prison for the maximum allowable time. Between the kidnapping and the gun, he would be gone for a long time. It had taken years to get here—the wheel of justice truly was glacially slow—but I could finally breathe easy.

Our four-year-old tornado came back through the house. I finished nursing and went out to the living room to join Grady and Gideon. Etta cooed, fascinated by her big brother, until I tortured her with tummy time as she howled angrily at me.

Later, Gideon and I collapsed into bed. By some miracle, both kids were asleep at the same time. Gideon wrapped his arms around me and pulled me close. I relaxed into his arms, breathing in the scent of him. The scent of safety, of home, of love.

"How did Lola's wedding dress turn out?" Gideon asked, sounding half-asleep already.

I smiled. "She's gorgeous in it."

"Wonder what her new husband's like," he mumbled.

"I guess we're all going to find out tomorrow," I replied.

"Can't believe Grandma hasn't given up. She's nearly a hundred," he grumbled.

"She's drunk on her own success," I said, and I laughed. I thought about that day eight years ago, when my life had changed. Thought about how vibrant Main Street looked these days, and all the new faces I ran into when I went into town. I thought of Lola, the woman she'd grown into in the past eight years. I hoped the man Etta had found for her was half as good as Gideon was. "You think her marriage will work out as well as ours did? She's still so young."

Gideon snored softly, already asleep. I kissed his shoulder, then turned around to check on baby Etta in the bassinet beside me, then glanced at the monitor to check on my son.

My family slept soundly, and a deep sense of peace settled over me. I'd never imagined life could be this good. As I snuggled into my husband's side, he turned toward me and pulled me into the circle of his arms—exactly where I belonged.

BONUS EPILOGUE
SADIE

A year after the fire at Life's a Stitch

I pressed on the accelerator and felt the extra weight of my car shift as we sped up. My now armor-plated car with bulletproof glass and extra bull bars front and back. Apparently, they'd had to rebuild the engine and improve the suspension to account for all the extra weight.

Flicking a glance at my husband, I arched a brow. "This seems like a lot. It feels like I'm driving a tank."

"You're doing great."

"I know I'm doing great," I replied. "But I don't think anyone's going to shoot me with a bazooka in Marswood Harbor."

"Just keep going and park outside your shop."

"Gideon."

"I need you to be safe, Sadie." He said it quietly, but I heard how important it was to him. Henry was in prison, but we were still awaiting his trial. The justice system was moving too slowly, and we were both still skittish after what had happened. This car was a reminder of how close I'd come to disaster.

Despite myself, knowing that I had my own tank to drive around town made me feel better. Gideon had given me that.

"Call it a belated wedding gift," he said.

"I think this is a gift to yourself."

In my peripheral vision, I saw the twitch of his lips. "Maybe," he conceded.

I drove onto Main Street and turned up the hill. The engine handled the extra strain beautifully, and we climbed up toward what used to be Life's a Stitch. I parked outside the glass-fronted shop, my eyes lingering on the new sign proclaiming it the headquarters of Sadie Bridal. My name in cursive font for everyone to see.

"Ready?" Gideon asked, glancing over at me.

I smiled at my husband and reached over to tangle my fingers with his. He brought my hand to his mouth and pressed a soft kiss there, his eyes full of warmth. I couldn't believe I'd thought him cold when I first met him. Guarded, yes. Slow to trust, of course. But cold? Gideon was as far from frigid as a man could get.

And when he looked at me like that, it made me feel very, very hot. My thighs clenched, but I forced myself to turn toward my shop. The building had been reconstructed after the fire, and there was no sign of the charred husk that used to sit here.

"Go on," Gideon murmured.

Throat tight, I slipped my hand out of his and slipped out of the car. Despite the weight of the armor plating, the door was easy to shut with a flick of my wrist, and I stood on the pavement to take in the newly renovated space.

Through the big windows, I could see beautiful hardwood floors and white walls. A small dais had been built in front of angled mirrors, with a reception desk in its original position. My heart thundered. I couldn't wait to get inside.

The jangling of keys made me look at Gideon. He held up a keyring and smiled as I reached for it. Unable to resist, I tilted my chin toward him and sighed when he pressed a kiss against my lips. His hand came up to stroke my cheek, and I melted against him.

"Thank you for everything," I whispered, throat tight. Gideon had taken the lead on the renovations. He'd liaised with the insurance company and made sure I was getting exactly what I wanted in the space. And as I unlocked the door and heard a steady beep, I realized he'd gotten exactly what he wanted too.

"The code is 0-7-0-6," he said as he flipped a plastic piece down to reveal a keypad on the alarm panel. "Press the numbers, then OK."

I pressed the code and stopped the alarm, then glanced up at him. "Our wedding date," I whispered.

He smiled. "We'll have to change it to something more secure, but..."

"It seemed right," I finished. Warmth flooded my chest, and I inhaled the scent of fresh paint and new flooring. I turned to take in the space, clasping my keys against my chest as tears sprung into my eyes. "Gideon," I breathed. "I can't believe it."

"The couch you ordered will be delivered this week," he

said, nodding to the corner of space behind the dais. "I didn't set up your gear because I figured you'd want to do it yourself."

I walked over to the big worktable on the far side of the room, in front of the windows where the light streamed in. My sewing machine was in its box, and stacks of fabric I'd ordered waited for me in their packaging.

My business was reborn.

After everything I'd been through, I had my fresh start. I turned and crashed into Gideon's chest, unable to hold back my tears. I'd already had two enquiries this week after announcing my business was reopening, and I knew that my wedding dress retreat idea would take off. Ida had already talked to her lawyer about setting up a formal business partnership.

Gideon's arms came around me, and I was surrounded by warmth and safety and him. I cried against the fabric of his black shirt, clinging to his shoulders, letting his hands coast up and down my spine as I tried to pull myself together.

"I hate it when you cry," he rumbled when I'd quieted down.

"I can't help it sometimes." I looked up, and Gideon smiled softly. His thumb brushed away the last of my tears, and then he kissed the wet tracks they'd left behind.

"Let me show you the rest," he said, tugging me toward the back of the space. Two doors were set into the back wall. The first opened onto a big, luxurious bathroom that future brides would love. The whole experience of coming into the shop would be exclusive and special. I couldn't wait to decorate the space and finally open the doors.

"I love it," I said, trailing my fingers over the white marble vanity.

"There's more," Gideon said, and he led me through the second door. I followed him across the threshold—and stopped short.

It was a mini Marswood Security command center. Screens lined the far wall, showing security footage of every single angle of the building, inside and out.

I planted my hands on my hips. "Gideon."

"We have motion-activated alerts set up for non-business hours, so we'll know if anything moves in the vicinity after hours. HD cameras, night vision, and sensors that detect smoke, gas, and temperature fluctuations. We'll set up the smartphone app so you'll have access to everything. I have a backup battery, so even if the power gets cut off, your system will remain active. The guys have you on continuous monitoring, so we'll know if anything happens."

"Gideon," I said, "That's creepy." I stared at the bird's eye view of myself in one of the monitors, then turned to the corner of the room to see a tiny camera.

"Let me show you how this works," he said. "Once you arm the system, these sensors go live," he said, sliding into the rolling office chair and tapping on the keyboard to bring up a dashboard. "There are three settings. Disarmed, Armed, and Work. The work setting is for when you're here alone."

I put a hand on his shoulder and listened intently as he walked me through the most high-tech security system I'd ever encountered. This thing could protect a vault of jewels. It was completely over the top.

And...I loved it.

I loved it because I knew that no matter what, Gideon had my back. He would recruit whatever resources he needed to keep me safe. And he wasn't locking me away in a high tower to do it; he was facilitating the growth of my business. He was encouraging me to grow and pursue what I wanted, making sure I was as safe as could be while I did it.

This man had a heart of pure, twenty-four-carat gold. I was as head-over-heels in love with him as I'd been from the start.

"Any questions?" Gideon asked, glancing up. His eyes were very blue, very earnest, and very serious. My heart squeezed and thumped like a writhing fish on the shore.

I slid my fingers along his jaw, feeling the ridges of the scarred skin on his left side. I traced his lips and watched his eyelids flutter shut. I leaned down and pressed a kiss to his lips. "I love you," I murmured.

His hands slid over my hips, squeezed, and then released. He stood up and kissed me, then nodded to the chair. "Sit down," he said. "I'll show you how everything works."

"Sure," I said, "but there's something I want to do first."

I could tell he was suspicious of me, and it made me smile wide and bright. I went up on my tiptoes and pressed a soft kiss to his lips, then lowered myself back down to my heels. He watched me, brows drawn slightly. I couldn't help the laugh that slipped from my lips.

And then I sank to my knees.

Gideon groaned. "Sadie," he said, but he didn't stop me as I unbuttoned his pants and slid the zipper down.

"I'm saying thank you," I chided.

"You don't have to thank me for doing what any husband would do."

I snorted. As if any husband would do all this. Wrap me up in his protectiveness while still allowing me to chase my dreams.

Handle all the paperwork and contractors and hassle so I could focus on designing and finding clients.

Reaching into his boxer briefs, I ran my hand along his cock. He groaned again, fingers tangling into my hair. I looked up at him, watching his lids drop down, his eyes glittering with need.

"You're so pretty when you're on your knees in front of me, Sadie."

I pulled him free of his underwear and licked his tip. "Am I?" I took him into my mouth and shivered at the sound of pure pleasure he made.

"So pretty when you've got my cock in your mouth," he rasped, fingers tightening on my hair. Then he grunted and reached behind me to tap the keyboard on the desk. I glanced up in time to see one of the screens go dark: the bird's eye view of us in this room.

"Don't want any of those assholes seeing this," Gideon said, hand returning to my hair so he could gather it up in a ponytail. He looked down at me, his free hand stroking my cheek. "My perfect, beautiful wife. Suck my cock, baby, and I'll make it so good for you after."

It was a promise I believed, but I didn't need to hear it. I was already wet, already clenching with unmet need. I softened my mouth and took him deeper, and then there was no more talking from Gideon. He only groaned and gasped and moaned until he couldn't hold back any longer. I swallowed him down, dizzy with desire, as he hooked his hands under my arms and hauled me up to the desk.

My skirt was flipped up, and my underwear provided no resistance. He shoved it aside, and then it was his turn to get on his knees in front of me. I gripped his wild, dark hair and lost myself in the sensation of his tongue and lips and teeth. Gideon didn't stop until I begged him to, until I was so sensitive my whole body twitched with every touch.

Then he gathered me into his arms and kissed me so I could taste myself on his lips. Pulling away, he held my chin and forced me to look in his eyes. "Now you learn how this system works," he commanded. "And then we go home and finish what we've started."

I smiled, cheeks flushing with heat, limbs loose with pleasure. "Yes, sir," I said, noting the darkening of his eyes and the way his hands lingered on my body.

It was only when we were back in the car and on the way home that I realized there was no nervousness inside me. I wasn't dreading what would happen next—and I hadn't dreaded sex for a long, long time. Maybe we would explore penetration this afternoon. Maybe we wouldn't. Sex was fun and free and connective. Whatever happened, I was safe in Gideon's arms.

My gruff, wounded, wonderful, protective, very hot husband. The love of my life. Mine forever, as I was his. I reached over and slid my palm over his thigh. He dropped his hand over mine, running his thumb over my knuckles.

"I love you," I murmured.

He lifted my hand and kissed the center of my palm. "Love you more, Sadie," he said. I wasn't sure how that could be true, but I believed him all the same.

WANT MORE? JACK AND EMBER'S STORY IS NEXT…

THE DEAL IS SIMPLE: Marry the woman I just met. Temporarily.

Ember gets her inheritance. I get my daughter's future secured. We play the happy couple in public, keep our hands to ourselves in private, and walk away clean.

Simple.

Except nothing about Ember Knightly is simple. Not her cool green eyes, her smart mouth, or those pencil skirts I can't stop dreaming about.

Playing the happy couple is easy. Keeping my hands to myself is a hell of a lot harder.

But walking away? That's where it falls apart.

Because my daughter's looking at her like she's already ours, and "fake" has never felt so real.

Then there's one storm, one night, one bed—and the look on Ember's face after, like she's already calculating how fast she can run.

She thinks she can keep enough distance to make it out of this marriage with her heart intact. She thinks we're on the same page.

She's the smartest woman I've ever met, but she's wrong.

Ember Knightly married me for the money, but I married her for keeps.

Get Book Two: The Marriage Mistake

LOOKING FOR
YOUR NEXT READ?

SAME VIBE. DIFFERENT TOWN.

ONE

Amelia Darcy was ready to crawl out of her skin. Red ants marched through her veins, leaving burning anxiety in their wake. They traveled the length of her body in an unending loop, through every artery, vein, and capillary, around and around and around.

Because he was *late*.

Huffing in a failed attempt to clear her mounting frustration, Amelia spun on her heels and continued wearing a line through the thin red carpet of the church's narthex. The single strap of her bridesmaid dress draped strangely over her shoulder. Why had her sister chosen an asymmetrical design? At least with two straps, the feeling would be mirrored on both sides of her body, which would be acceptable. Amelia hadn't been comfortable since she put the thing on.

She wouldn't even think about the color; that would only make her anxiety worse. Earlier, when Amelia had slipped on the lilac silk garment and caught sight of herself in the mirror, she'd fully recoiled. Against her pale, desaturated skin and her pale, desaturated hair, the pastel purple shade produced a distinctly corpselike effect. Even her eyes, which she'd always thought were her best feature, looked sunken, their pale gray irises turning dull as worn pewter. The makeup artist had tried to glue false eyelashes on her lids, cheerily claiming they'd brighten her face right up, but then Amelia had twitched and blinked so much the whole endeavor had been aborted. So she still looked like she belonged outside in the church's graveyard instead of the bridal party, except now with slightly irritated eyelids.

But today was Maggie's wedding day, and Amelia would wear a sparkly leotard and dance the cha-cha backward if it made her sister happy. It didn't matter what color her dress was, or how many straps it had, or if that number was one too few.

Wedding planning hadn't been fun, exactly, but Amelia had thrown herself into it. She'd made phone calls, coordinated vendors, ordered decorations, planned and attended a hellish bachelorette party, helped set up the church and the reception venue, and completed countless other tasks—all in the name of sisterly love. She'd taken her role as Maggie's maid of honor seriously.

The best man, on the other hand?

Not so much.

He hadn't shown up to the rehearsal dinner, hadn't helped with any of the preparations, and now, the only time that *actually* mattered, he was late. Two more minutes, and she'd lead the bridal progression down the aisle on her own. He could slink in whenever he arrived and watch from the back pew, for all she cared. If he showed up at all.

The strap on her shoulder slipped, so she yanked it back up. Stupid thing.

She'd strangle him when she saw him. Months—*months!*—of planning, and now the whole wedding hinged on the arrival of some mysterious best man. Nerves morphed into anger, and Amelia wanted to scream. She'd make him sorry for being so late. That was a promise. She'd strangle him with his own tie and enjoy every gruesome second of it.

Her feet stomped as she made another lap. And another. And another. Her teeth gnashed so hard a headache started pulsing near her temples.

A door creaked open behind her. Amelia whirled, only to let her shoulders drop in disappointment.

A dark-haired man poked his head out of the room where the bridal party waited. He lifted a brow. "No sign of him?"

"No." Her answer was curt. Her lips compressed, as if she could make the missing best man appear by drawing her mouth into a perfectly straight line. It didn't work.

"All right. I'll let them know." Marlon St. James didn't seem worried about his brother's tardiness. He certainly didn't seem surprised. Even the groom hadn't worried when she'd scurried to the altar to inform him his best man was missing in action.

Emory had given her a little half-smile and said, "He'll show. He's flying in this morning, probably hit traffic."

Amelia didn't share Emory's confidence. A scowl etched itself over her brow as she spun around to do another lap. She hadn't been able to get a straight answer from her sister's other bridesmaids when she asked about the best man. Sly looks and rolled eyes were the usual response to the mention of his name. Maybe a snort and a wry, "You know how he is."

But she didn't know how he was. She'd never laid eyes on the man. All she knew was he was *late*.

Murmurs swelled in the church as guests grew restless. She'd wait one more minute, and then they'd start without him. She'd apologize to Maggie and Emory afterward, but really, it was—

Hinges groaned to her left. Amelia turned toward the sound, only to be struck dumb by the vision unfolding before her.

The church's arched doors split down the middle, letting in golden sunlight through the widening gap. A man stood in the center, a hand on either door, silhouetted by the sun's honeyed rays. He pushed the doors all the way open to step through them then straightened, standing as tall and proud as a king returning from war. Or maybe a fallen angel, seeking vengeance.

Or a missing best man, finally deigning to make an appearance.

Leo St. James stepped into the church, the sunlight limning the edges of his body in gold while casting the rest of him in black, impenetrable shadow. He looked impossibly large. For no reason at all, Amelia's heart rattled.

The doors squeaked on their way shut and bit by bit, the best man was revealed to Amelia's hungry stare.

Because that's what was growing inside her—hunger. A ravenous ache pulsed in the very heart of her as she saw the strong lines of his face, his heavy-lidded green eyes, his softly masculine lips. There was a sort of disheveled grace to him, a quality that made him seem more than perfect. Like his appearance was a veneer her mortal gaze wasn't supposed to penetrate, his flaws purposefully chosen to make him seem simply human.

Slowly, sunlight disappeared behind heavy timber doors until a final groan and a click sounded. The best man watched her, a brow quirking at her perusal.

Suddenly she realized she'd been gaping. Her spine snapped straight. "You're late," she clipped.

His gaze didn't leave her face. "Am I?"

"And you're a mess."

Leo looked down at himself and seemed surprised to see the state of his clothes. "So I am," he muttered. "Got changed at the airport."

Edging dangerously close to mania, Amelia tried to wrangle her fleeing wits. She felt lightheaded and strange. He was very beautiful. But—so what?

He was also late, and that was nearly unforgivable. It was Maggie's wedding day, and nothing—especially not *him*—would ruin it. Even if this was "how he was." Whatever that meant.

Stomping toward Leo, she ignored the incessant thumping of her heart. He looked even worse—better?—up close. Rumpled. Deliciously so.

Before she could divine what they were doing, Amelia's hands rose to the bow tie hanging undone at Leo's neck. She couldn't fasten the bow until the top button of his shirt was clasped, so she clicked her tongue and pulled at his collar. He rocked forward when she yanked the fabric, letting out a short, low grunt.

From the corner of her eyes, Amelia caught the curl of his lips.

Smiling! At a time like this! Strangling him would be too

kind. He deserved to be tickled to death. Or stretched out on a medieval rack and submitted to the most horrid water torture imaginable. Or...or...have every one of his long, full eyelashes plucked out.

Her fingers trembled as they dipped near the hollow of his throat to do up the button. Stubble rasped against her knuckles, and a sharp jolt of heat traveled through her middle.

"This is...unexpected," he said, voice dropping to a low baritone that did interesting things to Amelia's inner thighs. Amelia's inner thighs needed to get ahold of themselves. "Are you sure we should be doing this in a church? You haven't even told me your name."

Fury was a rocket launching in her chest. Explosions created a cloud of dust and debris in her veins as anger took off inside her, because he didn't even seem sorry for being unforgivably late. He was *flirting*, at a time like this! Leo St. James, professional annoyance. Who did he think he was? Showing up at Amelia's sister's wedding, looking like a disheveled prince, then *joking* about it!

The. *Nerve.*

The man couldn't even dress himself, and he was trying to be cute with her?

"Oh, please," she hissed. "Spare me." She scowled at him, flicking her gaze upward to meet his eyes. It was a mistake. As soon as her gaze clashed with his, she saw the gleam that lived in his emerald-green irises. It promised everything dark and dirty, and Amelia wanted to let herself fall into those promises and never emerge again. Her anger was snuffed out in an instant as a wave of unfamiliar lust took over.

Strange. It wasn't like her to feel this way about men—not even the pretty ones. Flustered, yes. Anxious, definitely.

Aroused? No way.

Her body's reaction swung her back to anger, and she gripped the feeling with both fists. She was angry at him for being late. Angry at the bridal party for putting her in this position. Angry at herself for finding him attractive.

Maybe the stress of her sister's wedding was getting to her. Or it was the lack of sleep over the past six months. Her work had been intense, after all. Starting a business usually was.

A small shake of her head, and her mind felt slightly clearer. Today was her sister's wedding, and this absolute lump of a pretty boy was threatening to throw the whole thing off-schedule. He needed to get himself together, then she'd hold his arm and walk down the aisle ahead of the rest of the bridal party with a smile plastered on her face. Nothing else mattered.

She tugged the collar to straighten it, then set herself to tying the bow tie. It was the same soft lilac as her dress, but against his tawny skin, the color looked rich and creamy. Of course it did. Her frown deepened, and Amelia used the moment to settle her unstable emotions. She tied the fabric carefully, straightening the corners until a perfect purple bow stared back at her.

All the while, Leo's gaze pressed like a weight. He stood very still to endure her ministrations, arms at his sides, chin lifted out of the way. But she felt it—the heaviness of his stare. He didn't have anywhere else to look but at her, she reasoned, but it still made her want to squirm.

It was no surprise that Amelia would feel put out by a beautiful man's gaze. She wasn't exactly beating men back these days. She'd been focusing on her career; she hadn't had time to date. Never mind the fact that being this close to a man made Amelia feel like she had a bird trapped in her chest and noodles for limbs. Best to avoid these sorts of situations altogether. She wasn't known for being a man-eater. More like a man-evader.

Sipping in a short little breath, she frowned at his vest. It, like the jacket and pants, was a navy so dark it was nearly black. His white shirt bunched awkwardly between his vest and pants. He'd have to re-tuck it.

She pointed at the offending area. "Fix this. It looks like a deflated muffin top," she blurted—and there was the other reason she hadn't had much luck with men. Words sometimes fell out of her mouth without warning, and often they weren't exactly delicate. She'd come to learn that her lack of filter wasn't an attractive trait. There were many, many data points from failed dates and awkward interactions to prove it.

But Leo didn't seem bothered. In fact, he leaned ever so slightly closer to her, so she could smell the scent of soap rising from his skin. "I was led to believe that fixing my clothing was your job," he answered, and for a moment, Amelia felt off-balance. It was the velvet quality of his tone and the way his scent wrapped around her like a drugging cloud. Then she registered the laughter in his voice.

Despite herself, Amelia's eyes snapped up to his once more. He was *mocking* her. Thunder rumbled in the distance, and Amelia knew it was her temper.

She just wanted this day to go right. For Maggie. For beautiful, kind Maggie with the luminous smile. Her sister deserved this. She'd found Emory, and they'd fallen in love, and now they'd have a perfect wedding day. Amelia would make sure of it.

This was what she *did*. She identified problems, then parsed the data into something useful. Whether it was a complicated data set for a client, or a wedding venue scheduling for today's event, or ordering supplies for seventy intricate handmade centerpieces (which included twenty-five hundred and ninety individual components, ordered from four different vendors), Amelia could sort any problem into a tidy, efficient solution.

She'd made sense of the wedding preparations, and now it would all go off without a hitch. No matter what the man before her did or said.

Leo narrowed his eyes, seeing something written on her face. What, she didn't know. Maybe he could hear the thunder just as clearly as she could. Ozone crackled in the air between them, like that breathless, heavy moment before a strike of lightning.

With a gusted breath, Leo turned, and a belt jingled. Amelia averted her gaze from his broad back, blood rising to her cheeks. It was half humiliating, really, to be blushing at the mere sound of a belt buckle clinking. No wonder men saw her and took off running in the other direction. Middle schoolers had more poise than she did.

Leo spun around and spread his arms, a roguish grin holding up the corners of his lips. "Satisfied?"

Ugh. "Annoyed."

His smile grew, as did the trembling in Amelia's thighs.

Leo tugged his jacket sleeves and arranged his cuffs just so. He combed both hands through his hair, and the gently curled light-brown locks fell into the kind of perfect disarray that betrayed an expensive haircut.

Rings glinted on two fingers: the thumb of his right hand, and the index finger of his left. They were simple gold bands that shone in the low light of the room and drew attention to his hands. Beautiful hands for a beautiful man. He lifted his gaze to hers and arched a brow.

"Good enough," Amelia grumped, even though the more truthful statement would be *drop-dead gorgeous* or *positively edible.*

"Do I get to learn your name now?" The gleam was back in his eyes.

Nerves gripped Amelia in a tight fist. Giving him even her name was handing over more power than was wise. A man like Leo St. James would take one look at her and crush her vulnerable heart. She felt the urge to protect herself, but Amelia was a rational being, and she knew it was only her name. He'd learn it eventually. She forced the syllables out. "Amelia."

"Amelia," he repeated, like he was sipping fine wine and detecting all kinds of hidden notes in it. Touching a hand to his chest, he said, "Leo."

"So I've heard," she said, and something undefinable flitted across his expression. His smile widened, but his eyes grew shuttered.

Amelia frowned. Odd.

No time to figure it out. She had a wedding procession to lead, and she wasn't letting Leo St. James out of her sight for a second until Emory and Maggie were husband and wife. She reached out and grabbed Leo's wrist, tugging him toward the room where the rest of the bridal party awaited, not trusting him to follow without physical encouragement.

Then he shifted, and his hand slipped against hers. She made to pull away, but he intertwined their fingers before she had the chance to escape.

He was... He was *holding her hand.*

It was a shock to the system, intimate in a way she hadn't expected. That broad, warm palm pressed against hers. His long fingers curled and notched between her knuckles. The heat of it. The sheer *size* of it.

She paused halfway to the side door and stared at their joined hands. His golden tan against her pallid skin looked... wrong. Foreign, somehow.

It made her feel very, very hot.

ABOUT THE AUTHOR

Lilian Monroe adores writing swoonworthy heroes and the women who bring them to their knees. She loves making people laugh and is eternally grateful to have found people who share her sense of humor.

When she's not writing, she's reading (or rereading) a book, walking, lifting weights, or attempting to play the guitar with very limited success.

She grew up in Canada but now lives in Australia with her Irish husband. He frequently asks to be used as a cover model for her books, and she's not quite sure whether or not he's joking.

ALSO BY LILIAN MONROE

For all books, visit:

www.lilianmonroe.com

Manhattan Billionaires

Big Bossy Mistake

Big Bossy Trouble

Big Bossy Problem

Big Bossy Surprise

Forbidden Boss

The Wrong Boss

Dirty Boss

Tempting Boss

More surprise babies!

Knocked Up by the CEO

Knocked Up by the Single Dad

Knocked Up...Again!

Knocked Up by the Billionaire's Son

Yours for Christmas

Bad Prince

Heartless Prince

Cruel Prince

Broken Prince

Wicked Prince

Wrong Prince

Lone Prince

Ice Queen

Rogue Prince

<u>**Small Towns are the best towns**</u>

Four Steps to the Perfect Revenge

Four Steps to the Perfect Fake Date

Working with the Enemy

Faking It with the Firefighter

Conquest

Craving

Combat

Calamity

<u>**Small Town + Later-in-Life Romance**</u>

Dirty Little Midlife Crisis

Dirty Little Midlife Mess

Dirty Little Midlife Mistake

Dirty Little Midlife Disaster

Dirty Little Midlife Debacle

Dirty Little Midlife Secret

Dirty Little Midlife Dilemma

Dirty Little Midlife Drama

Dirty Little Midlife (fake) Date

Filthy Little Midlife Fling

Merry Little Midlife Matchmaker

Forty and Fighting Dirty

<u>Brother's Best Friend Romance</u>

Shouldn't Want You

Can't Have You

Don't Need You

Won't Miss You

<u>He'll do anything to protect his woman</u>

His Vow

His Oath

His Word

<u>Enemies to Lovers/Workplace Romance</u>

Hate at First Sight

Loathe at First Sight

Despise at First Sight

<u>Fake Engagement Romance</u>

Engaged to Mr. Right

Engaged to Mr. Wrong

Engaged to Mr. Perfect